PRAISE FOR

# The Peacock Feast

"[An] intricate, psychologically keen work . . . Enthralling."

—*The National Book Review*

"A dazzling panorama of a novel—moving from a Tiffany mansion to a gardener's tenement apartment to a sixties' commune to a death row unit to an old woman's beautifully decorated last room. The forces of social history and the forces of personal trauma weave the remarkable plot, and readers will be left applauding."

—Joan Silber, author of *Improvement*

"A great novel . . . You will be deeply moved . . . [and] may cry at the end . . . Gornick has given her readers a tale suffused with pathos and moral imperative, which tugs kindly and powerfully at our hearts."

—Lloyd Sederer, *New York Journal of Books*

"The deftness of Gornick's talent is visible . . . Finely observed and ultimately redemptive."

—*Kirkus Reviews*

"Embrac[es] an old-fashioned feel . . . Meant to be read and not binged . . . [It has] a sense of literary leisure at times evocative of the Gilded Age that anchors it."

—Jennifer Klepper, *Washington Independent Review of Books*

"An explosive moment that shatters generations, a buried trauma, the unspoken weight of history: In this original and beautifully rendered novel, two women, strangers to each other, hold pieces of a puzzle they can only construct together. Weaving fact and fiction to paint the evolution of a family over the sweep of a century, Lisa Gornick plumbs the connections that transform lives in a book that is both gripping and elegantly nuanced."

—Christina Baker Kline, author of *Orphan Train*

"A complex and extremely powerful multigenerational family story."

—Marion Winik, *The Weekly Reader*

"Delicately weaving Grace's present with Prudence's past, acclaimed novelist Gornick spins an appealing and enthralling family saga."
—Carol Haggas, *Booklist*

"Gornick braids the lives of three generations across a span of 100 years in this vivid novel . . . [Her] prose is strong throughout; this is an intricately threaded story of family, secrets, loss, and closure."
—*Publishers Weekly*

"[A] wonderfully complex, many-stranded novel . . . *The Peacock Feast* is marvelously rich in character, event and locale . . . A thoroughly rewarding novel and, though not terribly long, a truly mighty one."
—Katherine A. Powers, *Newsday*

"[An] intricate, emotionally complex and glorious chronicle . . . [A] magical novel."
—Jane Ciabattari, *BBC Culture*

"Spanning a century, two coasts, and two continents, this well-researched historical novel is moving and profound."
—Lauren Gilbert, *Library Journal*

"A perfect novel . . . Luxurious . . . It's a book that beckons readers to get lost in its tapestry."
—Jacqueline Cutler, *The Star-Ledger* (New Jersey)

"You cannot stop paying attention for a single sentence in this book. It's so beautifully woven . . . A masterpiece."
—Marrie Stone, KUCI's *Writers on Writing*

"Fun, trenchant, immersive . . . but on top of that I got historical and psychological mystery, art history, and several different lush settings . . . Exactly the book I needed."
—Rebecca Makkai, *Electric Literature*

"Every so often you come across a novel whose emotional range and complexity defies summary. *The Peacock Feast* is that kind of book . . . Intelligent and satisfying."
—Amanda Holmes, *the next book. . .*

"So dazzling, that I found myself rereading pages."
—Caroline Leavitt, *Carolineleavittville*

"Lisa Gornick's extensive background in clinical psychology gives her emotional tale about life-changing choices and reflection great texture and authenticity. This book will likely have the tears running and serve as an unexpected guide to a life of more mindful experiences. Grab this dark horse for yourself and your loved ones."

—Nathaniel Lee, *Bookstr*'s "Three to Read"

"[Lisa] Gornick has given us a beautifully written book, complex with characters' stories across four generations. For all the sorrow and heartbreak in her character's lives, we are left with understanding and hope."

—*The Literate Quilter*

"A story about how family embraces and breaks you . . . Yes, read it."

—Lolly K. Dandeneau, *bookstalkerblog*

"*The Peacock Feast* is one of those rare books that feels both grand and intimate, bringing the reader deeply into a very vivid past. Lisa Gornick has written an engrossing and impressive book."

—Meg Wolitzer, author of *The Female Persuasion*

"For the thrill of discovering a new favorite author, try Lisa Gornick's sweeping historical novel *The Peacock Feast*." —Dawn Raffel, *NextTribe*

PRAISE FOR

# Louisa Meets Bear

Chosen as a Fresh Pick for Your Book Club Meeting by Oprah.com

"Lisa Gornick is . . . one of the most perceptive, compassionate writers of fiction in America . . . [And] that's part of what makes *Louisa Meets Bear* such a wonderful, perfectly executed novel—it's not just the beautiful writing, it's the honesty behind it." —Michael Schaub, NPR

"Extraordinary . . . When you reach the final page, you'll be sad to leave Gornick's universe behind. Grade: A."
—Sara Vilkomerson, *Entertainment Weekly*

"Brilliantly constructed . . . Gornick captures all the heartbreak and joy of what it is to be human." —*Publishers Weekly* (starred review)

"Achingly eloquent." —Cathleen Medwick, *More*

"Extraordinary writing; I fell in love on the first page."
—*Library Journal* (Barbara's Picks)

PRAISE FOR

# Tinderbox

"This vivid portrait of a family unraveling is perfect for book clubs."

—Sue Corbett, *People*

"*Tinderbox*, will certainly be compared to Jonathan Franzen's acclaimed *The Corrections* . . . Gornick creates a world of characters every bit as complex and flawed—and as real—as Franzen's subjects."

—Jewish Book Council Book Club

"I clung to every page of *Tinderbox*; the writing is intelligent and sharp, and with each turn of the story, my investment surged. Gornick has translated the very real and tender chaos of family into a novel that's expertly constructed and engaging." —*Bustle*

© Sigrid Estrada

## A NOTE ABOUT THE AUTHOR

LISA GORNICK is the author of *Louisa Meets Bear*, *Tinderbox*, and *A Private Sorcery*. Her stories and essays have appeared widely, including in *The New York Times*, *Prairie Schooner*, *Real Simple*, *Salon*, *Slate*, and *The Sun*. She holds a B.A. from Princeton and a Ph.D. in clinical psychology from Yale, and is on the faculty of the Columbia University Center for Psychoanalytic Training and Research. A longtime New Yorker, she lives in Manhattan with her family.

ALSO BY LISA GORNICK

*Louisa Meets Bear*

*Tinderbox*

*A Private Sorcery*

# The Peacock Feast

# The Peacock Feast

Lisa Gornick

Picador
Farrar, Straus and Giroux
New York

Picador
120 Broadway, New York 10271


Printed in the United States of America
First published in 2019 by Sarah Crichton Books,
an imprint of Farrar, Straus and Giroux
First Picador paperback edition, March 2020

Grateful acknowledgment is made for permission to reprint lines from "Gacela of the Dead Child" by Federico García Lorca, translated by Edwin Honig, from *The Selected Poems of Federico García Lorca*, copyright © 1955 by New Directions Publishing Corp. Reprinted by permission of New Directions Publishing Corp.

The Library of Congress has cataloged the
Sarah Crichton Books edition as follows:
Names: Gornick, Lisa, 1956– author.
Title: The peacock feast / Lisa Gornick.
Description: First edition. | New York : Sarah Crichton Books / Farrar, Straus and Giroux, 2019.
Identifiers: LCCN 2018020553 | ISBN 9780374230548 (Hardcover)
Subjects: BISAC: FICTION / Literary. | FICTION / Family Life.
Classification: LCC PS3607 .O598 P43 2019 | DDC 813/.6—dc23
LC record available at https://lccn.loc.gov/2018020553

Picador Paperback ISBN: 978-1-250-25128-2

Designed by Jonathan D. Lippincott



1 3 5 7 9 10 8 6 4 2

Frontispiece: Peacock Feast, Laurelton Hall, May 15, 1914, from "Roman Luxuries at Tiffany Feast for Men of Genius," *The New York Times*, May 24, 1914

*In memory of my father, Fred Gornick—*

*Scientist, Explorer, Raconteur*

# Contents

# The Peacock Feast

# 1

# New York, 1935

*Shortly after Prudence's twenty-third birthday, now more than three-quarters of a century ago, her mother told her the story of Louis C. Tiffany dynamiting the breakwater at Laurelton Hall—his fantastical Oyster Bay mansion with its columns capped by brilliant ceramic blossoms and the smokestack buried in a blue-banded minaret—so as to foil the town from reclaiming the beach for public use. Prudence's mother was only weeks from death, and as she told the story, she wept. She wiped her nose on her bed-jacket sleeve, eyes pinpointed from the tincture of laudanum Prudence had given her.*

*Prudence had been born at Laurelton Hall, her father one of a battalion of gardeners who tended the glass genius's 588 lavishly landscaped acres, her mother one of a squadron of maids who cleaned the eighty-four rooms. They'd left when Prudence was four, her father assuming a position at the Tiffanys' Madison Avenue mansion, but she still recalled the fountain with a color wheel engineered by Mr. T so the water could be rendered different hues, the peacocks strutting across the lawn, the totem pole with a whale atop marking the bend in the drive.*

*Her mother, always tiny but by then the size of a girl, reached a frigid hand out from the bed. She rested it heavily on Prudence's arm. "I was in the largest of the third-floor bedrooms. No one slept there, but still, every week, they made me polish and sweep. When I lifted the window to shake the duster . . ."*

*Her mother shuddered. "Whitecaps and a terrible smell. Like bananas gone bad."*

*She retracted her hand and picked violently at the nubby coverlet.*

*"Stop. You'll make a hole."*

*"The explosion was so loud, I thought it must be the Germans come."*

*Like a faded photograph at the bottom of a box, the scene seemed to Prudence already known: The crackle of dynamite along the breakwater Mr. T had built to expand for his own family's use the strip of sand that lay like an ermine cuff between his gardens and the sea that had once been the favored bathing spot for the residents of Oyster Bay. The plume of spewing water over the granite rocks, flooding the beach on which the town had planned to erect thirty-five cabanas on land Mr. T believed was his and his alone.*

*Why was her mother telling her this?*

*Because there was no one else to tell: Prudence's brother gone now for more than a decade; Prudence's father dead the following year.*

*Her mother pulled the coverlet up to the tip of her chin. "June sixteenth, 1916. That was the cursed date."*

# 2

# An April Sunday, 2013

At Prudence's age, three weeks past her hundred-and-first birthday, the phone rarely rings, so that when it does, a little after two, she is startled, only realizing then that she has slipped into a doze in one of the wingback chairs by the library table where she'd been drinking the Earl Grey tea Maricel leaves in a thermos, always with the strict instruction *Mrs. P, you are not under any circumstances, not even Jesus showing up in this kitchen, to light that stove.* A section of the paper has slid onto the rug, and as she blinks into awareness, she remembers it is Sunday, Maricel's day off.

The phone does not ring most days because nearly everyone she has known is no longer alive. And for those who are, as she witnesses on her outings (she remains a surprisingly strong walker, though she does accede to Maricel's insistence on holding her arm), talking as a means of communication seems to have fallen out of fashion.

"Hello," she says, disarmed, as she so often is when she hears her first words of the day, by how like an old recording she sounds, scratchy and faint.

"Hello," she hears back. A woman's voice. Gentle but with a backbone to it. "I'm Grace O'Connor." The voice pauses, as though aware that Prudence's breath has halted on the inhale. "My grandfather Randall O'Connor, I believe, was your brother."

Prudence does not blink, as stilled as if she'd met a black bear on a path. She stares at the knobby knuckles of what had once been, she'd been told, lovely hands, at the highway of raised blood vessels visible through her parchment skin. *No. No thank you, I have no need of that* are the words she hears in her head.

"I think I am your great-niece."

There is no tacked-on silly laugh, and with this, Prudence senses a grown woman, which makes sense; her own grandchildren, had she had children, might have been, as she's often calculated, grandparents themselves. But her mind is not making those idle calculations now. Rather, wild impetuous animal, it has leaped back to the day, a rare pocket of vivid memory, when they received the first letter from Randall, then only fourteen. A letter, it appeared from the postmark, that had taken three weeks to travel from his lodgings in San Francisco to Hell's Kitchen.

That Randall had written at all had dwarfed the content of the letter, which contained little news save that he was staying with Charlie, a boy he knew from New York, and that he'd found a job as a florist's assistant. After her mother read the single page aloud, her father wiped his eyes with the back of his hand. "Well, he knows about flowers from me," he said, and her mother sucked her lips into her mouth, holding back, Prudence imagines, *Go to hell, Eddie, it's because of you, stupid drunk, that he's gone*. Her father had not been a stupid drunk, but when he did drink, he could get sloppy and mean, as he had the night Randall left. A night when he'd shoved her mother, and Randall, who boxed at the place around the corner and had a quick right jab, made fists, and her father, who had never hit them, swung at Randall.

*Grace? Is that what the woman said?*

Folded inside the letter to her parents was a separate one for her. *Pru, you're the smartest of us all. Just stay clear of our father when he's had a few. He's not a bad man but the whiskey makes him, well, I don't want to cuss.* There were a few lines about how Randall would see her soon, maybe not this Christmas, but Christmas the next at the most. But then Christmas and Christmas the next had passed without Randall's coming back and the spans between his letters grew longer and longer. When her father died the following year and her aunt sent a telegram to Randall's rooming house, his landlady cabled back *Moved*. A decade later, after her mother died, Prudence did not even know where to send a telegram.

But now the woman, Grace, is explaining that Randall, her grandfather, has been dead for nearly twenty years. That he had one child, her father, Leopold.

A shock passes through Prudence. Of course, she's known her brother must be gone by now, but hearing it, hearing how long it's been . . . She closes her eyes so as to do the arithmetic in her head. Randall was three years older than her. Twenty years ago, he would have been eighty-four.

"I am wondering if I might see you," the woman says.

See her? See a photograph of her? *Pull yourself together,* Prudence admonishes herself, by which she means gather up her thoughts, with their inclination of late to wander off like toddlers willy-nilly wherever they want. "Have a visit? You are wondering if we might have a visit?"

"Yes. Would you be willing?"

The *No. No thank you* returns. Dorothy Tiffany, the daughter of her parents' employer who'd once told Prudence, "We must shoulder failing those we love," would have come right out and said it: a firm *No.* But she, Prudence Theet, née Prudence O'Connor, cannot, cannot do that.

"When will you be in New York?" Prudence asks.

There is a pause, and for a moment Prudence thinks perhaps the line has gone dead.

"I'm sorry. I should have said this before. I am in New York now."

Prudence's heart pounds wildly, as though the black bear has reared onto its hind legs.

"Actually . . . Actually, I'm outside your building now."

"You're outside my building now?"

"Yes."

To Prudence's amazement, the bear turns and saunters into the trees, leaving something she hasn't felt in a long time. Something she would have to say is closer to elation than fear. Such a long time since she has done anything more spontaneous, more rash, than stopping with Maricel on one of their walks to buy an Italian ice from a cart.

She hears Maricel's scolding: *Mrs. P, it could be someone come to rob you. Or worse. Worse than that. There are evil people out there, they prey on elderly persons . . .*

But this is not people. This is her brother's grandchild. And if it is not, if it is someone come to do her harm, what difference will it make? She is in her final passage. There is no arguing about that. The only question is, a passage to where? Her mother, with her cries in her final days of "Eddie" and "Oliver," had believed to heaven. The latter name, Prudence had not recognized—an early love? A late love, such as she, Prudence, once had?—but her father, Eddie . . . Prudence had not reminded her mother that if there was a heaven, he might or might not be there.

"Well, then, please come up."

After the doorman calls to announce a Miss O'Connor, Prudence grips the arms of the wingback chair and pushes herself to her feet. Usually, her afternoons are dotted with catnaps, the outcome of her invariable 4:53 awakenings: nature's timepiece set in her brain stem with the exactitude her husband, Carlton, had once described to her of a school of salmon's return to the very waters where they'd been born so as to spawn and then die.

She rests for a moment, holding the edge of the library table and looking out at the great expanse of the Hudson, the West Side Highway hidden behind park foliage thick as bunches of broccoli. The New Jersey waterfront was largely undeveloped when she'd moved here from Park Avenue a few years after Carlton's death. Now high-rises are visible from her fifteenth-floor window and a driving range that from this distance might be a leprechaun's kerchief smoothed over the ground. Only the river is unchanged. In winter, there are ice floes and wind-whipped waves; in summer, skies dressed at sunset with plum and papaya stripes. A vista, it saddens her to think, that has brought her more consistent pleasure, provided a more enduring connection, than anything human or animal.

When Carlton died, she'd been thirty-seven, childless, her parents long gone, Randall drifted so far away, it was as if he'd disappeared. A few months later, on the insistence of Harriet Masters, in whose interior-decoration firm Prudence had worked prior to her marriage, she consulted the psychiatrist Harriet had seen after her husband—presumably heartbroken from one of the torrid affairs he'd conducted with the wives of his fellow club members but, Harriet claimed, more bored than distraught—hung himself in the attic of their Tuxedo Park home. When the psychiatrist asked about Prudence's friendships, she told him about Ella, with whom she'd briefly been intimate, and Elaine, with whom she'd worked at Harriet's firm. On occasion, she reported, she and Carlton had socialized with Carlton's business associates and college friends and their wives, most particularly Alfred, Carlton's mountaineering partner. Their most regular dinner companion, however, had been CCB, for whom Carlton had become a surrogate son after his own son, married to Dorothy Tiffany, had become debilitated from manic-depressive illness. At the end of the meeting, the psychiatrist diagnosed Prudence as suffering from an overwhelming loneliness that predated the loss of Carlton. The problem, he gently explained, was not a lack of companions, but that there was not a one with whom she could talk about anything not found in a newspaper, much less, God forbid, cry.

She picks up the fallen papers and the cold cup of tea, considers going to the bathroom to tidy herself, then dismisses the thought. She has never been vain, but it is unsettling to see herself in the mirror: the voluptuousness she'd once found so embarrassing on her diminutive frame now eroded to loose skin draped over bones and sinew, her formerly pumpkin hair still thick but now stripped of color, her milky skin now too fragile for soap or cosmetics.

Instead, she makes her way to the kitchen, where she turns on the tap and waits for the kettle to fill. How had this Grace found her? Maybe through that thing called Google, a ridiculous word, like something out of a children's limerick. If the Google device had existed during the years when she'd still thought she wanted to find Randall, would she have used it to do so? Or would her fear about what might happen if they saw each other again have prevailed as it had with Carlton's offer before they married to hire a private detective? "Perhaps after we're settled," she'd mumbled, but what she'd thought was if the detective was to locate Randall, what could she say to him? *You never came home the Christmas next? You left me to bury both of our parents?*

She puts the filled kettle on the stove and lights the burner. As always, there is the guilty pleasure of defying Maricel, guilty because she knows that Maricel's injunctions—the stove, the front door, the shower, what clothes to wear so as not to catch "the cold in your chest"—come only out of concern for her. She listens for the sound of the gas igniting, then adjusts the flame under the kettle. Well, if this is a murderer ascending now on the elevator, she can console herself that on her last day she did not add to the collection of small cowardices that have constituted her adult years. Cowardices that have seemed in their sum almost evil: the sins of someone too tepid, too bland, or perhaps simply too self-righteous for passionate crime.

Yes, if this is a ploy, she will be at peace with having risked her life to meet Randall's granddaughter.

*Do not hold your breath*, Prudence reminds herself as she unlocks the door. *You do not want to faint.*

Before her is a wiry woman with chapped cheeks and chestnut hair pulled back into a too-short, too-severe ponytail. She smiles, tiny lines webbing out from her eyes and a mouthful of perfect teeth.

Her brother had a son and this son had a daughter. Prudence leans on the doorjamb as she absorbs the astonishment of it. A daughter whom someone must have taken regularly to a dentist but is dressed now in pants a size too large and shoes too sensible for her age: early forties, Prudence guesses. A woman who—to Prudence's decorator's eye, accustomed to seeing beneath the finishes of a place to its bones—looks as if she shoos away beauty. A person for whom a renovation would be possible but who has no desire to undertake it.

She did not kiss the girl. Should she have? But now the kettle is whistling. "Come in." Prudence gestures toward the living room. "I'll bring us some tea."

Less than a minute, but already so much roiling that it is a relief to have this retreat to the kitchen, the distraction of the transgressive thrill of pouring the steaming water into the teapot she never uses now that Maricel leaves her tea in an aluminum thermos.

She places the pot and teacups on a tray and takes out the shortbread cookies Maricel keeps in the cupboard, more for herself than for Prudence, who has lost her appetite for sweets.

The tray. Can she carry it? But the girl—she is not a girl, but with what must be nearly a sixty-year age difference between them, it's the word that comes to mind—is now in the doorway to the kitchen. Without asking, she takes the tray.

Prudence trails behind her guest to the living room. From the rear, with her slender hips and flat backside, she might be mistaken for a boy. A quiet is nestled in her movements. It may be that she has spent time with people who are unwell. Or old people, it occurs to Prudence, like herself.

"By the window, if you don't mind," Prudence directs.

She watches Grace's gaze alight on the vase of dahlias, the blood orange and kingly purple having called to Prudence when she spotted them a few days ago in plastic bins outside a Korean market, a touch of color in the otherwise moon-toned room. Perhaps Grace learned about flowers from her grandfather—Randall had written that he worked for a florist—and now Prudence wonders if Grace knows furniture too, if she recognizes the chrome-and-glass tables as Eileen Gray, the slipper chairs in creamy leather as Mies van der Rohe.

Grace sets the tray on the library table. She waits for Prudence to lower herself into the wingback chair before taking the matching one.

*How strange*, Prudence thinks. No more than fifteen minutes since she was napping here, and now the room so dizzyingly occupied.

Grace reaches for the teapot.

"Let it steep a bit longer. Another two or three minutes." Prudence smiles to soften what she fears landed like an old-person's bark. "So, Grace, it is Grace, yes?"

"It is." Grace looks at her warmly but not insistently, as though gauging her approach. "How funny that we both have virtue names."

Prudence must have a quizzical look on her face because Grace adds, "Prudence, Grace."

"I quite hated my name growing up. I thought it suggested that

I was prudish or, even worse, prunelike. My brother, your grandfather, called me Pru, but that doesn't solve the ugly *prrr* sound. But *Grace*, that is lovely. It brings to mind the graceful Grace Kelly."

"Thank you. My namesake, though, was Grace Slick. A very different woman."

"The name rings a bell, but I'm afraid I can't say from where."

"A rock-and-roll singer. My mother saw her perform early in her career, with her band The Great Society. I suppose I should feel lucky she didn't name me Great."

"That would not have been nearly as charming."

"They named my brother Garcia, after Jerry Garcia. Jerry Garcia of the Grateful Dead."

"Even I know about them." Prudence gathers the shawl she keeps on the back of the chair around her shoulders. "So, Grace and Garcia?"

"People thought about us as a unit, our names connected with an ampersand."

"He's younger than you are?"

"By three minutes. We were twins."

Twins. Whenever Prudence hears of twins, she thinks of Dorothy Tiffany, who'd once told Prudence that she'd been obsessed with twins on account of her twin sisters, Comfort and Julia. She'd followed them around so incessantly, they'd taken to calling her Me Too. "That must have been interesting."

"It was like having a live-in best friend, though we were kind of opposites. Garcia was open and exuberant. I was cautious and bookish. He had what they would call now a learning disability, but I think it was just that his brain needed some extra time to develop."

Grace bites her lower lip, then swipes at it as if to stop herself. "My grandfather might have been more relaxed about it if there hadn't been such a contrast between us. For a long while, I hated that school was so easy for me. It seemed that it only made things worse for Garcia."

Prudence wonders what color Grace's hair was as a child. There's no hint of the Irish coloring she and Randall had inherited from their mother in Grace's olive skin, and she doubts that Randall's and her red had filtered down to Grace. Still, Prudence can see the family resemblance in Grace's small bones and in the trace of a curvaceousness that appears otherwise to have been beaten out of her.

"Did you spend a lot of time with your grandfather while you were growing up?"

"He raised us. He and Angela, our housekeeper. My father dropped us at his doorstep. Literally. He arrived in the middle of the night with Garcia and me not quite a year old—sick, wet, and hungry, my grandfather said—carried us into the foyer, and left. The story we were always told was that my grandfather took care of us himself that first night and was so worn-out by the morning that when Angela arrived, he lay on the kitchen floor and fell right to sleep."

"He must have really trusted her."

"She'd worked for him since the day he was married. My grandmother had hated the way her mother treated her household help, and she swore she'd never have anyone work for her, but then her parents gave my grandfather and her a house as a wedding present and it was too large for her to take care of herself. Rather than hiring what her mother called a 'colored woman' or 'a nice Irish maid,' she hired Angela, who was sixteen and just arrived from Mexico."

A nice Irish maid? Does Grace know that her grandfather's mother had been precisely that?

"My grandfather said that my grandmother treated Angela like a little sister. Instead of a uniform, my grandmother bought her six weekday dresses and two for Sundays, with matching ribbons for her braids. She took her to pick out the curtains for her room, taught her to read and to play basketball. It would have been impossible for anyone to adore my grandmother more than my grandfather did, but Angela came close."

Prudence pictures Angela's room: the flowered curtains a girl from Mexico who wears ribbons in her hair might choose. An orange bedspread with red fringe, the wooden cross she would hang over her bed.

"When my father was born, Angela became his nanny. She

lived in until he left home, and then my grandfather bought her a studio apartment a few blocks away. The day we arrived, she packed up her things and moved back into her old room on the fourth floor."

"She sounds like a wonderful person."

"She was. She and my grandfather were totally loyal to each other, but they could be like oil and water. Angela was always singing and hugging us and it felt as though she understood us completely, whereas my grandfather was reserved and meticulous and so insanely protective of us . . ." Grace sighs.

How, Prudence wonders, does one find the balance between too few and too many questions? So precarious, like a seesaw. Too few and Grace might think that Prudence is not really listening. Too many and Grace might feel she is being grilled.

What Prudence wants to say is, *You don't have to tell me everything.*

What Prudence wants to say is, *Tell me everything.*

"Where were your parents?"

"My father was off. Colombia. Hawaii. Thailand. Anywhere he could get drugs cheaply. First pot, then hallucinogens, then more pot, then more hallucinogens, and finally smokable heroin. He was the poster child for what they called when I was in nursing school the 'gateway-drug theory.' That less addictive drugs lead to more addictive ones. It's not always or even mostly true, but it seems to have been for him."

*Nursing school. So she's a nurse.*

"A few years ago, I requested his records from the detox center where he'd gone. Reading them, I saw that his history was more complicated. All mixed up with a lot of mystical ideas he had about drugs."

Prudence nods. During the sixties, she'd read about people who believed that drugs could open a door to creativity and higher consciousness. Even Harriet, by then old enough to collect Social Security, had tried marijuana, though she'd reported afterward it had only made her feel silly and too sleepy to do anything more than curl up on her couch.

"When I was five, my father came back to San Francisco. We'd see him every few weeks, but I was too young to know that he was strung out on heroin. If he wasn't wasted, he was in withdrawal, shaking or sweating, unable to sit still. At the end, my grandfather wouldn't let us be alone with him. Either he or Angela always stayed in the room."

Grace looks at Prudence as though apologizing in advance. "He overdosed when I was nine."

The wave of grief Prudence felt when Grace told her that Randall has been dead nearly twenty years now returns, this time, though, sharper and more intense. She envisions her brother holding his head in gnarled hands and children quietly playing in their rooms and a woman with long black braids crying as she stirs something over a stove.

"My grandfather didn't tell us, though, until we were ten."

"How could he not tell you?"

"He buried my father without us there and forbade Angela from talking about him. I was too young to be able to put into words that something was wrong. Angela lit candles all over the house, even the bathrooms, and on the Day of the Dead, she made an altar with my father's poetry books and drumsticks and a photograph of him as a baby with my grandmother."

"You must have thought that was very odd."

"Everything felt odd. It was as though the house had been put under a spell."

"And your mother?" Prudence asks.

"She had what they called then a breakdown but would probably be diagnosed today as a postpartum depression. Her parents brought her back to Houston around the same time my father left us with our grandfather."

Grace smiles, a rueful smile that seems intended to communicate, *This is a very old story. You don't need to feel badly for me.* It's a smile Prudence remembers having pasted on her own face when she first met Carlton's family and the people in his social set, who she feared viewed her as the orphan match girl.

"I think at first she believed that she'd get herself together and come for us. I remember her sending us letters and drawings and cassette tapes with children's songs when we were very little, but then we stopped hearing from her."

Grace glances at the teapot and then at Prudence, who nods.

"My grandfather told me that when my father died, he called her parents. They said she'd been in and out of hospitals and was living in a group home. He wasn't sure if they'd even tell her about my father overdosing, but she called him that same day to say that she was coming to the funeral."

Prudence raises her eyebrows.

"She never made it."

With Grace now pouring the tea, Prudence senses a curtain having been drawn on the past. *Come back, come back to this room, this April day,* Prudence admonishes herself. *Back to the girl adding cream only, as you requested, to your tea.* "I haven't even asked you what brings you to New York."

"I'm a hospice nurse, and I'm giving two papers at our professional association's annual convention. It's at the Sheraton Midtown."

Grace places the cup and saucer within Prudence's reach. "The truth is, I've been thinking for a long time about trying to contact you. I'm embarrassed to say how long. My grandfather died in 1993, and I thought about trying to find you then, but he'd been out of touch with you for so long. I gave in to inertia . . ."

Was she wrong about the curtain? The tea merely a pause?

"It was the sister of one of my recent patients who made me think about it again. Herman, my patient, was eighty-nine, and his sister, Rose, was eighty-five, and I saw how strong their bond still was. A few days before he died, she told me that he knew her better than anyone else ever had."

Grace looks at Prudence as though making sure she understands that this is the nature of Grace's work: all her patients die. "Rose showed me a very old photograph of Herman seated on a chair, holding her, the day she was born. She'd been born at home, and that afternoon a photographer had come to their parents' house. Herman was so small, so young, but he was gazing at her with this radiant love."

Prudence feels a heaviness in her chest, a thickness in her throat. She was born at home too, in the gardener's cottage at Laurelton Hall. Randall must have been there. But she's never seen any photographs of that day, heard any stories about it.

"Herman had been with Rose the day she was born, and she was with him the day he died. It made me think about you and how sad it was that my grandfather never saw you after he left New York."

Prudence's eyes tingle. Were her tear ducts not so dry these past few years, they would fill.

"Wondrous things sometimes happen in the hours after a person dies. In my more spiritual moments, I think the veil between life and death is for that brief span porous: the body still warm, fluids still flowing, but the soul escaped."

With the word *soul*, Prudence feels a chill. She thinks of the man, so long ago, who'd looked into his soul and seen the truth about her.

"A lot of families want to whisk the body away, but Rose and Herman's son asked if they could have a few hours before we called the funeral home, and then Rose asked if I would sit with them. It was late afternoon and the light was waning, but there was a kind of brilliance in the room. Herman's son was holding his father's hand and crying a little, but also smiling at his aunt Rose, who was talking about when she and Herman were children. Herman had loved their grandmother's apple cake and the first thing he ever built—he was a civil engineer and spent his whole life making things—was a wooden stool so his grandmother could reach the cake pans she kept on the top shelves in her kitchen. He painted it apple red, Rose said, to remind his grandmother to make the cake."

Grace drops a sugar cube into her tea. "When Rose told that story, I was overcome with wanting to find out what had happened to you."

"You must have been surprised to learn that I am still alive."

"I was. Surprised and happy. I only found your address the day before I left. Otherwise, I would have written you first."

"I'm so glad you did. Find me."

Grace stirs her tea. "Can I ask . . . did you have children?"

Prudence shakes her head no. Even now, so many many years past that turn in the road, it's hard to talk about.

"I think, then, that you are my only living relative on my father's side."

"Except for your brother."

Grace takes a long breath, then wipes her mouth with a napkin. "My brother died two years before my grandfather."

Prudence averts her eyes, not wanting Grace to see how stunned she feels. How can there be another death? Three generations: Randall, his son, his grandson.

"I want to tell you about Garcia, just not today," Grace says softly. "Perhaps I could come again? I'm here all week. Until Saturday."

"I would like that very much." Prudence chides herself for sounding stiff, a caricature of politeness, but it is true: She would like to see Grace again. Very much.

"When I went through my grandfather's things, I found a box of mementos in his study. He'd shown me the box many times when I was a child, but it had been at least ten years since I'd opened it and looked at what he kept there: things he brought with him when he came to San Francisco, newspaper clippings he collected afterwards, a packet of letters from you and your mother."

Most of Prudence's past is shrouded with the shapes of events no longer distinct, or faded with the emotional color gone. Now, though, the memory of the evening when Randall's first letter arrived balloons. She sees herself cutting a square from the drawing paper Dorothy Tiffany had given her and writing her brother back. Carefully printing the address for his rooming house on an envelope, walking on her own to the post office to ask how many stamps were required, after which there'd been the waiting, day after day, for the mail to arrive, despite knowing it would take two weeks for her letter to cross the country and, even if her brother responded immediately, another two for his to travel to her.

"I brought the letters in my suitcase. Actually, I brought the entire box. I could show you everything."

To Prudence then, it had felt like years, but most certainly several months before she received Randall's response . . . A white space . . . And then her mother crying as she composed a letter to Randall at the florist shop where his former landlady, having sent the one-word *Moved* telegram, had later written he worked. Crying because not only did she have to tell her son that his father had died, she could not say that his father had in his final hours asked about him. All she could write was that his father had fallen from a ladder at Mr. T's Madison Avenue mansion, crashing fifteen feet to the ground and bringing down with him the glass orb on the chain to which he'd uselessly clung.

Grace glances at her watch. "I'm so sorry, but I have to go. I'm meeting with the other people on my first panel. Could I come on Tuesday around six? Perhaps I could take you out to dinner?"

"I'll have Maricel, the woman who helps me, make us a light meal."

"I hate to trouble you . . ."

"She will be delighted to cook. With me, her culinary skills are a waste. What do you like to eat?"

"I'm afraid I'm a bit of a bother. I'm vegan."

"Is that vegetarian?"

"It's even more restrictive. I don't eat any animal products. But I could bring something . . ."

"Maricel could make us her rice and beans and her okra and a salad. Would that suit you?"

Grace stands. "That would be perfect. I've been vegan since my brother died. It was physical at first. I couldn't swallow anything that had been killed or taken from an animal. Then, it became political. It drove my grandfather crazy. He was a meat-and-potatoes man."

Prudence pushes herself up from her chair. She senses Grace watching her, not wanting to offer unnecessary help. "That's how we were raised," she says once she's squarely on her feet. "Corned beef and cabbage and always potatoes."

She's thankful that it's not the Sunday when Thomas, Harriet's grandson who is now Prudence's lawyer, takes her out to dinner. She wants to sit in her chair and look out at the water and absorb these snapshots of the man her brother became. When he'd leaned over to kiss the top of her head and then slipped away while her mother was berating her father for being a drunken fool, he'd been a boy. Not yet using a razor. Absorb that he married, apparently a wealthy woman if they were given a house as a wedding present, had a son who became a drug addict, raised his two grandchildren with the help of a Mexican housekeeper named Angela, ate meat and potatoes his entire life, died two decades ago.

While Grace waits for the elevator, Prudence stands, half in, half out of the hall, propping her door open with her back. The two of them smile and nod at each other until the elevator arrives and Grace disappears inside. Then, thinking of Maricel's instruction "You bolt both locks, Mrs. P, but not the chain. That you have to leave off so I can let myself in," Prudence, for the first time all day, does as directed.

# 3

# Prudence

## Laurelton Hall to New York, 1914–1933

The scant residues of Prudence's own experiences of Laurelton Hall are so overshadowed by the many residues of the photographs she's seen of the mansion, she can no longer distinguish between what belongs to her and what belongs to everyone.

A few scenes, though, congeal. In the earliest, she's at a hidden perch behind a potted lemon tree. A small boy, her size, crouches beside her clutching a feather. Girls in white dresses with silver trays aloft on their slender shoulders traverse the terrace. On each tray, there's a peacock, its rainbow plumage overflowing the back lip, the feathers tangled with its porter's long loose hair. The boy's tongue pokes her palm as she presses her hand over his mouth.

After Carlton's death, when she'd gone back to work for Harriet Masters, she'd made a trip one snowy March afternoon to the New York Public Library to research country homes of the era of Laurelton Hall for the obscenely expensive renovation of a client's house built a year later. Sitting in her wet galoshes in the chilly Periodical Room, she'd studied the page of photographs from a May 1914 copy of *The New York Times* about what must have been this very event she dimly recalled. It came as a jolt to realize that she'd been only two years old.

Although the occasion would come to be known as the Peacock Feast, on the engraved invitations Mr. Tiffany had sent to 150 "men of genius," he'd cryptically described the evening as an opportunity to view the spring flowers at his country estate. The all-male attendees—painters, publishers, architects, Tiffany's closest friends, his father's gemologist—had been transported by a private train from New York City to Oyster Bay, their arrival timed to precede sunset. From there, the men had been driven by a fleet of cars up the mansion's mile-long driveway planted especially for the spectacle by Tiffany's forty gardeners with purple and red phlox and white and pink laurels and blue and yellow tulips in arrangements that resembled stained glass.

The dinner, Prudence read, was heralded by a procession of five nubile young ladies trailed by children of descending heights showcasing the *paons en volière* (roasted peacock) and *cochon de lait farci* (suckling pig) prepared for the meal by the chefs of the Delmonico Restaurant from produce and animals raised at Laurelton Hall. As the famed Harry Rowe Shelley played the organ, a somber Miss Phyllis de Kay, whose father was in attendance, led Tiffany's three youngest daughters and one of their friends, all five costumed in white Grecian gowns affixed by straps that crisscrossed their breasts and encircled their buttocks, from the terrace to a palatial dining room laden with apple-tree branches and overlooking the Sound, now with night having fallen, sparkling with lights. Miss de Kay wore a headdress constructed from a peacock, its face draped over her forehead so the gaping beak rested between her eyes and the crest of head feathers formed a small fan above. She and the two girls behind her carried what must have been extraordinarily heavy platters on each of which a roasted peacock whose full plumage had been artfully reattached was arrayed, while the other two girls bore enormous bouquets of long peacock feathers.

Studying the caption under one of the photographs, Prudence saw that it was Dorothy who shouldered the third peacock, which she held, as though in silent protest, a bit lower than the others. Unlike her twin sisters, ahead and behind her, her face was hidden by her long hair, her gaze on the creature's head, but Prudence could sense Dorothy's misery in the sharp bend of her elbow and the tight way she stood, as though herself one of the Laurelton Hall columns with their glazed capitals.

Behind the girls were six children, Tiffany's grandchildren and the grandchildren of his friends, also in white gowns with scarves that flowed from their heads to their ankles. Gripping lit torches, they sprinkled rose petals from wicker baskets on the 150 men of genius seated at large octagonal tables. At the rear were four even smaller children dressed as portly cooks with long aprons tied around their pillow-padded middles, each holding a platter on which sprawled a suckling pig.

In the photographs, the peacocks' glazed eyes had not been visible, but in Prudence's memory, the little boy crouched with her behind the potted lemon tree had cried in horror. Even at two, she must have known that they should not be there, secretly watching, because she'd put her hand over his mouth.

Prudence's next memory of Laurelton Hall is of being held aloft by her father as she watches a bride emerge from a gleaming black car. She remembers the car door opening and a white-slippered foot and then the burst of applause from the servants and guests. Not until Prudence met Carlton, whose parents, close friends of the groom's father, had attended this very wedding of Dorothy Tiffany and Robert Burlingham, had Prudence attached a date to the image: September 1914, just a few months after the Peacock Feast. A date Carlton recalled because it had been his first year at Groton, when he'd been ashamed of how homesick he felt and how strange the mostly northern boys seemed, as strange as if he'd gone to England for boarding school, which he might have had the war not begun.

Carlton's mother's first letter had included a report of the trip she and his father had made to Oyster Bay for the wedding, just days after they'd left him at school. A small affair, she wrote, only family and close friends with a brief ceremony at the church in Cold Spring Harbor and then a simple wedding breakfast at the Tiffany home. Prudence had blushed when Carlton told her that his mother had described how Tiffany's servants had framed the entrance to the dining room: the women with starched aprons and bouquets of pink peonies in their white-gloved hands, the men with carnations dyed the same pink pinned to their black lapels. Blushed to think that Carlton's parents had perhaps glimpsed her own parents, positioned within Tiffany's design.

The scent of the wisteria hanging from the beams and in huge pots on the tables in the Laurelton Hall dining room had been so overwhelming, Carlton's mother reported, it was frankly nauseating. Between the lines, Carlton could read his mother's disapproval that the wedding had been unfitting for the son of CCB, such a prominent figure in New York City politics, not to mention for a Tiffany, and her resentment that she'd been deprived of a grander affair that would have included a wedding gown with a sixteen-foot train and a lavish dinner dance with a full orchestra to which she could have worn a gown herself. That she'd traveled all the way to Oyster Bay to see Dorothy in what had been her mother's plain wedding dress (a dress befitting the marriage of Dorothy's mother, a woman who at thirty-five had been presumed a spinster, to a widower) and to then be served a breakfast not very different from what might be on her own table Easter morning.

Prudence's last memory of Laurelton Hall begins with a smell: the scent of fermented apples in the kitchen crate where she is feverishly sleeping, her mother at work on the third floor while Molly, the cook, watches over her. Molly, with her yeasty breath, her hands dusted with flour as she spoons cold water into Prudence's mouth. Molly lifting her onto the outhouse seat.

Then screaming. A terrible quantity of screaming. Molly, she thinks it is Molly, holding Prudence's mother, making her swig from what Prudence knows now but would not have known then was a whiskey bottle, tucking a blanket around her mother, slumped over in the back of one of Mr. T's cars. It is Prudence's first time in an automobile, but young as she is, she is aware that she must hide her excitement, and then everything changes and they are no longer living in the gardener's cottage but in the apartment in Hell's Kitchen.

Her father leaves every morning, taking the streetcar to the fifty-seven-room Tiffany mansion on the corner of Madison Avenue and Seventy-second Street. It's her father's job to tend the tropical plants in the top-floor studio, with its freestanding four-hearth fireplace that majestically rises to the double-height ceiling. On occasion he comes home late and mean from a bar where he goes on paydays with the other men who work at the Tiffany house. Her mother leaves the apartment only to shop for groceries or attend mass with her hair covered by a white lace scarf. She sleeps with the matted top of a peacock feather under her pillow.

Soon, Prudence is in school, and her memories thicken to include other children and classrooms and snowstorms and a horse she sees fall to its knees on a cobblestoned street and then roll onto its side with white froth on its lips. All of this, it seems, a prelude to the night when her father shoves her mother and Randall raises his fists.

Her mother cries out, "You cannot strike your father. You cannot. God will curse you, and we've had enough curses on this family."

"Let 'im, let the little bastard try," her father taunts, and then he takes a swing at Randall, who ducks, and her father loses his balance and falls backward, hitting his head on the table.

Her mother tends the knob that forms on the back of her father's head. "Go, Prudence, quick, fetch me some ice," she calls out, but Prudence is sitting on the edge of her bed in the room she shares with her brother, watching him pack his rucksack: two pants, two shirts, his newsboy cap, the Irish fisherman's sweater their grandmother had made for their father and that is now Randall's, his copy of *The Call of the Wild*. On top he places the flat wooden box, the length and width of a school notebook but thicker, with a brass clasp he sometimes lets her open to see the white stones and the glass tile and the upper portion of a peacock feather, not ratty like the one under her mother's pillow but carefully dusted, with its eye still royal blue.

"Christ almighty," her mother yells as her father vomits on himself. "Prudence, get me a wet cloth," and her brother is leaning over and whispering in her ear, "I love you, Pru. I'll write you," and she is staring at the floorboards, too terrified to say anything back.

Prudence writes her first and only poem the day after Randall leaves:

My brother is missing.  
We don't know where he's gone.  
I don't feel like kissing.  
Mother cries until dawn.

She reads the poem over and over again that first week while she stares at the bed where her brother slept, knowing that he won't be coming home in a few days as her father claims. The poem, she discovers, transforms her misery from brute pain, a pressure in her chest that makes her feel that she must lie down and curl her knees up to her stomach, into something she can hold in her mind.

With Randall gone, her mother stops going to church and sends Prudence to the grocer's with a list. Dreading finding her mother in bed on her return from school, Prudence takes to visiting her father at his job. She comes in through the servants' entrance, and if Mr. T is out, as he usually is in the late afternoons, the under-butler lets her go unaccompanied up the back stairs to the three-story-high studio where her father might be pruning the plants that grow like a toy rain forest in a greenhouse alcove, or on a ladder polishing the lamps that hang on wrought-metal chains made of little figures of elephants and monkeys and birds. Sometimes she brings pieces of brown package paper and, using a pencil from her school satchel, sketches the room: the fireplace with the chimney like the trunk of a very old tree, the goldfish bowl suspended over a fountain, the paintings, some of them, she discovers, Mr. T's own work.

Only once does she actually see Mr. T. She is drawing in the corner of the room when she hears heavy footsteps. Her father's body stiffens in alert. Frightened, she ducks behind a settee, but it is unnecessary since Mr. T only pokes his head in as though looking for someone and then leaves without even greeting her father.

One afternoon, a lady arrives. At first, like Mr. T, she peeks into the studio, but then, spotting Prudence's father, she comes in.

"Eddie, I didn't know you worked here."

"Yes, Miss Dorothy. Pardon me, Mrs. Burlingham." Her father puts down his tin watering can, wipes his hands on his canvas apron. "It's been seven years now."

The lady touches his arm with her bare hand. "Please call me Dorothy. You've known me since I was a girl." She shakes her head slightly. "It is just too peculiar to hear you call me Mrs. Burlingham."

When Dorothy notices Prudence sketching in the corner, Prudence's heart pounds out of control. Will her father lose his job because she is here? Will the lady drag her downstairs to be whipped by the frightening Mr. T?

"Is this your daughter, Eddie?"

"It is. Prudence. She comes here sometimes after school."

The lady approaches her. Even at eleven, Prudence knows that Dorothy, with her bob and brown dress with no adornments aside from a thin belt and a white collar, is not glamorous in the way that a rich lady should be. Moreover, her eyes make her seem simultaneously odd and exotic: deep set under heavy brows, with an expression that is warm but also detached, as though she were observing Prudence through a pane of glass.

When she smiles, though, a mother smile, everything changes. She crouches so she can examine the sketch Prudence is working on of the four-sided fireplace. "You handle perspective very well. And you've captured how magical and almost frightening the hearth looks. Like something out of a fairy tale."

"That's exactly what I was thinking!" Prudence blurts out. "It always makes me think of 'Jack and the Beanstalk.'"

"A place where an ogre might roast small children . . ."

Prudence glances over at her father to see if he objects to her talking with the lady, but he has taken his watering can to the greenhouse alcove and is tending the potted orchids. "Or maybe where a sad giant would live all alone?"

"You are kinder than I am. My daughter Mabbie likes to draw too. But she is only six. Not nearly as skilled as you are."

A week later, the lady returns with a rag paper sketchbook and a box of pastels. "These were on Mabbie's easel, but she doesn't need them. Now you can draw the plants and the flowers. I suspect you'll make them look so real, I'll be able to smell the blooms."

On the day that Randall's first letter arrives, Prudence comes home with her father from the Tiffany mansion to find her mother no longer in bed but making dumplings for the chicken she has gone to the butcher herself to buy. Her mother reads Randall's letter aloud, then watches while Prudence takes the separate one folded inside for her into the room that she'd shared with Randall and is now hers alone. Later, Prudence dries the dishes while her mother washes, grateful that her mother has not asked to see Randall's letter to her. Instead, her mother inquires, "Who is Charlie? Your brother wrote that he is staying with a boy named Charlie," and Prudence feels important that she knows: the boy with the lock of black hair that fell over his forehead, he wore a newsboy cap, smoked cigarettes on the train platform. Randall had talked about how Charlie had just picked up one day—"Got himself out of this hellhole"—and gone to San Francisco.

When she looks over, her mother is dabbing her eyes with the hem of her apron. Later, her father puts his arms around her mother, and for the first time since Randall left, she does not pull away.

It is from a tall ladder in Mr. T's studio that her father, the following year, falls. Her mother says he must have lost his balance, reaching to dust one of the glass globes, but a footman spreads the rumor that Eddie came back from lunch having had a nip or two. He dies in the ambulance. Her mother is nearly catatonic, leaving Prudence, now twelve, to handle with her aunt the arrangements.

The morning after her father's death, one of Mr. T's lawyers, a ruddy-cheeked Mr. Bromston, comes to the apartment with instructions to send the funeral bills to him. He removes neither his overcoat nor his top hat and addresses her mother with a tone of sternness and contempt that frightens Prudence. Was her father's death a crime? Will her mother be taken to jail in his stead?

Some of the staff from the Madison Avenue house attend the wake in Prudence's mother's parlor—not the butler, whom her father used to call behind his back Mr. Too-Good-for-Us, but one of the footmen and two of the chambermaids and Mr. Feeney, who during the years her parents were at Laurelton Hall had run the furnace housed in the blue-tiled minaret and now tends the cars Mr. T keeps in the city.

Mr. Feeney makes a little bow to her mother, immobile in the chair by the grate with her hair combed by Prudence's aunt and only an ounce or two of water fed to her in a spoon having passed through her lips since Prudence's father's fall. When Prudence asks if she can bring Mr. Feeney a glass so he can have some whiskey with the other men, he tells her, "Thank you. No, I don't partake no more." He narrows his eyes as if to say, *If only these other lugs would do the same,* and Prudence thinks he would mean her father too if he were still here.

"Would you like some tea, then, Mr. Feeney?"

"What a polite girl you are . . . If it's not too much bother, some tea would do me good."

After Prudence brings him a cup of tea and a saucer and a biscuit to go with it, he pats the spot next to him on the divan. "Sit, keep me a company," he says, and then he tells her how her father had been the only gardener at Laurelton Hall whom Mr. T permitted to touch the plants he selected and arranged himself each week for the fountain courtyard. And how after a maid had been attacked by one of the peacocks that roamed the property, it had been Prudence's father who'd gone to Mr. T to say that the birds needed to be fenced off.

"They're beautiful beasts," Mr. Feeney says. "Made Mr. Darwin sick that it's the males who have those colorful feathers and that it's the ladies who choose. But they can be vicious, especially when they're in heat. Heard tell of them gouging out eyes."

Mr. Feeney sips his tea and takes a delicate bite of the biscuit. "He loved his peacocks, Mr. T. Every fall, after they molted, he'd have his gamekeeper, Riley, gather the feathers. Riley would wash them and dust them with talcum, and then it would be your father who'd make them into bouquets. Hugest one you ever saw in this urn on the mantelpiece in the drawing room. So we were all afraid to ask. Your father was just as scared as the rest of us, but he knew it was dangerous for Mr. Tiffany's daughters and grandchildren, and for youse too, for those birds to be wandering free, so he screwed up his courage and told Mr. T. And next thing we knew, the peacocks was moved to the back of the property."

For a few foolish hours, Prudence imagines that Mr. T or maybe his daughter, Miss Dorothy, the lady who gave her the sketchbook and pastel crayons, might come to the wake or the funeral, something she longs for but also dreads on account of her mother looking like a madwoman in her chair by the grate.

Mr. T does not come, but on the morning of the funeral a letter arrives for Prudence from a Mrs. Robert Burlingham. Not until she begins reading does Prudence understand that Mrs. Robert Burlingham is the very same Miss Dorothy.

*Dearest Prudence,*

*I am so sorry to hear about your father's tragic accident and death. I am in Connecticut with my four children, and my youngest, Mikey, is quite ill. Otherwise, I would most certainly attend the funeral.*

*I have such fond memories of your father. I used to love watching him change the disks in the color wheel under the fountain at our house. My father always had such strict instructions about them, and he was always happy after he saw the results your father achieved.*

*When I was fourteen, I went off to a boarding school in Catonsville, Maryland. It was a girls' school called St. Timothy's, and even though I'd pleaded to be permitted to go, once there, I quite hated it. We'd been raised as free spirits in many ways—ruffians collecting flowers and oysters—though my father was a tyrant about punctuality and our not causing disarray in the house. I was terribly homesick and would count the days until summer holidays.*

*My second summer, my father was abroad on a trip he made with a designer from his glass factory. I was crushed!*

*Every morning, I would find your father in the rose arbor and tell him about my miseries: how much I missed my mother, who'd died three years earlier, how my twin sisters, Julia and Comfort, had one another while I had no one, how horrid it was of my father to go away while I was home on holiday.*

*Your father would let me rattle on and on, and then he'd reassure me that the heart does mend. I remember him telling me how unhappy he was when he left his mother behind in Ireland, coming here alone at fifteen. I couldn't believe that he'd not seen her since. I know he didn't mean to make me feel ashamed of my complaining about my father being gone for just a summer, but it helped me that he did because he made me think of what my mother would have said: that we must never forget how very fortunate we were compared with the poor sad people living a hundred to a tenement building with the stench of open toilets and the unbearable heat of summer. I saw how much I had to be grateful for.*

*The last time I recall seeing your father at Laurelton Hall was the night before my father's "Peacock Feast." My father's companion, Patsy, had insisted we practice the procession. Your father brought this big box filled with peacock feathers up from the barn and out to the terrace, and he helped my sister Julia and our friend Francesca Gilder pick the ones they would carry. He made a little pile of the feathers that were too short or a bit damaged, which he said he'd give to his children. I remember thinking.how lucky they were to have a father like him.*

*Please express my deepest condolences to your mother.*

*Fondly,*

*Dorothy*

Prudence has never seen a letter with so many words in it. As with the three letters Randall wrote just to her, she feels special having received it. But it also makes her feel bad. Does Dorothy think that Prudence's family are like the poor sad people living with stink?

It seems that Dorothy has nicer memories of Prudence's father than Prudence does herself.

She is glad that Dorothy did not come to the wake.

Her mother's sister stays with them for four days after the funeral, but then she has to return to her own family on Staten Island. "If your mama doesn't start eating by the end of the week," she instructs Prudence, "you go to the pharmacy on the corner and have them call me at this number. That's the grocer on our block. He has a telephone and he'll send his boy to bring me to the line."

Prudence nods.

"Let her stay in her bed for the rest of today and tomorrow, but after that make her get up and at least wash and sit in the parlor."

By the morning, though, Prudence's mother is up. She's fixed her hair and made a pot of oatmeal for breakfast that she douses with cream and sugar and then fries with butter into little cakes the way Prudence likes. Prudence eats two and watches carefully as her mother swallows a few bites from one.

"Shoo," her mother says. "Off to school."

Every month, a clerk arrives with an envelope from Mr. T's office. Her mother tips the boy a nickel. After he leaves, she counts the bills. "Unless we want to live on soup for the rest of our days and never have us a new dress," she tells Prudence, "I'm going to have to get a job."

By Prudence's thirteenth birthday, her mother is installed as a seamstress in the Wanamaker's furniture department. She'd learned to sew from her own mother, who'd been apprenticed to a milliner in Cork, and she knows from her first job, at the Tiffany factory in Queens, where she'd been one of the fastest girls piecing together the lampshades from the small bits of colored glass, that she is good with her hands. Once married, though, Prudence's mother had been let go, as was the policy for the girls who worked there. Her supervisor, Clara Driscoll, fond of Bridgey, as she'd called Prudence's mother, had arranged for Prudence's mother and her new husband to be interviewed for positions at Laurelton Hall.

"Clara Driscoll's the one who designed the lamps," Prudence's mother says. "Never got credit, but she did all the drawings, came up with the new designs each season. And half those famous windows too." One Sunday, Clara, who was an avid bicyclist, took Prudence's mother and two of the other girls from the factory to the plaza surrounding Grant's Tomb, where, she announced, she was going to teach them how to ride a bicycle. She owned her own bicycle, and she rented a second one from a shop nearby. The other girls were afraid to even climb on, but Prudence's mother, the smallest of the three, nimbly mounted the bicycle, and in half an hour Clara taught her how to ride.

Her mother laughs as she tells Prudence the story. "Clara beamed like I was her babe taking a first step. She was so proud of me. A few weeks later, she invited me to come bicycling again with her, but by then I'd met your father, and Sundays were his only day off and . . ." She sighs. "I was like any girl, I thought having a beau was the most important thing."

"Did Clara have a beau?"

"She was widowed. A young widow. Mr. T made her leave when she remarried."

Her mother is paid piecework at Wanamaker's. In the summers and during her school vacations, Prudence helps her, covering buttons for divans and sewing beads on the edges of pillows. One day, the department supervisor, a corpulent woman named Mrs. Clarkson, looks over Prudence's shoulder while she is sketching during the lunch break, and after that Prudence is allowed to do some of the drawings the salespersons give to the customers. For these, she is paid separately, not much, but enough to buy her mother a spring coat and herself an Easter hat.

When Prudence is sixteen, Mrs. Clarkson encourages her to enter a citywide drawing contest for a college scholarship. Prudence has not thought about attending college and is astonished when she comes in first place.

The woman who administers the scholarship invites Prudence

to her office. "You are a beautiful girl," the woman says in a carefully enunciated voice.

Prudence feels red blotches rising from her chest to her cheeks. Is the woman making fun of her?

"You don't understand it now, and that is a good thing because it will allow you to focus on your work, which is very good. Excellent, in fact."

Once her mother is asleep, Prudence examines what she can see of herself in the scratched mirror over the bathroom sink: her curly red hair, her pale skin, her violet eyes. She looks nothing like the screen actresses she and her mother admire, her hair so much redder than Clara Bow's or Marion Davies's, her body save for her chest so much slighter than that of Bebe Daniels or Billie Dove. And never ever could she imagine having the bold gaze of a Norma Shearer or Dolores del Rio.

She puts the awards letter at the bottom of her undergarments drawer, with Randall's letters and the one from Dorothy Tiffany and a sheet of paper onto which she copied from a book in her high school library a poem called "A Graveyard," which her English teacher had read aloud:

> the sea has nothing to give but a well excavated grave.
> The firs stand in a procession—each with an emerald
> turkey-foot at the top—
> reserved as their contours, saying nothing;
> repression, however, is not the most obvious characteristic
> of the sea;
> the sea is a collector, quick to return a rapacious look.

After her teacher read the poem, by a woman named Marianne Moore, she said, Prudence looked up *rapacious* in the dictionary kept on a stand at the back of the classroom. She felt a pit in her stomach as she read the definition: "aggressively greedy or grasping." It made her think of the lawyer who had come to their house the morning after her father's death—as though he'd been calling her mother this awful word.

She can hardly utter it in her mind.

*Rapacious.*

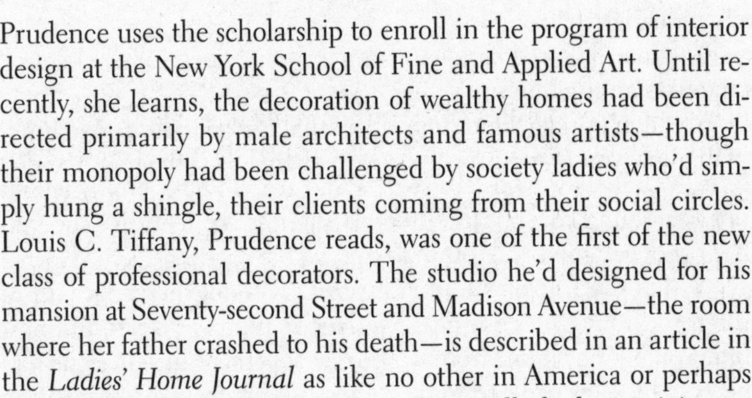

Prudence uses the scholarship to enroll in the program of interior design at the New York School of Fine and Applied Art. Until recently, she learns, the decoration of wealthy homes had been directed primarily by male architects and famous artists—though their monopoly had been challenged by society ladies who'd simply hung a shingle, their clients coming from their social circles. Louis C. Tiffany, Prudence reads, was one of the first of the new class of professional decorators. The studio he'd designed for his mansion at Seventy-second Street and Madison Avenue—the room where her father crashed to his death—is described in an article in the *Ladies' Home Journal* as like no other in America or perhaps the Western world. Along with Laurelton Hall, she learns, it is considered his masterpiece.

Mr. Feeney visits every Sunday at teatime. A lifelong bachelor whose nails, Prudence's mother marvels, are always so clean despite his mechanic's work, he lives with a "cousin" in Washington Heights who is a waiter at Delmonico's—one of the restaurant staff who served the roasted peacocks and suckling pigs after they'd been paraded through the dining room. While his cousin prepares for the restaurant's early Sunday dinner, Mr. Feeney sits in their parlor, complimenting Prudence's mother on her dress or the scones she makes in anticipation of his visits. If her mother thinks of Mr. Feeney as a suitor, she never mentions it, but neither does she acknowledge that Mr. Feeney's cousin is no blood relation.

Like Clara Driscoll, Mr. Feeney calls Prudence's mother Bridgey. Prudence sees that her mother looks forward not only to Mr. Feeney's attentions but also to the gossip he brings each week: the details of Mr. T's declining health, the visit of Mr. T's daughter Dorothy from Vienna, where all four of her children are in treatment with the daughter of the famous Professor Freud, who is treating Dorothy herself. Although Mr. Feeney doesn't say so directly, it seems clear that Dorothy has left her husband, whom Mr. Feeney, lowering his voice, says suffers from "nerves" and is now living with his parents when he is not in a sanatorium. "She stayed two days, and then turned right back around," Mr. Feeney reports. "Can you imagine? Being rich enough to take an ocean liner back and forth for a two-day visit?"

A few weeks before Prudence turns twenty-one, Mr. T dies. Prudence's mother reads the news in the paper, then hears the details from Mr. Feeney, who tells her, "Word came that Dorothy would not be coming back for the funeral. Suppose she feels like she said her goodbyes good enough in those two days she was here."

When the first of the month passes without the usual visit of the clerk from Mr. T's office, Prudence's mother goes to the post office on her way home from work to see if perhaps the envelope had been mailed instead and for some reason not delivered. Returning empty-handed, she leaves her hat on the hook by the door, changes into her housedress, and busies herself with peeling potatoes. "Maybe they are a bit topsy-turvy there with his death just last month," she tells Prudence. But the following week, when there is still no visit from the clerk or envelope arrived in the mail, she hands Prudence a card with the lawyer's name, Mr. Franklin Bromston, and the address of his office and asks her to go during her school lunch hour to inquire.

Her mother has done so well since that first week after her father's death: working, keeping house, going to Staten Island each Saturday to visit her sister, never protesting during the semester Prudence had studied at the Paris branch of her school even though, Prudence's aunt confided, her mother had cried herself to sleep every night from "missing you, Prudence, dear."

"Mum, can you go? I feel embarrassed to be inquiring."

Her mother looks at the floor. "People like those lawyers scare me. I wouldn't be able to get out a word."

In the morning, Prudence puts on her navy crepe dress with mother-of-pearl buttons that run from the belted waist to the velvet collar. She powders her nose and pins her hair in a tight bun. Midday, she takes the subway to the address on the card, and then the elevator up to Mr. Bromston's sixth-floor office.

From behind a desk in the anteroom, an elderly man peers at her over pince-nez spectacles perched on a bulbous nose.

"Excuse me, sir. I'm here to see Mr. Bromston."

"Do you have an appointment?"

Prudence's mouth turns dry. How had it not occurred to her when her mother handed her the card that she should make an appointment? "No, sir."

"And what is this in reference to?"

"My father, Edward O'Connor, worked for Mr. Tiffany."

The man raises his eyebrows and purses his lips in a way that makes Prudence wonder if he knew her father. It's hard, though, to imagine her father in this room.

"Mr. Bromston is lunching at his club." The man studies an appointment book open on the desk. After what seems like a long time, he adjusts his spectacles and looks up at Prudence. "Mr. Bromston might be able to briefly see you before his first afternoon appointment." The man points to a bench on the far wall. "You may wait there."

At the end of an hour during which Prudence is too intimidated to ask if there is a ladies' room she could use, the man beckons her to follow him.

Mr. Bromston's office is long and narrow, like a tunnel, and terribly overheated. For a brief moment, Prudence thinks no one is in it. Then she sees Mr. Bromston, nearly hidden behind a colossal desk. Save for his stern expression, he does not look like the lawyer she recalls from the morning after her father died. That man had been portly, too large for their parlor. This one is skinny with a few strands of hair brushed horizontally across the top of his otherwise bald head.

He motions for her to take the chair catty-corner to the desk, a ladder-back that, to Prudence's dismay, makes her chest jut out as she sits.

"You are not married?" From his tone of voice, he might as well have asked, *You are a prostitute?*

She shakes her head no.

"So, it is Miss O'Connor."

He taps his pen on the desk. "Miss O'Connor, I do not have all day."

She's so thirsty, she's afraid the words will stick in her mouth. "I am sorry to bother you, but we did not receive our money from Mr. Tiffany this month." She swallows, then licks her lips. "My mother asked me to inquire."

Mr. Bromston narrows his nearly lashless eyes. Unable to control herself, she glances down to see if a button has popped open on her dress.

When she looks up, Mr. Bromston is dipping his pen into an inkwell. For a moment, she thinks he is going to write a check, but instead he takes a sheet of letterhead from a bin. He writes something on the paper and with a sharp flick of his frighteningly thin wrist sends it flying across the desk.

She raises her hand to block the paper from falling onto the floor, then leans forward to see what's written on it. It's a single word, printed all in capital letters: *EXTORTION*.

"Do you know what *extortion* means, Miss O'Connor?"

His voice is now loud.

"Yes, sir," she says, though in truth she does not understand it any better than she had the word *rapacious*, other than to say that it is equally horrid.

"We will not tolerate any extortion," Mr. Bromston says, each word evenly spaced and accompanied by the marching beat of his pen again tapping the desk. "Did you hear me, Miss O'Connor?"

She is so hot, she fears she might faint.

"Enough is enough. It has been going on seventeen years, these payments to your family."

Beneath her navy dress, her undergarments are damp, and when she speaks, she sounds reedy like a child. "Excuse me, sir. I don't think it's been quite that long. My father passed nine years ago."

Mr. Bromston peers at her as though deciding if she is a liar or simpleminded. "It is 1933, Miss O'Connor. The payments to your family began in June of 1916. Do you require a piece of paper and a pencil to do the arithmetic?"

*Do not cry*, she tells herself. *You must not cry.*

He folds his hands. "You convey the message to your mother, your brother, whoever the devil you live with: Enough is enough."

Her chin bobs up and down as she imagines telling her mother that the clerk will no longer be coming each month.

"The gravy train, Missy, is over." His voice is now booming. "Do you hear me, *Miss-eee*?"

When he stands, she sees he's hardly taller than her.

He points to the door.

"Now go."

# 4

# Randall & Leo

## San Francisco, 1923–1962

In the story on which Grace and Garcia were raised, a true story though scrubbed of some of the ugliest details, their grandfather Randall had come West at fourteen, stowing away on trains from New York to San Francisco. It was six years before the Crash, when the number of itinerant men quadrupled, but a substantial core had long lived hopping flatbeds: men without families or regular jobs, some of them mean and dangerous, especially if they'd been drinking all day, but most friendly enough. Proud to have a skill to show a young person: how to hoist onto a moving car, how to forward-heave a rucksack and then jump off without breaking bones. Willing to tell a boy which conductors wouldn't give trouble as long as there was no harm to the cargo or paying customers during the ten days it took to cross what her grandfather always called "our great land." The only unfortunate incident had come not at the hands of a fellow rider or guard, but from a fertilizer explosion in an adjacent car that had left him hard of hearing on his left side.

Not until Grace was older did she understand that her grandfather did not mean "our great land" in the sappy knee-jerk patriotic way it is usually used, but rather as a shorthand for the awe that had overtaken him as he'd gazed out at the golden grasses of the prairies, the forked cacti of the desert, the godlike sequoias of the Northwest. An old man, or perhaps just a man who looked old then to her grandfather, had taught him the names of the wildflowers, names her grandfather never forgot: yellow coreopsis, agave, purple cone.

In San Francisco, her grandfather met up with Charlie, a pal from the Hell's Kitchen neighborhood who'd also been a newsboy, the two of them in those days watching each other's back. Charlie worked in a florist shop, and it fell to him to go every morning at three to get the flowers that the farmers from the sunny spine of the state would bring to the market south of the city. At first, her grandfather hadn't even had a proper job: he would help Charlie, and in exchange Charlie would let him sleep under the bed in his dormitory-like room and give him a few coins every day to buy bread and beer.

"You drank beer at fourteen?" Grace asked.

"We drank anything anyone would give us. Beer was cheaper than milk, which is what I really wanted, but it filled the belly."

When the boy who swept up and handled the constant trash was let go for taking a few discarded blooms for his mother, Charlie recommended Randall to Mr. Crowell, the shop owner. Soon, it was noticed that Randall seemed to have a way with flowers. "I guess those years at Laurelton Hall, growing up in a place with forty gardeners, rubbed off on me." Randall was promoted—if you could call it that since there was no more money and only longer hours—to florist's apprentice, which he had the wisdom, even at fifteen, as he was by then, to recognize as an opportunity.

Crowell—a dour, small man with hands etched with scars from shearing mishaps—had a loyal following of San Francisco society matrons who never questioned his Victorian approach to floral design, with its focus on opulent displays of compact bundles of richly colored, symmetrically arranged stems placed in ornate containers—an approach he'd appropriated during the three Dickensian years he'd spent as an apprentice himself in a renowned shop in London. After six months as the boy who fetched the flowers from the buckets, then the boy who trimmed the stems, Randall was entrusted to do the "finishing off": adding the greenery to the bouquets and floral arrangements, the twisted wire to the corsages, the paper wrappings like a bishop's hat.

Within a year, Randall was promoted again, to assistant florist, with his own apprentice to do everything he had done before himself. The work was largely cookie-cutter centerpieces for ladies' luncheons and church benefits, but as Randall began to read on his own, most particularly the writings of the innovative English gardener and artist Miss Gertrude Jekyll, who advocated an informal, naturalistic but design-influenced attitude to flowers in the home, he tried out these sparer, subtler arrangements on a few carefully chosen clients. As he correctly intuited, particularly receptive to this fresher style was Mrs. Cecelia Brown, an elegant, tall woman who as a child had summered in the south of France with an aunt who'd taken her for dinner with Matisse in Collioure, had married into a Chicago railroad family, and was now mistress of a nine-bedroom mansion with dizzying views of the bay, not yet marred, as she would later lament, by the Golden Gate Bridge.

When Mrs. Brown requested of Mr. Crowell that Randall design the flowers for the Pacific Heights Ladies Auxiliary Charity Costume Ball, an important event in the San Francisco calendar of which she was the chair that year, Crowell fired Randall on the spot, intimating that Randall had stolen something. It was an error in judgment on Crowell's part since the slander so outraged Mrs. Brown, she decided to set Randall up with his own shop and commenced a campaign to have all of her friends switch their business to him. In a matter of days, she'd found a storefront for Randall on Jackson Street and funded the initial rent and equipment as an advance on the fees for the flower arrangements at the ball. It was 1928 and Randall was nineteen years old.

Grace's grandfather weathered the Depression by working eighteen hours a day. He hired a widow to greet customers and keep the books and help out with the cleaning up, but he did everything else himself: the trips to the flower market before dawn, cutting the blooms, the arranging, the wrapping, the prodigious disposal of garbage, even the deliveries when his customers could not send their drivers to the shop. The cottage-style centerpieces he'd done for the costume ball had received attention in the society pages, and he never lacked for customers. In 1931, Mrs. Brown invited him to accompany her to England, where they visited Miss Gertrude Jekyll and Mrs. Brown financed Randall's acquisition of many of Miss Jekyll's simple vases. Back in San Francisco, Randall used the vases as a platform for what became his signature dishabille mode of flowers languidly arranged like the courtesans in the Matisse paintings Mrs. Brown had shown him.

For a while, Grace wondered if her grandfather had been Mrs. Brown's lover before he'd met Grace's grandmother, but later she surmised that her grandfather, exempted from the war due to having failed the hearing test, had been the escort, with Mrs. Brown's encouragement, for many young ladies whose beaux were officers abroad.

And so it happened that in the fall of 1942, Randall, then thirty-three, was commissioned by Mrs. Brown to escort Carolyn Duprew, a willowy, anemic-looking blonde of twenty-two whose pilot fiancé was overseas, to a private club's annual dance. Both Carolyn's father, Winston, a gout-ridden banker with an affected English diction, and Carolyn's mother, Anita, a shrill woman whose Mississippi family was renowned for treating their help like the slaves they'd once owned, would be in attendance as well.

It was Winston who an hour into the dance was informed by an air force officer, who, having come to the Duprew house, had been directed by their butler to the club, that the plane piloted by his daughter's fiancé, Boyd Alexander, had been shot down over the Libyan Sea.

With his cheeks red from alcohol and elevated blood pressure and his voice raised over the orchestra, Winston asked Randall to accompany him to the men's lounge, where he blurted out the dreadful report.

"Bloody awful," Winston kept saying over and over. He pulled on his bow tie. "And bloody hot in here, wouldn't you say, chap?"

With the *chap*, Randall realized both that Winston Duprew did not recall his name and was panicked about what to do now: scared both of his daughter, who had fainted in public on more than one occasion, and his wife, who was prone to dramatic displays of emotion.

"Well, sir, if you would allow me to offer an opinion . . ."

"Absolutely, young man. Any advice here would be most appreciated. Carolyn is going to just take it terribly. I'm thinking maybe I should have a doctor on hand. Don't they have injections they give for this sort of thing?"

"Perhaps we could finish the evening and I could bring Carolyn home and you could then tell her once she's back in your house?"

Winston stared at Randall as though he'd discovered how to turn lead into gold. "Brilliant. Of course, of course, that's what we'll do. I'm going to take my wife home now so I can inform her . . ." Winston Duprew shook his head side to side, as though imagining what that would entail. "And we can prepare ourselves," by which Randall felt certain Winston meant *I can get out of this bloody dinner jacket and belt down a few whiskeys first*. "You follow along with Carolyn as soon as it seems a decent hour to leave."

"Yes, sir. Sounds like a solid plan."

Then, Winston looked at Randall with what appeared to be sheer terror. "But you'll stay until after we tell her, right, chap?"

For a moment, Randall had the impulse to say *Are you a downright idiot? I just met your daughter tonight*. But then he thought about it from Carolyn's point of view: what would it be like to learn the news of her fiancé's death with only her wheezing father and pompous mother there?

Carolyn Duprew surprised Randall by having no reaction other than a slight shudder of her shoulders. Her father was sweating profusely, and it was her mother who was sobbing, in part because she'd already put a 50 percent deposit on a wedding gown for her daughter by a man who'd been Madeleine Vionnet's most prized designer before war rationing had shuttered the Parisian couture houses. Anita Duprew—a woman who could not understand that a consommé and a Waldorf salad would be more elegant than the lobsters à la Newberg and the filet mignon with sauce *à la beurre et champignons* she served at her luncheons (meals deemed showy, "vulgar," as one of Anita's guests was overheard whispering)—was simultaneously famously cheap. It would slay her to lose the exorbitant sum she had additionally paid to have a hundred pearls individually pierced so they could be sewed to the bodice and along the fitted wrists of her daughter's wedding dress at a shop so exclusive one needed an introductory letter before an appointment could even be made.

Carolyn accompanied Randall to the front door. She extended her hand and thanked him for taking her to the dance. She apologized for his having had to witness . . . she raised an eyebrow rather than completing the sentence. Then she smiled sweetly and Randall's heart split in two.

The following Sunday, Randall called on Carolyn Duprew, who scandalized her mother by announcing that she and Mr. O'Connor would be going for a walk and tea. The moment they were out of sight of the house, Carolyn took Randall's arm, leading him to the steep Lyon Street steps, which she raced down, laughing like a schoolgirl. They made their way to the bay, walking east to Fisherman's Wharf, and then taking the cable car up to the Mark Hopkins Hotel, where they had tea and little cakes, and then cocktails and caviar toasts, as Carolyn told Randall how she'd come to be engaged to Boyd Alexander.

A third cousin twice removed on her mother's side, Boyd Alexander was from a Hattiesburg family who'd gone from owning cotton plantations with north of a thousand slaves to owning banana plantations in Colombia with workers as imprisoned as slaves. Stationed for his pilot training in Oakland, Boyd had obeyed his mother's instructions that he must call upon the Duprews. At first, Carolyn had been charmed by Boyd's Southern manners and his self-assurance, but it was as though he'd inherited a streak of the cruelty from the great-great-grandfather who was his namesake, a man known for the relish he'd taken in personally whipping his slaves—men, women, and children—rather than leaving the job for his foreman.

Randall's fists formed rocks when Carolyn told him that she'd been in her second year at Mills College in Oakland, an art-history major and on the volleyball team, when Boyd had forced himself upon her and she'd become pregnant.

"I know, looking at me now, you'd never think I could play volleyball, but when I started at Mills, I had twenty more pounds on me and I was the strongest girl on the team. I could do a dozen boy's push-ups and run three miles without even getting winded." She sighed. "Now I look like a character from a Brontë novel. Like a strong wind could blow me over."

When she'd realized she was pregnant, Carolyn had confided in her mother, begging for help to arrange an abortion, but her mother had refused both the abortion and to acknowledge what had happened as a rape rather than a moral failing of Carolyn's. Instead, her mother had insisted on an engagement, with the plan that Carolyn would go away before she began to show and the baby then given up for adoption, after which Carolyn would return for a proper wedding. The Carolyn before her pregnancy would have fought this plan like an alley cat, but she was felled by a vicious morning sickness that her mother told everyone was a stomach ailment. At thirteen weeks, she miscarried, losing a dangerous amount of blood on account of her mother not calling an ambulance, out of concern, Carolyn felt certain, that with a hospitalization, the news of her pregnancy might become known. That was eight months ago. She'd become so anemic, all she'd been able to do was lie on the couch with a novel, a relief only in that it was an excuse not to see Boyd before he shipped out.

"So, you see," Carolyn said, "here I am, having to playact grief for a man I despised, having to playact being sickly when I'm really recovering from having been maltreated during a miscarriage that resulted from a rape. And down the road, what is there in store for me? Having to playact being a virgin to my future husband . . ."

She took a long sip of the sherry she'd ordered. "You are the first person aside from my mother and our doctor who I've told the true story. My mother made me swear to not even tell my father."

Randall put his hand over hers. He had to bite his tongue not to ask her to marry him on the spot.

Unable to begin a courtship under the circumstances, Carolyn and Randall devised an arrangement whereby she became his tutor, teaching him French and the art history she'd learned during her two years at Mills College. Three evenings a week, they met in her father's library with the leatherbound books Anita had ordered to fill the shelves and that neither she nor Winston ever opened. After Carolyn and Randall had completed the day's lessons, together they read books on the history of architecture and landscape design and the monographs of Frederick Law Olmsted on the role of public parks in the acculturation of immigrants to American democratic ideals and customs.

When Randall introduced Carolyn to Gertrude Jekyll's work, she responded even more passionately than he and Mrs. Cecelia Brown had—such a liberating contrast to her mother's cloyingly bright and overly decorated home, where Carolyn had never felt there was a square inch of serenity or sincerity. A mother with one of Miss Jekyll's gardens, Carolyn thought, would have wept when her daughter told her she'd been lured into a shed by a claim of newborn kittens by a man who smashed his beefy hand over her mouth and went at her with such force, there were chafe marks on her buttocks and thighs afterward. A mother with one of Gertrude Jekyll's gardens, where the lanes were bordered with roses and the lettuces and peppers flowed into the cutting flowers, would have found a reputable doctor to do an abortion, would not have responded by sending a deposit for a wedding gown that would cost more than her maid's annual salary.

A year after Boyd's death, Randall asked Winston Duprew for his daughter's hand in marriage. Winston, thick as he was, had sufficient horse sense to know that Randall, with his intelligence and stable nature, would be a good match for Carolyn, who, after what he believed she'd been through—stomach ailments, the tragedy of losing Boyd—he thought deserved some happiness. Anita, however, was apoplectic, acceding only after Mrs. Cecelia Brown, of whom Anita was both in awe and afraid, paid her a call during which she intimated that were Anita to act like a bitch, Cecelia might leak the true story about Carolyn. How Cecelia Brown had found out, Anita Duprew would have given a pinkie finger to know. That scoundrel doctor who'd come to the house when Carolyn miscarried? Carolyn herself?

The latter was, in fact, the correct answer. Carolyn, having anticipated her mother's objections to her marrying Randall, who, despite his success, her mother viewed as a déclassé shopkeeper, had invited Mrs. Brown to tea. They'd met at the teahouse in Golden Gate Park, a place Carolyn had been certain neither her mother nor her mother's friends would frequent, with the Japanese family who'd run it for half a century now in an internment camp. "Oh, my dear. My dear child, how absolutely horrid," Mrs. Brown said after Carolyn revealed what had happened with Boyd. Carolyn had seen in Mrs. Brown's eyes genuine sadness for her, which turned to outrage as it dawned on Cecelia Brown the role Anita Duprew had played in the girl's ordeal and the measures she would take to block her daughter's marriage to Randall for being Irish and Catholic and having no family—*no family* meaning to Anita Duprew no family wealth. Randall did have a family, a mother and a sister, whose name, Prudence, Cecelia Brown now recalled. In that moment, she had half fallen in love with Carolyn herself, for her spunk, for wanting to spend her life with Randall, whom Mrs. Brown viewed as the finest young man she knew, with more grit and better character than any of the sons of the society set to which she and Anita Duprew belonged.

"Anita, sweetheart, beloved," Cecelia Brown added, taking Anita's hand and thinking, *What a wicked woman. I hope her servants poison the disgusting turtle soup she still believes it fashionable to serve.* "Just think, you will now be able to use the deposit on the dress by the man from the Madeleine Vionnet house. With Randall supervising, the flowers will be divine. You will be the goddess of Pacific Heights."

In the year since Boyd's death, Carolyn had put on some weight and regained her color. With her golden hair and her green eyes and her rounded upper arms, she looked to Randall like one of the farm girls he'd glimpsed twenty years before from the flatbed of a train and then fantasized about: girls rising to milk cows or sweep porches or hang laundry, strong and generous and content with the joys of warm sun and plump babies. When she asked Randall if he would mind terribly waiting for their wedding night to be intimate—it would mean so much to her to have what she was going to think of as her first experience after they were married . . . that first time . . . she raised her chin and inhaled deeply and held her head high . . . that was not making love, that was an assault—his eyes again welled with tears, not from sadness and anger as they had when she'd told him about the rape, but because he loved her all the more for having the courage to say this outright.

As a peace gesture, Carolyn allowed her mother to plan the wedding. Walking with her new husband into the ballroom at the Fairmont Hotel in the dress with the hundred pearls sewn to the bodice and wrists, she squeezed Randall's hand, as if to say, *Just a few hours. After this, we will have our own lives.* Alone that evening in the four-story Victorian on Locust Street that Carolyn's parents had given them as a wedding present, which was where Carolyn wanted to spend their first night as man and wife, Randall, who'd anticipated treating his new bride with caution and patience, had felt his cup runneth over as he discovered how lusty and adventurous she was in their marital bed.

To her mother's horror, Carolyn worked side by side with Angela. Together, they did the sweeping, the dusting, the polishing, the laundry, the ironing, the shopping, the cooking, the baking. Late afternoons, they would go to the Julius Kahn Playground, where they played tennis and, scandalizing the neighborhood, basketball too. Evenings, while Randall tended to the shop's bills and correspondence in the second-floor library, Carolyn would set up the dining room as a school with a chalkboard on an easel and a stack of ruled paper. She taught Angela to read, to do arithmetic, the rudiments of American history. When they were done with the lessons, Carolyn would cajole Randall to join them in the music room, where she would play the piano while Angela, who had a beautiful voice, would sing lamentful Schumann songs in a German Carolyn had phonetically transcribed.

The first two years of his marriage, her grandfather told Grace, were blissfully happy. He and her grandmother traveled, not to Europe, on account of the war, but to Yosemite, the land championed by their hero Frederick Law Olmsted, to Hawaii, and to Mexico, where they took Angela to visit her family in Veracruz.

Shortly after Carolyn turned twenty-six, she announced to Randall that it was time for them to have a family, at which point the honeymoon ceased as their intimate life acquired the goal of conception, a goal that they both worried they might not reach during the two years they ardently tried before Carolyn became pregnant. Given her earlier miscarriage, she was put on bed rest for the last three months of her pregnancy, during which Angela, by then nineteen, took over entirely with the housework and cooking and care of Carolyn.

Grace's father, Leopold Duprew O'Connor, was born in February of 1948. Her grandmother lost so much blood that an emergency hysterectomy was performed immediately after the birth. Afterward, anemic again, Carolyn yielded more to Randall and her mother than she had before, not because she doubted her judgment, but because she was acutely aware of the limits of her energy, how every step she took felt as though it were with a hundred-pound load on her back.

Knowing that there would be no second child, Randall and Carolyn lavished Leo, as they called the baby, with their love and attention. Angela became Leo's nanny, and Emmaline, who had worked for Carolyn's mother, took over the housekeeping and cooking. By the time Leo turned two, Carolyn had regained a good deal of her strength, but afternoon outings with Leo were left for Angela. Every morning, Angela listened to Mr. Randall's directions. She must be certain to hold Leo's hand from the moment they exited the house to the moment they reached the park lest Leo get distracted and run into a passing car. She must be certain while in the park to never take her eyes off him: there were disturbed people who abducted children. Most of all, under no circumstances was she ever *ever* to take him by the water: neither the bay to the north and east, or the ocean to the west. Whereas the other children in the neighborhood frequently passed summer afternoons at the city's beaches, carefree stretches with inner tubes and picnic blankets and buckets and pails, Mr. Randall strictly forbade any such excursions. The Pacific is too rough, he informed Angela with the same tone of voice he might have used had he said *Everyone, quickly, to the basement. There are bombs falling overhead.* Children could be swept under by the waves or the undertow.

Despite three adults hovering over him and his father's prohibitions, Leopold was a normal child. He had friends in nearby houses, he attended birthday parties and a little nursery school in the neighborhood. His mother taught him to read and to play the piano, and his father taught him to play baseball and golf, which

Randall had taken up to please Winston. There were trips each year, the three of them—his red-faced grandfather, his serious father, and himself—to Carmel and to Palm Desert, trips Leo enjoyed as much for the enormous swimming pools and the Shirley Temples his father would permit him at the cocktail hour, which for his grandfather began at four, as for the golf itself. Every Sunday, they had dinner with his grandparents, and every Sunday, when the meal was done, his grandfather would ask if Leo would like to see his collection of World War I souvenirs: a bayonet, a green metal helmet, an Austrian newspaper.

At six, Leo was enrolled at his grandfather's alma mater, the all-boys Presidio Academy, to which he was driven every morning by his grandparents' chauffeur on the insistence of his grandmother, who thought it unseemly for children to take the public bus to school. He wore a navy blazer, with brass buttons his grandmother instructed Angela to polish, a white button-down shirt, and pleated trousers. Once monthly, his grandfather took him to his own barber to have his hair, still blond but already turning brown underneath, cut into what the boys at school called the Presidio crew: short on the sides but with a little length on the top so they didn't look like cadets.

The boys, addressed by their teachers by their last names, ate in a dining room, served by elderly black men they called by their first names. The headmaster, who'd been a classmate of Leo's grandfather, would sit with the faculty at the table at the front of the room. "Mr. O'Connor," he would admonish Leo, "if you do not cease the slouching, you will strangulate the growth of your spine, and your name will not be joining your grandfather's and mine on the basketball-team placards displayed in the front hall." The headmaster tactfully avoided mentioning Leo's father, who had stopped school at twelve, but passionate reader that he was (each year, Leo's parents chose an author to read together: Shakespeare, Melville, Tolstoy, Ibsen) would, as Leo became old enough to make such discernments, strike him as better educated than his Yalie grandfather, whose reading diet was limited to the *San Francisco Chronicle* and *Life* magazine.

Leo's father left interactions with the school to be handled by

Leo's grandfather and mother. The only time Randall interceded was when Leo was seven, the age the boys at Presidio Academy commenced mandatory swimming instruction, which his father opposed as adamantly as play by the ocean and intended to have waived for Leo.

Leo was required to attend the appointment his father made with the headmaster to deliver these directions. With his classmates, Leo had visited the school's basement pool. It smelled like a wet dog, and Leo, dreading what the older boys reported was freezing water, was hoping his father would prevail in having Leo excused.

The headmaster tamped the tobacco in his pipe and positioned his lighter next to the bowl. He fixed his eyes on Leo's father. "Mr. O'Connor, it has been a mandate at Presidio Academy since I was a student here with Leopold's grandfather that every boy must pass the swimming test before he is advanced to the fourth grade. It is a question of the safety of the boys that they know how to swim. Two of the survivors of the *Titanic* were Presidio boys, and I am certain that is attributable in part to our program."

"The ships these days I can tell you from my own Atlantic crossing are well outfitted with rescue boats."

"Mr. O'Connor, you must certainly acknowledge that there are occasions when a man should know how to swim. And it is a manner of honor for a Presidio boy to not only know how to swim but to have mastered lifesaving. We have many documented cases of Presidio boys and men who have jumped into a river or ocean to save someone who was going under."

Leo's father appeared to be in physical pain. He looked at his knees. Leo wanted to pound the headmaster with his fists, but he also desperately had to pee and was afraid that might come unbidden with any sudden movement.

When his father looked up, his face was impassive. "What safety precautions do you take in the swimming pool?"

Sensing victory on the horizon, the headmaster softened his tone. "We have two teachers who are certified lifeguards watching the boys at all times. We have never hewed to the barbaric practice at our fellow boys' schools of throwing students into the deep end and having them discover the dog paddle on their own. No, that teaches the boys nothing. During the first week of instruction, we present the basics of breathing without the lads even dipping a toe in the water."

Leo watched his father nod. Was that approval? Approval that Leo have swim instruction under the condition that he never go in the water?

"After that first week, we introduce swim boards, with which they learn how to float and to kick. Then the instructors teach them how to put their heads under the water and breathe."

With this last sentence, Leo feared his father might faint the way Leo had seen his mother do on occasion.

The headmaster stood. He chuckled slightly, a chuckle that sent shudders down Leo's spine. "Mr. O'Connor, we have never had any injuries of any sort in our swimming pool aside from a scraped knuckle or stubbed toe. We will expect to see your son outfitted for his first lesson the Monday after next."

Leo turned out to be an excellent swimmer. Wiry like his father but with his grandfather Winston's broad shoulders, he was, the gymnasium teacher informed him, a natural for the butterfly stroke. Swim class was at the end of the school day, and on those occasions when his mother would pick him up, she would nuzzle his chlorine-scented hair and hug him. If she was feeling strong, they would walk home together or ride the cable car to Nob Hill for ice cream at one of the Italian cafés, where his mother would amuse him with shaggy dog tales. Saturday afternoons, while his father was in his shop, Leo and his mother and Angela would go to Golden Gate Park, where they'd visit the secret redwood grove, measuring with their arm spans the circumferences of the largest trees and then sitting on the damp ground, the three of them, leaning on one another and inhaling the ancient feral scent.

On the afternoons when Angela picked him up from school, he would on his arrival home find his mother in the painting studio she'd set up overlooking the rear garden, landscaped by his father with cabbage roses and trellised vines. With Leo gone most of the day, Angela had insisted on taking over the evening-meal preparation from Emmaline. Dinners consisted of delicious spicy foods, which his grandmother grumbled about sotto voce when she and his grandfather joined them, her ire inflamed by his grandfather's enjoyment of Angela's empanadas and corn breads and especially her flans.

In short, it was heaven.

Grace's father's heaven came to an abrupt halt when he was eight and his mother got sick, a cancer Leo understood only to be somewhere in her belly. His father refused to acknowledge what his mother never doubted: that she would soon die. Unable to bear any mention of this, his father would exit the room if she even alluded to the time after she would be gone. Sometimes, in the middle of the night, Leo would hear the front door opening as his father, unable to sleep, left for a walk and then, on his father's return, his mother's soft voice.

Afternoons, Leo would climb into her bed, burying his face in her silky nightgown. She would run her fingers through his hair, now more brown than blond, kiss his cheeks, and turn her body, which felt thinner and thinner with each passing week, into his.

Then one day Leo came home to find his mother propped up with pillows on the sofa in the parlor, a lace shawl spread over her like a blanket. It was a room filled with beautiful paintings and chairs covered in cranberry velvet, not a place where any of them ever sat, save with company, much less reclined, as his mother was doing now. She motioned for him to close the pocket doors. He put his forefinger through the brass tab and pulled the heavy panels, one by one, until they met in the center, sealing the two of them alone in the room. His mother shifted to make room for him, smoothing the spot on the sofa where she wanted him to perch by her side.

When she spoke, it was so quietly, he had to lean in to hear. "Your father disagrees with my talking openly with you about my dying, but that is only because he is so sad. If he were able to think more clearly, I am certain he would agree that we must prepare you."

Leo stared at the chino fabric of his school pants, loose over his skinny thighs, while his mother stroked his hand. His mind went to the baseball the other boys from the neighborhood would be gathering to play in the Julius Kahn Playground.

"Leo."

His mother wouldn't allow him to go alone, but he was certain Angela would take him. He wanted to go, but he didn't want to leave his mother. It was the first time he was aware of wanting two things at one time, and it felt strange, as though with the experience he was losing something he would never again have.

"Leo," his mother repeated. The baseball slipped away. He looked up to let her know that he was listening. "What I want more than anything is for you not to be afraid."

His mother's eyes were glistening in the dim light. He sensed that she was telling him something important, and that she'd rallied herself to leave her bed and lie on the sofa so as to say it. He struggled to understand, but it was as though he had to translate each of her words from a foreign language into one he knew, and after that, the sentences would not come together as a whole. He could feel his brows knitting, and then for a moment his vision was blocked as his mother's hand passed over his forehead.

"I am going to die. Your father refuses to believe it. But it is true, and I want to help you to be ready."

He nodded solemnly, and for a split second, the baseball came back and he was nodding goodbye to that too, but mostly the nodding was to encourage his mother to go on because, even at eight, he could tell this was something important to her and he loved her more than anything else in the entire universe.

"I am going to explain to you what it means to die."

"I know what it means."

"Yes, darling, I'm sure you know a lot. But I am going to explain what you do not know and what no one knows until you are about to die yourself, and then only if you are not too scared to think about it."

"You are not too scared?"

"No, darling. I am not scared at all. What I am scared about—and *scared* is the wrong word—what I am worried about is you and your father. If I weren't worried about the two of you, I would be at peace. My life has been short but, for the most part, it has been a very lucky one. I grew up with everything a girl could want. I adored school, was good at sports, loved art. And then I met your father, for me the most wonderful man in the world. So smart, so creative, so brave and kind. We have been very very happy together."

His mother brought his hand to her lips and kissed his knuckles. "And then I had you. My beautiful, clever, loving son."

"You are not worried about Angela?"

"Yes, I am. But just a little bit. Angela grew up with death being part of her everyday life—her mother lost half her babies before they reached the age of three—so she understands death better than we do. And she will have you and your father to take care of, and it will be a big and busy job for her."

"How do you know she will stay?" Now Leo was crying and he felt worried that his mother would think he was crying because of Angela, not her, worried that he might lose Angela if . . . no, his mother was not saying *if . . . when* she died.

"I know Angela will. I know beyond any words she could say to me."

"How do you know?" He felt that he had to understand this, be certain that there would be Angela before he could talk any more with his mother.

"Because she loves me. She loves me because I have loved her like a little sister and I have taken care of her. And since the moment you were born, she has loved you. She was the first person to hold you, even before I could, because I was very weak then. She will never leave you and she will not die." His mother smiled. "Well, she will die. Everyone dies. But not for a long time. Probably not until you have grandchildren."

Leo nodded again.

"Now, you must tell me what you understand about what it means when someone dies."

He realized he did not know. He did not know beyond the very little he'd learned at the Sunday school his grandmother insisted he attend. But at the Sunday school, mostly they were taught Bible stories and Christmas carols. No one had said anything about what happens when you die aside from Jesus having come back to life. Would his mother come back to life?

"You go to heaven?"

It was as though he could see through his mother, not only inside her but through and beyond her. He could feel her love the way he could feel rain in the air before drops brushed his skin. He could taste the tears in her thoughts.

He studied her face. She looked tired. Very tired. And for the first time, she looked old. Very old. As ancient as the redwoods in Golden Gate Park.

Was she going to die today? This afternoon?

His mother winced. She touched her dry lips. "Darling, go ask Angela to bring us some cold drinks. Tell her I want water, but you may have a pop or a lemonade."

He felt guilty that he was relieved to have a reason to run out of the room, to the kitchen, where Angela was at the stove stirring one of the soups that were all his mother could now eat. He hurled himself into her hip, and she nearly burned herself before she turned off the stove. She drew him into her lap on the kitchen chair, and he wept into her warm body, listening to her murmuring, "*Niño, mi niño*," until he was able to give the instructions for water for his mother and a lemonade for himself.

By the time he and Angela arrived in the parlor with the drinks, his mother was asleep. He'd not dared to ask Angela to take him to the Julius Kahn Playground to play baseball, too afraid that his mother would die while they were gone.

His mother lived for another seven months, having waited to die, Leo thought, for him to turn nine the week before. There'd been many more talks about death, so many he'd grown quite accustomed to them.

At first, the talks had centered on what precisely would happen. A time would arrive when she would no longer be able to eat or drink and the doctor would give her so much medicine to keep her from feeling pain that she would slip into a sleep from which she would not awaken. Her breathing would sound funny, maybe like an old man snoring, she told Leo.

"That will be funny, won't it? It might even sound like I'm gurgling."

They were in her bedroom. He was seated on a stool next to the divan where his mother lay. He did not think it would be funny.

"Then, at some point, I'll take a big gasp and stop breathing altogether. It will be like going to sleep forever."

"You never wake up?"

"No, you never wake up."

"What if you have to go to the bathroom or you need to itch?"

His mother ruffled his hair. A few months ago, she would have laughed from her belly. Now she feebly smiled. "That's the good thing about dying. You don't have to go to the bathroom anymore. There are no more itches." She'd not said, *And no more pain*, but he'd understood that too.

"And then what happens? After you stop breathing?"

"The doctor will take his fingers and close my eyelids."

"You can't do that yourself?"

"No."

"Can I do it for you?"

"I don't know if they'll let you. But do you want to do it now?"

"Yes."

She made herself very still and stared up at the ceiling. He leaned over her and put his middle fingers on her eyelids and pushed them closed. "That's all you do?"

"That's all you do." She stroked his arm. "Now there's one more thing I want to tell you. I don't want you to worry about being here at the exact moment I die. Maybe you'll be at school. And that will be just fine. I don't want you missing your classes to sit next to me waiting for me to take my last breath."

"But I'm going to want to be with you when you die."

"I know, darling. And maybe you will be. But no one can say precisely when that will happen, and it would be awful for you to be cooped up in a dark, airless room with all of the adults weeping and carrying on, which I'm afraid they will. I don't want you falling behind with your schoolwork and not getting to see your friends. It will be hard enough on you without your having to catch up with your assignments and getting weak from not running around every day the way boys your age should."

Leo started to cry. He could not bear the thought that he might not be there when his mother died. For a moment, that seemed even worse than her dying itself.

"And here is the most important thing, so I want you to listen very, very hard and then we'll talk about it again tomorrow and next week and maybe more than that."

She handed him a tissue, waited for him to dry his eyes and blow his nose. She looked at him, as though gauging if he was ready to hear what she was going to say.

"I'm going to always be with you."

He felt a moment of panic. Was she saying she would become a ghost?

"Oh, darling, I'm sorry. That must have sounded spooky."

It seemed like another life when he'd loved having his heart race: their hide-and-seek games with his mother jumping out from the back of a closet with a loud "Boo"; pretending they were French tourists when they rode the cable cars, answering the conductor with "*Merci, monsieur,*" Leo hardly able to contain himself until they got off at the top of Russian Hill, when he would squeal, "Mama, he believed us!"

"What I mean is that I will live on inside of you. You will be able to have conversations in your head with me. You are old enough to know what I would say about things."

His chest felt heavy, as though something were crushing him. He could hardly breathe. He wanted to throw himself onto her, but he was afraid he might hurt her. He wanted to stamp his feet, but then Angela would hear the noise and race in and make him leave his mother to rest. "I am not. I am not old enough. I do not know what you would say."

"I will give you an example. You are sitting at the dinner table and Angela has put some lima beans on your plate, and you think they look like rabbit turds. You don't want to eat rabbit turds, you only want to eat the roast beef and mashed potatoes. What would I say?"

"'Just take a bite. Just give it a try. You didn't want to try a raspberry the first time you saw one, you thought it looked like a gross hairy bug, and then you loved it.'"

"Exactly!" His mother laughed, a strange laugh, and Leo

could tell she was forcing herself and that it was difficult for her. "You know exactly what I would say. And you will be able to ask yourself, 'What would Mama say?'—and I will answer in your head."

"Okay." He could feel his brow furrowing. It still seemed a little spooky. "Do you promise?"

"I promise until the end of time. And there is something even better that I haven't told you yet."

"What is that?"

"There are things you will want to talk with me about as you get older, things that don't interest you now, like girls . . ."

He made a face.

"I know it sounds impossible now, but it won't be long before that will change. Or what kind of career you should pursue. This is the most wonderful part. Even though you don't know now what questions you might want to ask me, when the time comes, I will understand and you can ask me and we will be able to have conversations in your head."

"So it's like you don't really die. You just don't have your body anymore."

His mother closed her eyes. Was she too tired to go on? When she opened them, she reached for his hand, inside which he held a crumpled tissue. "No, darling. I really will be dead. You must never forget that. I really will be dead—but if you allow me, I can live on inside of you, as part of you."

Hearing the sweetness, the hesitation, in her voice, he burst into tears again. "But, Mama, of course, I will allow you." And then, forgetting all about his mother's sore belly and the pain the weight of his torso against hers might cause, he flung himself on her and wept and wept and wept while she murmured to him and made circles on his back with her thumbs and then dried his face with the edge of her shawl and kissed his forehead.

Years later, long after he stopped letting her talk to him because he didn't want to hear what she would say, he would still feel her lips on his brow.

"I will always watch over you," she'd told him. "You will always be in my heart, and I will always be in yours. Only, after I die, it will be Angela or your grandmother's driver who will pick you up from school, Angela who will sit with you at dinner, your father who will check your homework and read to you at night."

He'd nodded solemnly. She'd made it sound like something simple, like a changing of the guard, but when it happened, it was nothing like that. His grandmother screamed at the funeral. His grandfather stumbled and fell on the way to the cemetery, spraining his wrist so that Leo's memories of the day would include his grandfather's arm in a blue canvas sling. Angela lit candles in every room of the house so no evil spirits would slip in as his mother's soul slipped out to join the other world.

As for Leo's father, his grief intensified his fears about what might happen to Leo, funneling into anything that involved water. Leo was not permitted to accept an invitation to spend a weekend with his friend Gary's family at their house on the Russian River. On the day his fourth-grade class went on a field trip to Point Reyes to study the geological anomalies, his father insisted Leo remain at home. "My son," he informed the school secretary, "will be unable to attend. He will return to classes tomorrow." His father strictly forbade Angela from leaving him alone in the tub. So intimidated was Angela by his father's ironclad prohibitions, she seemed to avoid even water vistas when they went out together.

In his head, Leo would talk with his mother about his father. "He won't let me do anything. He won't let me go to swim parties or to another boy's house unless he calls first to make sure we won't be going to the beach."

His mother, in his mind, would take his hand. "I know, darling. It's irrational. He's not afraid for himself. He crossed the Atlantic with Mrs. Brown before we were married. It's only because he loves you so much and he's so afraid that he could lose you too."

"I'm not going to drown in the bathtub!"

"Your father would tell you how many children do."

Then he would think about his father, so gaunt since his mother died, Leo could see his eye sockets, and Leo would imagine putting his arms around his rosewater-scented mother, and he would let go of the anger at his father for another few days, resisting saying aloud the jabs he'd devise while his father struggled to fill the dinner hour with conversation. *Am I allowed to drink this glass of water? Or is it too dangerous? What if I cough and water gets into my lungs? Aren't there cases of children who've croaked from that?*

Not until many years after her grandfather had died was Grace able to see the man as a whole rather than as a jumble of pieces, some of them extraordinary and some so difficult, she understood why her father, Leo, had to break loose or die of suffocation—though not why he'd had to break loose and then still die.

By then, she was several years into her work as a hospice nurse. Ben, her friend from nursing school who'd dropped out of a Ph.D. program in philosophy to do what he called real work rather than mental masturbation, had given her his paperback compendium of Nietzsche's writings. Reading the aphorisms, she was struck by how she'd grown up without philosophical inquiry. Her grandfather had been prodigiously intelligent. After her grandmother's death, he'd continued their joint studies as a solitary autodidact, expanding his reading to include world history, botany, economics. Every day, he read the *San Francisco Chronicle* and then a goodly portion of *The New York Times* and *The Wall Street Journal*. Every month, he read *Scientific American* and *The Atlantic* and *The New Republic*. He parlayed his studies of finance into shrewd investments of the money he made himself and of the trust from her grandparents that he managed for her brother and her, had an understanding of aesthetics that he expressed in his floral designs. But, he'd never stepped back to ask, What makes a life worth living?

Instead, her grandfather had operated on principles that were for him a prioris. They were good ones—he was uncompromisingly honest in business, he treated his employees and customers with respect, he extended a hand to others—but he never viewed his assumptions as choices, as about himself. For him, they operated automatically, like photosynthesis or osmosis or thermodynamics. Never ever had she seen him question anything he'd done. Never ever had she seen her grandfather wonder what to do.

Never, that is, until her grandfather heard what Garcia wanted, what he was asking of them. Then she'd seen him falter. Briefly, very briefly, but it was the most frightening thing she'd ever witnessed: this man—who'd never budged in his dictates, his injunctions, his mores—broken, defeated.

# 5

# An April Tuesday, 2013

*Joy!* Riding the elevator up to Prudence's apartment, two days after their first visit, Grace feels the elation always there after she's given a presentation. Her first panel, this afternoon, now over: her paper well received and, most important, *done*, the anxiety dissolved.

The paper was on fantasies about the moment of death. Almost all of her patients and many of their family members have fantasies about how the end will go. Only a few of those whose remaining time is measured in weeks or days, not years or months, imagine the mystical accounts in the bestselling inspirational books: a golden light, a soft voice guiding one through a tunnel, an ambrosia scent of indescribable delight. For most, what they imagine is closer to a horror movie: there is no air, as in drowning or being strangled. A pain so excruciating, they lose consciousness . . . and then nothing.

Grace has learned that there's little relation between the fantasy of the final moments and how at peace the dying person and his or her loved ones are with an end looming near—that those anticipating a mystical conclusion are no more likely to have grappled with their goodbyes than those fearing the horror-movie finale. Her job, as she conceives it, is to help a family move the needle, no matter what is imagined, a few notches so as to alleviate the suffering of the last days and the suffering to come for those left behind.

On rare occasions, Grace finds herself privy to something that transcends the focus on the final breath: a dying person so at peace that death is as natural as leaves falling from trees or the waning of the moon. Herman Green, whose sister, Rose, had prompted Grace to wonder what had happened to Prudence, had been such a person. He'd lived alone in the house he and his wife, whose end he'd shepherded three years before, had built an hour north of the city until he had a stroke that landed him in the hospital and catapulted him down the rabbit hole of no return: semiparalysis that made him unable to speak, a broken hip that rendered him bedridden, and then a pneumonia that necessitated breathing supports. When Herman's doctor proclaimed the discharge options to be a nursing facility or home hospice care, David Green, Herman's only child, without hesitation arranged to move his father into his San Francisco apartment.

As she always tries to do when severely ill patients are being transported from a hospital back to their or a relative's home, Grace visited David's apartment the day before to make sure everything—the equipment, the medications, the care plan—was in place. Usually families were overwhelmed by the details of the transition, but David Green was calm. Over the phone, she'd learned that he was fifty-one, divorced, an evolutionary neuroscientist, his two-bedroom apartment a five-minute bike ride from his lab. "My father can have my bedroom," he said as he showed her around, "and I'll sleep in my home office." Gently, she suggested that a hospital bed would be more comfortable for his father—and looking at David's height, an extra-long one, she surmised.

While she placed the order for the bed, the foam pad to prevent bedsores, the oxygen tank, the adult diapers, the disposable gloves for the aides, David disassembled his own bed frame. A single bed, she noted. Like her own.

"You're handy," she said when she got off the phone.

David Green pushed his thinning hair back from his eyes. "Nothing compared to my dad." He pointed to the standing desk in his office, where he would reassemble the bed frame. "He built that for me just last year. He brought all the wood here himself, cured and stained and precut to size, from his workshop. But he taught me a lot." The look she's learned to recognize of a grown child whose love for a parent has been spared the tannin of resentments spread over his broad boyish face. "We built tree houses and sleds and a go-cart when I was thirteen and certain I was going to be a race car driver. Then, when I became interested in science, he helped me build my first microscope."

During the twenty-seven days Herman lived after he was installed in his son's room, he never left the hospital bed, never uttered a word. Still, stopping by each day, Grace had come to know Herman better than patients she'd worked with for three times as long who with a brittle timbre to their voices could have filled volumes with the stories they told casting themselves as heroes or heroines. She'd never heard Herman's voice, but she'd seen his eyes: the way he communicated without language his deep appreciation of the running eulogy David delivered to him over those final weeks.

"I never thought about what you did for me, Dad, until I was fully grown. It just seemed a given, like snow being cold or cherries sweet." Tears had streamed down David's face as he told Herman, "You weren't one of those fathers who insists that his kid be a planet to his sun, polish his shoes with the same chamois cloth, cheer the same baseball team."

Herman held David's hand. He mustered a tiny smile beneath the oxygen nasal prongs. Grace rose to leave them alone, but David looked at her with wet eyes that said *Please, bear witness to me*. So, while David told Herman stories about what Herman had done for him, she sat at the foot of the hospital bed crocheting, as Angela had taught her. Miniature afghans she made for infants in the neonatal intensive care unit run by Sunny, a Korean doctor who, when they'd met a decade ago, she might have fallen in love with for his rejecting any limit on what he'd do for a newborn with a leaking heart. Might have, that is, had sex worked between them. Given that it had not, she'd been relieved when Sunny and Ben, her nursing-school classmate, became a couple, and she could settle into being the friend they insist sleeps over Christmas Eve so she can in the morning open the stocking they've made for her.

She listened while David reminded Herman of the Westinghouse Science Talent Search competition when Herman had stayed up all night checking David's calculations for the caloric intake of mice raised in the presence of television versus not. While David told Herman that he would never forget that when he finally let his parents know that he was dropping out of medical school after they'd already paid two years' tuition because he now understood that what he wanted was to study the evolution of the brain and what it tells us about intelligence and the essence of being human, and for this, he needed to study neuroscience, not medicine, his father had said only, "I'm glad, son, that you figured it out."

Bedridden, in diapers, having to be fed with a baby spoon, Herman had remained until his last breath the adult in the room, never abdicating the responsibility he felt for those he loved. Even at the end when he was sleeping nearly all the time and had passed into a state, Grace explained to David and the aides, in which even yogurt was too hard to swallow and impossible to digest, he would rouse himself each time his sister arrived with her shopping bags filled with containers of the foods she'd cooked for him. He'd let Rose feed him a few spoonfuls of her chicken soup and applesauce, squeezing her arm and nodding his thanks until Grace, concerned about how difficult it was for Herman to breathe with the food in his throat, how it could cause painful diarrhea, would take the bowl and say perhaps Herman would have more later.

And now, her great-aunt, Prudence, 101 years of age, is greeting her at the door with a kiss on each cheek. With no signs of being near death.

"Here"—Prudence nods at the bench in the foyer—"you can put your things here. Are you hungry? Shall we eat now?"

Grace is hungry, she'd been too nervous to eat more than a handful of nuts for lunch, and she guesses that Prudence is on the early schedule of most people her age.

"Yes. Let me help you."

Grace leaves her jacket and the tote with the wooden box that had belonged to her grandfather on the bench and follows Prudence into the kitchen. From the way the food is so carefully prepared, the bowl of rice and beans and the platter of okra both covered with plastic wrap on the counter, the cucumbers in the salad peeled with scores of decorative skin on the thin edge of the slices, Grace, having hired and fired countless caregivers for her patients, sees that Maricel is a gem.

Prudence points toward her dining room. "When I'm alone, I eat at the library table in the living room, but Maricel insisted we dine here."

A long, narrow table is set with two gold place mats and pressed white cloth napkins. Angela, too, had ironed the table linens, as well as the bed linens and all of their clothing including Garcia's undershirts. Grace waits until they're seated to inquire about the paintings, a series of abstracts hung along one wall.

"I bought them at an Art Students League show, not long after I moved here." Prudence smiles sadly. "Carlton would have hated them. For him, anything not clearly representational was suspect. Even Whistler was suspect."

"My grandfather was the same. Except when it came to gardening and flower arranging. There, he was sort of a maverick. One of the early advocates of more artful and natural designs."

Grace senses Prudence's attention, feels her holding back from pressing now, still early in the evening, for more details. Usually, Grace is the one counseling timing: alertness to when an invitation to tell more will open or close a door. So unfamiliar to be on the other side, with the caution directed at herself.

Prudence tells Grace about her single trip to California when her employer, as a way of keeping her firm afloat during the Depression years, had marketed a line of dishware similar to the Franciscan ceramics manufactured there. Prudence points at the platter with the okra, a piece from the Desert Rose pattern that she'd brought back from the factory.

Seeing Grace's gaze pass over the platter, Prudence suspects that it looks prim and old-ladyish to Grace. Or, and somehow this seems even worse, Prudence never having abided by decoration's taking an arch tone, having always believed in sincerity and simplicity, perhaps it strikes Grace as kitsch.

How different Los Angeles had seemed to her, she tells Grace. Everything so far apart. They'd had to hire a driver to get from place to place. What she doesn't say is how strange it was that it had never occurred to her to try to see her brother on that trip.

"San Francisco is much smaller. You don't need a car. I have one, though, because I sometimes need to get somewhere quickly . . ." Grace sighs. No matter how hard she tries to steer clear of her work, she finds herself in one of these death cul-de-sacs: alluding to panicked caregivers she races to at midnight to help administer painkillers they are afraid to inject even though she's taught them with oranges, to adult children who want her to officially proclaim a death, but, it so often seems to her, really just want her with them in those numinous hours when the room is filled with the airs of a person passing.

And here she is, unable to stop herself from noting that Prudence has eaten no more than two hundred calories: a few bites of the okra, a few forkfuls of the rice and beans, two cucumber slices. How many times has she instructed families not to get into food struggles with their dying loved one? People eat what feels best at this stage, she teaches. Not that there is any evidence that Prudence is in her final weeks.

After Prudence puts her fork down for what is certainly the last time, Grace clears the table. She loads the dishwasher while Prudence busies herself organizing a tray for them with a pot of tea and again a plate of the shortbread cookies.

"I think we've satisfied Maricel's wish that we use the dining room," Prudence says with a little smile. "Let's have this in the living room."

Grace carries the tray to the library table under the window, then gets her tote from the foyer. She sits in the wingback chair, across from Prudence, letting the tea steep as Prudence instructed on her first visit.

"When did you last talk with my grandfather?"

"Talk with Randall? That would have been the night he left. Good God, ninety years ago."

Prudence rests her eyes on the river. "As you get old, really old, your age, how many years have passed, seems surreal to even you. If someone were to tell me there'd been an accounting error and, in fact, I am sixty-one, I would think, yes, of course."

She looks back at Grace. "But perhaps you didn't mean that literally? Perhaps you are wondering when we were last in touch?"

Grace nods. She's not sure exactly what she meant.

"There were letters the first year Randall was out West, but they dwindled. My aunt sent him a telegram after my father died, which we later learned he never received because he'd moved. I can't recall when his letters entirely stopped, only that by the time my mother died, I had no idea how to reach him."

Grace serves the tea. She remembers that Prudence likes cream but no sugar. It takes only one hand to count the people for whom Grace has known how they like their coffee or tea. Her grandfather. Angela. Kate, her best friend since fifth grade. Garcia.

Garcia: No milk and three lumps of sugar.

She can feel the edges of the wooden box inside the tote at her feet. When she packed it in her suitcase, she'd not asked herself if it would be a good thing to show it to Prudence were they to meet. Now, though, it seems like a boulder in a rushing river. You stop here. You go back. Or you pick your way around it, you edge your canoe or your kayak or your raft through the narrow channel between the boulder and the bank. You trust there are not rapids on the other side, a foaming hundred-foot drop.

A dozen times a year, she sits across from spouses or grown children or, most heartbreakingly, parents who ask her, Should we tell Grandma or Dad or Junior that she or he has an inoperable tumor or stage-four cancer or Lou Gehrig's that will leave her or him without the ability to walk or talk or swallow? A dozen times a year, she hears family members wonder if it would be kinder to spare mother, husband, brother, or daughter this information during their numbered days. Six months, six weeks, six days. And a dozen times a year, she presses her hands together and says that she understands their concerns, but knowing we are facing death—*This is only my philosophy, you should consult your spiritual adviser, if you have such a person*—is an inalienable right. No one, she says—*And again this is only my view*—should deprive another person of bringing his or her life to completion.

Usually, there are nods and then tears. Sometimes, though, the response is doubt and confusion, and then she has to explain how much can happen in the final span: forgivenesses, amends, love never expressed. And how this is a blessing not just for the dying person but for the entire family. But now, here she is, questioning if she should show the box to Prudence, if after ninety years of not seeing her brother, it would be a gift or the reopening of a wound to rifle through these items that for her brother were the remnants and reminders of what he'd had before he'd left her behind.

Grace leans over, the blood rushing into her head so she sees dark circles and flashes of light, feels the queasiness always there the first years after Garcia's death. She takes the wooden box from the tote and places it on the table in front of Prudence.

Prudence stares at the box, the very box, she realizes with a start, Randall took from the shelf in the room they'd shared to put in his rucksack. It crosses her mind that if she opens this box of her brother's, her heart might stop. She dares not look at Grace, dares not let the young woman see what she fears is passing over her face.

The box is heavier than Prudence expects. She lifts it to her nose, inhales the wood, then presses the narrow side with the brass clasp to her chest, to the place where those first weeks after Randall left, his absence had formed a hollow. Morning after morning, she would wake with a feeling of confusion, and then the awareness would wash over her again that he was gone and between her heart and her gut would be the terrible vacuum.

Were the girl, the young woman, this Grace, not watching her, Prudence would again bring the box to her face. She would investigate if her brother's scent remained in the wood. Were Grace not here, she might even lick the wood so as to taste it, something she could not do in front of anyone: how exaggerated and bizarre that would seem. Instead, she places the box back on the table.

Grace looks away, as she has learned to do with families after she has told them her thoughts about the right to know we are dying. For most people, she is putting into words something they already understand, and averting her gaze grants them the privacy to gather up their wisest and most generous and strongest selves, but for others—and these are the ones she worries about later, after she has moved on to her next case—it spares them having her see their terror that the boulder is approaching and no one on this side knows what is beyond.

Through the window, she sees the red orb of the sun on the horizon, the river glistening with the end-of-day light. The eastern coast of what her grandfather had called "our great land." She's been here a handful of times before without ever trying to find her great-aunt. And her grandfather, hadn't he been back here as well, for a night or two, bookending the ship crossing he'd made with Cecelia Brown? Had he thought to see his sister and mother? Was his mother even alive then?

On the rare occasions when Grace had stayed home sick from school, her grandfather would leave his florist shop at noon to check on her. Thinking it would entertain her, he would bring the wooden box from his study. He would drag the armchair in her room next to the queen-size canopy bed where she would lie like an invalid princess, a carafe filled by Angela with water she would boil and then cool to room temperature, refusing to add the ice Grace's grandfather would urge.

Her grandfather would place the wooden box on Grace's lap. Before she opened it, he would ask her to list the items inside.

"There are the stones you took from the beach in front of Laurelton Hall," she would solemnly answer. "A blue tile your father gave you, copies of newspaper articles you found at the library. There's one about a wedding and one about a big party."

"The party was the Peacock Feast, and it happened before the wedding, but they were just a few months apart. The year?" her grandfather would ask, as though this were a Mensa test.

Grace would furl her brow and try to recall, and Angela, crocheting in a corner of the room, as she would do when either Grace or Garcia was sick, would make a *tsk-tsk* sound to discourage the quizzing. Annoyed, her grandfather would tell Angela to go, she could put a little bell by the bed and Grace could ring if she needed anything, but Angela would refuse to budge from her seat.

"Mr. Randall," she would say, "in my country, a mother does not leave a sick child alone." Grace's grandfather would scowl, secretly pleased that Angela was so vigilant, but not wanting to encourage her belief that the death angel might creep into the room if she were not keeping watch. Her belief that had she ignored his instructions to leave him alone with Mrs. Carolyn in what turned out to be her last moments, had she stayed, she would have wrestled the dark messenger to the ground or brokered a bargain that he take her instead.

"Nineteen fourteen?" Grace would venture.

"Yes, May twenty-fourth, 1914, was when the article ran, but the affair itself was on May fifteenth."

Grace would open the box and find the stapled papers with the caption her grandfather had written in his careful hand. While her grandfather watched, she would study the photographs: the five girls in long white dresses, three carrying what looked like live peacocks but had been, her grandfather told her, roasted with the feathers inserted afterward for their presentation; a girl wearing a hat constructed from the head of a peacock, her face so pale and still, she might have been carved out of marble; a group of children costumed in chef's hats with pillows under their aprons that made them plumper than the stuffed pigs they each held.

By the time Grace was thirteen, she could list most of the other items in the box: more newspaper articles, the top of a peacock feather, a photograph of her grandfather as a boy of four or five seated on a blanket with two identically dressed babies, a packet of letters tied together with a gold ribbon. By then, though, she'd felt too old to have her grandfather at her bedside when she was home sick from school, and in any case, her grandfather was preoccupied with Garcia, who, having failed seventh-grade math and barely scraped by in English and history and science too, had been tested by a neuropsychologist, who recommended an even smaller, more flexible school than the one Garcia had attended since leaving the Presidio Academy, where his father and great-grandfather had gone.

Now, again, a dart of worry. Has she made a mistake bringing the box? In nursing school, they'd been taught that a starving person should be treated with caution. You have to start with a spoonful or two of broth. A full meal could overwhelm bodily systems.

"Would you like me to just show you one or two items for today?"

Prudence nods. There's a hint of fear in her eyes, a look that reminds Grace of her grandfather when he'd come into the diner where she worked on his trips to visit Garcia, wary of what news she might report. It washes over her that this woman across from her is her grandfather's sister: the same heart-shaped face, the same violet-tinted eyes.

Grace reaches over and draws the box toward her. Using her thumbnail, she flips up the little brass hook and opens the top.

A faint smell wafts from inside the box. Prudence inhales a potpourri of something musty, something salty, something turning to dust. A scent cradling a century past. With it she sees her mother's face. Her mother's face from before they moved to the city: laughing so her teeth show and her eyes crinkle, unbraiding her red hair and brushing one hundred strokes. Her freckled calves on the beach where the servants were permitted with their families when Mr. T and his wife and children were away. Her mother sucking out the pits from the orchard plums and spitting them into the dirt before giving Prudence the fruit. Lifting her onto one of the ponies outside the barn. "Such a big girl, Prudence, you're such a big girl." Prudence with her socks and shoes off, her toes deliciously free to burrow into the cool, damp dirt while her father inspects the beds of lilacs, her mother leans over with her nose inside one of the blooms.

Grace is looking through the photocopies, searching for a particular one it seems. When she finds it, she folds back a page and hands it to Prudence.

There are photographs, children and young women in costumes, but Prudence locks on the handwritten words at the top. In a hand as familiar as her own, her brother had printed *The Peacock Feast, May 15, 1914.*

When Prudence opens her eyes, Grace is sitting quietly across the library table. The photocopied pages are still in Prudence's lap. She is embarrassed that she drifted off.

"How long was I asleep?"

"Not long. Maybe ten, fifteen minutes."

"I hope I didn't worry you. I wake so early these days and then spend the rest of my days in and out of little naps. Like a baby, I'm afraid."

"I am worried about you. Not that you fell asleep. As you said, that's normal at your age. About your living alone."

"I have Maricel. She comes every day but Sunday. She watches over me like a mother bear."

("Thirty hours out of one hundred sixty-eight," Maricel, who has been on a campaign this past year to have her sister work for Prudence on Sundays, chides. "Nothing . . .")

"But what if you fall or something happens when she's not here? Could I at least arrange a medical alert system for you? Then, if you were to fall or need help, someone would be notified."

"If I fall, it will hardly be a tragedy. I've lived a long, long life. I'm like one of those cans that's past its sell-by date."

What Prudence doesn't add is a long, long life that started so abundantly, then withered and drooped, leaving her now with only Maricel and her beautiful things.

"I'll come back Thursday. Around five? If that is okay?"

"Please do. I would like that." Not until after Prudence has said the words does she realize that they are true.

"I could leave the box here."

Prudence nods. She remains in her chair by the library table while Grace clears the tea things. She hears the water running in the sink, thinks how at Grace's age, she was already a widow.

When Grace returns, she leans down to kiss Prudence goodbye. How lucky her brother had been to have this lovely granddaughter.

"I'll let myself out. The door locks automatically, doesn't it?"

"It does."

After Prudence hears the door close, she looks again at the papers in her lap. She was so riveted by her brother's caption, she didn't recognize that this is the very article she came across sixty-some years ago in her wet galoshes in the Periodical Room at the New York Public Library—a bitter era of her work when the items she'd purchased for her wealthy clients had so essentially felt like coded declarations of wealth, she'd come to think that rather than waste their money on Sheraton sideboards and Chippendale chairs, they should simply pin to their backs a sign stating their net worth.

Looking more carefully, she sees that her brother stapled together what is actually two articles: The first, published just two days after the event, is a short description of the menu and a list of the young ladies and children in the pageant. The second, published a week later, has nearly a full page of pictures of the procession.

Prudence finds Dorothy's name under one of the photographs. She's carrying one of the peacocks. Her thick hair grazes her waist, and the band of the Grecian-styled gown is wrapped around the top of her thighs in a way that reveals the shape of her behind. There are no images of Tiffany from the evening, though Prudence dimly recalls a picture of him she'd come across that same March afternoon from the Egyptian Fete he'd given the year before the Peacock Feast: dressed like a pasha in silken pantaloons, his impervious wide forehead rising up from dark brows to a fez perched atop his head.

Her lids are growing heavy and she is drifting, drifting again. Drifting into fantasy or waking dream or memory, how would one ever know?

Hidden behind a wall, she watches a parade of peacocks. Together, they screech, move their rumps, and fan their enormous feathered tails. A thousand blue eyes shimmer and shake.

There's a sound at Prudence's ear. A little boy, her own age, crouched beside her, their fingers entwined, is crying.

# 6

# Leo & Jacie

## San Francisco, 1963–1965

At fifteen, Grace's father, Leopold, turned wild. It was the spring of 1963. He was in ninth grade, in the most accelerated classes—honors geometry, honors Latin, honors chemistry—and he and his best friend, Gary, would next year be co-captains of the junior varsity basketball team. Until then, Leo's rebellions had been restricted to the conversations he'd had in his head with his mother, who'd always humored him: *Be patient, be tolerant, your father loves you, another few years and you will make your own decisions.* Leo did not know about the lysergic acid experiments being carried out in Menlo Park to the south or that the Haight would become the sanctuary for seekers and lost souls from Maine to Texas, but he could sense it. It was as though he'd been given truth glasses and the life he led in the Presidio and Pacific Heights suddenly looked absurd: the navy blazer he wore to school, the tennis whites required on the courts at his grandparents' club, the striped tie for Sunday dinners—costumes of a bygone era.

In March, Leo rolled, as he had since school teams commenced, from basketball into lacrosse. One May day, when lacrosse practice was canceled because the field was too wet, Gary, who didn't play a spring sport, asked if Leo wanted to come along to Kelly's Cove, the surfing spot south of the Cliff House restaurant, where Leo's grandparents, with strict instructions from his father that they were not to walk with Leo down to the beach, often took him for Saturday lunch. For the past month, Gary, their friend Jimmy, Jimmy's year-older brother, Shane, and Shane's friend Will had been learning to surf under the tutelage of a guy they called Flab, who gave lessons and loaned boards in exchange for a twenty they'd pool together from their allowances.

Leo's heart pounded so hard, he could only nod in response. "But I don't have a bathing suit with me."

"Take yours from the locker room," Gary said. "Marshall"—the locker room attendant—"will think you're bringing it home to wash."

Leo felt a rush of gratitude, a memory surfacing from six years before, when he'd returned to school after his mother's funeral. While the other boys had been awkward with him, some even avoiding him, not out of meanness but because they didn't know what to say, Gary had come right over to him. Even then, Gary had been the tallest in the grade, a little uncoordinated from not having possessed his height, but beneath his clumsiness, which the teachers mistook for a touch of dim-wittedness, a serious thinker, the boy who even at nine saw the themes in the chapter books they read and wondered about such questions as, Must we have war? He put the flat of his hand on Leo's back, and in Leo's memory, Gary hadn't left his side for the rest of that year. Gary would line up beside him when they were told to walk in pairs. He'd patiently read Leo the spelling words over the phone: *their*, *there*; *choose*, *chews*; *great*, *grate*; *bear*, *bare*. When they had to shimmy up a rope and Leo clung two feet above the shiny gym floor, unable to lift himself any higher, Gary had coached him, "Come on, Leo. You can do it. Grip with your thighs and reach your hands so it's easier to pull."

Shane had been given his father's old Ford for his sixteenth birthday. It was the first time Leo had been in a car with a kid driving. Will took shotgun, and Gary, Jimmy, and Leo climbed into the backseat. The air pounded on Leo's face from the rolled-down windows and the radio blasted the Beach Boys' "Surfin' U.S.A." and Will raised his arms in a triumphant pump. It was thrilling.

In the parking lot at Kelly's Cove, Jimmy handed Leo one of the fishy wet suits from the trunk. Leo copied the others as they stepped into the legs, yanking the crotch up as high as it could go, and then wriggled into the arms. He couldn't tell even Gary that he'd never walked on a beach or felt the ocean.

"That's Flab." Gary pointed at a guy with hair bleached dry as a Brillo pad, huge arms, and a belly that hung over his surfing shorts.

"Sissy kindergartners," the guy hollered.

"He never wears a wet suit," Gary explained.

"Can't handle the cold water cuz you ain't got hair on your cocks."

When Leo's foot touched the sand, he thought his heart would stop. *Leo,* he heard his mother say.

It was overcast, the ocean a good fifty yards away. Enormous and gray with white froth on top.

*Leo.*

"Fuckin' waves," Shane yelled as he ran with a board toward the water.

*Leo, stop.*

He wanted to stop. He wanted to do exactly what he heard his mother telling him.

*You must, for your father's sake. And, darling, the water does look very rough.*

His eyes welled with tears. He imagined Flab's snickering if he turned back. Gary and maybe Jimmy would understand, but Shane and Will would join Flab in thinking him a sissy.

*Go away,* he shrieked in his head.

*Go away* . . . and to his amazement his mother did precisely that.

Leo was a month behind the others in the surfing lessons and a decade behind them in knowing how to swim in the Pacific, but basketball and lacrosse had taught him to control his lanky body (Leo left his butt at home, his friends would tease) in three dimensions. To his surprise, once he was in the water, his fear disappeared.

"Give Big Daddy your ears, little girls," Flab announced. "This kid is going to be the best of all of youse." Translated into the new language that Leo, without his mother's voice in his head, would soon be using with ease, he didn't give a fuck if he got smashed in the head with a board. He'd win if he caught a wave and he'd win if he broke his spinal cord and died getting pounded by the surf. That second thought—that he'd win too if he died—came as a surprise to him: he'd never thought about himself as depressed, and he felt quite certain he wasn't. He just didn't care enough about living long to give up living now. He'd lose only if he stood like a scaredy-cat watching the surf from the shore.

Afterward, Leo had to confide in Gary about his father's water insanity. "I'll be grounded until I'm twenty if he discovers I came here."

"Wow, man, I never knew that. You should've told me." Gary looked at him with the concern of the pediatrician he would go on to become. "I knew your father was wound tight, but I never realized it was like that."

"Remember the time he wouldn't let me come with your family to the Russian River?"

Gary nodded.

"Same deal. He didn't want me by the water."

In the end, though, it was easy. After surfing, Leo would go home with Gary. He'd shower in Gary's bathroom, washing the sand and sea off his body, leaving his suit with Gary's. He'd wave goodbye to Gary's mother, then walk the six blocks to his own house, his hair dry by the time he got home.

*Go away,* he'd shouted to his mother that afternoon. *Go away.* Not knowing that it would be as in the fairy tale where the fisherman's wife wishes that everything she touches becomes gold and is left with her meat and water turned to metal. That his mother would go away for good. That never again would he hear her voice.

In the fall, when they all went back to school, Leo and Gary and Jimmy to tenth grade and Shane and Will to eleventh, their surfing ended as abruptly as it had begun. Gary, the worst surfer of them all, with his long feet and thick torso, tired first of the clammy wet suits, lugging the boards across the wide beach, getting knocked around in the freezing water. He'd lost interest too in basketball, instead spending his free time listening to early rock and roll, the Elvis Presley and the Drifters they'd grown up on, and the British bands everyone was following now.

Leo's classes were a drag, but he'd always been a good student. He felt that he had no choice. He had to do well for his father, who had told him that the two heartbreaks in his life were Leo's mother's death and that he'd left school after sixth grade. Math came easy for Leo, which he knew made him lucky, but his real love was books. He'd read the Hardy Boys and then, somehow getting them confused, Thomas Hardy. From there, Upton Sinclair and, in no particular order, as he discovered the authors through older boys or a teacher or his own perusing of the library shelves, Arthur Miller, Dylan Thomas, Bellow, Roth, Kerouac, Ginsberg.

Over winter break, Shane, who'd become the school's pot dealer, turned Jimmy and Leo and Gary on to marijuana for the first time. For Leo, it was a sensation of being unmuffled. Arriving home at midnight, he nearly gasped from the scent of the gardenias on the entry-hall table. The corn bread Angela had left on the kitchen counter was so buttery, so savory, so ecstatically delicious, he lingered with it in his mouth, then ravenously ate the rest down to the crumbs he gathered by licking his forefinger and scraping it along the bottom of the pan. Afterward, he sat in the parlor, looking at the photos from when he was first born: his mother's joy in him darting out from the pictures even now, nearly sixteen years later. The album was still in his lap when Angela woke him and sent him upstairs to sleep.

By the summer, Leo and Gary were getting high nearly every day. For Leo, it felt as if a trapdoor inside him had been pried open and the bird of sadness that since his mother's death had slept curled inside his gut could now fly out. It wasn't that he ceased grieving his mother. Rather, smoking a joint in Gary's car parked on the top of Twin Peaks, looking down at the green swath of the Presidio, his backyard all of his life, and out toward the beaches where they'd surfed last summer, he felt his view enlarge. He could see his mother's death as part of a tapestry. Could see the train that had brought his father from Hell's Kitchen in New York across the Great Plains and over the Rockies to San Francisco, then still a small city. Could imagine the years of his father's relentless work to build his florist business, to catapult himself into a position that had let him woo Leo's mother. He could see himself linked by the threads that went from his mother to his grandmother Anita and from there to his slave-owning great-great-grandparents; by the threads from his father to his servant grandparents—with a shock, he realized he didn't even know their names, only that they'd been gardener and maid for the glass designer Louis C. Tiffany—and from there to his Irish great-great-grandparents who'd lost half their children in the potato famine. He could see himself quitting basketball and lacrosse, writing on the outside of his World History binder, *Death to jock brain*.

With the grass, the revelations tumbled out, one after the other, like stones sliding down the face of a mountain.

"I'm going to be a poet," he said to Gary.

"That's cool. That's a cool thing to do."

Gary, who'd been learning guitar from a guy, King, who worked at a record store in North Beach, told Leo that he'd discovered that music was not about playing notes written on a page but about playing the melody inside himself.

Leo felt a surge of love, 100 percent stoned love, for Gary, for King, for his father, even for his lacrosse coach, who would not understand why he was quitting the team. "Yeah, I totally get that," Leo said.

"But you know what?" Gary continued. "It's not going to be my life. I don't have that kind of talent. You have to be an original to be an artist. I'm not an original."

Gary propped his forehead on the steering wheel and started to cry. It kind of spooked Leo. "I'm okay." Gary looked over at Leo. "These are good tears. They mean I'm being honest with myself."

At the end of Leo's junior year, Shane, off to Europe before starting Williams, turned his marijuana business over to his brother Jimmy and Leo. "Gotta have a partner," Shane told Jimmy. "Someone covering your back. Otherwise, clients mess with you." Shane had picked Leo because he'd seen the streak of fearlessness in him when they'd surfed Kelly's Cove. Leo had a way of sizing up people that struck Shane as a bit ruthless, but in a good way. "Unlike you, goofball," he said to his brother, "Leo won't give the dope away to every deadbeat who bellyaches, 'Hey, man, front me an ounce, I'll sell it and make it back for you by the end of the week.'"

It shocked Leo how much money he made. He bought a used VW with a tape deck already installed that he told his father (what difference did one more untruth—he couldn't bring himself to use the word *lie*—make?) Shane was loaning him while he was back East. With no need for a job, he announced that he was going to spend the summer studying for the SATs. He'd use the money he'd saved from his grandparents' birthday checks for his pocket expenses.

In July, Leo went with Gary to see a band, the Great Society, that King had told Gary to check out. Gary was lukewarm on the band, but Leo thought the singer Grace Slick, with her low velvet voice, was amazing.

As the band started a song called "Darkly Smiling," a girl in a long skirt that looked as if it had been made from an Indian bedspread and a halter top that exposed the sides of her large, soft breasts squeezed in next to Leo. Leo was a good six inches taller than the girl, but he could tell she was a little older. She swayed with the music, her arm dusting his on the downbeat.

"You're darkly smiling," he said.

She peered at him with chocolate eyes and a twisty grin that suggested he was being woven into a web of thoughts in her head. "Darkly, sparkly." There was a hint of a Southern drawl in her voice. She raised her hands over her head, and her breasts lifted. "Like fireworks."

Leo offered her a toke from his joint. She held the joint between her thumb and forefinger, staring at the lit end.

"That chick is tripping," Gary said into Leo's ear.

Leo took the joint back from the girl before it burned her fingers.

By the end of the concert, she was crying and shivering, and when they asked who she'd come with, she pointed at the ceiling, then whispered, "You." Gary draped his sweatshirt over her shoulders. He leaned down so he could look directly in her eyes while he asked where she lived. To Leo's surprise, she answered, reciting her address as though some part of her brain had stayed sufficiently on guard to recall that vital information.

Gary put his hand under her elbow, and the three of them

walked to Leo's car. The girl climbed into the back. She curled into a ball with her head hanging off the seat. She was whimpering. "Man," Gary said. "Someone's got to be with her until she comes down."

Leo could tell that Gary, who had to get up early for his summer day-camp job, had had enough of the crazy chick. "I'll drop you, and then take her home. Maybe she has a roommate who can look after her."

When they pulled in front of Gary's house, the girl was moving her fingers to what looked like the "Itsy Bitsy Spider" song. "You sure you can handle this?" Gary asked.

"No prob. Besides, I think she's coming down now."

The girl's address was a Victorian house in the Haight. Leo left her in the car while he rang all the bells. A guy called out the window, "Gene? Is that you?" Leo hollered back that he wasn't Gene, but he had a girl with curly dark hair in his car who said she lived here.

"She's the studio on the top floor."

"Does she have a roommate?"

"Nah."

"Any friends here who could be with her? She's kinda fucked-up."

The window closed. The air was damp in the bone-chill way it could get in San Francisco in summer.

Leo used the pay phone on the corner to call his father. For the first time in a long while, he told his father the truth. "I met this girl, she's high on something, and I don't want to leave her alone."

"What do you mean, 'high on something'?"

"I think she took LSD. She lives by herself and I'm going to stay with her for a while."

"Leo, where are you?"

"I'm in a phone booth on the corner of Haight and Clayton."

"I'll come meet you."

"No, Dad."

"You have to take her to an emergency room."

"That would freak her out. She just needs someone to be with her for a few hours. Okay, Dad. I'm going to hang up now. I'll be home in the morning."

"You can bring her here."

"I love you, Dad."

Leo walked back to the car. He could feel the tears lodged in his sinuses. Before his mother died, he'd said *I love you* to both of his parents and to Angela every day. Now, he couldn't remember the last time he'd said those words to anyone.

He opened the back door and shook the girl, who was still doing the "Itsy Bitsy Spider" thing with her hands. "Where are your keys?"

Obediently, she sat up, reached inside her bag, and pulled out a macramé key chain.

"Give them to me."

She handed the keys to Leo and followed him to her front door and up the stairs to her apartment.

Leo unlocked the door and flipped the light switch. The walls glowed, each a different fruit hue, and watercolors were taped to them in clusters. In the middle of the room was a mattress covered with a cloth like the girl's skirt, and in the corner, an easel with a drawing of a mandala. Next to the window was a table with macramé plant hangers in various stages of completion, and a plate with three yellow papayas.

The girl collapsed onto the mattress, crawled under the bedspread, and closed her eyes.

Leo sat at the table. Behind the spools of twine was a transistor radio. He turned it on. It was set to the classical station his mother had listened to. He rolled a joint, took a few drags, and put it out.

The girl tossed and turned while Leo remained at the table listening to piano music that felt as if someone had put a microphone inside his heart and was broadcasting his emotions: sad but with the sensation of being more fully alive than he could ever recall. When the piece was over, the announcer said it was Glenn Gould playing the *Goldberg Variations*. Leo wrote the name in the notebook he had taken to carrying with him now that he knew he wanted to be a poet.

The girl's moans were just barely audible over the music. She flung off the bedspread and tugged on her halter top until it opened, exposing her breasts. They looked like sand castles topped with wet circles, and Leo felt the start of an erection. He covered her with the bedspread, and she curled back into herself, her knees raised to her stomach.

After the girl had fallen into what seemed to be a deep sleep, he rummaged through the bag she'd had with her at the concert. Inside was a paperback by someone named Anaïs Nin, a tin of patchouli hand cream, a hairbrush, and a small sketch pad with some drawings of a powerful-looking tall woman with long blonde hair and feather earrings. Written in bubble letters beneath one of the drawings was *Lake*.

At the bottom of the bag was a wallet. Leo hesitated before opening it, before taking out the license. Before reading the name, after which the sleeping girl would no longer be the sleeping girl.

A Texas driver's license. Jacie Klein. DOB 5-25-46.

She was nineteen, twenty-one months older than he was.

Grace's not-yet-father lay on the floor next to her not-yet-mother. She turned toward him, opened her eyes for a split second, and darkly smiled.

When Jacie woke, well into the afternoon, she wrapped the Indian bedspread around her and got a T-shirt from the bureau next to the table. She and Leo sat on the mattress, Jacie cross-legged and Leo with his legs stretched out, while they drank the coffee Leo had made from beans he'd found in the refrigerator of her galley kitchen and ate the papaya slices he'd cut and the rice cakes he'd spread with peanut butter he'd taken from her cabinet.

A year ago, she told Leo, she was sitting with the twins she babysat on the lawn in front of their house showing them how to draw unicorns and mermaids when an ice cream truck pulled up. "Now that I was headed to college, my mother had wanted me to get what she called a *real* job for the summer. Working in a store or waiting tables at their country club, something where I'd be around kids my own age. 'You might meet a boy,' she said. But I'd spent the past four summers taking care of Max and Rachel, since they were two, and I just wanted to do that again."

Jacie twirled a strand of hair around a finger. Even Leo knew it was not the kind of hair girls wanted: too frizzy, too untamed.

"This blond guy got out of the truck. He reached his arms over his head, and then he lit a cigarette. I'd never smoked a cigarette, but he made it look like a Zen thing to do, like whittling a stick of wood or rolling a pie crust. A few minutes later, he stomped out his cigarette and leaned over to pick up the butt. As he stood up, he caught my eye. And that was it. It was like Prince Charming in *Sleeping Beauty*. Dale, I didn't even know his name then, had broken the spell, and I woke up and knew that I was going to do something amazing with him."

Two weeks later she'd left Houston with Dale, emptying her bank account of the nearly thousand dollars she'd saved and leaving her parents a note that she was going with Dale to New York to visit a friend of his, and from there they were driving cross-country because Dale wanted to see both the Atlantic and the Pacific. They were taking the new truck his father had bought but not yet outfitted for selling ice cream, and they'd sleep in the back and buy food at grocery stores. She knew her parents didn't think he was a suitable boyfriend for her (they'd met Dale once, after which her mother had said, "He seems like a nice boy, only, honey, he's had such a different life from you . . ."), but Dale, she wrote, was an excellent driver. They should not worry at all. Not one bit.

When she called home that first night, her parents went completely bonkers. Her father, a gastroenterologist used to directing his patients and his staff and his family, all in the same even but officious tone (Jacie's brother had a pitch-perfect imitation that would elicit a play slap from their mother), demanded that she tell him—"Immediately, Jacie"—where she was, then threatened to call the police when she refused. It was the first time she'd not done what her parents told her to do, and she had to remind her father that she was eighteen and could legally travel on her own. Her mother had been so hysterical, all Jacie could make out was "Vassar," the college where she was supposed to go in September.

Leo studied the girl across from him. She was definitely not beautiful. Most definitely not the girl he'd imagined losing his virginity with, but he knew that this was what would happen. Soon, maybe even today.

"My mother had tried to convince my father that I should go to art school. 'She just wants to draw and read novels and poetry,' she told him. 'What is the point of insisting she take economics and chemistry?' But my father refused to even discuss it. Both of his children required proper college degrees."

Jacie cocked her head. On her face was a tiny smile, bemusement, it seemed, at her father's bullheadedness, but also sadness at having disappointed him, and Leo could tell that she loved him in spite of his refusing to see her for who she was. Was it the same with his father? No, his father saw him for who he was, only he forbade it: forbade Leo to venture out of the protective corral, so that there'd been no choice save to become a liar and sneak.

"I was so terrified by the idea of going away to college, my mother and the college counselor selected the three schools where I applied without even asking me. After I got my acceptance letter from Vassar, I had the hiccups for a week. I kept imagining myself sitting alone in a dining room with a huge vaulted ceiling stuffing forkfuls of mashed potatoes into my mouth while everyone else sat together laughing and talking. When I told my brother, who'd been at MIT for two years by then, he snapped at me that I was being an imbecile. 'What are you going to do?' he said. 'Stay in Houston and live at home and go to a community college? Spend your Saturdays on a chaise lounge by the pool while Mom stuffs envelopes for the League of Women Voters and Dad scoops out the drowned mosquitoes? That will be like remaining in high school.' I'd been too embarrassed to say *Yes, that sounds pretty good.*"

Listening to Jacie, Leo felt mesmerized. Gary was by nature honest and the opposite of a braggart, but Leo had never before heard anyone else so lacking in vanity. He thought about how he should go down to the pay phone and call his father, but he didn't want to leave the tripping girl—well, she was no longer tripping, now she seemed like a regular girl, the kind of girl who never got in trouble at school and never caused her parents any worries until suddenly she had. Well, not exactly regular. There was that weird book in her bag and the watercolors taped to the walls and the table covered with macramé.

Jacie reached over and massaged Leo's temples with her thumbs and forefingers. He closed his eyes, unaware until that moment that his head was throbbing. She kissed him softly on the mouth in a way that was somehow both sensual and chaste, then leaned back.

"When we got to New York, I left Dale with his friend and took the subway to the Bronx to visit my father's mother, Bubba. She's my favorite grandparent, and every Christmas when we came to New York, I would sleep in her bed with her and she would buy the least expensive seats possible for *The Nutcracker*: we'd be so high up, the dancers would look like grasshoppers. The whole subway ride, I practiced in my head saying I was traveling with a friend, but when I saw her, I burst into tears and told her everything. I was afraid she'd insist that we call my parents, but all she said was 'Bubbala, this is your time to have adventures. Let me tell you about an adventure I had when I was your age.'"

Leo tried to imagine his grandmother Anita talking with him about having had an adventure, but he could not get past her penciled brows and her pancake powder and her pinched expression when his grandfather praised what she thought of as Angela's peasant cooking.

"Bubba and her friend Shirley had taken a bus to Atlantic City. Their first night there, they dared each other to eat clams. They'd grown up kosher, and her friend Shirley was so scared God would strike her dead on the spot, she raced outside after her first bite and threw up. But that, Bubba told me, was not the most important part of the trip. Something much more important than eating clams had happened."

"What happened?"

"She had sex."

Jacie laughed. It was the first time Leo had heard her laugh: from her belly, the way he dimly recalled his mother laughing before she got sick. "Bubba looked like the cat who ate the canary. 'I know, it must be surprising,' she said, 'to think that an old lady like me had sex before she got married. But I never regretted it. His name was Morris Dreyer. A very intelligent boy with soulful eyes.'"

Jacie bit into a piece of the papaya Leo had cut. He reached over and wiped a dribble of goo from her chin.

"My grandmother told her friend Shirley the next day, and Shirley slapped her and called her a whore. Bubba slapped her back and called her a bitch. Bubba said that she'd never told anyone since. But now," Jacie said, "there are four of us who know. Shirley, Bubba, you, and me."

"Five. Morris Dreyer. Don't forget him."

When Jacie laughed again, Leo wondered if sex with her would feel as good as making her laugh. It was so strange, but he already felt as if he loved her, as though he had leaped right over infatuation and the tempest of romance and falling in love to simply loving this Jewish Texan girl whose parents, she would later explain, had left the Bronx, where they'd both grown up, so her father could join a gastroenterology practice in Houston. Houston in 1943 seeming to Jacie's parents like another country, a world apart from the Bronx kitchen tables where letters were read from relatives in Bessarabia or Odessa about the slaughter of Jews by the Romanians or, for those families from Vienna or Berlin or Frankfurt, about the deportation to what they could only think of as work camps but knew in their hearts were no such thing.

"After I heard about Morris Dreyer, I realized how disappointed I was that I'd given up my virginity to someone who I'd never think of so fondly sixty years later."

Jacie paused. Was she looking for his reaction to her not being a virgin, or his reaction to her regretting her first time having been with Dale?

"Telling Dale, after we'd been here for a few days, that I wasn't going back to Houston with him was the hardest thing I'd ever done. He took it to mean that I thought he wasn't good enough for me. 'You read books,' he said. 'You'll probably marry a doctor like your dad.'" Jacie looked down at her lap. "The truth, though, was actually worse: we'd run out of things to say by the time we reached the Rockies. I was so bored, I thought I was going insane."

The day Dale left, Jacie told Leo, she'd found a sublet for a room in a group house on Ashbury Street run by a man-size girl named Lake who made earrings from feathers and wore silver rings on all of her fingers. Lake took Jacie to an Indian emporium, where she bought two long wrap skirts and an embroidered tunic and a pair of harem pants Jacie thought made her look like a jester but Lake proclaimed totally cool. Within a few days, Jacie got a job at a coffee shop on Market Street. She set up a drawing table in her room, and another girl who lived upstairs taught her how to make macramé plant hangers, which the household sold along with Lake's feather earrings on Saturdays at the San Jose flea market. Jacie had lived in Lake's house until the guy whose room she was subletting came back from India. After that, she'd moved here.

Leo touched Jacie's folded leg. The twenty-one months between them seemed like a ravine: she'd been on her own for a year; he was still a kid living at home. But it also gave him power. His life had not yet started. He could still do anything. She'd already pulled off the highway, Vassar a turn long passed, grown acclimated to scraping by.

He knew this should give him pause, that he should be checking out how stable or unstable she was before he took off his clothes.

"I love Grace," she said.

"Grace?"

"Grace Slick. The singer last night."

"'Darkly Smiling,' I liked that."

"That's my favorite song of hers. I'm going to do a drawing of it."

"How do you draw a song?"

"You draw how it makes you feel."

Leo nodded. He could see the crossroads, the two routes clearly marked. The prudent route, the one his mother would have advised he take were he still able to hear her voice: Stand up right now, kiss the girl on the top of her messy hair, and head to his car. Give the quarter pound of pot and the scale that was in the box under his bed to Jimmy and say *I'm out* and start doing stairs and get in shape and tell Coach he could count on him for lacrosse this year. Bring his grades up, go to Stanford, which is where Mrs. Brown, whose alum husband had left a sufficient bequest that she had some influence there, had told his father Leo should go. Become a lawyer or a banker, inherit his grandparents' money, and marry a beautiful, well-educated girl. Have three children, the eldest, a daughter he'd name Carolyn after his mother. And maybe then, his mother would forgive him for having abandoned her two summers before at Kelly's Cove and she'd talk to him again.

Or he could take the *other* route, the route with no name, only an arrow pointing to what he was already doing: unzipping his jeans and standing naked before Jacie. Helping her pull her T-shirt over her head, touching her breasts, putting his mouth over the amazing brown nipples, then climbing under the Indian bedspread with her where he cried as he entered her and she held him and told him that they would be together forever now.

The last thing Leo heard before he drifted off into what afterward seemed like the deepest sleep he'd had since his mother died was Jacie whispering, "When we have our daughter, we'll name her Grace."

# 7

# Prudence

## An April Wednesday, 2013

In the morning, Prudence sits at the library table with a cup of the tea Grace took care remained in the thermos and Randall's wooden box. She flicks open the brass clasp and takes out the small blue tile. She presses it into her palm. Her brother had been seven when they moved, old enough to roam the property on his own. Had there been a pile of tiles behind a shed or a sack of them at the back of a barn? Had a piece broken off from a mosaic and he'd pocketed it?

She sets the tile next to her teacup and takes out two of the newspaper articles: one a clipping from the original paper, the other a photocopy. She looks at the clipping first. It's from a 1957 copy of *The New York Times*, about the fire that burned Laurelton Hall to the ground. In 1957, Randall was forty-eight—over thirty years since he'd moved West, but apparently still reading the New York papers. She tries to imagine him cutting out the article from the then-inky pages, the face she'd known as a child advanced through time with a neatly trimmed mustache now added on.

As with the article about the Peacock Feast, Prudence dimly recalls having read this piece before. By 1957, Tiffany had been dead for a quarter of a century and Laurelton Hall, having fallen into disrepair, had been sold a decade prior for a paltry price. It must have been from this story that she'd learned that the fire had left little standing aside from the minaret that housed the steam furnace.

She's quite certain she's never seen the photocopied piece, from a June 1916 Oyster Bay weekly. How had Randall found it? Had he written the periodical's offices? The feature recounts the extended argument between Mr. Louis C. Tiffany and the town regarding the beach fronting Laurelton Hall. Prudence's mother had told her about this fight, but not the legal details Prudence reads about now regarding the interpretation of riparian rights: the statutes governing access to and use of a body of water. According to the article, Mr. Louis C. Tiffany had won a first set of cases that gave him exclusive claim to the beachfront, a location that prior to this ruling had been a public bathing place. He'd constructed a breakwater that rerouted the water and expanded the sand by fifty feet and moved an old schooner there to serve as a bathhouse for his family and guests. The town of Oyster Bay had, however, persisted in its objections, and the original rulings were overturned. Mr. Louis C. Tiffany did not deny that on the eve of the land's return to public use, he dynamited the breakwater, destroying the beach.

An icy sensation spreads across Prudence's chest and down her limbs as she reads. Her mother, just weeks before her death, described the explosion. At the time, her mother had been mostly in a laudanum fog, but every few hours, in the brief interlude between the drug's waning and the pain's waxing, she would bob back into consciousness and have a moment of lucidity.

She'd opened the window to shake out her feather duster, her mother said, and she'd smelled the dynamite. Like bananas gone bad. Then she'd felt the explosion in the soles of her feet.

"The arse'ole," her mother said, "the devil arse'ole."

Maricel finds Prudence still sitting at the library table with the contents of the box spread before her. Her mahogany brow wrinkles, the only sign on her otherwise smooth face of the nearly four decades that have passed since she was a high jumper plucked from her village school to train with the Guadeloupe team, which she might have accompanied to the Olympics had she not become pregnant at seventeen with her eldest, Alina.

Like Grace's grandmother, Prudence had also entered her marriage not wanting to have anyone working in her home—though most definitely for different reasons. Once, when she'd told Carlton how uncomfortable she felt having someone else wash her undergarments or prepare her meals or scrub her toilet, he said, "Well, it's understandable," leaving unspoken what she'd been certain was the second half of the sentence, *with your parents having been servants themselves.* Not until she sold the Park Avenue apartment after Carlton's death, moving here to the smaller West End Avenue one, was she finally able to let go Louise, the maid who'd worked for Carlton since before they were married, and Mrs. Meechin, the cook his mother had sent from her Virginia home.

Prudence had reluctantly hired Maricel the month she turned ninety-two. At ninety-four, she'd acceded to Maricel's pestering that Prudence let her come every day, ten to three, save Sundays. At first, Prudence had thought of this as a favor to Maricel, who, having wanted for her children the braces and summer camps and private colleges of the children of her employers, had for decades taken as many jobs as she could cobble together: days caring for babies and toddlers and the ill elderly, nights cleaning schools and clinics and offices. Even now, with her son and two daughters largely grown, Maricel cannot sit still, as though any hour when she is not working is a dollar bill ripped to confetti, her nervous system so acclimated to industry, leisure has become impossible.

Over the nine years Maricel has worked for her, Prudence has pieced together Maricel's story since she came to this country at eighteen. Leaving her firstborn, Alina, an infant, with the mother of Alina's no-good father, Maricel took a job a cousin had found her as a live-in nanny. Her employers had treated her like indentured labor, docking her pay for the sandwich she ate at lunch, expecting her to take care of a baby and a toddler while doing all the housework. The job ended after Maricel darted across the kitchen to intercept the toddler from touching a hot stove and the mother screamed at her for breaking a glass that toppled in the commotion. Blood rushed into Maricel's head and she lost control of her tongue and called her boss a "fat bitch" and, in her mind, the worst insult of all, "a terrible mother." She left that day, ignoring the weeping woman's pleas to stay: panic about how she would take care of her children herself.

For three years, she'd wired each Friday most of her week's earnings to Alina's grandmother. When the no-good father died in a bar fight, Maricel brought Alina to live with her in the Bronx, where she'd moved in with a man from her island. A kind man with a union job as a sanitation worker, but simple, she's told Prudence, still a country person, who married her and adopted Alina and then gave her two more babies. All three of Maricel's children earned scholarships for college and have launched their boats: Alina to Mount Holyoke, married now with her first child on the way; Maricel's son to Haverford, from where he'd rolled into an investment-firm training position; and her youngest, a beauty, in the acting program at Northwestern.

"What's all this?" Maricel asks, pointing at the library table.

"My great-niece brought some things to show me. She asked me to thank you for the delicious dinner. She particularly enjoyed the okra."

Maricel does not respond, but Prudence can tell that she is pleased. She's showed Prudence photographs from when she was a high jumper, her long, athletic legs hurtling over the bar. Now she complains about her ample stomach and thighs, the result, she both blames and boasts, of the goat curries and rice with red beans that her husband adores and that she spends her Sundays cooking.

A year after Maricel came to work for Prudence, Prudence had broached the idea of their making a trip together to Maricel's island, Les Saintes. How different it would be to visit the Caribbean with someone from there rather than sequestered on a resort as Prudence had been during her seventies and eighties when the cold months in the city had begun to wear on her but her taste for adventurous travel had dissipated.

Maricel, though, had been hesitant. "What if you get sick? There's only a clinic on my island. You'd have to be transported by boat to Basse-Terre."

Behind Maricel's concerns, Prudence had sensed that Maricel would be ashamed for Prudence to see her island home: no tropical idyll, Prudence surmised, but rather a hilltop shanty with a concrete patio and water fetched from the single faucet that served the hamlet.

*You are talking to the daughter of a woman who was a maid*, Prudence had wanted to say. *My mother wore a black skirt and a starched white apron and was not permitted to address her employer.* But Prudence had feared the story would come off wrong, the way telling someone who's ill about the time you were ill never ends up feeling right.

"Let's get you your shower, Mrs. P," Maricel says.

Afterward, Prudence and Maricel have their morning tea from a freshly brewed pot, and Maricel tells Prudence that an agent is coming to see her daughter Larissa's upcoming show at Northwestern. If he signs her, Larissa says, she might be able to get some work in a commercial over the summer.

"But now she's decided that she will stay in Chicago after she graduates. She says there will be more opportunities for her there with all of the small theater companies."

Maricel and her husband have been to Chicago only once, the spring of Larissa's first year when Prudence gifted them airplane tickets and a hotel room in Evanston. Maricel cried when Prudence told her. "But, Mrs. P, how will you manage without me here?" she asked, reluctant to accept the trip until Prudence pointed out that it was only for a weekend, just an extra day that she'd be without Maricel's help. She would ask Thomas Masters to set their dinner for that Sunday.

Prudence knows about the string of bad boyfriends Maricel's eldest daughter, Alina, had while she was at Mount Holyoke. She knows about Alina's abortion because she'd advised Maricel on how to arrange it, at a clinic where Alina would receive counseling first and be able to have her mother accompany her. Prudence knows about the time Maricel's son drank too much and got sick outside his dormitory, and how he had to go before the disciplinary committee. She knows that Maricel worries that Larissa is a lesbian. And through it all, always prefacing her remarks by saying Maricel is the mother, she clearly knows best, Prudence has reassured Maricel that they are great kids. All of them. Maricel wouldn't want kids who didn't rebel at least a little, would she? How would they figure out what is important to them? How would they grow to be their own selves?

*Their own selves.* She'd flushed hearing herself utter these words. Like a drunk preaching moderation.

"Thank the Lord I was a child before I became a parent because I'd have died of shame if I'd understood then what I put my mother through." Maricel shakes her head. "My poor mama. She turned gray with me. There I was, the island track star, sneaking off to drink rum with the crazy boys of our hamlet. She knew I'd end up with a bun in the oven. She locked me in the house and only let me out for school and practice."

Prudence knows how hard Maricel has worked. How very, very hard. The remorse she carries at not having been with either of her parents during their final days. Yet, to Prudence, Maricel's life is enviable. Yes, she's had her worries about each of her children, but she's proud of what she's achieved—raising three good children, each with a good future—and her heart is full. Very full.

No one could say about Maricel what Prudence so often thinks about herself: that she is like a wildflower. She has brought trivial, unremarkable, forgettable pleasure to the few people whose paths have crossed hers. She has furnished homes for wealthy people, some astronomically rich, a few with decent taste, too many motivated only by a vulgar wish to display their bank accounts. Rooms that are either now worn and frayed or long ago redone. But she has created nothing for which she will be remembered. It will make no difference when she is gone.

It has surprised Prudence this past year to find herself returning again and again to the question that, with death surely near, no longer feels adolescent but surprisingly urgent: What is the purpose of life? She knows she is ill equipped to approach what has been a central question for philosophers for millennia. Still, she has found her way to what seems to her the most sensible answer: There is no purpose to life. Like a tree, like a rose, like a rhinoceros, she has decided, we endure, more or less, in the expected time frame. Like going to a restaurant and selecting a meal, the best we can do is choose to live as well as we can.

And here, she faults herself. She has done little harm, but she has done little good. She has nibbled a bit at the dishes placed before her, but been too wary to try anything pungent, complex, satisfying.

Prudence is playing what she still thinks of as Carlton's Bach on what she still thinks of as his piano, the restraint of the *Inventions* and *Little Preludes* easier for her now than the colors of the Chopin and Debussy she once loved, when Maricel comes in to do a final tidy of the living room. During their walk today, Prudence had felt a buckle in her left knee, but her hands are intact, her fingers sufficiently nimble for the familiar repertoire she plays. She stops playing as Maricel approaches the library table, still covered with the contents from Randall's box. It bothers Maricel to go home with the apartment disorderly in any way. "Leave it," Prudence says. She smiles to soften what she fears sounded like an order. "I will put everything away later. As soon as I finish looking through it all."

After she is done with her piano practice, Prudence stretches out on the couch, as is her habit at this hour. With the afternoon's warm weather, Maricel has kept the window slightly ajar. Prudence listens to the muffled sounds from the street. She finds it comforting to hear people outside. How terrifying to be all alone in a cabin on a mountaintop or a cove by a sea . . .

When she wakes, the room is white with harsh afternoon light, her mouth acrid from daytime sleep. Slowly, carefully, as she's learned she must, she swings her legs over the side of the couch and stands.

She settles into her chair by the library table and takes the packet of letters held together with a gold ribbon from the box. Letters, Grace said, that her grandfather had saved. The ribbon, Prudence wonders, from his shop?

A faint mildew smell rises from the paper. She unties the ribbon and counts the letters. Sixteen, stacked in chronological order.

To her surprise, the first, written when she was eleven, is from her.

*May 14, 1923*

*Dear Randall,*

*We were all very very happy when we got your letter and know now where you are. Father told me that there are big hills in San Francisco and that it is like an island. Is it an island? I told Mother that I remember Charlie, and that he is a nice boy. Don't worry. I didn't tell her that he smoked cigarettes!*

*I'm sorry if this will make you feel badly, but Mother has been crying so so much. Maybe you can write again soon. I think that will help her not be so worried about you.*

*I wrote a poem the day after you ran away. I showed it to Miss Gordon. She's my fifth grade teacher. She said it is very good but very sad.*

*Your loving sister,*

*Pru*

When she reaches the end of the letter, Prudence touches the paper to her cheek. She sees the yellow oilcloth with the border of red flowers on the table where they ate their meals, her hands as she cut the square of paper from the drawing pad Dorothy Burlingham had given her, the black inkwell. The words dimly familiar, the child who'd chosen them so long ago both her and not her.

She flips through the stack of letters, finding only one other from her. Had she written only twice, or had Randall kept only these two?

*August 10, 1925*

*Dear Randall,*

*Mother and I were so happy to get your last letter. I am glad you like your new rooming house and that you have such a good job. Mother was very bad off right after Father died, but she's better now. She got a job at Wanamaker's as a seamstress in the department where they sell furniture. Customers choose the fabric for their chairs and sofas. It is summer vacation now and I am working with her. It's good because she is paid by the piece, and what I do goes to her count. Since Father died, we get an envelope every month from Mr. T, but the money from Wanamaker's is a big help.*

*Do you have a girl? Mother says she thinks you do. She says you're sixteen now, and Father was a looker in his day so maybe you are too.*

*Your loving sister,*

*Pru*

The other letters, save one from her aunt, are from her mother, sloppy and with many misspelled words: *troly, teech, lawyr.* The earliest ones tumble, each of them, into an accusatory tone: How could Randall have left his parents to worry so? Then, after Prudence's father died and her mother got her job at Wanamaker's, the tone changes, as though her mother snapped out of feeling sorry for herself. Even the handwriting is more controlled and the sentences improved:

*The soupervizer is now leting your sister help with some of the sketches. Your sister has a very nice way with drowing . . .*

Only once in these later letters does her mother deviate from this breezy, cheerful style. After giving the news that Prudence has won a citywide drawing contest with its prize of a four-year scholarship, the letter shifts, literally, from blue to black ink:

*I never said this to you, but I shood of. Don't think I don't know it was a grate hardship for you that your father forbid you to speke of certen things. You thawt your father blamd you, but he knew deep down that you was a child.*

Prudence feels her lids growing heavy, her breath deepening. She sets the packet of letters inside the box, draws her shawl from the back of the wingback chair around her, and closes her eyes.

# 8

# Prudence

## New York, 1933–1937

After Mr. T's lawyer flicked the paper with that single ugly word *EXTORTION* across his desk and boomed, "The gravy train, Missy, is over," there were no more envelopes. It was 1933, the fourth Depression year, a few months before Prudence's graduation from the New York School of Fine and Applied Art, when, thanks to a recommendation by one of her teachers to Harriet Masters at Masters Design, Prudence would be one of only three students in her class to receive a job offer.

Harriet Masters had been among the first women who'd come to interior decorating as a professional rather than as a society matron. She'd grown up in a Tudor monstrosity in Tuxedo Park, which she'd inherited and where she still lived. On her twenty-first birthday, Harriet had married a doctor, Akron, who, having failed his medical boards, worked in a research laboratory. Akron had horrified her with his prodigious sexual appetites, and she'd been relieved when she quickly become pregnant and could, under the accepted practices of the day, cease relations. Her son, Stewart, was a delicate and sickly boy who surprised everyone by reaching puberty early and shooting up six inches over a summer. That fall, with Stewart off to junior boarding school and Akron out more nights than not, Harriet enrolled at the New York School of Fine and Applied Art, from which she graduated in 1926 at the age of thirty-six.

Disillusioned with his research job and filled with fantasies of long European buying trips (solo, so he would be free to carry on his dalliances), Akron announced he would join Harriet in a decorating business, which she named Masters Design. Harriet hardly had the nameplate affixed to the door when Akron hung himself, leaving behind a notebook of incoherent poetry about his heartbreak over a Mrs. Annette Jergins's refusal to leave her husband, heir to a munitions fortune, and marry him. The existence of Mrs. Annette Jergins had not surprised Harriet—it had been three years since she and Akron had last been intimate—but she was surprised that Akron had thought to lash himself to another woman, who would undoubtedly be less permissive in domestic arrangements than she'd been. "Your father was always an imbecile," she told her son.

With her family's assets largely in property, Harriet's wealth was mostly insulated when the market crashed two years later. By then, she had a staff of twenty-three employees at Masters Design. Interior decorating work ground to a virtual halt, but Harriet refused to lay off any of her employees. Instead, Harriet, whose aesthetic talents were modest but whose business acumen was impressive, utilized her staff to design furniture, linens, wallpaper, and dishware: decent-quality knockoffs that could be profitably sold at 50 percent of the originals, the richer her clients, Harriet having discovered, the more they appreciated a bargain. There was no justification for adding someone to the payroll, but Harriet had succumbed to a former teacher's plea that she find a position for the school's most talented graduate that year, a girl, he whispered, who most truly needed employment: it was only her and a seamstress mother.

Prudence began as Harriet's assistant. Discovering the true nature of the work—clients aspired for their homes to look like the homes of people at the outer reaches of their social circle or like the pictures they'd seen in society magazines—came as a disappointment to Prudence, who'd imagined designing rooms never envisioned before, not spending most of her time ordering plumbing fixtures and upholstery fabrics. When Prudence rallied the nerve to mention this to Elaine, Harriet's assistant before Prudence and now a junior decorator, Elaine laughed. "You thought you'd be an artist. No, we are the personal shoppers for rich ladies too insecure about their own taste or with too many houses and too many luncheons to select their own curtains and lamps. Yes, I know, in school they don't tell you that it's more bookkeeping than drawing. Wake up, sweetie. This is why it's called a job. It's work."

Two years after Prudence started at Masters Design, her mother got sick: a woman's cancer detected after she lost her appetite, her limbs turned to matchsticks, her abdomen swelled to watermelon size. The cancer was fast-growing, and when the doctor informed Prudence her mother had only a few more weeks, Prudence told Harriet that she was regretfully resigning so she could care for her.

By then, Elaine had been promoted to senior decorator with her own projects, and Prudence had moved into Elaine's former position. Together, they were handling the interiors for a Newport mansion being built by a man who owned the stockyards in Chicago rumored to have been visited by Upton Sinclair before he wrote *The Jungle*. Prudence had pictured their client as short and stout with a cigar plastered to his lips and a meaty smell emanating from his skin, but he was as stringy as a street urchin and rumored to eat only raw fruits and raw vegetables. In Elaine and Prudence's first and only meeting with the client (after that, he'd always sent one of his accountants), Prudence had been confused about what he wanted for the Newport estate—a historical reproduction of a French or British country house? A relaxed home where he would be able to retreat with his wife and many children? "It's simple," Elaine had later explained. "He wants the place to look as expensive as possible while spending as little as possible. Think gold foil and Dutch-masters reproductions. Think rich cheapskate, ignorant but cunning."

"Don't be ridiculous," Harriet said in response to Prudence's resignation. "Elaine can do the site meetings, and you can organize the orders from home. I'll send Billy"—Billy was Harriet's driver—"to pick them up from you." Prudence looked at her feet, embarrassed by how grateful she felt.

Her mother was worst at night. Moaning, she would toss and turn and fling off her blankets. Prudence would give her the strongest tincture of laudanum the doctor had said was permitted and lace with brandy the chamomile tea her mother was still able to drink.

Some nights, though, it seemed that neither laudanum nor brandy scraped the surface of her mother's pain. Then, Prudence would feel her own exhaustion, an exhaustion that was more of her spirit than her body. The shame she felt about her self-pitying thoughts: She was twenty-three. She should be up with a talcum-scented baby, not a dying woman with a nauseating rot emanating from her lady parts.

It was nursing in its purest form, without hope of cure, with hope only of alleviating suffering. Warm compresses laid between her mother's hip bones. Massages for her mother's feet, the toes purple from lack of proper circulation. Hours spent reading aloud. Singing to drown out the moans.

Even as a young child, Prudence had never truly believed in God, though she'd not dared to say the words aloud until after her father died. She'd understood that she was not alone, that others questioned the existence of a deity, because of the existence of evil: If He is there, why did we have the Irish potato famine? If He is present, why do babies die? None of this had bothered her. There could be a God and He could just be mean. Or there could be a God with pain part of His greater plan. What had bothered Prudence was more elemental: If there is a God, who created Him? How could something come from nothing?

Her mother had looked at her wide-eyed when Prudence said this, as though for the first time she were seeing that her daughter was more she-goat than human. It would have been easier if her mother had slapped her or threatened to wash her mouth out with soap. Instead, she'd turned back to her mending, resigned, it seemed, to the idea that Prudence, like Prudence's father, who'd never gone to church after they'd left Laurelton Hall, was also an infidel.

Now, though, with her mother's unbearable moaning, Prudence prayed. *Please, please, God, Lord, Jesus, Allah, whoever is there, tell me what to do. Should I put a pillow over her head? Should I strangle her with the sleeve of her bed jacket?*

On the third night of her mother's moaning, it came to her.

Damn the doctor's instructions. Her mother needed more. More laudanum. More brandy. The two together.

Prudence poured an ounce of brandy into one of her mother's nicest glasses, from a set that had been a Christmas gift from Prudence's father to her mother. It was still two hours until the next dose of the laudanum should have been given, but she added three teaspoons instead of the prescribed one.

"Open up," she said to her mother.

Her mother sealed her mouth and looked off. A few coarse hairs were on her upper lip. Afterward, Prudence would tweeze them.

"You want me to, Mother, don't you?"

Her mother weakly nodded. She parted her lips. Using a spoon, Prudence gave her the laudanum-laced brandy. Within minutes, her mother's face relaxed.

At first, it looked as if her mother had slid into sleep, and Prudence wondered if it would be her mother's final rest and if she would be at peace with this, with having induced an earlier death. Earlier by what? Two days? Three? But after less than a minute, her mother stirred. She pushed with her hands on the mattress, trying to hoist herself up.

With the top of the mattress raised from her mother's efforts, Prudence saw something blue poking out. She slid her fingers beneath and pulled out the decayed top of a peacock feather.

Seeing the feather, her mother reached out a hand. Prudence gave it to her. Dimly, she recalled her mother having slept with a matted peacock feather under her pillow those first weeks after they'd moved here when she'd never left the apartment. Now she buried it in her nightclothes.

Prudence lifted her mother so she was propped against the pillows and filled a glass from the carafe on the bedside table with the water she boiled each morning, holding it to her mother's lips.

Her mother drank a few sips, then gripped Prudence's arm. "He was a bastard. What he did to me."

Prudence put down the glass. She stroked her mother's hand. She didn't want to hear about her father's misdeeds. "He did his best, Mum. I know he was rough on Randall, but I think Randall would have left anyway. His friend was already there, in San Francisco."

"Pulling down me bloomers, sticking his ugly thing into me, with me a married woman with children already."

Prudence could hear herself sucking in air. She dropped her mother's hand. "Who are you talking about, Mother?"

"Calling me a dirty thing. An Irish pig."

She stared at her mother's face. The doctor had warned that the cancer might spread to her mother's brain. Had that happened?

Prudence felt her heart pounding in her chest. To a man who had his daughters parade with roasted peacocks on silver salvers, her mother would have seemed like one of his sixty thousand belongings.

Her mother's eyes drooped shut, a thread of spittle avalanching toward her slackened chin.

The morning before Prudence's mother died, she asked for Randall.

"He's coming, Mother," Prudence lied.

Prudence gave her mother the prescribed dose of laudanum, made her a lukewarm tea with honey and a small amount of brandy. She spooned the tea to her mother slowly, kissed her dry forehead.

When the tea was done, her mother looked directly at her. "I wonder if he still has those red curls."

Then she shut her eyes for good.

A month later, Prudence learned from Harriet Masters that the fifty-seven-room Tiffany mansion on Madison Avenue had been purchased by developers, who planned to knock it down. Prudence felt surprisingly sad. Her father had died in the top-floor studio, but in many ways her own life had begun there during the afternoons when she'd sketched in the pad from Dorothy Tiffany while her father dusted the hanging glass lamps and tended the extravagant plants.

Shortly after, Harriet gave Prudence her first solo client. Ella Jameson was a Smith graduate who spoke French and Italian and was a generous patron of the arts. She and her doting husband, Lawrence, had recently purchased a town house near the newly developed Gracie Square neighborhood so as to be close to the Brearley School, which their two daughters attended. Ella wanted modern furniture. "No damask, no ferns! No Louis anything!"

Prudence showed Ella photographs of a parlor and dining room done in the Manhattan Style.

"Perfect. Only I don't want to be bothered with any of the decisions. I have the benefit for my daughters' school, two painters I've promised to help find dealers, an Italian singer who just fired the German pianist she was supposed to play with at a concert here next week . . ."

Prudence ordered a Jean-Michel Frank white sofa for the parlor and Breuer Cesca chairs for the breakfast room. She had curtains made in African-motif fabrics for Ella's older daughter's room, found a Calder-inspired mobile for the younger girl. "Oh my," Lawrence said when he saw the Eileen Gray end tables. "Made from steel. But I suppose it makes sense. It will be so durable."

Ella pecked Lawrence on the cheek. "Such a love, isn't he?" she said to Prudence, who registered Lawrence's relief that Prudence had kept his grandmother's oval claw-foot dining table and the furniture for his library, his armchair reupholstered in a fabric similar to the original.

In the spring, Ella invited Prudence to a dinner party at her house. Prudence, just turned twenty-four, had been to the opera as Harriet's guest and had spent time in the country homes of her clients organizing paint colors and modernizing kitchens, weeks during which she had taken meals with her clients' families (though Elaine had warned that it might be with the staff; this had happened to her on a few occasions), but she had never been to a dinner party. Elaine helped her select a dress, but no one could help her with what she most worried about—the conversation. How would she be able to talk about the subjects she imagined Ella's guests so easily discussing: Stravinsky versus Rachmaninoff, the situation in Europe, the best hotels in Florence and Nice?

Not until afterward had Ella told Prudence that the raison d'être for the evening was to introduce Prudence to Lawrence's Harvard classmate: the eccentric but still quite eligible thirty-seven-year-old Carlton Theet. Four days a week during eight months of the year, Carlton ran the New York office of his Virginian family's textile company, which he'd astutely positioned to receive the uniform and parachute contracts from the war he anticipated would come. The balance of his time was devoted to his quiet but ardent aspirations of mastering the entire repertoire of Bach piano music and reaching the summit of the tallest mountain on each of the seven continents.

Having heard Ella's introduction of Prudence as "the talented decorator who did absolutely everything for us—you know I would never have the patience to pick out draperies or pillows!", the first question Carlton asked Prudence was "And what are your opinions on *Gesamtkunstwerk*?"

Prudence felt the familiar awful flush rise from her chest to settle in her cheeks. Was the man giving her an oral examination? Black spots clouded her vision and she feared she might have to close her eyes.

Carlton peered at her. She saw that he saw that she did not understand and that it would breach what he considered good manners to acknowledge this. "I'm asking because my parents are friends of the Burlinghams. Perhaps you've read in the papers about the urban-improvement projects championed by Charles Culp Burlingham, CCB as most people call him?"

The name did ring a bell, something to do with the election of Mayor La Guardia two years ago, but overcome as she was with dizziness, she could not recall anything more.

Was he now going to ask her thoughts about the mayor?

"My father shares none of CCB's politics—he considers them socialism and quite abhorrent—but they roomed together at Harvard and remain friends. When CCB's son married Dorothy Tiffany, my parents attended the wedding at her father's country home, Laurelton Hall. It's renowned for being an embodiment of *Gesamtkunstwerk*: a total work of art, with Tiffany having designed every item from the desk blotters to the wallpapers to the fountains."

Prudence felt so hot, she feared she might break into a discernible sweat. Was this the test: Would she admit that her parents had been servants there? That her father had cut the wisteria that had hung from the dining room rafters on the day of the wedding, that her mother had made up the beds? She imagined blurting this out, and Ella then taking her arm and leading her to the kitchen to have her meal there with the servants.

"I quite like the idea," Carlton continued, "but my mother thought Mr. Tiffany was tyrannical in its execution."

"I've seen photographs," Prudence said, feeling like a liar about to be exposed. But was not saying something the same as a lie? And, in truth, all she'd retained from her own experience of the estate were shards of memories. What she knew about Laurelton Hall in any specific way had, in fact, come largely from the photographs she'd seen in magazines.

"Mr. Tiffany had much the same idea for the studio he built in his family's mansion on Seventy-second Street," Prudence continued, relieved to be able to add what she hoped was a respectable contribution to the conversation. "Now, though, the house is being demolished."

"For goodness' sake, why?"

"With Mr. Tiffany having passed, no one is living there. The family has sold the property, and Mr. Candela is going to build an apartment building on that corner."

After dinner, Carlton on piano accompanied Lawrence on cello in what Lawrence explained was the Gounod melody, known from the Ave Maria, overlaid on Bach's Prelude in C from *The Well-Tempered Clavier.* Despite Prudence's untrained ear, she sensed that Carlton's technical skills outstripped his musicality, constricted by a tension in his limbs and a rectitude that prevented him from fully immersing himself in the music, but she was moved by his close attention to Lawrence, the way Carlton adjusted his tempo and volume to the slight shifts in the cello. Seated on one of the swivel Le Corbusier chairs she'd purchased for Ella's music room, Prudence noted the intimidation she'd first felt with Carlton dissolving into a benign protectiveness. She could see herself beside him at the Steinway piano, placing a light hand on his shoulder and, as he signaled with a sharp downward movement of his chin, turning the page of his music book.

A week later, Prudence was in her small office at Masters Design making a list of which vendors she needed to write to again to inquire about the status of deliveries for the Newport house when Elaine ushered in Carlton with a package under his arm.

"May I?" he asked, pointing to the chair opposite Prudence's desk. Behind his back, Elaine raised an eyebrow and gave an arch smile.

"This past Tuesday, I lunched with Charles Burlingham. I believe I mentioned him to you?"

Prudence nodded.

"He told me that his daughter-in-law, Dorothy, had written to ask if he would arrange for one of her father's watercolors from the Madison Avenue house to be given to the daughter of one of her father's gardeners."

Carlton glanced at the package he'd leaned against the desk. For the second time with this man, in what was only their second meeting, Prudence felt the terrible heat rising up from her chest as she imagined, again, that the moment had arrived when she'd be exposed: Harriet marching in, perhaps with an outraged Ella in tow. How dare Harriet entrust the daughter of a gardener to decorate her home? My God, Ella had given Prudence keys to her house, access to her most private rooms.

When Carlton looked up, however, what she saw in his eyes appeared to be an apology, an apology for having mentioned something he knew that she would have preferred not to discuss.

"It would have been indiscreet at Ella and Lawrence's dinner for me to hold forth on Robert and Dorothy, but it is a tragic situation. Robert has not accepted the reality that Dorothy is not coming back from Vienna. She has started an entirely new life there with the Freud family. All of her children have been in psychoanalysis with Professor Freud's daughter, and she is apparently training to be a psychoanalyst herself."

It made no sense—how would Carlton know about Mr. Feeney

and his Sunday visits to her mother?—but Prudence could not shake the thought that Carlton was aware that she'd heard much of this before.

"Dorothy wrote that she'd been very attached to one of her father's gardeners and that his daughter as a child had shown promise herself as an artist. When CCB said the name, I realized it was you. I told him I'd deliver the watercolor myself."

Carlton lifted the package onto Prudence's desk. She avoided his eyes as she untied the twine and unwrapped the brown paper.

The watercolor, impressionistic in style with thick brush marks, was of a field of daffodils in a frenzy of colors. In the foreground was what looked like a man in worker's garb, his face obscured as he bent over to examine one of the blooms. In the background were three redheaded children, barefoot with a small ball they were kicking between them.

Prudence looked up. Carlton was studying the painting upside down. He knew her. He knew who she was. Yet he was still sitting here, across from her in the chair on the other side of her desk.

"I'd like to write to Mrs. Burlingham and thank her. Could you provide me with an address?"

"Of course. I will ask CCB and will send it to you."

Carlton stood. She could see his eyes lingering on the painting, on, she imagined, the children in the background, refraining, she felt certain, from asking, *Perhaps one is you?*

Prudence hung the watercolor on the wall across from her desk. A few days later, a note arrived from Carlton with Dorothy Burlingham's Vienna address. Immediately, Prudence wrote to her.

*Dear Mrs. Burlingham,*

*Thank you for the beautiful watercolor by your father. It is especially meaningful to me because of what appears to be a gardener tending what might have been one of the fields at Laurelton Hall. I am very grateful to you for sending it to me.*

*I was very saddened to hear that your father's home will soon be demolished: I have so many memories of his studio there, with the huge four-sided fireplace, and of your kind visit to bring me your daughter's pastels and sketchbook.*

*I am afraid you might be disappointed at the road I have taken. I did not pursue becoming an artist; instead, I studied at the New York School of Fine and Applied Art so I could work as a decorator. I have a good job now with the Masters Design company. With the economy as it is, not too many people are doing large-scale redecorating, but we still have a few major projects, and I am in charge now of one of them. I do a little bit of sketching, but most of my time is spent as the intermediary between the craftsmen and the clients.*

*Your father-in-law's friend Mr. Theet delivered the painting to me and kindly provided your address. He told me that you are training to be a psychoanalyst. It must be so very interesting.*

Prudence paused. What she wanted to write were questions that were impossible to ask: Are you happier since you left your husband? Do your children accept your decision? Why did you not come back for your father's funeral?

What she wanted to say was, I so admire your courage.

Instead, she wrote:

*I purchased Professor Freud's book on dreams, and although I can't claim to understand all of it, I find it fascinating. What he said about how dreams hide what we are really thinking, changing our unacceptable thoughts into ones we can tolerate, made me shiver.*

*Thank you, again, for the wonderful gift.*

*Most sincerely yours,*

*Prudence O'Connor*

Prudence was not surprised when a few days later a second note arrived from Carlton, asking if she might accompany him to a concert at Carnegie Hall. It was a program from the first book of the

Bach *Inventions*, and as they stood together in the lobby, having a sherry before the concert, Prudence observed the man at her side. He was, she noted, even more uncomfortable than she was herself. Once the music began, however, she saw his face relax, his shoulders release, his hands land on his lap, one forefinger keeping count. Afterward, over a dinner at which he abstemiously ate ("Please," he urged, "order whatever you like"; he, unfortunately, could abide only a chop and a vegetable at this hour), he dissected the performance: the pianist's success in bringing the melody in the left hand onto an equal footing with that in the right; the approach he'd taken to Bach's precision such that it felt godly, filled with echoes and shadows, not militaristic as performers too often interpreted the work.

Listening to Carlton, Prudence felt something warm and soft flow through her, feelings broken loose from a hard block where they'd been congealed since Randall left. It was not physical attraction but rather affection. Affection for this high-minded man.

It had never occurred to Prudence that a man like Carlton—someone whom her mother would have called a gentleman—would ever be attracted to her, but Carlton clearly was. Why? Did her lowly social status make him feel more secure? He didn't strike her as a person who suffered from insecurities. Perhaps, Prudence thought, he found her soothing, like the simple foods he apparently preferred.

What would it be like, she wondered, to live with a man of such refined sensibilities, of such ingrained asceticism? So very, very different from her parents, for whom abstinence was motivated by economy; from her clients, for whom it was not even in their vocabulary. On her visits to the Japanese rooms at the Metropolitan Museum of Art, she'd often lingered in front of the pen-and-ink sketches of monks who resided in bamboo huts with only a tatami mat. Is that what it would be like with Carlton? Would she ascend to a plane where no horse falls to its knees with white froth on its lips, no mother calls out, "Get me a wet cloth," no brother packs his belongings into a rucksack and moves three thousand miles away?

By the time Prudence received a letter back from Dorothy, she'd moved from the Hell's Kitchen apartment where she'd lived alone after her mother's death to a garden apartment on Eighty-second Street near York Avenue, not far geographically from the brownstone where Ella and Lawrence lived, but socially a world away. The new apartment had its own entrance through a gate that opened with a key that Prudence copied for Carlton after he become her first lover. Having dined at his club, Carlton would arrive at nine, departing by dawn to return to his own apartment on Park Avenue and Seventy-seventh Street, directly across from the residence of CCB and his wife, Louie, and their son, Robert, Dorothy's abandoned husband, who now lived with his parents when he wasn't away at a sanatorium.

*Dearest Prudence,*

*I am so glad you appreciate the watercolor. That is why I sent it to you—with the hope that it would be more meaningful to you than to anyone else.*

*You mustn't disparage your work as a decorator. As you may know, my father was, in fact, one of the first professional decorators, a business he opened with Mrs. Candace Wheeler, and then continued with other partners. He had many important commissions, including the White House renovation for President Arthur, Mark Twain's home, and the Presidential Palace in Havana. Of course, it is true that given my father's temperament, he never took marching orders from anyone. He designed the rooms according to his own vision and utilized the glass tiles and wallpaper and furnishings produced in his own factories. I know that most decorators are not given such leeway.*

*Psychoanalysis has always been interested in art, and you are right to distinguish between art and decoration. Art, it seems to me, has to do with the expression of the artist's personal vision. If it is good, it must, like an analysis, include the dark side of human nature: Aggression and Thanatos, the death drive, are as strong as Love and*

*Eros, the life instinct. Even my father, who in his older years was fond of saying that he refused to look at the ugly, must have understood this in his younger years when as a painter he frankly depicted scenes of poverty. Decoration avoids these destructive forces, creating surfaces that at their best are serene and pleasing. My father often quoted Mrs. Wharton's book on decorating and the principles she espoused of simplicity, serenity and appropriateness.*

*Not to say that our home at Laurelton Hall was designed with those principles! You were perhaps too young when you lived there to remember the dizzying hodgepodge: the Chinese room, the Moroccan minaret, the English gardens, the Persian fountains, the Japanese swords, the Native American displays. My sisters and I often thought that our father had gone quite mad, like one of those hoarders one reads about on occasion in the newspaper who is discovered months past his death hidden under the trash he accumulated.*

*I have gone on way too long. Perhaps it is because you touched me when you were a girl, and I am so pleased to learn that you have made a life for yourself—forgive me for speaking so plainly—that is larger than that of your parents. You must always maintain your own work, never allow a marriage to be the center of your life. I say that from sad experience, having married a wonderful man—intelligent and idealistic and a devoted father—whom I have to live apart from due to the destructive impact of his episodes of severe mental disorder on our children.*

*Should you ever come to Vienna, I would be most happy to receive you in my home here. Until then, dear Prudence, enjoy my father's watercolor.*

*Affectionately yours,*

*Dorothy Burlingham*

When Prudence discovered seven months after she and Carlton had met that she was pregnant, her first fear was that Carlton would suspect her of that awful word *extortion.* She began to cry as she delivered the news. Cry and then shake from the February chill that had infiltrated her rooms.

Carlton was drinking a snifter of the brandy he kept in her kitchen, where they were standing. She had an Earl Grey tea cupped in her hands.

He put an arm around her and stiffly hugged her. Then, gently, he explained that he could never have children.

She did not understand what he meant. That he was incapable of siring a child? That she was fabricating the pregnancy? That she had another lover? Her cheeks burned. She lowered the tea to the table, loosened her shawl.

"It is a decision I made a long time ago," he said. "Not to be a father. I have told you my principal life ambitions, including to reach the summit of the highest mountain on every continent. Thus far, I've succeeded in North America and Europe. I intend to broach Africa and Australia in the next three years. If the war does not interfere."

Prudence gripped the edge of the table. Was Carlton saying he would rather climb a mountain than have a child, or he would rather climb a mountain than have a child with her?

"There are men who are willing to father children and leave them to be raised by the mothers. I am opposed to that arrangement. And even when I will be home, there are my other ambitions: To master the Bach piano canon. To enlarge my rare-book collection to include Asian manuscripts. It would be cruel to a child to insist on the silence I require while practicing. To forbid a child from touching my books."

She thought about her own father, the evenings and wages he'd spent at the corner bar, but also the dim memories she had of him before they'd left Laurelton Hall. Holding a rope while she sat atop a pony in a little corral behind the barn, taking her to see the peacocks shimmying their tails in the sun. She thought about Mr. Tiffany, who'd paraded his daughters for his spectacle parties. Yet Dorothy had written about him with affection and admiration.

*If these men could be fathers whose children still loved them, why can't you?* she silently cried.

Carlton took her hand. He was unbending, but not because he did not understand her feelings. He did understand, and it pained him to cause her pain. But he could not budge without compromising himself in a way that he viewed as an assault on the very integrity of his being.

If she did not have an abortion as soon as it could be arranged, he told her, slowly but without any fissure of doubt, he would cease all contact with her. Immediately. Permanently.

# 9

# Leo & Jacie

## San Francisco, 1965–1966

It is dusk when Grace's father, Leo, wakes in the bed of Grace's mother, Jacie. Jacie is curled with her back toward Leo. The room is dank from the window he cracked hours before when he made coffee and cut papaya slices and spread peanut butter on rice cakes. Everything feels different, as though in his sleep he's been ferried away from childhood, where his body belonged more to his mother and Angela than to himself, to another shore where he slept naked, for the first time, with a girl.

Still, there is his father, his father on the coast left behind, who has no way of knowing that Leo now resides in another country, on an entirely different continent. His father agitatedly moving bills and invoices from one place on his desk to another, sorting magazines and newspapers, vigorously attacking the garden with his pruning shears, driving Angela crazy by affixing pieces of blue tape to the places where the grout should be scrubbed with a toothbrush and a ladder used to dust the upper moldings. Picking up the telephone to make certain the line isn't dead. Parting the sheer parlor curtains Leo's mother hung so many years ago to peer out at the street. Looking for him.

He covers Jacie with the bedspread, puts on his clothes, and walks down to the pay phone. In the streets by his father's house, the air is scented with lilacs and pine trees and the sea. Here, it is garbage and dog shit and rotting wood.

He reaches in his pocket for a dime, dials his home number.

His father picks up on the first ring. "Leo?"

"Yes, Dad."

"Where are you?"

"On the corner of Haight and Clayton. I told you that last night."

"Leo, listen to me. You are to come home immediately."

"No," Leo says softly. He thinks about Jacie having told him that before she left Houston with Dale, she'd never before not done what her parents instructed her to do. Has he ever directly refused one of his father's dictates before? Yes, in his actions—surfing, smoking pot, selling pot, cutting classes—but never outright with his words. "I'm going to stay here a couple of days."

"Stay where?"

"With this girl. The one I told you about last night."

"The drugged girl you helped home?"

"She's fine now. She's really not messed up. She's an artist and very smart."

"How old is she?"

"A little older than me. Nineteen."

There is a heaviness in Leo's chest. The last time he felt this terrible with his father was after his mother's death, when he'd been aware that the one thing his father couldn't bear was Leo's sadness. At nine, Leo had been unable to articulate the paradox, but he'd felt it: his father so fully grasped the dimensions of Leo's grief—not only a boy's loss of a mother, but the loss also of the luminous joy with which she'd infused their home—that he couldn't bear to see it on Leo's face.

A kid Leo's own age, skinny, with a wolfish look, is sitting on a stoop across the street, rolling a joint. Maybe if he gives the kid a few bucks, he can sit with him, passing the joint back and forth and watching the sky to the west now streaked with orange and magenta and graphite.

"I gotta go, Dad. I'll call you in a couple of days."

On Monday, after he knows his father will have left for his shop, Leo goes alone to the house. Angela gathers him into her arms. "You naughty boy. Your father has been worried sick about you. Three o'clock in the morning, I hear him walking around. I come downstairs, I make him hot milk and chamomile tea. I give him corn bread. This morning . . ." She makes a *tsk-tsk*. "Dark circles under his eyes. Like when your mother was sick."

"I'm fine. Look at me, right?" He circles around, and Angela swipes at his backside. "I'm almost eighteen."

"It is August. You are not eighteen until February."

"How old were you when you came, *by yourself*, from Mexico?"

"That is different. I came to live with my brother and his wife. And from there, to here. I had your mama . . ."

"How about my father? He was fourteen when he left home. He traveled across the country, hitching on trains. I'm just a mile away."

Leo climbs the stairs to his room. He takes the quarter pound of pot and the scale from the bottom of a box stored under his bed that his mother had, now so long ago, labeled *Leo's Art Work*, a dozen of his poetry books, and a week's worth of clothes laundered and pressed by Angela, puts it all in a suitcase, and moves in with Jacie.

By the end of the month, they are Leo & Jacie, apart only when Jacie is working a shift at the coffee shop or Leo is delivering pot to someone, and he sees that he was wrong. He has not skipped over falling in love. It's just that it's different from what he'd imagined and hard for him to fully grasp.

What he knows for sure is that he loves bringing her to orgasm, hearing her gasp and feeling her skin turn moist from a pleasure she tells him she'd never known existed before him. And that she is the most interesting girl he has ever met. She reads all the time, mostly women writers he's never read himself: the Anaïs Nin he'd seen in her bag, but also Virginia Woolf, Isak Dinesen, Djuna Barnes, Flannery O'Connor, George Eliot. Some days she stays in bed until dusk, reading, with a cup of Moroccan mint tea beside her. And some days he'll wake to find her cross-legged on the floor, sketching with charcoal pencils on one of the drawing pads her mother sends, or standing at the easel with watercolors, or packing up to go to a painting studio with sufficient ventilation for her to use oils. When they're out, she'll order a cheeseburger, but mostly she cooks with the vegetarian items—tempeh and garbanzo beans and soy milk and wheat berries—she'd learned about when she lived with Lake. At night, she listens to music, again mostly women artists, and works on the macramé planters she still sells at the San Jose flea market with two girls who have rooms in Lake's house.

Living with Jacie, Leo tells Gary, is like doing a foreign exchange program. She's a culture unto herself.

"That's so cool," Gary says. "Most girls our age are such followers. They all dress the same, listen to the same music, sound the same. Jacie's an original."

"Sometimes, though, I feel like she doesn't need me. After she left Houston with this ice cream truck guy, she lost all fear."

Gary looks at him coolly. "No, man. You're wrong there. She needs you. Remember what she was like the day we met her? Fucked-up. You're her anchor."

In September, Leo goes back to school. It's his senior year. His father threatens not to pay the tuition balance if Leo doesn't move home. "Your choice," Leo says. "I guess, then, I'll have to go to public school."

Randall hasn't met privately with the Presidio Academy headmaster since Leo was seven and he'd come in to object to the swim requirement. Now the headmaster points out that if Randall doesn't let Leo finish his senior year, Randall will be cutting off his nose to spite his face. "At least, Mr. O'Connor, with Leo here, we can keep an eye on him. I will let the faculty know about the unusual circumstances and ask that they be on the alert if your son shows any strange behaviors." Randall knows that the headmaster's primary concern is to secure Leo's tuition balance, but also knows that what the man says is true. Randall agrees to continue paying Leo's school fees.

Leo drives the VW from Jacie's apartment to Presidio Academy every morning. In the past, he's always joined the cross-country team in the fall so he'd be in shape for basketball in the winter and lacrosse in the spring. The day after he fails to show up for the first cross-country practice, the lacrosse coach corners him at lunch and tells him to come by after school.

The basement athletic office smells of the chlorine from the pool down the hall and the rank contents of the lost-and-found box by the door. Coach sits with his feet up on a metal desk, his neck looking all the more reptilian on account of his crew cut, not the modified version the boys have, but the razored one he's kept since his years in the Marines.

"I hear, O'Connor, that you're living with some hippie girl."

The way Coach says *hippie* makes it sound unsavory, like *skanky* or *hooker* or *slut*. Leo looks at the baseball bobble dolls on the shelf behind Coach's head. It seems surreal to Leo that he's spent so many years in this building.

"You said it was your grades kept you from playing last spring. A dumb-shit decision. You could've been team captain this year."

Coach crumples a piece of paper and tosses it through a hoop on the door. He peers at Leo. "Christ, kid. You look like crap. You gotta work out. Get back in shape."

Leo is starting to space out. The office has no window and it feels as if it has no fucking air. He forces himself to focus. "I'm not going to play this year either."

Coach looks at him with more astonishment than anger. He's had plenty of boys drop out, but never a starter, a boy who might even be recruited for a college team—though with Leo's not having played his junior year, not so likely anymore. "Why? Why would you do something moronic like that?"

"I don't want to play lacrosse anymore."

Coach crumples another piece of paper. "Is there some other sport you want to play? You can't go out for baseball for the first time as a senior. They might put you on the team, but you'd never get off the bench."

"No. No other sport." Leo cannot tell this machine of a man, dull-witted but well-intentioned, that what he wants is to come back every afternoon to Jacie's apartment and read William Carlos Williams and Federico García Lorca, whom he can now understand in Spanish, and this new book of poetry Jacie bought him by a woman named Diane di Prima. Smoke a joint and go up to the roof and write in his notebook fragments of thoughts and poems until Jacie gets home from her job and comes to find him, after which they'll go back to the apartment, hot with the afternoon sun, where he'll take off her clothes and bury his face in her damp breasts and wait for her breathing to sharpen and her thighs to go soft. That he'll then go see one of his customers, guys who he sells quarter pounds to now that Jimmy has quit the business and Leo is on his own—enough to handle what he smokes himself and the rent and concert tickets for Jacie and him. Jacie will meet him at the vegetarian Indian place on Divisadero Street and they'll eat *saag paneer* and *chana masala* and drink rosewater *lassi*, and then he'll sit at Jacie's table and do his homework while she does her macramé until they climb into bed together, both of them naked under the goose-down comforter he's bought them now that it's cooler at night, the rice shades open so they can watch the moon.

A week before Leo turns eighteen, his father asks him to come to the house for dinner on the night of his birthday. It's February, seven months since he moved in with Jacie. He's refused to give his father their address, but he says yes—if he can bring Jacie. It will be his father and Angela's first time meeting her, her first time at the house where he grew up.

Leo has never before seen Jacie nervous about her appearance. She irons the floor-length Indian skirt she wore the night they met, the one that looks like a bedspread, and shaves the pills off a black turtleneck. She washes her hair and wraps it wet around her head, securing it with bobby pins and then sleeping with it that way so as to tame the frizz and curl. After she gets dressed, she timidly asks Leo if she looks okay. "You look beautiful, Jacie," he says, but in truth he knows she will seem dumpy next to Mrs. Cecelia Brown in her Chanel suit, whom his father has invited along with Leo's grandparents, Gary, and Jimmy.

Seated in the parlor before dinner, Leo realizes that it's the only occasion he's observed Jacie with what he thinks of as adults. He is surprised by how polite and natural she is, talking with Mrs. Brown about the Houston art museum where, Jacie explains, her mother is a docent, and with his grandfather about her father's medical practice. His father, Leo can tell, is pleased, despite himself, by Jacie's appreciation of his garden, her interest in Leo's mother's sheet music, still stacked atop the piano. Only his grandmother seems overtly disapproving—disapproving, Leo is certain, of Jacie's clothes, her hair, the very idea of a girl living with a man, even if that man is her eighteen-year-old grandson.

Halfway through dinner, Leo catches Gary's eye and they sneak up to the roof for some tokes from a joint.

"My old man would never say it, but I think he kind of likes Jacie."

"No, duh," Gary says.

"What do you mean, 'no, duh'?"

Gary looks at him bemusedly. "Well, she's kinda like your mom."

Leo holds back from snapping, *Are you nuts? My mom was blonde and slender. Beautiful.*

"Artistic. Independent."

Leo feels a wave of shame. He's no better than his grandmother, who'd looked down her nose at his father. Glued to the surface. Gary means in essence: how Jacie refused Vassar because she neither could nor would ever attend League of Women Voters meetings in stockings and sensible pumps; how Leo's mother married a man whose father had been a gardener and mother a maid because she loved and believed in him.

In early March, Leo's midterm grades, which have already been sent to the handful of colleges where he managed to get applications in on time, arrive in his father's mailbox, each having slipped at least half a grade from the low they'd reached the last marking period. His father doesn't say it, but Leo knows he is thinking that Leo can now kiss Stanford and Berkeley goodbye. A week later, a teacher passes the headmaster a tip he heard from the most suck-up of the twelfth-grade boys: in his locker Leo has a plastic bag filled with joints that he is selling by the dozen count.

When the headmaster calls Leo in to tell him that his locker has been searched and marijuana has been found, Leo offers no defense.

"I am certain," the headmaster says, glancing over at the plastic bag now on his desk, "that you know the next steps. I will telephone your father. There will be a disciplinary meeting."

"And I will be expelled. Don't waste your time. I'm withdrawing." Leo stands. He points at the bag. "Keep it. It's good shit. My goodbye gift."

After ten days, Leo goes to see his father. He parks the VW by the Lyon Street steps and walks partway down. He smokes a joint while he watches the fog curling around the towers of the Golden Gate Bridge, which he used to tell his mother should be called the Red Gate Bridge. He is glad that she is dead so that he doesn't have to see her sadness at his throwing everything he's had overboard.

They sit in his father's study, his father behind his desk and Leo in the chair opposite. His father has clearly lost weight, the cords in his neck now visible. On the credenza are photographs Leo hasn't seen before of floral arrangements his father must have designed for events this past year.

Leo scans the shelves of books his father read with his mother and then, since her death, on his own. The wooden box with the peacock feather and the old newspaper articles and the letters from Leo's father's mother and sister is still on an upper shelf. Leo can't remember when he last looked inside that box. Could it have been before his mother died? He dimly recalls the other items inside. Stones from the place where his father had been born. A blue tile.

His father tells him that he has hired an attorney. In the negotiations with the school, the headmaster has agreed not to turn over the evidence from Leo's locker to the police under the condition that Leo, "so as to protect the honor of the school," withdraw his college applications. If Leo complies, the school will offer no information to the college admissions offices, but if he does not, a letter will be sent stating that Leo has been expelled.

Leo knows that he should be listening more carefully to what his father is saying, but in truth, it doesn't matter. Leo has had no intention of going to college in the fall. He'd put in the applications because it would have been more work to explain to everyone why he wasn't. He and Jacie have already decided that they are moving north, to Mendocino, to live on a commune started by Pippy, a girl Jacie met through Lake. Learning that Pippy had gone to Vassar, Jacie had decided it was a sign that Pippy's commune was the place they should go.

As soon as Leo saves up a little more money, he is going to stop smoking, go squeaky-clean and Zen and maybe even vegetarian too. He'll buy camping gear and they'll head north. Once they get settled, he's going to turn some of his poems into song lyrics and take up the drums, since he's decided that percussion is poetry without words.

"Okay, Dad," he says. "I'll withdraw everywhere."

In June, Leo sells his last cache of pot. He smokes a ceremonial final joint and gives his scale and other paraphernalia to Shane, home from Williams for the summer and happy to have his clientele back. Leo and Gary get a job on a painting crew.

For most of the summer, they work on a Victorian in the Mission District. The house belongs to a lady with long silver hair and drawstring paisley pants who insists on serving them lunch: oversize bowls of homemade soup and millet bread she bakes herself. They sit in her garden, slurping their soup under the palm tree that shades the table.

"How's Jacie doing?" Gary asks.

Leo feels a stab of jealousy. Ever since his birthday dinner when Gary had said that Jacie was like Leo's mother, Leo's been aware that Gary seems to have a bead on Jacie, sometimes noticing things that Leo himself hasn't seen. Even that first night he'd met Jacie, at the Grace Slick concert, it was Gary who'd known that she was tripping. At times, watching the two of them quietly talking, he thinks Jacie is closer to Gary than to him. Once he even told her that. "Leo," she cooed, putting her arms around him, "I love Gary. He's an old soul, one of those people who's lived a lot of lives. But I could never sleep with him. He's like the yang of my brother: my brother with his hostility washed away."

"Why are you asking?" Leo says.

"She just seems kind of out of it."

"I think she's adjusting to my being clean. She's never known me when I wasn't getting high. Her sleep's all messed up. If I get up to take a piss, I'll see her sitting at her easel or in a chair by the window, staring out at the street."

When Gary puts down his spoon to listen closer, Leo wants to slap him. Slap him or smoke a joint. Instead, he pushes back the bowl of soup. Fuck, he is going to go nuts if he has to eat another bowl of this lady's gassy soup tomorrow.

He doesn't tell Gary that it's actually much worse than staring out the window at three in the morning—that Jacie switched to the afternoon shift at the coffee shop so she can go back to bed after Leo leaves for work. He has no idea how much of the day she sleeps, but there have been evenings he's come home to find her still in her nightshirt, not having made it to work at all. Some days, she has no appetite, eating nothing until dark. Other days, standing at the kitchen counter, she can eat an entire box of oatmeal-raisin cookies. When she gets to the last few, he'll see her miserably chewing, as though finishing the box is at least finishing something. Afterward, she'll cry that she is getting fat, and the truth is, she is getting a little thick around the middle.

At the end of August, Gary leaves for Johns Hopkins and Jimmy heads south to UCLA. By then, Jacie seems to have snapped out of it. She's gone back to the morning shift at the café and has started walking home from work. They decide to spend the fall and winter saving up money and move to Pippy's commune in the spring.

Leo signs up for a poetry workshop he sees advertised on a flyer at City Lights bookstore. In the evenings, Jacie works on her pastels and he does the exercises from the workshop: write a sonnet, a villanelle, a poem in iambic pentameter.

Grace Slick leaves the Great Society and joins the Jefferson Airplane. Leo and Jacie go to an Airplane concert. When Slick sings "Somebody to Love," Jacie squeezes Leo's hand and doesn't let go. Later, after they have sex, she looks so searingly at him, he forces himself not to roll over, not to fall asleep as he wants to do. To instead prop up on an elbow and ask "What's the matter?" He refrains from adding the beat of the *now* that's in his head: What's the matter *now*?

"I know you are going to leave me. Not now"—that same *now*— "but one day."

Leo puts his arms around Jacie, tries to draw her to him, but she pushes back so she can see his eyes. "You can be honest. It would help. Then I could trust you. I could trust that for now you are here with me."

He feels confused and then irritated.

"I don't mean this month or anytime soon. Just one day, you're going to wake up and want someone different. Prettier, skinnier. Less depressed. Someone who can live with you in that big house of your father's and looks right to be your wife."

He's never thought this way. But now that she's said it, he does think about it. It is hard to imagine Jacie fitting into the life he had with his father and grandparents. Perhaps if his mother were alive, it would be different. She would have appreciated Jacie for her intelligence and artist's soul. For the softness at the center of her being. His mother's view of Jacie would have prevailed, at least for Leo's father, over the narrow-minded one of his grandparents.

The softness at the center of her being. He's not had that idea before, but it strikes him as profoundly true. True about Jacie and true about Gary too: the reason they connect with each other in a way that he cannot with them. Cannot because whatever was once soft in him is now hard.

"Hush. Go to sleep." He kisses the top of Jacie's frizzy head and turns to the wall.

# 10

# Prudence

## New York, 1937–1938

When Carlton told Prudence that he'd found a doctor, a man with a small office in White Plains, to do the procedure, her only request was that he not tell CCB about the abortion.

Carlton paused before he nodded his assent, and in that pause, Prudence saw both Carlton's attempt to decipher what she was asking and that she was right: it had occurred to him to confide in CCB. For over a decade, Carlton had been CCB's sounding board about both Robert, whose manic agitations could exceed CCB's powers of restraint, and Dorothy, who believed it necessary to keep an ocean between the Four (as CCB referred to his grandchildren) and their father's mental instability, a decision that had caused Robert enormous pain. Only with CCB, who'd revealed so much about his own family, would Carlton ever consider discussing a matter so personal.

It was not that Prudence was afraid of CCB knowing she'd become pregnant outside of marriage. The conservative customs he and Louie maintained in their home notwithstanding, he was dedicated to the betterment of those without his advantages, an empathy, she'd often thought, he'd acquired from his own episodes of melancholia. She felt certain that CCB understood that women have unwanted and accidental pregnancies and that they are no more to blame than the fathers of these unborn babes. Nor did she believe that he would condemn an abortion. What she was afraid of was that CCB might find occasion to tell Dorothy, not out of malice or an instinct for gossip, but because Prudence's situation would be a way of engaging his daughter-in-law in an intimate conversation, as he worked hard to do for the benefit of his son and grandchildren. And it was this that was unbearable: the thought of Dorothy knowing Prudence's cowardice in acceding to Carlton's will. Of Dorothy seeing Prudence's lack of faith in her capacity to have a child on her own. Her unwillingness to let go of Carlton and the life he offered.

In her mind, Prudence argued her case with Dorothy: *Working for Harriet, I earn a decent wage, but after I pay the rent and put aside enough for carfare and groceries, it requires diligent and relentless budgeting to be able to purchase a pair of shoes or a gift for anyone.*

*You, born with so much, with ponies and pillars topped with ceramic peonies, with money to take an ocean liner whenever you please, you cannot know what it is like to never be able to attend a concert or travel.*

*You cannot know what it is like to want more . . .*

Prudence blushed just imagining uttering these words. She felt too ashamed to even finish the thought. To suggest that she was giving up a baby so she could go to Carnegie Hall or Rome.

Carlton hired a car to drive them to White Plains. When the nurse brusquely instructed her to follow along, "miss," she saw Carlton looking at her, knew he wanted her to catch his eye and take his concern for her into the makeshift operating room, wanted her to believe, as he most sincerely did, that the abortion was not the measure of his affection for her but rather an immutable limit, like that of a Jewish person, as he'd observed once of a colleague at a funeral mass, unable to put a proffered Communion wafer on his tongue. Those were her last thoughts, the blood and body of Jesus Christ our Lord, as the chloroform mask was lowered over her mouth and nose. She woke with the nurse pressing a cloth between her legs.

She bled for two months. Although Prudence could not bring herself to confide in Elaine, she sensed that Elaine, seeing Prudence's cheeks drained of color, knew. "You need iron," Elaine announced. Sundays and Wednesdays, Elaine took to cooking liver steaks, wrapping the offal in wax paper, and bringing it to work the next morning for the maid Harriet retained at Masters Design to warm for Prudence's lunch.

Carlton's marriage proposal three months later—by then, her body had righted itself—was accompanied by a speech during which he explained in further detail his aspirations. As he'd previously stated, his goals—the ascent of the highest peak on each of the seven continents, the mastery of Bach's compositions for piano, the expansion of his rare-book collection, and, in general, a life of aesthetic and intellectual refinement—were not compatible with raising children. He loved her and, were she to marry him, would cherish and care for her until the end of his days, but he would soldier on to find a different woman to be his wife if she could not accept this condition.

"There are so many men who do both. Have families and pursue their ambitions."

"Because they neglect their children."

"No," she quietly said. "There are men who do both."

"Name one."

"Mr. Tiffany. My father told me he always came home by five to be with his children. They would accompany him while he inspected his flowers each evening."

"They would accompany him. Trail behind him. That is not what I would want for a child."

She'd not felt that she could argue further with Carlton. What was the point of adding the example of Teddy Roosevelt, who Harriet, having worked on his home in Oyster Bay, a short drive from the Tiffany mansion, reported had set aside an hour each day before dinner to play with his children on the lawn? Carlton would produce a superior contradictory piece of evidence provided by CCB and Louie, intimates of Teddy's cousin Franklin and his wife, Eleanor.

Instead, Prudence told herself that after a few years of their being together Carlton would change his mind. He would see the depth of her desire and bend. There was time. It was not as though she wanted children at this very moment. She had her work, her own clients now.

Carlton, though, did not want her to work after they were

married. He wanted to remain in his Park Avenue building, across the street from CCB and Louie, but to move into a larger apartment where he could have a library to house his rare books, a music room for the grand piano he intended to purchase, and staff lodgings. Prudence would need to take control of the renovation and decoration for their new home, then organize their domestic routines and social commitments. In addition, he wanted her to accompany him on some of his mountaineering travels. As for her own pursuits, she could take classes at the Art Students League and lease a painting studio.

"Isn't that what you've always wanted?" he asked.

Had she ever said that to Carlton? But she could not admit what she felt: that painting seemed beyond her. Not technically. She could envision learning how to mix oils, copying the great masters' works, making slight variations of her own. But creating her own paintings? Not imitations but a canvas that expressed her own vision? That seemed impossible. There wasn't enough inside her.

She thought about what Dorothy had written her about the difference between art and decoration, imagined asking Dorothy where paintings come from. *You have to be a whole person*, she felt certain Dorothy would reply. *Unafraid of who you are, light and dark. As able to see the evil in yourself and in the world as the beauty. Look at Rembrandt's* Portrait of Himself, Dorothy would say. *Look at Velázquez's depiction of the pampered Infanta Margaret Theresa in* Las Meninas. *At Whistler's* The Gold Scab: Eruption in Frilthy Lucre, *with his once patron depicted as a taloned peacock.* This, Prudence knew, was precisely what she could not do.

And could she give up her work, as Carlton would insist? Dorothy Burlingham had said in that same letter that a woman must maintain her own work. It was a lesson Prudence had learned early on from her mother, a lesson her mother claimed she'd learned herself from Clara Driscoll, her supervisor at Tiffany's glass factory in Queens. "Clara always said to us, 'Girls, you have to be able to put bread on your own table.' That's why I was so happy when your father took the position at Laurelton Hall—because I could work there too." Prudence could still see the look of shame on her mother's face as she continued, "Then, after everything happened,

I just couldn't work anymore. I know this is horrid of me to say, and I hope the good Lord doesn't smite me for it, but after your father died, my strength came back. It had to, for your sake. And once it did, the first thing I thought was 'I'm getting me a job again.'"

But hadn't her mother also told her when Prudence had wondered if she should do as Mrs. Clarkson at Wanamaker's suggested and apply for the citywide drawing contest, "When good fortune visits, you don't spit in his face. You offer him a cup of tea."

Carlton was a good man. He drank in a gentlemanly manner. He didn't gamble save for an occasional cribbage game at his club. Never ever would he strike her or anyone else.

Was not Carlton's marriage proposal good fortune visiting? Would any sane woman of Prudence's circumstances not marry him?

With their marriage in the fall of 1937, Carlton and Prudence began to dine weekly with CCB and Louie. Robert was in and out of sanatoriums, taking meals when he was home with his male nurse in his quarters upstairs. On one occasion, Prudence heard something crash, and CCB excused himself from the table. Later, Carlton told her that CCB had instructed the nurse to give Robert an injection of a sedative.

Prudence found Louie, with her blinded eye and cane and the lymphedema rumored to be hidden under her invariable black skirt and overcoat, fearful to look at but fascinating for the intensity of her opinions. Louie's strongest opinions were about her daughter-in-law, Dorothy. Twelve years had passed since Dorothy had left with the Four for Vienna, but Louie had still not forgiven her for not having told Robert or CCB or Louie in advance, the news delivered by radio telegram after Dorothy and the children were at sea.

Both CCB and Louie railed about the atrocious education the Four had received at the Matchbox School that Dorothy and a friend had started in Vienna. At ten years of age, CCB reported, Mabbie, the second oldest, had written him a letter in which she spelled *first* as "ferst" and *goes* as "gose."

"Do not misinterpret me," CCB said. "I admire what Dorothy

has done with the children, and I can see that their treatment with Miss Freud has been useful to them as well. But it has gone too far. It is too late now for Bob, he is already twenty-two, but it would have been better for both Michael and him to attend a good boarding school where they could have played sports the way boys should. And the girls too. Dorothy should know that. She was in boarding school herself for five years at St. Timothy's in Maryland."

CCB paused to carve the roast, which their butler then served.

"The summer before Robert and Dorothy married," CCB continued, "I had a conversation with her father about precisely this subject. It was Louie and my first visit to his eccentric estate."

CCB knew that Prudence's father had been Tiffany's gardener at the Seventy-second Street mansion, but did he know that he was talking about the place where she was born? That she and her family had been living there then?

"The evening was awkward due to Tiffany having put up roadblocks to Robert courting Dorothy. When he'd first realized that Dorothy was serious about Robert, he forbade her to see him for a year. If after a year they still had feelings for each other, he blithely said he'd reconsider." CCB glanced over at Louie, who was scowling now. "Louie was very upset about it."

"It was a monstrous thing to do," Louie added. "Robert was so dejected, he left to do an internship in Panama. And then, after he and Dorothy did as her father demanded and didn't see each other for an entire year, Tiffany refused to give his permission when they said they wanted to marry."

"For what possible reason?" Carlton asked.

"Pure selfishness. If Dorothy got married, he'd be left alone in that mansion on Seventy-second Street with no one to order about or watch him strut." Louie snorted. "He only relented after Dorothy's half sister Mary announced that she and her family would take one of the apartments in the building."

"Louie, dear," CCB said. "That's speculation."

For a moment, Prudence wondered if CCB might have the candor to say what seemed so obvious to her: perhaps Dorothy's father had sensed Robert's instability.

"After dinner," CCB continued, "Tiffany invited me to accompany him to the courtyard so he could have his evening cigar. It looked like something out of an Ottoman palace with a gurgling fountain and a domed ceiling and a pipe organ housed on one of the balconies." CCB shook his head. "I still remember how careful he was to flick the cigar ashes into the cup of his hand so they wouldn't fall on the tiles. I couldn't understand why he didn't ask a servant for an ashtray or why he didn't keep an ashtray there. Afterwards, I realized there had been no ashtray because he thought it would mar the effect he'd created in his courtyard."

CCB motioned for the butler to bring him another piece of the roast. "I'd only met Tiffany on a few occasions before, and in the past he'd talked mostly about his factory and new developments in glass manufacturing. I'd even wondered if he was hoping I'd give him some legal advice about a patent issue to which he'd alluded. That night by the fountain, however, he talked about Dorothy. He told me that she'd been unhappy her first year at St. Timothy's, but she prevailed and went on to captain the girls' basketball team. Being away from home, he said, had done her a world of good. He didn't hesitate to tell me that he'd discouraged her from returning for her last year because by then none of his daughters were living with him and he felt lonely."

"The same reason that he objected to Dorothy's marriage," Louie said triumphantly. "Nothing to do with Robert whatsoever."

"You have a point, dear," CCB said. "But Robert told me it was also because Dorothy's father didn't want her to receive a diploma since then she would have been able to attend college, which he opposed for all his daughters."

Prudence felt herself blushing for Dorothy: to have been so controlled, so thwarted.

"Now Miss Freud depends on her in the same way her father did." A tightness crept into CCB's voice. "I supported the suffragists. I believe in the equality of women in the eyes of God. But Miss Freud has set herself up to be the father for the Four. That, I find an outrage, not only against my son but against nature."

Prudence put down her knife and fork. *Against nature?* Was CCB implying that there were "relations" between Dorothy and Miss Freud?

"Through my intercession, my grandson Bob did come back to attend Harvard, but he was so ill prepared, academically and psychologically, he couldn't make it through his first year. I insisted that he attend summer school, and that led to his being reinstated, but then he made a visit to Vienna in August and it was all for naught. He decided that resuming his analysis with Miss Freud was more important than returning to Harvard." CCB shook his head, as though still in disbelief. "Now, he has met a young lady, and I fear this will be the end of Harvard for him. I think his mother would rather he marry at a young age and remain in close proximity to her than that he return to complete his education."

CCB pushed back his chair. "To make matters worse, now that Dorothy has been diagnosed with tuberculosis, Robert is in support of Bob staying in Vienna. He thinks having Bob nearby will hasten her recovery."

Prudence wanted to inquire about Dorothy's tuberculosis, but Carlton interjected before she was able.

"But that is outrageous. She must put their children first, no matter her physical condition."

At home, Prudence queried Carlton about Dorothy's health, but he did not seem to know any details aside from saying that Robert had been obsessively worrying about Dorothy, who he still believed might one day resume their marital life.

For weeks, the Four were a recurrent subject in their nightly dinner conversation. Prudence was moved that Carlton had joined CCB in being so concerned about the fate of Dorothy and Robert's children. Was it possible that this reflected a softening in Carlton, an opening for them to revisit having children themselves?

It took days for her to gather up her courage to ask. At dinner, she fielded Carlton's watchful eyes as she picked at Mrs. Meechin's lamb chops, then waited for Louise to clear the table and for the evening tisanes to be served.

"Hearing how important CCB's grandchildren are to him, does it ever lead you . . ." She paused. "Does it ever lead you to question our not having children of our own?"

Carlton cocked his head. He looked at her as though she were pathetically slow, a person who could not follow the developments in the second act of a play or grasp that a moment of quiet signaled a transition between movements in a symphony rather than its end. "To the contrary. Observing CCB's life, all of his talent, how much more good he could be doing in the world, all I can think is how tragic it is that he has fallen into this great sinkhole of his son's mental derangement and now the derangement that his son has passed on to his own children. It makes me even more convinced that propagation should require the most serious of consideration—were we not so sentimental, an examination or an interview before an expert panel—rather than being the assumed course as it is for dogs or cows."

She feared a bead of sweat might dot her forehead. Nothing Carlton had ever said suggested that he thought his own family line or genealogy had a blight. Was he implying that her family had a strain of insufficiency that would make her having children inadvisable?

Perhaps there was. Even if the whisperings that her father had been drinking the day he fell to his death in the Tiffany house were no more than malevolent gossip, she had only to think of Randall's last evening at home to know that her father had undeniably drunk to excess. And might not a doctor view the weeks when her mother had been unable to dress or leave their apartment and her deathbed utterances—what she'd said about Mr. T, her muttering about the souls she would soon see—as evidence that she'd been mentally unstable?

"I think I'll go to bed early," Prudence said.

Now that Prudence was married to Carlton, her relationship with Ella Jameson changed. With Prudence no longer one of Ella's noblesse oblige projects, it was as though their differences—Ella, seven years older, with nine- and ten-year-old daughters—dissolved.

As a child, Prudence had been too afraid of finding her mother unwashed in her bed or her father belligerent after a visit to the bar to bring girlfriends home. Then, after her father died and her mother got her job at Wanamaker's, Prudence had been too busy working there herself after school to have a close girlfriend. Even with Elaine, who came from a home where there'd often been insufficient milk for five children, Prudence had never spoken about Randall or the envelopes from the Tiffany offices. Although she'd been certain that Elaine would not have condemned Prudence's decision to have an abortion, Prudence would not have been able to tell her how she felt, having done it.

The friendship Ella offered was intoxicating. With a gloved finger, Ella would tip Prudence's chin skyward so she could better see the hat Ella's milliner declared would best suit Prudence's face, would hold Prudence's hand while they sat side by side to be measured by Ella's shoemaker for evening slippers. "Your feet"—Ella laughed—"they are no larger than my daughters'!" They took Ella's girls ice-skating, attended Broadway matinees, walked arm in arm through the Greek and Roman wings of the Metropolitan Museum of Art while Prudence shyly explained what she'd learned about classical design. Ella told Prudence about the boy she'd loved when she was fifteen, and although Prudence could not reciprocate with stories of her own early loves, they amused each other with their accounts of their husbands' idiosyncrasies: Lawrence's refusal to touch fish, the way puppies could make him cry; Carlton's insistence on sleeping with the window open on even the bitterest of nights, his morning tonic of apple cider vinegar and cayenne pepper. On the days when they did not visit, they would each post a note before dinner so on the following morning the cream envelope of Prudence's stationery would be on Ella's breakfast tray and the pale pink one of Ella's on the table next to Prudence's tea.

Then, in the span of a dinner at Ella and Lawrence's brownstone, a Thursday evening with Prudence and Carlton the only guests, everything changed. Even now, three-quarters of a century later when nearly all of Prudence's memories have been reduced to snapshots, the night remains vivid in her mind: the amber of the sherry they had before the meal, the robin's-egg blue of Ella's dress, the forest green of the chicken Florentine.

After the men retired to Lawrence's library for cigars, leaving

Ella and her alone in the dining room, Prudence described the lunch she'd had the previous day with Harriet. Harriet had urged Prudence to come back to work, and Prudence had repeated what she'd said a year before when she'd resigned: Carlton objected to his wife working.

"Harriet nearly neighed. 'You cannot,' she lectured, 'allow a husband to have that much control. Even if you don't want to work, you cannot allow him to believe that it is because of him.'"

Ella smiled. "I can see Harriet throwing back her shoulders as she said that." Ella sipped her coffee, and Prudence, her thoughts muddled from the second glass of wine Lawrence had pressed upon her, regretted having declined a coffee for herself.

"Harriet then spent the rest of the luncheon complaining about how it was her job to teach taste to rich people."

Before Prudence had even completed her sentence, she saw Ella's face cloud and then seal. The terrible heat rose from Prudence's chest to her neck, bright red she was certain, and she thought about the afternoon she'd been with Randall when they'd rounded a corner to witness a horse collapse on the street. "Why, oh why, did we take that route?" she'd asked Randall that night, unable to rid her mind of the anguish she'd seen in the animal's eyes.

Ella excused herself so she could check on her daughters. Prudence miserably remained at the table. As soon as Ella returned, Prudence would apologize. *Of course, I've never felt that way with you. You have the most exquisite taste. If anything, the instruction has gone the other way.*

The next person to enter the room, however, was not Ella, but Carlton. Looking exaggeratedly at his watch, he announced that the evening had slipped away and they must—"Prudence," he said with a sharp note in his voice—must leave immediately.

It was as though a train had arrived and she was being rushed from station to platform. She followed Carlton to the foyer, where Ella stood with her maid, who was holding their coats. Lawrence, his cheeks ruddy from the port he and Carlton had enjoyed after the meal, opened the front door and stepped onto the stoop.

It was lightly snowing.

"And not even Thanksgiving yet!" Lawrence said. "Ella, you'll have to get the sleds out for the girls."

Ella did not comment on the snow. Without looking at Prudence, Ella offered the side of her face for a farewell kiss, placed a hand on Lawrence's back to shepherd him inside, and closed the door of her house.

As always, Carlton insisted they walk the five long blocks and six short ones from the Jamesons' home to their apartment. The streets were hushed from the hour and what was becoming a blanket of snow. Not wanting Carlton to see her shivering, Prudence buried her nose in her upturned collar and hugged her arms to her body. Standing up to the elements had been a cornerstone of his blue-blooded upbringing: summer mornings diving from the dock of his grandparents' Maine lake house into frigid waters; winter trips to Montana when they'd slept in hunters' cabins with the wind wailing like a wounded animal. From the age of six, he'd been forbidden by his father from crying, tears met with a swift paddling. Now, as an adult, he carried the same attitude into his climbing expeditions. The route was meticulously planned to minimize dangers and maximize safety, but whatever discomfort or fear he or his fellow trekkers experienced once under way was to remain unspoken.

Thomas, the night doorman, greeted them with small talk about the snow. Unable to abide the rules Ella kept in her own household that the help must await her return no matter the hour, Prudence allowed Louise, who lived in, time off on the evenings when she and Carlton were out. Louise, Thomas whispered to Prudence, had not yet returned.

Carlton unlocked their apartment door, pecked Prudence's cheek, and went immediately to bed. Prudence put the kettle on to boil in the kitchen and drew a bath.

Soaking, she brooded about the dinner. Afterward, she sat at her writing desk in her dressing room with a cup of chamomile tea and wrote to Ella.

*Dearest Ella,*

*I left your home after your delicious dinner with a most heavy heart—afraid that I had offended you with the remark I repeated from Harriet Masters. Please know that I did not intend that remark to be about you: You have the most gorgeous taste and if there is anyone who has been the teacher between us, it is you.*

*Carlton insisted we walk back. The city was beautiful in the snow, but I needed a hot bath and a steamy cup of tea afterwards! I hope you and your beautiful daughters are fast asleep and will awaken to a winter wonderland.*

*Affectionately yours,*

*Prudence*

The letter felt false—not the apology, that was genuine, but the breezy way she'd depicted the walk home and her mood now. She didn't want Ella any more than Carlton to know about her cold, wet feet or that her misery about the evening had only grown stronger in the hour since her arrival home. Intimidated by Ella's chilly goodbye, she'd signed the letter *Affectionately yours* instead of *With dearest love* or *As ever, always yours,* as she and Ella usually did.

Prudence put the envelope on the hallway table for Carlton to mail when he left for work. Ella would receive it late morning. Surely she would post her reply by teatime.

By the second Saturday after Prudence had sent her note, Ella's lack of response was her response. At a performance of *Rigoletto* that evening, Prudence was relieved to shed tears under the guise of Gilda's abduction and Rigoletto's horrified awareness that he had been complicit in his daughter's capture.

During the intermission, Carlton looked at her curiously. She'd learned that he was perceptive, but opposed to acknowledging the shifts of her emotions, as though doing so would be indulging a weak strain in her character. Instead, he discussed his plans for his next trip. In September, he would travel to Tanganyika to climb Kilimanjaro with a guide who'd devised a new ascent. Unlike McKinley, which Carlton had climbed the year before they met, Kilimanjaro could be summited without special mountaineering skills. Even she, were she to physically prepare, would be able to do it.

She clutched the champagne glass Carlton had handed her. Had he developed the idea that she would climb Kilimanjaro with him? Before they'd married, she'd tolerated coats that failed to keep out the wind and boots that let in the damp, but she could no more imagine sleeping in a tent on cold, rocky ground than she could gutting an elk, as Carlton had learned to do at nine years of age, or knocking a man unconscious, as Carlton had told her a guide had once done with a climber who'd panicked on a rappel and was endangering them both.

When the bell rang informing them that it was time to return to their seats, Carlton took her still-full glass.

"I saw Lawrence last night," he said as they settled back into their box.

Her stomach tightened. It would be like Carlton to engineer telling her something disturbing when the opportunity to respond was limited by lights soon to be dimmed.

"He wants to buy a summer home on St. Regis Lake, not far from the Vanderbilt family camp, but apparently Ella refuses."

"Why is that?"

"Some sort of row with the mother of another Brearley girl whose family also summers there." Carlton gave one of his half smiles, an expression that someone who didn't know him might experience as odd or even condescending, but which Prudence understood to be his diffident way of sharing his appreciation of an irony or a bit of black humor. "I have the feeling that if you cross Ella, that is it. She can cut you off for good."

Over the following days, Prudence felt herself sinking into an impenetrable loneliness. She, Prudence Theet, née Prudence O'Connor, daughter of servants, had unwittingly insulted Ella Jameson, inhabitant of a world populated by the likes of the Vanderbilts. That Prudence had sincerely and almost immediately apologized made no difference.

Rather than feeling indignant at this injustice, Prudence was ashamed. Ashamed that she had so dearly wanted Ella as a friend and had deluded herself into thinking it possible. Despite the poverty of her experience with having a friend, Prudence felt certain that friendship should encompass generosity: the generosity of spirit that allows for turbulence and disagreements. For forgiveness. Or perhaps—and this seemed even more painful—the breach with Ella had nothing to do with anything Prudence had said, but more with Ella's having tired of the novelty of an intimate outside her circle, a circle Prudence existed on the periphery of only because of her marriage to Carlton.

The loneliness sank into her gut, making food revolting: beef looked like feces and chicken was a dead bird and vegetables dirty debris. It disturbed her sleep, so she would wake at four. Creeping into her dressing room, she would watch the sky lighten. One morning, at dawn, she saw a flock of swallows slashing the sky in a V formation. For a few moments, her spirits lifted as she imagined the birds an advance guard for the larger group, but the thought dimmed to be replaced by concern that they were an errant congregation that had lost their bearings.

With Prudence's cheekbones hollow and her clavicle sharply outlined above the neckline of her dresses, Mrs. Meechin took to putting extra butter in Prudence's dishes, Louise to bringing her hot chocolate made with cream. One morning, as she sat struggling to eat a few bites of the greasy eggs, Carlton announced that Dr. Hinley, CCB's private physician, who came now every day to care for Robert, would be arriving shortly to examine Prudence.

Before Prudence could object, Carlton looked at her sternly. "I am not asking you. I am telling you."

Dr. Hinley took her blood pressure and listened to her breathing with a stethoscope. He examined her throat and her ears. He palpated her abdomen, tested her reflexes with a tiny hammer he kept in his doctor's bag. Then he and Carlton retired to Carlton's library for coffee and Mrs. Meechin's raisin buns, over which he presented Carlton with his diagnosis of Mrs. Theet: feminine melancholy, perhaps linked, he carefully suggested, to her infertile state, which he presumed from their lack of children, exacerbated by what he surmised to be residual anemia from what Carlton described as a miscarriage. Hinley prescribed bed rest, liver on alternate days, iron pills, and, in a month's time, a trip to Arizona, where the dry desert air and the sunshine, he told Carlton, would be beneficial to his wife.

Not wanting to go to Arizona, where she feared the sun scorching her fair skin and a terrible silence over the desert landscape, Prudence forced herself to eat the liver Mrs. Meechin prepared, to stay in her bed no matter how many hours she stared at the ceiling. She lectured herself: *You were alone before Ella. You were fine then. You will be fine again.*

In December, Louie Burlingham died. By then, Prudence felt not so much recovered as altered. It was a relief to have Carlton's attentions turn to CCB and to his own parents, who came from Virginia for Louie's funeral and then remained with Carlton and Prudence for the holidays. Without informing Dorothy, at a clinic for the treatment of her tuberculosis, Robert peremptorily left for Vienna.

Alone now, CCB dined with the Theets on Christmas Day. Carlton had accepted Prudence's wish to give Louise and Mrs. Meechin the holiday off so they could spend it with their own families. Prudence knew, though, that it embarrassed him that she served the meal—his embarrassment compounded by his mother's evident disapproval of what to her was an unseemly situation, but then alleviated by CCB's lavish praise of the potato gratin and jellied salad prepared in advance by Mrs. Meechin and the beef Wellington and plum pudding Prudence had made herself.

Throughout those first months of 1938, Carlton carefully followed the deteriorating situation in Europe. Not only was he anxious about the reports on CCB's behalf with Dorothy and the Four in Vienna, but he was concerned about the tickets he'd booked for June: a delayed honeymoon trip he'd meticulously organized to commence in Paris and then continue on to Geneva, Lago Maggiore, the Pyrenees, and Nice, where they'd board a boat to the Peloponnese.

In early March, Robert, shattered by the news that Dorothy

would remain in Vienna to help execute the Freuds' departure to London, returned to New York with only Mikey, his youngest son. A week later, when Germany invaded Austria, both Robert and CCB were terrified that Dorothy and the three children still with her would be arrested on account of their association with the Freuds. Not until April, after they received word that Dorothy and the children had departed for Italy, was there some respite from their fear. Still, every conversation with CCB, who now dined in Carlton and Prudence's home Wednesdays and Sundays, turned to Dorothy's machinations in tandem with Princess Bonaparte to move the Freuds safely to England, and then to Robert's increasing agitation as it became clear that his wife was intending London to be her new home as well.

Summer arrived in May that year, the azaleas in the park flowering by the first week, the annuals in the urns at the entrances of the Park Avenue buildings in full bloom. For Prudence, the blossoming around her felt like a chastisement about her own barrenness. She envisioned herself as a pony in a ring, round and round through the seasons, each year the same, each without destination.

The nights were hot and airless, and her insomnia was only worsened by her awareness of Carlton's scrutiny of it. For hours on end, she lay corpselike with the sheets flung to the side. In a week, they would depart for Europe. She dimly recalled having slept as she'd never before slept on the crossing she'd made to Europe when she was a student at the Paris branch of her school, and she desperately hoped this would be the case again.

One particularly bad night, she was still awake as dawn approached. The velvet curtains of their bedroom were ajar, and a sliver of light from a streetlamp formed a narrow triangle on the wood floor. Soon Carlton would wake. She feared he would roll toward her, as was his habit in the early hours, putting his hands under her nightclothes, using coitus interruptus during the days he deemed at risk of conception from the charts he kept of her menstrual cycle.

The evening they would board the boat would be sixteen

months to the day since she'd had the abortion. Now all she could think of was why, why had she gone along, allowed Carlton to convince her to lie on that table? Let that doctor clamp the chloroform mask over her face?

She'd grown up with enough women struggling to feed their children to know that there are circumstances when a woman ends a pregnancy because there are already too many mouths to feed or because she knows in her bones that she cannot survive another laying up—that she would be birthing a child who would be motherless. But none of this had been the case for her. She was young, she was healthy. She could have taken care of her (for she felt quite certain that the baby had been a girl) without Carlton. Harriet and Elaine would have helped, she could have found a woman to care for the baby while she was at work. They would have had to live humbly, far outside of what the Ellas would deem society, but she could have managed.

Her skin was burning, whether from heat or shame, she could not distinguish. What she knew for certain was she must—must—get some morning air. Moving quietly so as not to wake Carlton, she dressed quickly in last night's clothing, not yet put away by Louise, and a hooded cape to cover her loose, uncombed hair.

In the kitchen, she poured a glass of tepid water from the pitcher. It was almost five thirty. In half an hour, Mrs. Meechin would arrive to begin breakfast.

Not wanting Thomas, who would be standing in his white gloves and doorman's hat at the building entrance, to see her—it would be like him to make a point of commenting to Jenkins, the day doorman, who would then make a point of passing what he'd heard along to Carlton—she took the back stairs and exited through the delivery gate on Seventy-seventh Street.

As she rounded the corner of Park Avenue, a movement in a window across the street caught her eye. It was the building where CCB lived now with only Robert. A portion of a curtain was flapping outside an open window.

A man was at the window. He seemed to be leaning out. Even from this distance, Prudence could tell that he was in pajamas. Blue-and-white-striped pajamas.

She counted the stories to the open window. The fourteenth floor, CCB's apartment.

The man, though, was no longer there. Had it been Robert? CCB? It must have been Robert. CCB would not wear striped pajamas like a convict. He would not peer out the window at this hour.

Then the man reappeared. The window raised higher. A smear of blue and white sluiced the gray dawn. Were there not the horrid slapping sound as the body hit the pavement, Prudence would not have been certain it had even happened.

There was a scream. Unable to move, to breathe, she stared across the avenue at the blue-and-white pajamas, streaked now with red.

The doormen from CCB's building raced out from the lobby. "Jesus, Mary, and Joseph!" one of them cried. A man ran across Park Avenue and knelt on the sidewalk. He stripped to his shirtsleeves and spread his jacket over the body.

Not until Carlton was assured by Dr. Hinley that with the barbital CCB had been given he would now sleep for several hours did Carlton return to their building. It was then that he learned from Jenkins what he'd been told by Thomas: that Mrs. Theet had unfortunately witnessed Mr. Burlingham's tragic death.

It was midmorning. Carlton found Prudence in bed. Despite the day's heat and a hot toddy prepared by Mrs. Meechin after Prudence had been escorted by Thomas back to the apartment, Prudence's teeth were chattering.

"Jenkins said Thomas never saw you leave the building. He could not understand how you were even there."

She pulled the sheet over her face. She could not bear being interrogated. She could not bear Carlton's accusing tone.

"Go away," she whispered, the sound Robert Burlingham's body had made as it hit the pavement still resounding in her ears.

When a detective came at the end of the day to take her account of what she had witnessed, Prudence thought this was Carlton's way of exacting her punishment for having crept out at dawn without telling him. Like a naughty child, she would have to report her misdeeds. In the twelve hours since Robert's leap, her mind's eye had been filled with his blue-and-white pajamas soaked with red. Now she described the curtains flapping, a man leaning out, the window lifting.

Had she understood what was happening? the detective asked.

She shook her head no, tried to explain it was all so fast. But after the detective left, she realized this wasn't true. Before she'd even counted the floors, she'd recognized that the open window was in CCB's library. Before the window raised higher, she'd been certain that the man leaning out was Robert. Before the scream, before CCB's doormen raced outside, she'd known that the horrid sound was Robert's end.

# 11

# Grace

## An April Wednesday, 2013

Grace gives her second paper on the third morning of the conference: "Employing a Hospice Model for Families of Death Sentence Recipients." Even here, with the state, not nature, the executioner, a meaningful ending, she argues, is possible.

Last week, she'd read an earlier version to Sunny and Ben. When she got to the historical material about executions hardly distinguishable from carnival acts, Ben had bellowed, "No! Gracey, we are nurses. If you were giving this at a philosophy conference, sure: go for the jugular. When I was a graduate student, I went to lectures where I wouldn't have been surprised to see a kooky deconstructionist brandishing a gun at someone calling Paul de Man a Nazi . . ."

Sunny patted Ben's hand. "I think"—Sunny held the copy of Grace's paper she'd set down on the coffee table—"what Ben is saying is that you might cut the sentences with 'townspeople gathered to witness hangings' and 'bleachers set up to watch a man strapped in an electric chair.'"

Heeding her friends' advice, she sticks to the family issues: how a parent or wife or child can say goodbye to a loved one on death row. How an inmate—she controls herself and does not add, *too commonly, a black man or a cognitively limited youth*—whether innocent or guilty, can face his own end. Again, she controls herself and does not say, *his own murder.*

Although she has presented versions of this paper before and experienced nasty Q&As afterward, it still astounds her that the same people who don't believe women have a right to end a pregnancy zealously support a judge warranting an execution. Today, when someone asks for her thoughts about euthanasia in the context of her hospice work, a *Fuck it* rises up in her, unleashing what she knows is imprudent candor about how her work as a hospice nurse has turned her into an ardent believer in the sanctity of life and the immorality under any circumstances of taking death into one's own hands. This belief yields her strange bedfellows: capital-punishment opponents and animal-rights defenders and antiabortion activists. "My death-sentence-protester, vegan, right-to-lifer girl," Kate calls her. Kate, whom she wishes were here with her now as all hell breaks loose for the remainder of the Q&A with persons who commonly abhor one another allying to berate those whom they usually view as in their camp, and Sandy, the chair of the panel, valiantly but unsuccessfully attempting to find higher common ground.

Grace has promised Sandy she will join her and the other two women on the panel for lunch. Now, though, after the angry reception to her remarks, she wonders if they will want her to come along or if they'd prefer to gossip without her there. She looks quizzically at Sandy, who puts a hand on her arm and raises an eyebrow.

"You could probably use a glass of wine," Sandy says. "I know I could."

Grace nods, not wanting to admit that she doesn't drink. The first of what had turned into a round-robin of emails about the choice of a restaurant for lunch with links to reviews and strict instructions to hit *Reply All* had arrived a few weeks ago as she was using her phone to order an additional oxygen tank for her patient Herman. She hadn't realized she'd sighed out loud until she glanced up and saw David watching her.

"Sorry. Nothing to do with your father. I'm giving some papers at a conference in New York next month, and the panel participants are already thinking about where we're going to eat afterwards. It makes me a little nuts."

"I get it. Paula, my ex, was a serious foodie, and it drove her crazy that I couldn't get excited about her scoring us a reservation at a restaurant so hot, she'd tell me, she'd had to put her phone on autodial and devote a morning to even getting through to the reservationist." David raised his eyebrows bemusedly. "'You have no idea how lucky we are,' she'd say, but the truth was, after a day of teaching and meetings with my fellows and lab assistants, I was happier cooking for us than going somewhere with two Michelin stars."

"What do you like to cook?"

David looked at her curiously. "You put your finger on the problem. If I'd been cooking from one of the recipe books Paula gave me for birthdays and Hanukkah, it might have passed muster. But I don't use recipes. I don't even keep music on. I just let my thoughts drift. I've come up with half of my ideas for research projects while I was chopping onions and the other half while I was chopping garlic."

Herman's eyes were closed; it was hard to tell if he was sleeping or too exhausted to lift his lids. "I cook the foods my mother cooked when I was a kid: roast chicken and lasagna and pot roast and pineapple upside-down cake. Your basic Eastern European suburban-American Jewish fare."

"Foods like your aunt Rose cooks?"

"Exactly. In fact, my mother's the one who taught my aunt Rose how to cook. Rose loves to tell the story that she couldn't even make a cup of tea when she got married, and that my mother came over and organized her kitchen and wrote out five recipes for her on index cards so she'd have something to serve my uncle Barney for dinner. When we got married, Rose gave the index cards to Paula, who politely thanked her and then later threw them in the trash because, she said, they were disgustingly spattered with grease."

Grace took Herman's pulse. She swabbed his cracked, colorless lips and the inside of his mouth with a little pink sponge attached to a stick, moved the rolled towel from under his left side to his right, and repositioned his body. From the ribs visible now in his back, she guessed that he'd dropped fifteen pounds in the two weeks since he'd left the hospital and that it would be only a matter of days before he'd stop eating at all. She would have to ask David to call Rose and tell her to not bring any more food.

"Eventually Paula gave up on me as her restaurant companion.

Instead, she would make the reservations for lunches or dinners with her colleagues or clients—she's a trusts and estates lawyer, so there were lots of those."

Herman emitted a little snore. David leaned down and kissed his father's forehead. "I've decided that the key to marriage is whether you can eat companionably. Before people sleep together, they should take a test to figure that out. Paula and I would have failed terribly. Even when we did have a meal together, it infuriated her that I'd object to her keeping her phone on and out at the table. She was compulsive about checking facts on Google, and it caused her physical pain to leave an email unanswered for a full ten minutes."

He took off his glasses and wiped them with his shirttail. "I tried to explain to her that everything I know about the brain suggests that we aren't wired to tolerate hours on end responding to pings and alerts. That it's impossible to have sustained thought with that kind of constant interruption. One of our worst fights ever was during a dinner at home when somehow we got onto talking about a movie we'd seen years before starring Tab Hunter and Debbie Reynolds. Neither of us could remember the name, and Paula was insistent that she look it up on her phone. I was hell-bent on convincing her that our conversation was what mattered, not the name, and then I quoted this study I'd just read that even having a phone on the table diminishes the quality of communication between people."

David settled his glasses back on his nose. "It was stupid and stubborn on my part, like waving a red cape before a bull. She started screaming that I was a fucking control freak, and then she dumped the bowl of spaghetti and meatballs I'd served her in the trash and stormed out."

On David's dresser was a photo of him with Paula and his parents taken, he'd told Grace, at the ceremony for an award he'd been given for his first book. Paula had on a pink strapless dress, and both her dark hair arranged in an updo and her toothy smile appeared lacquered on.

"She came back five minutes later and apologized, and I apologized for having been so insufferably pedantic, but the truth was, she thought my talk about creativity and reflection requiring solitude was a lot of romantic bullshit, like a college sophomore quoting Rilke."

Rilke. She'd read portions of Rilke's *Letters to a Young Poet* to Garcia after he'd asked that she bring some of their father's books to Huntsville. There'd been a sentence her father had underlined: *Search into the depths of Things: there, irony never descends* . . .

For a moment, she was tempted to ask David if a person could have too much solitude, a brain too many hours of silence, but she's learned over the years to resist being lured by the intimacy of sitting at the bedside of someone dying into forgetting her role: she is the nurse, the guide through the final days. Being lost on her own journey is of no moment.

After what had seemed to Grace like an endless number of emails, the group settled on a faux-French bistro, where it's harder than she anticipated to find something she can eat. She mumbles about having had a big breakfast, inquires if the tomato soup has cream, which it does, eliciting a lactose-intolerance sidebar, and then, not wanting to draw further attention to herself, orders a green salad and french fries.

When the conversation turns to shopping, one of the women exclaiming over Woodbury Common, another over some stores in Williamsburg, and then to children and homework loads and college counselors, Grace slips into her default mode at these sorts of meals, nodding along and contributing timely murmurs while her thoughts wander—which they do, today, to the photos her grandfather showed Garcia and her of the pillars from the loggia at Laurelton Hall. Topped by capitals of glass and pottery flowers with stalks slender as asparagus, the pillars had been restored after the fire at the Tiffany estate and are now installed in the American Wing of the Metropolitan Museum of Art, where Grace hopes to go once she finishes this interminable meal.

# 12

# Jacie & Leo

## Mendocino, Summer 1967–January 1971

The month before Leo and Jacie move to Mendocino, Pippy, founder of the commune where they have been planning to live, calls Jacie. Disgusted with the way the men—acting as if they know more about framing a barn or staking a garden or running pipes—boss the women around, Pippy has decided to make the commune women's land. "You can come," Pippy says, "but not your guy."

Pippy tells Jacie about another commune, Riva Krik, twelve miles north, run by this kind of mystic, Peter, who'd been a minister and then lived for a while in Cambridge, where he had his mind blown with a lot—Pippy laughs, "*a lot*"—of psilocybin and LSD. After he had a vision of himself floating over a dell of redwoods, he moved out here to start Riva Krik.

"I'm going to see him later this week," Pippy says, "at a swap meet we have each month. I'll tell him about you and your guy, but you should write him too."

Pippy gives Jacie Peter's address, and Jacie writes to him that afternoon. She draws a border of vines and farm animals and uses pastels to decorate the envelope with astral designs. The following week, she receives a letter back.

> *Art Girl! Bring your man and your camping gear and your paints. If your energy is in sync with ours, you can stay in one of our cabins. Each cabin has a bed that fits two and a wood-burning stove, but there's no running water or*

*electricity in any of them, so pack flashlights and candles and blankets and whatever bourgey stuff you can't live without.*

NAMASTE

*Peter*

*ps Everyone gives 25 bucks a week for our collective expenses, so bring some money too. Cash appreciated.*

By the time they arrive at Riva Krik, it's been a year since Leo has smoked any pot. It's June and the fields are dotted with yellow and purple wildflowers, and the ground is scratchy and dry. Neither Jacie nor Leo has ever slept in a tent, much less pitched one, but they manage with the help of another couple: Susan, once a cheerleader at her Iowa high school and now with her shirts stained by breast milk, and Tim, a carpenter with a union card and a bushy beard flecked with wood dust.

Peter, they learn, is attached to Goddess, who keeps a tepee at the edge of the land where she brews medicinal herbal concoctions she sells at a flea market in Fort Bragg on Sundays. Goddess's hair is in dreads and her skin is weathered like someone's from the Andes and no one knows how old she is. The land, Tim tells Leo, was bought by Goddess after her parents, diplomats in Saudi Arabia, were killed while on a Kenyan safari by militants who'd attacked the tourist group. The story, Tim believes, is a cover for the murder having been directed at Goddess's parents, really CIA agents.

At the end of Leo and Jacie's first week, Peter announces that he and Goddess have decided: "The energy you kiddos emanate is in sync with Riva Krik." He leads them to a cabin close to the Shiva Spa (the bathhouse with three compost toilets, a wash sink, and separate shower areas for men and women) and a short walk from the Karma Kookhouse (the kitchen and dining room).

With Jacie and Leo, there's a core seventeen of them, and then usually another two or three people staying for what might start as overnight and turn out to be a couple of months. A tribe, Peter calls them. Working off the money grid, he says, they avoid the exploitation of their surplus labor by the fascist capitalists. He gives Leo a copy of Philip Slater's book about the corrupt use of possessions as a measure of achievement.

The commune meets daily at sunrise to meditate together, to listen to what Jacie thinks of as one of Peter's sermons, and to divvy up the collective chores, written on a chalkboard by painfully thin Cathy, who dropped out of Duke medical school to become a weaver but has held on to the orderliness that got her there. Leo apprentices himself to Tim, who teaches him how to cut down a tree with a handsaw, cure the wood, and make tongue-and-groove planks, and Jacie takes to helping Susan with the two children she's had with Tim: four-year-old Malika and eight-month-old Fellini.

If Jacie is not on the post-dinner-dishes crew, she helps Susan give the children their baths in the Shiva Spa wash sink, then reads to Malika while Susan nurses Fellini. After the children are asleep, Jacie and Susan wash Fellini's cloth diapers in a laundry area Tim has fashioned outside the cabin, using water they heat on the wood-burning stove. Susan vigorously scrubs each diaper, and Jacie then wrings them out and hangs them on the line to dry in the morning sun. Once they're done, Susan, too exhausted most nights to even brush her teeth, goes immediately to bed, while Jacie heads to the painting studio Tim and Leo built for her: a shed with shelves for her art supplies and a large window with a view of the towering redwoods on the hills behind Riva Krik. Looking out, she can see the glow of the campfire across the field, where Leo sits cross-legged with Peter and a few of the other men, some of them sharing a pipe, but not Leo, who seems happier now that he's drug-free.

On occasion, a cowbell rings, a signal that they are to gather in the meadow outside Goddess's tepee either for what Peter calls a consciousness-raising circle or for pressing news. Usually the news is that the pump has broken again or a storm is coming and they need to protect the vegetable garden, but each time Jacie fears it's about one of the children, if not Fellini or Malika, then Alda or Bennett—the children of Gardner, the commune mechanic, and Helen, who takes care of the goats.

When the cowbell rings on this hot September afternoon, Jacie is in her art shed, working from charcoal sketches she's done of Malika on a watercolor portrait. Trying to capture the sweet spot the child occupies between a sage knowingness—as though she came into the world with an understanding of birth, sex, death—and her innocence of the ugliness in the human heart. Greed, jealousy, schadenfreude—a word Jacie learned in high school and has never forgotten: the idea that a person would take pleasure in someone else's misfortune striking her as among the most frightening things she's ever heard.

Arriving at the meadow in front of the tepee, Jacie finds Leo seated between Peter and Goddess with the others in a circle around them. Peter moves a bit to the side and motions for her to take the space he's made next to Leo.

Goddess chants, and the members of the circle join hands and sway in unison.

Then Peter speaks. "I have brought everyone here because capitalism abhors appreciation. If bosses appreciated workers, truly, not in condescending, trivial employee-of-the-month ways, they'd have to pay them their genuine due, which would mean giving workers the profits from their labor. As a commune, as a collective, we must fight this culture of no gratitude."

Peter sucks on his unlit pipe.

*The man should still be a preacher,* Jacie thinks.

"The time has come for us to express our gratitude to Leo and Jacie for joining us, for giving us their hearts and bodies."

Jacie glances at Leo. He looks stunned. Stunned and confused.

"Leo," Peter says. "You have put aside the ego of a boy of privilege to work with your hands. You have made a wise choice in letting our good man Tim be your teacher. Carpentry is noble work. Jesus was a carpenter. You have opened your mind to the books I have given you. You have been a man to your woman."

Peter takes an aluminum-foil packet from his pocket. Jacie's heart pounds and her armpits dampen as she watches Peter crumble the sticky substance into the bowl of his pipe, as she smells the hash burning. He puts the pipe to his mouth and turns to Leo.

She looks imploringly at Peter. Surely he has forgotten that Leo has been clean now for fifteen months, but the look she gets back is opaque, as though a screen has been lowered between them.

Leo takes a long toke on the pipe.

After the hash has made its way around the circle, Peter asks Leo and Jacie to come to his cabin. He unfolds a paper and hands it to them. It's a property tax bill from the Mendocino County clerk.

"We owe nineteen hundred dollars."

Leo smiles at the tax bill as though Peter has granted him the honor of seeing a sacred text.

"We need you to ask your parents to help out. A grand from each, and we'll be good for the taxes."

Jacie turns hot with anger. Leo's mouth is locked in a stoned grin, and she hopes he doesn't blurt out they don't have to go to their parents, they brought money with them: she from her waitress job, Leo from his pot business and then from painting houses.

For the first time since they arrived at Riva Krik, she feels bad about being here. Hurt that Peter and Goddess want to milk Leo and her. Ashamed that she doesn't want to pay more.

The following morning, after the communal meditation, Leo takes nineteen hundred dollars from the leather pouch they keep under a floorboard in their cabin. "We'll give it to Peter together," he says, taking Jacie's hand.

Seeing the money, Peter laughs and then, pudgy as he is, surprises Jacie by doing a handstand on the lumpy dirt outside his cabin.

"Lunch, kiddos, on me," Peter announces. Jacie has the sense that *lunch on me* means "lunch on Riva Krik." They pile, Peter and Goddess and Leo and Jacie, into Leo's VW and go to the Cobweb Palace, the inn in nearby Westport, where, even though Goddess is a vegetarian, they all eat lamb chops and Caesar salads made with imported anchovies.

Peter orders a bottle of French wine. "Marx never intended to rid the world of pleasure. The idea is not that the revolution will abolish the good life. The idea is that everyone will share in the good life." Peter raises a glass of the Bordeaux. "To the revolution. The good life for all."

With the second bottle of Bordeaux, Leo envisions himself bobbing in a river of history, scarlet and murky as the wine. For the first time ever, he tries to imagine his father's parents—the grandparents he never met. He tries to imagine his father's sister—the aunt Leo also never met, but whose name, Prudence, he now recalls. He thinks about the capriciousness of his father having been taken under wing by Cecelia Brown. Yes, there'd been his father's hard work and his talent for floral design, but without that piece of luck, his father would have remained a florist working in someone else's shop, would never have become a society favorite with fashionable commissions, a respectable escort for his mother. There would never ever have been an intersection of the O'Connor and Duprew family lines.

How remarkable it would have seemed to his father's parents that a grandson of theirs grew up as a prince in Presidio Heights, attending a school with the sons of the wealthiest families of San Francisco, his meals prepared and his school shirts ironed by Angela, beloved but still their maid. How heartbreaking it must be for his father that his son now chooses to live like a laborer in a one-room cabin in the woods of Northern California with a girlfriend who dresses in what must look to his father like rags.

The first winter is terrible. No matter how many layers she wears, Jacie cannot get rid of the chill in the marrow of her bones. Morning to night, her hands and feet are freezing and she feels as though she is trembling beneath her clothes. The children pass between them a perpetual cold that keeps Fellini up at night with a hacking cough. Jacie has barely recovered when the second winter, harsher than the first, arrives. By summer, she can't button her jeans. She throws up in the mornings and is so tired, she is back in bed by noon.

Susan takes Jacie to the Fort Bragg hospital for a pregnancy test.

Five days later, Jacie returns with Leo, who squeezes her hand too hard while a Dr. Knight inserts three gloved fingers in her vagina and puts a stethoscope on her abdomen.

"Any history of twins in either of your families?" Dr. Knight asks.

Jacie shakes her head no.

"She's pregnant?" Leo says.

"Twins?" Jacie murmurs.

"Pregnant, that's definite. Twins, I can't be sure. We don't have ultrasound equipment here. You'd have to go down to the city for that. But I've been doing this for longer than you young folks want to know, and I'd say get yourself two cribs."

Jacie's eyes open wide. She feels gripped with terror. Terror at the thought of caring for one much less two babies in the dead of winter when she is due. How will she nurse two babies? How will they keep the cabin warm? How will she wash so many diapers? When she starts to cry, Dr. Knight mistakes her tears for overwhelming happiness.

Leo drives them back to Riva Krik. She leans against the window on the passenger side of the VW, fighting off nausea and more tears. She wants to go back to Houston and lie on a chaise lounge by her parents' kidney-shaped swimming pool reading Anaïs Nin while her mother flips through her *Smithsonian* magazine. She wants to sit on the grass drawing unicorns and mermaids with the Jackson twins. She wants Bubba to bring her red grapes and the Stella D'oro cookies with the chocolate-button centers.

When the cowbell rings in the afternoon, Jacie drags herself out of bed and walks to the field in front of Goddess's tepee. Peter gestures for Leo and her to join Goddess and him on a bamboo mat in the middle of the circle. *Again*, Jacie thinks. *Weren't they just here, being massaged into paying the tax bill?*

*No. Not just. Nearly two years ago.*

She lowers herself onto the mat. She can no longer sit crossed-legged, all of her appendages, it seems, having swollen to half again their size, and her skin has an unpleasant smell, like dried blood mixed with the decomposing leaves and goat dung littering the field. A few drops of rain fall on her head.

"Riva Krik Tribe," Peter begins. "Leo and Jacie are taking the next turn on the life wheel. They have made a baby and their baby is two." Peter smiles benevolently at Jacie. "Goddess tells me it is a blessing for Riva Krik to have twins come to us." From here, Peter launches a sermon on Castor and Pollux, how one of them was conceived by a mortal father, the other by the rape of Leda by Zeus disguised as a swan. With the thought of being mounted by an oily swan, Jacie feels a rush of nausea and fear. She inhales deeply and looks up at the gray sky and then out at the giant trees beyond the clearing.

"And now, kiddos, is there anything you would like to say?"

Leo stands. Jacie squints at the father of her children. His hair has fallen over his eyes and his jeans are loose on his butt. "Thank you, Peter. Thank you, Goddess. Wow. Castor and Pollux. That's wild." Leo brings his hands together and lowers his chin, as though bowing to them.

Only Susan addresses what is on Jacie's mind. "Don't worry, Jacie. You've been so generous with us. Now it's our turn to help you." Jacie thinks about Lake, how she got the guys who lived in her house on Ashbury Street to get off their lazy backsides and scrub the tub and mop the kitchen and pick their crap up from the floor. But Susan is not Lake. Nights, she washes diapers while Tim sits by a campfire, passing a pipe with Peter and now Leo too.

Jacie goes into labor on a Sunday in February, two weeks after Leo's twenty-second birthday. It is a record-breaking cold for this date in Mendocino: twenty degrees, according to the thermometer Gardner has hung outside his and Helen's cabin. Leo drives Jacie to the Fort Bragg hospital, where after nineteen hours of labor, Dr. Knight does a C-section.

The nurses wipe the cheesecake film off the babies and wrap them in blue and pink blankets. The girl is six pounds three ounces. They hand her to Jacie. The boy is five pounds eight ounces. They hand him to Leo.

Jacie kisses the forehead of their tiny baby girl. For the first time since she learned she was pregnant, she is flooded with a joy so intense it fills her all the way to her throat. "Grace," she whispers. "'Darkly Smiling.'"

Leo kisses the forehead of their tiny baby boy. “Garcia,” he whispers. “‘On the Road Again.’”

When the sun finally arrives in April and it’s warm enough to take the babies outside, Jacie is not much smaller than she was before she delivered, her stomach still so distended, she barely fits into the loose dresses she’d worn when she was pregnant. Getting up three, four times each night to feed the twins, shaking Leo to rouse him to help, sometimes successfully but too often not, she tries to find the joy she’d felt seeing her son and daughter for the first time, but all happiness seems to have remained in the hospital in Fort Bragg. She cries while she nurses Grace. She cries while she burps Garcia. She cries while she rocks the one, then the other, to sleep.

Cathy makes a schedule so that every afternoon one of the men comes to help Jacie, which mostly means they carry the babies around in a double sling Gardner has fashioned while they do whatever they usually do, and then every evening one of the women arrives to assist with baths and bottles and washing clothes and diapers.

All spring, Leo blasts Jefferson Airplane’s *Volunteers* album from a record player in the music shed he and Tim built and Gardner then wired with electricity from a used generator he found at the Fort Bragg swap meet. Even from inside their cabin, Jacie can make out the lyrics from “The Farm,” a song with Jerry Garcia on guitar and Grace Slick doing vocals.

Leo sings along: “‘Yes it’s good livin’ on the farm.’” An unlit joint hangs like a cigarette from between his lips. He dances across the cabin, holding a baby in each arm. “‘Ah so good livin’ on the farm.’”

Jacie watches the babies nuzzle into Leo’s chest. She takes the boiling water with which she’s sterilizing bottles off the wood-burning stove and climbs back into bed. The sheets stink from sweat and baby throw-up and what smells like shit. She hates the song. She hates Jerry Garcia. She hates Grace Slick. She hates living on the farm.

In August, Kitty, a skinny girl with stringy blonde hair and a hollow between her bottom ribs and the snap of her cutoff jean shorts, arrives at Riva Krik carrying a huge backpack with a pup tent and sleeping bag strapped to the top. She tells Peter she's nineteen and taking a break before she moves to San Francisco to join a dance company, but Goddess, who considers everything on what is her land to be her business, goes through Kitty's tent one morning while Kitty is on Karma Kookhouse duty. "Seventeen," she announces to Peter.

Peter tokes on his pipe. "How do you know?"

"Delaware driver's license. Ninety-two dollars in her wallet and a teddy bear inside her sleeping bag."

Peter raises his eyebrows.

"That ridiculous tent is probably from her kid brother's Boy Scout camp."

"And?"

"Runaway," Goddess proclaims.

Kitty's second week at Riva Krik, Leo volunteers to play his bongos while she does her daily hour-long dancer's stretches. The exercises begin with Kitty flat on her back and a leg stretched upward so her knee grazes her nose, and they end with her legs flipped over her head and her knees hugging her ears.

The babies are now six months old and eating cereal and mashed fruits and vegetables. After Jacie gives them breakfast, she takes them outside, Grace in an outward-facing carrier strapped over Jacie's still-huge belly, Garcia in her arms. Kitty is arching her spine in a yoga cat-cow while Leo sways and drums behind her. She undulates, her tiny stomach lowering as she offers up her tiny butt.

Jacie can smell her own acrid breath. A wet stink spreads from her armpits to between her heavy breasts. She imagines Leo's tongue poking into Kitty's tight vagina and Kitty moaning the way she does when she straddles her legs and leans forward, resting her forehead on the ground.

A week later, there's a night Leo tells Jacie that he's going to the music shed to listen to records and play his drums. When Jacie wakes at three and finds herself still alone in the bed, she leaves the babies asleep in the cribs Tim helped Leo build and runs to the field where Kitty's pup tent is set up, not far from the creek.

Jacie pounds with her fists on the canvas opening, zipped closed from the inside. She can hear Kitty's voice: "What is it? What's happening?" And then Leo's: "Shhh, just be quiet."

Jacie tries to rip open the zipper, but succeeds only in dislodging one of the tent pegs. Still screaming, "Leo, cheater," she throws herself face-first into the creek.

Susan and Tim take the babies into their cabin while Leo and Gardner lift Jacie from the creek and Goddess and Peter watch.

Goddess points at Kitty, her naked body wrapped in the Mexican blanket she lays on the ground each morning while she does her stretching exercises. "The cops could arrest you," Goddess tells Peter, "for harboring a minor."

Gardner takes off his shirt and drapes it over Jacie's wet shoulders. Her nose and chin are scraped and she's no longer crying, just staring straight ahead.

Leo cups Jacie's elbow. He walks her across the field to the music shed. He takes a Jefferson Airplane album from a milk crate, places the needle on the track where Slick covers Crosby's "Triad."

Holding Jacie's hands in his, Leo accompanies Slick: "'I don't really see why we can't go on as three. We love each other—it's plain to see.'"

She stares at him. So much noise is in her head, she can't hear her own thoughts.

Leo stops singing. He lifts the needle from the record and looks squarely at her. "Jacie, I'm twenty-two. I'd never been with anyone except you."

She sees herself slitting her throat. Her blood running onto the ground like a fat pig's at slaughter.

She grabs the record from the turntable and stomps on it.

Peter calls a Riva Krik meeting to address "the tensions brewing now in our tribe."

"In our family," he adds.

Goddess leads Jacie to the middle of the circle, then beckons for Leo and Kitty to follow. Drawing a vial of ayurvedic scent from inside the folds of her skirt, Goddess places a drop on each of their foreheads and massages the scent into their temples. Kitty lasciviously lifts and lowers her shoulders. She points her toes and touches her nose to her knees, her tiny tank top riding up her narrow rib cage.

Jacie follows Leo's eyes as they lock on the band of tight skin between the bottom of Kitty's top and the top of her jeans. Jacie can feel the rolls of fat on her own middle, can hear her babies crying in Gardner and Helen's cabin, where ten-year-old Alda is watching them.

Peter addresses Kitty. "Your kundalini is flowing." He means every male on the commune and a few of the females too want to fuck her, though only Leo has actually done so. "But we are in a cycle of tending to babies and plants. We are not good soil for you," by which he means someone is going to get seriously hurt if they don't get her out of there. Kitty, he announces, will be given a hundred dollars and driven to Pippy's women's collective, where she can stay while she figures out where to go next.

How it happens that Leo ends up driving Kitty in the VW with the two car seats in back, not to Pippy's women's land but to the town of Mendocino, where he checks into an inn at the edge of town, no one will be able to say. Only that he does not return that night.

In the morning, Jacie leaves the babies with Susan. Knowing Leo and what he would do, she hitchhikes to Mendocino, where she goes to every bed-and-breakfast and every inn until she sees the VW. She finds Leo and Kitty in a room they've not even bothered to lock, fucking in an armchair with Kitty's legs looped over Leo's shoulders at the precise moment Jacie arrives.

From under her shirt, Jacie takes a penknife she uses to open paint cans. She lunges at Kitty, driving the knife into her child-size thigh. Jacie stares at the extraordinary amount of blood that sluices down Kitty's leg—thankfully lifted, or Kitty, whose screams bring the innkeeper, might have gone into shock—then bolts out the door.

In the evening, the sheriff and his deputy follow Leo, who has spent the afternoon in the Fort Bragg emergency room with Kitty, back to Riva Krik. The sheriff blasts his siren as they bump down the rutted road. "The little scrape—Skinny Boy says it happened while he and Skinny Girl were *quote* playing around," the sheriff tells Peter, who meets him at the patrol car. "Required thirteen stitches. Skinny Girl says she's nineteen and was living here this past month, but I'm betting sixteen—and if I'm right, I hope you got yourself a good lawyer."

Peter asks if they have a warrant, at which point the sheriff, who's muttering, "Stinking, dirty hippies," under his breath, lets his jacket fall open to expose that what he has is a gun.

The sheriff and the deputy walk the property, making a list of everyone who lives on it. "Who did the plumbing?" the sheriff asks when he sees the pipe running from the well to the Karma Kookhouse and Shiva Spa.

"Licensed plumber," Peter says.

"Electric?"

"Licensed electrician."

"You filed with the county."

"In duplicate."

"Bullshit," the sheriff says.

"Bullshit you got a warrant."

When the sheriff and his deputy get to Leo and Jacie's cabin, the deputy leans down to look at the babies.

"How old are they?" he asks.

"They just turned seven months," Jacie says.

"Twins?" the sheriff asks.

"Yeah," Leo says.

"Yes, sir," Jacie adds. She sees the sheriff sizing up the babies and her: the crust on the edge of Grace's nose, Garcia's stained onesie, the raw scrape on her chin from when she threw herself into the creek two nights ago.

"Listen up, Mama. You listen good to me. I got my eyes on you now. I'm giving you and Skinny Boy a break, and you should be kissing my ass for that. Next time I see these babies, they better be looking like a Gerber ad. Otherwise, you're going to be explaining what's going on here to Child Protective Services."

Leo cries. He doesn't want to lose the babies, doesn't want his children growing up as he did without a mother. He tells Jacie that he loves her. Kitty was nothing, just a slutty runaway girl. It was the drugs. He's going clean again. He'll tell Peter that he can't share pipes anymore. He and Jacie have sex for the first time since the babies were born. It's been so long, she bellows when she comes and then sobs afterward.

At the commune's sunrise meeting, Leo repeats in front of everyone what he's told Jacie. He chops wood to prepare for the coming cold weather. He caulks the cracks in the cabin the way Tim has shown him. He brings all their sheets and blankets to a laundromat in town. He changes diapers. He washes diapers.

The babies pull themselves up. Grace takes a step with Jacie holding both of her arms. Garcia claps his hands in time with the beat of his father's bongos.

They let the babies sleep in the bed with them. Leo spoons one and Jacie spoons the other. They wait for the babies to fall asleep, then spread a blanket on the floor to make love.

In January, at eleven months, Garcia and then Grace come down with bad colds. The colds turn into coughs so violent they throw up their food and cannot sleep. The babies get rashes on their faces. Then they get fevers. No one has a medical thermometer, but Susan says she can tell their fevers are high.

Leo and Jacie bring the twins to the emergency room. The pediatrician on call diagnoses Grace with a bronchial infection and Garcia with pneumonia. They both have severe diaper rash and are dehydrated. Leo holds Jacie while she weeps. With the freezing weather, she hasn't washed her hair in a week. It hangs around her face in greasy clumps.

The babies are admitted. A woman from Child Protective

Services arrives. She has white hair shorn like a sheep's and a clipboard with carbon-copy papers. A full minute passes each time she reaches the bottom of a page and prepares to move to the next one.

Jacie answers each question "Yes, ma'am" or "No, ma'am."

When the forms are completed, the woman says she will do a home visit once the babies are released from the hospital. Then she will write her report.

"What happens after that?" Leo is scared but his fear sounds like belligerence.

"That, young man, depends on the report."

After four nights in the hospital, the twins are released. Jacie is given an appointment card with the name of the woman from Child Protective Services who will come the following Monday at nine.

Sunday night, Jacie tells Leo she has a headache. Cathy gives him a bottle of aspirin to bring to her. Leo puts the babies to sleep in theirs cribs rather than in the bed where Jacie lies with a pillow over her eyes. He sterilizes bottles, sweeps the cabin, scrubs the diaper pail, lays out fresh clothing for Grace and Garcia for the morning.

Leo wakes at minutes past midnight. There's an awful smell. He bolts from the bed, thinking it's one of the babies. Then he sees Jacie facedown on the floor. She's moaning, her head in a pool of yellow vomit. Next to her is the bottle of aspirin, turned on its side and empty.

Tim and Gardner carry Jacie to the truck. They drive her to the Fort Bragg ER, where the admitting nurse recognizes her as the mother of the twins there last week and the attending doctor orders her stomach pumped. Cathy cleans the cabin floor and Susan and Goddess help Leo dress and feed the babies and then buckle them into the car seats in the back of Leo's VW.

At five in the morning, Leo rings the bell of his father's house, a car seat with a sleeping baby in each hand.

Randall comes to the door in his green tartan bathrobe. He is sixty-one and it is the first time he has laid eyes on his grandchildren.

Leo nods at his father, who steps aside. Setting the car seats on the foyer floor, away from the open door, Leo returns to the VW to get the duffel packed with the babies' clothing, diapers, formula, and bottles. He carries the bag up the stairs to his father's front door and puts it between the two sleeping babies.

"This is Grace," he says, pointing to the car seat on the left. "And this is Garcia."

When Leo goes back to his car, Randall assumes it is to get something else. He bends to examine the babies. Their long dark lashes. Their bow-shaped mouths. The one Leo said is Grace smiles in her sleep. Garcia fingers the straps of his car seat.

A car ignition turns over. By the time Randall stands to look outside, the VW is gone.

# 13

# Prudence

## Summer 1938–1972

The day after Robert Burlingham's death, Carlton announced that he'd rebooked the tickets for their European trip, their late honeymoon on which they were to have departed in six days, for November. "Of course," he informed Prudence, "you would not be able to go now."

She felt foiled: If she said that she wanted nothing more than to sail in six days, to not be here in their bedroom with the view when she opened the draperies of the sidewalk where she'd seen Robert's blue-and-white pajamas soaked with blood, Carlton would view her as either callous or at risk of a nervous collapse.

"My primary concern is about you. But there is CCB too. I could not in good conscience leave him so soon. If Louie were still alive, it would be another matter, but without her . . ."

Carlton sucked in his cheeks: his way, Prudence had learned, of putting a brake on himself. "Dorothy, CCB says, does not intend to travel from London for Robert's funeral. The Freuds will arrive next week from Paris, and she feels that she must stay with Professor Freud's sister-in-law until they do."

Was Carlton aware, she wondered, of what she recalled having heard from Mr. Feeney: that Dorothy had not come back for her father's funeral either? Would that information make Carlton more or less damning of Dorothy, whose loyalties he condemned as stronger to Miss Anna Freud than to her husband? To Professor Freud than to her father-in-law.

Prudence chastised herself—how small, how selfish—that her thoughts went to the trunk of dresses she and Louise had so carefully packed. To the evening strolls she'd envisioned on the promenade in Stresa overlooking Lago Maggiore. With Italy striking Carlton as morally questionable, Stresa was the only place in that country he'd consented to their visiting—and then only at the fussy Grand Hotel des Iles, more Austrian than Italian in sensibility, where he'd stayed as a child with his parents, his suppers taken in the suite he'd shared with his governess since children were not permitted after six in the dining room. From Stresa, Prudence hoped they would be able to visit the Isola Madre, where, Ella had once told her, a ramshackle palace with a puppet theater and trompe l'oeil frescoes was surrounded (like Laurelton Hall, Prudence had thought) by gardens with citrus trees, wisteria, and peacocks. There, on the magical Mother Island, Carlton, always so dutiful, so maddeningly proper, might, Prudence fantasized, be infected by its *Midsummer Night's Dream* spirit. Might, for just a day, or even an hour, let go of his Nordic ideals. Be liberated from his terrifying goodness. Back at the hotel, he might—it was possible, was it not?—be overcome with an animal passion and (she felt ashamed even imagining it) take her, not in the polite and cautious way of their usual relations. And from this, there might be conceived a child he would want.

Carlton spent the summer mastering the Bach three-part inventions. Two hours, every evening in the music room, until she thought she would go mad hearing those mathematical variations. She wanted Chopin, she wanted Debussy. She wanted the Arno, the Tiber, the Seine. She wanted a baby.

In August, Prudence and Carlton accompanied his parents for a week's stay at the Calverton Hotel in Virginia Beach. Their bathroom had a tap for ice water piped from a tank on the roof, and a tub with the option of salt water. Every evening, an orchestra played on the veranda. Prudence knew that Carlton hoped that the amenities and amusements of the hotel would be therapeutic for her. Not wanting to disappoint him or draw attention to herself, she made an effort to appear cheerful during the days spent in the family's cabana on the beach and to then dress festively for the five-course dinners.

At night, she would wait to hear Carlton's light snoring, for him to turn away from her toward the wall. Quietly, she would move onto their balcony overlooking the Atlantic, the whitecaps shimmering under the sliver of moon and then disappearing with the cover of the ghostly night clouds. Here in Virginia, with the servers in the dining room all white men, the Negro staff kept to the kitchen and the laundry, it sank in that Carlton's family were Southerners. His grandparents had owned plantations, grown cotton. Had slaves. She, now a Theet too, was sleeping on a bed with satin sheets in a room with iced water from a tap on account of wealth made from humans sold like horses, like scythes, like bushels of peas.

The week before the November departure, CCB asked Carlton if he would bring papers to Dorothy in Hampstead, on the outskirts of London, to be signed. "The ship lands in Southampton. It will mean adding an overnight in London before we make the crossing to France," Carlton announced, refusing out of allegiance to CCB to acknowledge the annoyance Prudence knew he felt at the change in their itinerary. She kept her face impassive, not wanting to reveal the excitement she felt about visiting Dorothy, whom she'd thought about so often but not seen since the afternoon in the Tiffany mansion on Seventy-second Street when, with her father still alive, she could not have been more than twelve.

"Dorothy is sharing an apartment with her daughter Tinky, who has apparently dropped out of Bennington. Her son Bob and his new wife have taken the flat above them, and the Freuds live down the block." Carlton cracked his knuckles. "It's their own little social experiment."

The following evening, they dined with CCB at his house. During the day, the news of Kristallnacht had arrived. CCB was so overwhelmed with alarm about how close Dorothy and his grandchildren, having only left Vienna a few months before, had been to danger, Prudence was nearly brought to tears herself—tears for

CCB, who had endured so much with the deaths of his wife and his son, and now this relentless worry about his daughter-in-law and grandchildren.

When CCB excused himself midway through the meal, Carlton requested a telephone from the serving girl so he could call Dr. Hinley, who arrived with a tranquilizer that would help CCB to sleep. Over the next day, Prudence feared that Carlton would again cancel their trip, but after CCB's second night of rest aided by another dose of the tranquilizer, CCB was sufficiently stable in Carlton's judgment for them to depart.

They landed in Southampton on a Monday afternoon and were in London by teatime with the plan, organized by Carlton in an exchange of telegrams with Dorothy Burlingham, of visiting her the following morning. She would send a note to their hotel with precise directions.

Arriving at their hotel, they were handed an envelope. To Carlton's surprise, it was not from Dorothy but from Miss Freud.

> *Dear Mr. and Mrs. Theet:*
>
> *I would be most appreciative if you would pay me a brief visit prior to your meeting with Mrs. Burlingham. My parents and I are installed at Twenty Maresfield Gardens in Hampstead, a few houses away from Mrs. Burlingham, who is at Number Two. Perhaps you could arrive at ten o'clock in the morning.*
>
> *Yours sincerely,*
>
> *Annafreud*

Carlton furrowed his brow. Prudence knew that he did not like being asked now for a second time to alter his plans, all the more so with the request coming from Miss Freud. But little could be done that would not create a scene, which would be abhorrent to him.

She would have liked to walk somewhere for dinner, to take a stroll in this city where she'd never before been, but Carlton had reserved them a table at the hotel's restaurant. Afterward, she sat in the lobby while he arranged with the concierge a taxicab for 9:15 a.m. sharp to bring them to Hampstead. Halfway across the lobby, she could hear the word *sharp*.

Back in their room, she left the curtains slightly parted so she could look out from the bed, past Carlton, at the nearby Westminster Abbey. The moon hung low and white between the spires, and she remembered how her mother, the year Randall left, had been swept up in the marriage of Prince Albert to Lady Elizabeth at this very place. Every evening, her mother would await Prudence's father's return home with the evening paper so she could read the latest news about a girl who'd at first refused the marriage proposal of a prince because she feared being no longer able to speak her mind, and who'd then on her wedding day brought thousands of women, including Prudence's mother, to tears when she'd laid her wedding bouquet on the Grave of the Unknown Warrior as tribute to her brother who'd died in the Great War.

Prudence turned from Carlton and the abbey and closed her eyes.

At No. 20 Maresfield Gardens, they were greeted by a plump woman in a white apron, Mrs. Fichtl, the Freuds' housekeeper, who had accompanied the Freuds from Vienna. Gesturing, Mrs. Fichtl indicated that Prudence and Carlton were to follow her into a small reception room.

Miss Freud had a disregard for feminine style that Prudence knew made Carlton uncomfortable and then sometimes (imperceptible to others but perceptible to Prudence) hostile, as though these choices were an affront to civilized conventions. "I apologize for the chill," Miss Freud said in her heavily accented English. "My father is seeing a patient in his consultation room, on the other side of the hallway, and even in this weather, he keeps the French doors ajar. The cool air soothes his sinuses, so inflamed from his jaw cancer. No matter what I do, the chill seeps in here."

Prudence's stomach clenched. How could one sentence include so many words—*sinuses, inflamed, cancer*—that Carlton would view as unacceptable for polite conversation?

Miss Freud smiled, revealing her slightly browned, slightly crooked small teeth. She shifted her gaze to Carlton. "But perhaps you would be so kind as to leave your wife for a little talk with me? I am sure you have many things to discuss with Mrs. Burlingham."

Without waiting for Carlton's assent, Miss Freud spoke in German to Mrs. Fichtl, and to Prudence's astonishment—she'd never seen anyone order Carlton to do anything—he was ushered out of the room by the housekeeper, who, Miss Freud announced, would indicate to him the direction on the lane to Mrs. Burlingham's house.

"Come along, Mrs. Theet, we will have our conversation upstairs in my consultation room, where it will be warmer."

Later, Prudence would read that the garden onto which the French doors in Professor Freud's office opened had beautiful flowers and high trees. That day, however, she saw neither the professor's office nor the professor himself, though she did hear noises that sounded like a nose blowing and then a phlegmy cough as she followed Miss Freud up the broad staircase and past the cushioned window seat on the landing to her own consultation room.

Prudence's eyes went immediately to the divan, with pillows at the head and a blanket folded at the foot. She'd heard that patients in psychoanalysis lay on a couch. Is this where Miss Freud's patients lay? The children too?

Miss Freud closed the door. She motioned for Prudence to take an armchair across from the divan. Miss Freud sat opposite, in a chair adjacent to the head of the divan, and took her knitting from a basket on a side table.

She untangled her yarn before she spoke. "I understand, Mrs. Theet"—Miss Freud looked up from her lap—"that you witnessed Mr. Burlingham's suicide. Perhaps you could tell me what happened that morning."

Prudence watched the now-moving knitting needles. She'd not talked about that morning with anyone save the detective Carlton had brought to interview her, but, to her surprise, the thought of doing so was not entirely objectionable. Where, though, to start? With her fear that morning of Carlton's reaching for her when he woke and the nausea at the thought of his coitus interruptus? With the doctor in White Plains? With Carlton's pronouncement that he could never have children?

"I'd had trouble sleeping and went out for some fresh air."

She paused. Could she really continue?

"As I turned the corner onto Park Avenue, I saw a figure at a window in the building across the street. It disappeared for a moment, then reappeared, and . . ."

Prudence's throat and nose filled. "There was a horrid sound."

She closed her eyes to keep herself from crying out.

"Horrid."

Miss Freud made a noise like a reverberating *m*.

"I knew it was Robert. I was terrified of seeing him so broken and bloodied. Embarrassed that I'd snuck outside and witnessed it."

"Why were you embarrassed?"

She'd not told the detective how she'd crept like a criminal from the bedroom, exiting through the delivery entrance with a cape over her shoulders and the hood covering her untended hair.

"I felt guilty. I know it doesn't make sense. I'd never even met Robert—only caught a glimpse of him once, when we were at dinner at his father's house. He stormed past, in some kind of state, just as we arrived for cocktails, which upset his mother since she liked to think of Robert and Carlton as cousins of a sort and that she'd invited us so they could see each other."

"Was it the body that embarrassed you?"

"But it's not as though I'd not seen a dead body before. When my father died, there was a wake at our house with an open casket. And I was with my mother when she died, three years ago."

"Just you?"

"I have a brother, but I haven't heard from him in a very long time."

With the mention of Randall, her thoughts shifted to Laurelton Hall. Was Miss Freud aware that Dorothy had known Prudence's father from when he'd worked there?

Of course, she was aware. There was nothing about Dorothy, Prudence imagined, of which Miss Freud was not aware.

Without knowing Prudence's connection to Laurelton Hall, Harriet had once mentioned that her husband, Akron, after reading about Tiffany's reception for 150 men of genius, had fallen into a jealous rage at not having been included. "As though the two poems he'd published merited him a spot. A few months before, seven poets, Yeats and Pound among them, had gathered on someone's estate in England to eat a roasted peacock. Akron must have thought that eating a peacock would unleash his own talents." Harriet had snorted. "Of course that table too was solely men. Well, what woman would eat a peacock? I've heard that the meat is disgusting."

Anna Freud rested her knitting in her lap. "You look as though you are recalling something."

"One of the evenings Mr. Tiffany held at Laurelton Hall. Miss Tiffany, Mrs. Burlingham, I mean, was part of the entertainment."

"Perhaps you are thinking about the event Tiffany called the Peacock Feast. It took place in 1914, and Mrs. Burlingham was twenty-two then. But you are right, she was still Miss Tiffany. She did not marry until that fall. It was humiliating for Dorothy and her sisters: marched barefoot like slave girls before their father's male guests."

"It is all a bit muddled in my mind. I do, though, remember watching the procession from behind a wall next to the terrace."

"How old were you?"

"I was two."

"And you were alone?"

Where was her father? Standing guard, perhaps, over the pots of orchids in the fountain courtyard. And her mother? Assigned, perhaps, for the evening to help in the kitchen.

Was Randall with her? Randall would have been five. Instructed, perhaps, to watch her, to keep the two of them out of sight.

But she did not recall Randall. What she recalled was another child, a boy, young, small like herself, clutching a peacock feather.

And then, suddenly, like a wave rushing over her head, she did not want to be there, in Miss Freud's consultation room. She wanted to leave. Immediately.

"Mr. Burlingham asked us to speak with his daughter-in-law. We brought some papers for her to sign."

How absurd she must sound. Miss Freud knew the reason for their visit. "I'm very sorry, but my husband will be expecting me."

Dorothy rose, smiling broadly, when Prudence entered the sitting room. "Why, look at you! Last time I saw you, you were only a girl." She took Prudence's hands between her own. "I am so glad to see you again. And thank you for taking time from your honeymoon to serve as my courier."

Dorothy motioned to the third chair drawn up to the small table, where Carlton was seated with his tea. His face was impassive, but Prudence felt certain that he was silently fuming that her visit with Anna Freud had extended their stay in Hampstead beyond the hour he'd budgeted.

"Do you take milk or cream or sugar?"

"Cream only, please."

"As I told your husband, I am delighted to finally meet him. My father-in-law is so very fond of him. He thinks of him as a son. And to learn that he has married the daughter of Eddie! As I wrote you after your father died, he was very dear to me."

Not wanting to see in Carlton's face the discomfort Prudence was certain he felt with the allusion to her father's servitude, she avoided his eyes. *And so?* she wanted to say. Loudly say. *Is there something disgraceful about my parents having been employed as a gardener and a maid? It's not as though my father was a convict and my mother a prostitute.*

She felt astonished by her thoughts; it seemed that the time she'd spent in Miss Freud's consultation room had released a wild woman from inside her. A wild woman who yelled, *It's me. Me who is disgraceful: locked in your prison of manners. It's you. You who treats me like a prostitute. The receptacle of your sexual relations, but never the mother of your child.*

"I think I wrote you about this?" Dorothy continued. "About the second summer when I came back from boarding school? I'd been so homesick at St. Timothy's, I honestly thought I might die from it. Of course, I'd forgotten that I'd been the one who'd begged to go. My father had refused at first, relenting only when my older sisters petitioned him on my behalf."

Dorothy seemed bemused by her younger self. "After all I'd suffered that year, I couldn't believe that he was away in Europe when

I arrived home. I spent an entire afternoon trailing behind your poor father while he weeded the kitchen garden, venting my anger about my father having gone off for three months with Clara Driscoll, who ran his Queens factory, and Dr. Parker McIlhiney, his chemist. Leaving me behind."

Dorothy sipped her tea. "Years later, your father witnessed what was my one act of rebellion before I married. It was the day before my father's Peacock Feast, and we were on the terrace practicing the pageant my father had choreographed. His companion, Patsy, was urging me to wear the peacock headdress, but I refused. My sister Julia had worn it at my father's Egyptian Fete the year before, and she'd told Comfort and me how vile it was, with the red eye looking down at her and the beak scratching her forehead and the oily feathers leaving a terrible smell in her hair. I remember your father winking at me and thinking he understood how I felt."

Dorothy smiled. "I didn't know your mother, I'm afraid I can't even recall her name, but I can still see her in my mind's eye . . ."

Could she tell Dorothy that her mother's name was Bridget, that she'd worked with Clara Driscoll, had been Clara's favorite girl? That Clara had taught her mother to ride a bicycle?

"Your mother was so little and so very, very pregnant. 'Mark my words,' my sister Comfort said. 'She is having twins.' Comfort crowed when she was right."

Prudence felt a surge of disappointment that, in fact, Dorothy did not remember her mother. Had confused her with one of the other redheaded maids. She knew Carlton would dislike her correcting Dorothy, but she felt that she must. "My mother *was* tiny. But she never had twins. There was just my older brother, then me."

Dorothy raised her eyebrows. She looked quizzically at Prudence.

Prudence did not want to see the censure she imagined on Carlton's face, but when she glanced at him, he seemed not to have been listening. Instead, he was looking pointedly at his watch, which he now tapped. She would not, no, she would not allow him to bully her into leaving. For what reason? So they could arrive at the British Museum at the precise hour he'd planned for showing her the Magna Carta?

"I remember your wedding," Prudence said. "My father helped carry the flowers to the church, and I cried because I wanted to go with him. He put me on his shoulders so I could see your dress when you came back to the house."

"My father was so fussy about those flowers. For the luncheon, I requested simple bunches of lilacs, but my father insisted that the centerpieces be coordinated with the dishes and table linens." Dorothy sighed. "He was a perfectionist, and perfectionists can be despots. His aesthetic judgments were more important than any silly sentiments I might have."

Carlton was now jiggling his knees. *Stop*, Prudence wanted to say. *Listen. You, you are the same: your two-part inventions, your three-part inventions, your rare-book collections, your mountain peaks.*

"When did your family leave Laurelton Hall?"

"It was June of 1916." Prudence does not include the date, the sixteenth, the way her mother always had.

"That was the summer of my father's epic battle with the town of Oyster Bay about the beachfront." Dorothy turned toward Carlton, as though signaling that the conversation would now shift to the land of commerce, where he would find his bearings. "My father could not tolerate being crossed, and he felt that the town was crossing him, egged on, he was convinced, by Teddy Roosevelt, who hated my father for not sharing his progressive politics. All of us—my older sisters, Comfort, Julia, myself—were in sympathy with the town. Why *shouldn't* the people of Oyster Bay be able to swim at what had once been the public beach, but we were too cowed by my father to speak up. I felt ashamed for not saying what I thought, but I was too overwhelmed then between Bob, who was such a difficult baby, and Robert, who was having one of his breakdowns, to say my mind."

With the mention of Robert, Carlton lifted his chin, as though he was back on sentry duty. Dorothy continued, the conversation directed now, it seemed, at him. "In the past, CCB had always stepped in when Robert went into one of his manic or depressive states, but this time, he was himself in a depression. It was a terrible time: three generations—Robert's father, Robert, and our baby—all so unstable. My mother-in-law never liked me, but she did her best to help, though her focus, naturally, was on her husband. When CCB got better, by the end of the summer, he and Louie insisted that Robert and I move closer to them, to a building right across the street from the brownstone where they were living then."

Did Dorothy know that now Prudence and Carlton lived across from CCB? That it was because of this that Prudence had witnessed Robert's jump to his death?

"What a disaster that was. Once, while I was out, CCB could hear Bob crying all the way from the street, and he swooped in and fired the baby nurse. When I arrived home, the nurse was gone and CCB was sitting there with Bob. So very intrusive . . . But I was dependent on Louie and him for their help with Robert, who could get violent when he was in one of his states, and I didn't dare object. The following summer, my father gave me a small piece of land just west of Laurelton Hall, and I built a little cottage so I could have an escape from it all."

How had it never occurred to Prudence before, in those dinners with CCB criticizing Dorothy for abandoning Robert, for keeping him away from his own children, that Dorothy must have been scared of her husband? For a moment, Prudence felt infused too with fear—fear that Carlton, who'd never raised his voice at her, much less a hand, might strike her when they left.

Carlton stood.

"Now that I think of it," Dorothy continued, "that's when I first noticed that your parents were gone."

Whereas it seems to Prudence that she remembers nearly verbatim the half hour she spent with Anna Freud and the subsequent hour with Dorothy, the rest of the trip exists now only in snippets: the garlic langoustines speckled with parsley at the restaurant at the Hotel Negresco in Nice; the shade from the palm trees on Isola Madre (which had not affected Carlton in the way she'd fantasized); the lapping of the water as they walked a path along Lake Geneva while Carlton outlined Alfred's views on the various ascents to Mont

Blanc, snowcapped in the distance; the dust on her hands and neck as they trekked through the ruins of the Temple of Apollo in Corinth.

The following summer, Prudence heard from CCB that Dorothy was in New York for the birth of her first grandchild. Prudence sent an illustrated book of Hans Christian Andersen fairy tales for the baby, and although the gesture was genuine, she also secretly hoped it might prompt Dorothy to invite her to tea—which it did not. Shortly after, Prudence read in the newspaper about Sigmund Freud's death, in the same house where she had visited with Miss Freud, and Carlton told her that Dorothy, desperate to return for the funeral, had pled with CCB to help arrange her passage, which CCB was unable to do owing to the war. Prudence hopes that she wrote a condolence note to Miss Freud, but she cannot recall if she did, only that by the time she and Carlton left in August of 1940 for their second trip to the Calverton Hotel in Virginia Beach, Dorothy had succeeded in traveling back to London, where she took up residence, CCB reported, with Miss Freud.

Not long after the war, Carlton's parents died in short succession: his mother first, his father seven weeks later. With his inheritance in hand and his concern that it would distress his father were he to withdraw from active involvement in the business now moot, Carlton installed a cousin as CEO and devoted himself full-time to his projects.

To Prudence's relief, Carlton seemed to have relinquished the idea that she join him for his trip to Kilimanjaro, which he and Alfred climbed the following year. On their return, they began to plan their next ascent, Mount Kosciuszko in Australia. She tactfully begged off when Carlton urged her to accompany him on what would be a four-month journey: such a long time to leave the apartment unattended, she murmured. In truth, she looked forward to the times while Carlton was away. Unencumbered by meal planning and the social engagements that evaporated when he was gone, she could go every morning to classes at the Art Students League, at peace by then with what she viewed as her own mediocrity, but having turned a corner to finding the act of standing with paints in front of an easel gratifying no matter the results.

A year later, Carlton set out to climb Mount Aconcagua: the

highest peak in the western and southern hemispheres, but nowhere as difficult as McKinley, he informed her. Alfred had developed a bad knee that prevented his making the trip, so Carlton arranged to be accompanied by an Argentinean guide, who wrote that he advised they take the Ruta Falso Polacos, the False Polish Route. Carlton hoped to reach the summit on his fiftieth birthday.

Carlton must have designated Alfred as his emergency contact because it was Alfred who received the telegram sent by the guide from a small village in the Andes that there'd been an accident. Señor Theet had fallen during a rappel. There was no further information.

Alfred took the next flight to Santiago, dissuading Prudence from coming with him on account of his being able to travel more quickly to the base camp without a woman in tow. For the first few days, she sat morning to night with CCB, ninety-one but with his mind still entirely intact, while he arranged with the American ambassador in Argentina for a search of all hospitals within a hundred kilometers of Mount Aconcagua. Prudence was relieved when she could provide a piece of requested information, something useful, but then seized with fear when she was asked to gather Carlton's dental records.

Alfred remained in Argentina for nearly a month. With no international telephone service in the mountain villages, he sent news via a series of telegrams. Like stitching and unstitching a needlepoint, a picture would take shape only to unravel a few days later. At first, the other guides told Alfred they had never heard of the man who'd accompanied Carlton. Then, one admitted that Carlton's guide had fled, perhaps to Bolivia.

Not until Alfred's return did he tell Prudence what he'd learned shortly before he'd left from a Swiss climber, who'd been a week behind Carlton on an ascent. An American had fallen into a ravine, the Swiss climber had heard from the porter who'd transported his own gear. The fall had taken place not during a rappel but en route to the summit. The American's guide had been unable to rescue him.

"Do you believe this?" Prudence asked.

Alfred took her hands.

"Please. Tell me. I need to hear the truth."

"I doubt that anyone will find a body, so we will never have proof." Alfred looked away. "But I do. I believe this is what happened."

A month later, Elaine gingerly asked if Prudence thought perhaps Carlton might have chosen to disappear. "He was about to turn fifty, you read stories sometimes about how that happens . . ."

Prudence burst out laughing. It was the first time she'd laughed since she'd received the news about Carlton. "I'm sorry. It's just that it's impossible to imagine Carlton doing something so impetuous. Honestly, I'd be happy to learn that he'd fallen in love with an Argentinean girl and was now living in a mountain village." She didn't add, with a houseful of babies to come.

Harriet took Prudence to lunch. "I won't take no for an answer. We're drowning in work and I need you. I'll double your salary and you can have the new girl as an assistant." Prudence had no financial necessity to return to her job, but she reminded herself that she had enjoyed her work before her marriage and been disappointed when Carlton had insisted that she give it up. And working would give her reason to be out of the apartment where, without Carlton, she felt more uncomfortable than ever rattling around while Louise and Mrs. Meechin, neither of whom she felt able to let go, washed her lingerie, made her oatmeal, cleaned her bathroom.

It was the heyday of the International Style in furniture, and Prudence found that she had an instinct for integrating a few of these pieces into otherwise traditional rooms. She disliked anything in plastic, but she would use the Saarinen Womb chairs and ottomans in a soft bouclé, the Mies van der Rohe Barcelona chairs in ivory cowhide, and the Prouvé EM tables in black metal and oak veneer. Placed alongside her clients' English sofas and Empire sideboards, often inherited pieces that it would have felt decadent to discard, the rooms became young and fresh without losing the personal quality that makes a home rather than, no matter how tasteful, generic lodgings.

Within a year, Prudence was in as much demand as Harriet.

For her clients, she and Harriet would agree in advance on the contractual arrangements, which Harriet would then present in a meeting they would both attend. Having always viewed Harriet as a fearless maverick, Prudence was surprised when time and again Harriet, faced with the client, would alter what they'd previously agreed upon to be more palatable. The change struck Prudence as a betrayal and fundamentally an act of weakness. If afterward she would delicately note it, Harriet would offer a vague explanation or even deny the terms on which she and Prudence had previously agreed.

At first, Prudence saw red when this would happen. Lying was as inconceivable to her as walking into a shop and taking an item without paying. In response, Prudence took to documenting the agreements she and Harriet made in memorandums. Before they would meet with the client, Prudence would give Harriet a copy: "Just a little reminder," she would say, "of what we discussed."

Three years after Prudence returned to work, Harriet received her largest commission ever: to decorate a car manufacturer's newly built Detroit mansion fashioned after a Burgundy château. Dismissing Prudence's reservations—the client's wife wanted only eighteenth-century furnishings, which Prudence found overly ornate, the colors insipid—Harriet assigned her as the lead decorator: "You'll be excellent. Just stay clear of anything Bauhaus."

The job, it turned out, included babysitting the car magnate's wife, Claire, thirteen years younger than he but no longer very young and, since their daughter's birth six years before, addicted to Miltown, "mother's little helper"—a helper, in Claire's case, on top of the governess, housekeeper, lady's maid, cook, gardener, and chauffeur. In his private negotiations with Harriet, the client arranged that his wife, accompanied by her maid, would join Prudence in early January on an extended shopping trip to Paris and the south of France, presumably to acquire furnishings and fabrics, but in truth, Harriet surmised, an opportunity for the husband to pursue an affair with a Chicago cabaret singer.

During a week in Paris, Prudence guided Claire through the

purchase of twenty-four Louis Quinze chairs, three hundred yards of Scalamandré fabrics, and a small Jacques-Louis David oil. By the time they reached L'Isle-sur-la-Sorgue, a town renowned for its Provençal antiques, Prudence felt like someone sick from too much goose-liver pâté.

In the middle of their second night in L'Isle-sur-la-Sorgue, Claire's maid banged on Prudence's door, screaming, "Mrs. Claire, Mrs. Claire is dying."

Mrs. Claire, it appeared, had swallowed the entire bottle of her Miltown after the phone conversation with her husband she'd had from the telephone cabinet in the lobby. Prudence raced to the front desk, where the night clerk summoned a Docteur Jean-Christophe Lemier, a slender man with long eyelashes and elegant wrists who spoke excellent English, heritage of the two years he'd worked at a clinic in Manchester after the war. Docteur Lemier administered an emetic to void the contents of Claire's stomach. Two days later, Claire and her maid returned to Detroit, from where, Harriet reported, the Chicago cabaret singer had hightailed it, leaving Prudence to select a dozen rooms' worth of bedsteads and armoires.

The morning after Claire's departure, Prudence received a note from Docteur Lemier. Would she grant him the pleasure of dining with him this evening? If so, he would call on her at twenty o'clock.

For the prior two days, Prudence had eaten alone in the hotel dining room. She'd never sat before on her own in a restaurant other than a coffee shop, and although she'd felt self-conscious (both nights, there'd been a solo gentleman at a corner table who stared at her intermittently), she'd enjoyed the solitude after ten days of Claire's inane chatter. Reluctantly, she said yes to the invitation. Perhaps the doctor wanted to tell her some information about Claire that it was Prudence's responsibility to hear.

They ate at a restaurant overlooking one of the town's canals. Although Docteur Lemier inquired about the unfortunate American woman, Prudence quickly realized that he'd not invited her to dine for this reason. With another man, she might have frozen in response, but the doctor was so comfortable with his intentions and so respectful and accepting of her reserve that she felt no pressure from him, only his interest in her, leaving her more at ease than she would have imagined had she done so in advance.

A widower with two young daughters—Nicole, nine, and Simone, just seven—Jean-Christophe, Prudence learned, was thirty-eight, three years her junior. Two years before, after his wife had died of a rare blood disorder, he'd returned from Paris, where he'd been a pediatric surgeon, to his parents' house in L'Isle-sur-la-Sorgue. Here, he'd joined his father in a general medical practice conducted from a glove factory that had been converted into a small clinic. Jean-Christophe's younger sister was the nurse; his older sister, who had three children, handled the books and was the receptionist. His mother watched the five grandchildren after school and with the help of her bonne prepared the midday meal at which the three families ate together every day.

Jean-Christophe was an amateur musician. As a child he'd studied piano and cello with a man who'd once played with the Paris Opera. In Paris, his daughters had been studying violin with a Japanese teacher. When they moved here, Jean-Christophe took over their lessons. On Sundays, he played in a quartet with his younger sister, a childhood classmate, and the music teacher from the local high school.

He inquired about Carlton: which composers he'd liked, the repertoire he'd played. "Musical tastes are so personal," he said. For him, Bach was too mannered, too cold. He loved Debussy and Gershwin and was working on "Clair de Lune" and *Rhapsody in Blue*, which he thought of as twin pieces born from a shared womb.

He talked about Anne, his wife: her beauty and intelligence, the exquisitely sensitive mother she'd been. Before she died, she'd made each daughter a photo album with pictures of herself—as a child with her parents, as a teenager skiing with friends, at her wedding—and then with each girl from her birth until Anne's last month, when she ceased allowing photographs, not wanting her daughters to have images of her with her eyes sunk into their sockets and her hair thinned to straw. She'd recorded birthday messages for both girls until they would be twenty-one, written letters to be read on their wedding days and at the births of their own first children.

At the end of the evening, Jean-Christophe invited Prudence to join his family the following day for their midday meal. The bonne served the four courses—the vegetable tartines prepared by Jean-Christophe's mother, the fillets, the vinaigrette salad, the platter of cheeses—while the adults discussed the day's *Le Figaro*, which the sisters found too conservative, and the children chattered about classmates and soccer matches. Sitting quietly, Prudence marveled at the generosity and acceptance the family seemed to extend to one another. Where were the sibling rivalries, the resentments between parents and children? None of it was evident in the family dining room, in the parlor where the adults sat afterward with their coffee, in the brush of Jean-Christophe's lips to his mother's forehead or the arm he draped across his father's shoulders as they walked back to their clinic.

It was the first time Prudence had ever fallen in love—in love not just with Jean-Christophe, but with his life. His days working side by side with his siblings under the tutelage of their father, who believed it his duty to treat everyone in the prefecture, to take as compensation a few crates of peaches or a butchered pig if that was all that could be afforded. Jean-Christophe's evenings supervising homework and music practices and baths, reading aloud to his daughters a chapter from *Le Comte de Monte-Cristo* or some Jacques Prévert poems, and then, before kissing them each good night, telling a story about their mother, the girls talking about her with such ease, it was as though she'd gone early to her bed down the hall.

Falling in love felt to Prudence closer to an illness than a blessing. An infection that left her unable to think of anything other than Jean-Christophe and his family. Save for her concerns about the terrible blushing that had thankfully abated with age, for most of her life she'd been free of the extremes of either vanity or insecurity, her assessment of her physique as good enough having remained unchanged since the first time she'd studied herself in the scratched mirror of the Hell's Kitchen apartment. Now, though, she worried that Jean-Christophe would find her physically distasteful, slight, insubstantial next to the photos she'd seen of the statuesque Anne with her halo of blonde hair. An old woman in comparison to Anne, who had been at her death eleven years younger than Prudence was now.

"You are so beautiful," he told her, "like a porcelain doll, but unbreakable." He'd known he could fall in love with her, he said, when he'd seen her that first night at the hotel: how she'd handled Claire, not shirking from what had to be done, helping to restrain her while he administered the emetic, then gently wiping the weeping Claire's nose.

He unpinned Prudence's hair and brushed it out in long strokes. He undressed her in full daylight, kissing her in places where Carlton had never put his mouth, places she'd always assumed would have revolted any man. Jean-Christophe inhaled her. He lavished her with his tongue. He adored her breasts, still firm from never having been suckled by a babe, the deep indent of her waist, the red tufts under her arms, her small buttocks. Carlton had been gentle in bed, but he'd never inquired about her pleasure, never seemed to want her save early mornings when he'd wake with an erection, or on the rare occasion when he'd come home from his club after a night that had entailed substantial spirits. With Jean-Christophe, she could sense his desire always there. Even when they were fully dressed, seated next to each other at his mother's table, she could feel it in the touch of his fingertips to her shoulder blade, in the pressure of his thigh against hers.

In the four years since Carlton's death, she had never inquired. Now, though, with Jean-Christophe a doctor, she asked him to tell her what would have happened to Carlton's body if, as she believed, it had been left in a ravine in Argentina.

"Do you really want to know?"

She nodded.

"The flesh and organs were probably eaten by vultures."

They were in her hotel room, his daughters asleep a kilometer away at his parents' home, where he would return before dawn to help them prepare for their school days.

"The bones decompose and become part of the soil. From the soil, wild grasses and flowers grow, and these are eaten by birds and small animals." Jean-Christophe studied her face. "*Ma belle*."

"Go on." It was as though he were telling her a fairy tale.

He smiled sadly. Had he thought about all of this with his beloved Anne?

"The birds are perhaps then eaten by larger animals, some of which are then hunted by local peoples."

"Who eat them?"

"Yes."

"So Carlton is now part of someone else, someone in Argentina?"

"It is not so linear, so concrete, but, yes, our bodies are matter, and matter does not disappear. It takes new forms."

"And our souls? Do you believe that they continue too?"

Jean-Christophe's parents attended mass every Sunday and he usually joined them, bringing his daughters. A wooden cross hung in the family dining room. One of his sisters had considered becoming a nun. But he and his father were doctors, their feet rooted in science. At lunch, the family discussed politics, the writings of Sartre, films.

"*Ma chère*, this is a longer discussion." He kissed her. It was late. "This we will talk about at another time."

He brought her to a special spot, a sheltered ledge overlooking the river, half an hour outside town. It was mid-February. Harriet had insisted Prudence take some time "to recuperate" after "the incident" with Claire, but it had been a month now and Prudence would need to return soon.

He'd prepared a picnic: cheeses, pâté, bread, canned pears from the tree in his mother's garden, a bottle of wine, a thermos of hot coffee. He made a fire, spread a blanket atop the ledge, draped another over her shoulders.

He told her that he wanted her to remain. To marry him. He gave her a book his daughters had drawn for her about two sisters who bring their pet chicken when they visit New York.

Her chest tightened when she read the book. She bit her tongue to keep from weeping at the drawings—the little red chicken, the

Statue of Liberty holding a bouquet of flowers. She could feel the yearning of Jean-Christophe's beautiful girls that she allow them to love her.

"I can't have children. I am too old."

"You will adopt my girls. You will be a mother to them."

"And there is my work."

"You could run an antique store in town. There are so many American and British dealers who come here . . ."

He stroked her arm. He cupped her elbow, pressed his nose into the hollow between her breasts.

She tried to picture herself living here. Walking Nicole and Simone to school past the waterwheels and the old men having their espressos in the cafés along the river, helping Jean-Christophe's mother and the bonne with the midday meal, listening to Jean-Christophe play his cello after his daughters were in bed. A *galette des rois* for Epiphany and ski trips to the Alps during the girls' winter holidays and for Easter chocolate fish and chocolate rabbits the children believed were brought back from the Vatican by the church's flying bells, "*Tu dois voir,*" Simone had enthusiastically explained, pointing to the bell tower in the twelfth-century church where the family had their own pew. Three weeks each summer at a seaside cottage in Corsica, where the girls ran wild like ponies and returned with their skin tawny and their hair streaked with gold. Chestnuts and truffles and La Toussaint in the fall, then *réveillon* with oysters and a roast goose and a hazelnut *bûche*, the children with their minds on the gifts to be brought by Père Noël.

And what was there on her balance sheet for New York? The Japanese prints at the Metropolitan Museum? The shoemaker Ella had introduced her to? Harriet, who would be disappointed. Elaine, who would miss her. CCB, now ninety-five? None of it added up to one squeeze of her hand by Nicole or a moment when Simone would rest her head on Prudence's shoulder.

She stared at the fire, now white embers. It was too fast, she told Jean-Christophe. She needed more time to get used to the idea. She couldn't, *snap,* leave New York, her work, reinvent herself as a French matron. As his wife.

He cried. He told her it was not too fast. She could leave New York. For God's sake, he'd left Paris. He told her it was not her work. He'd given up being a pediatric surgeon to join his father's practice.

"It is love. You are afraid of love."

She buried her face in Jean-Christophe's chest. With Carlton, she'd remained in her own cocoon. With Jean-Christophe, they'd be like the pictures she'd seen of twins before birth, curled together head to foot.

"You can bring the girls to New York for their spring holidays. They will have so much fun. You can stay with me. I have plenty of room. We'll take them to see the ballet and the Museum of Natural History and the Empire State Building. Then, I will come here for August. After that, we'll see. We'll see . . ."

At her apartment on Park Avenue, she'd been greeted by a blue aerogram.

> Ma chère *Prudence,*
>
> *My heart breaks writing you this, but we must say a permanent adieu. I have thought long and hard and looked into my soul—and I know that you will never move here, never be a mother to my motherless girls. I cannot subject them to the arrangement you have proposed. I am young, I have love in my heart. There is nothing,* rien, *that I want more than to have you as my wife and the mother of my girls, but if you are not able to do that, then I must have faith that I will find a woman who will.*
>
> *I ask you,* ma chère *Prudence, not to write to me. It is too painful to continue this way.*
>
> *In sadness, devotedly yours,*
>
> *Jean-Christophe*

Prudence climbed into her bed with the letter. She wept. She wept more than she had when she'd realized that Carlton was most certainly dead. At night, she pressed her nose to the window, looked down at the pavement where she'd seen Robert Burlingham in his blood-splotched blue-and-white-striped pajamas. This is where she must stay?

In the morning, she called Harriet. "I seem to have caught something on the airplane coming back." Harriet sent flowers. Elaine met the first shipment of the Louis Quinze chairs at the dock and arranged for their portage to the car manufacturer's Detroit château.

After two days of chamomile tea and Mrs. Meechin's chicken soup, Prudence ventured out. She walked north on Park Avenue. The cold crept in at her neck and wrists. Her eyes watered.

She hailed a taxi, not certain of her destination until she settled into the backseat. "The Cathedral of Saint John the Divine," she said, surprising herself at the choice. Because it had expunged the Tiffany chapel once installed there as too extravagant for communion with God? Because it was the most Gallic edifice in the city, a structure that might have been built in Rouen or Reims or Rennes? Because it was on the edge of Harlem and she was unlikely to see anyone she knew there?

She sat in the chilly, cavernous nave and listened to the organist practice. In his letter, Jean-Christophe wrote that he'd looked into his soul. He'd used the word *faith*. He must have faith that he'd find a woman to be the mother of his motherless girls. They'd never had the conversation about what he thought happened to the soul after death.

She had tea at the pastry shop across from the cathedral, ate an apricot hamantasch. A mother held her young son up to the counter so he could tell the waitress which cookie he wanted.

With Carlton, she'd deluded herself that he would change, come around to their having a child. Jean-Christophe loved his daughters too deeply to impose his delusions on them. She'd privately berated Harriet for being cowardly with clients about financial arrangements. But that was simply money. Jean-Christophe had seen that she was a coward of the heart.

She returned to work the following Monday. Harriet showed Prudence the thank-you letter with a five-thousand-dollar bonus check that had arrived from Claire's philanderer husband to the staff at Masters Design for "handling what was above and beyond your job." In particular, Prudence's virtues were extolled.

Harriet looked beseechingly at Prudence. "I could assign Elaine to complete the project."

"No, I'll finish it. But in the future—"

"Of course." Harriet cut off Prudence before she put into words that never again would she take on something she found so distasteful.

In truth, though, Prudence's reaction to Claire and the furnishing of her Detroit mansion was larger than the nausea she felt at the tawdriness of it all. The whole enterprise of decorating someone else's home struck her now as essentially flawed. For a home to have true beauty, it had to reflect the sensibility of its owners, be a repository for their history. It needed to tell the story of its occupants. Otherwise, it was no more than a showroom with perfect surfaces, vacant beneath. She'd heard laughable but it seemed to her actually sad stories about portraits of aristocratic-looking strangers hung in the dining rooms of men whose mothers had never owned more than two dresses to rotate on Sundays. Not that there weren't circumstances when she felt her work to be valuable: the items she'd selected for the pied-à-terre of a German couple whose philanthropic work for leper colonies had prevented them from yet visiting their New York apartment; the practical rooms she'd assembled for a widowed judge clueless about where to buy a tomato, much less a sofa, and color-blind to boot. With these jobs, Prudence had done her best to ghostwrite a personal expression of her client—but these were exceptional cases: individuals whose inner lives could not find expression inside four walls.

She considered resigning, but she disliked living solely off the income from Carlton's estate. With her commissions a fraction of what they'd once been now that she left the mansions and country homes to the other decorators, she sold the Park Avenue apartment and bought a smaller one at a third the price and half the size on West End Avenue. It was the smaller apartment that had provided both the excuse and the impetus to give Louise and Mrs. Meechin notice, accompanied by generous severance packages and her help finding new positions, which they both did in short order, leaving Prudence perplexed as to why she'd delayed the change for so long.

She'd moved to West End Avenue, where she's lived ever since, in March of 1957—the same month, she realized this morning when she took the article about the fire from her brother's wooden box, that Laurelton Hall had burned to the ground. Holding the newspaper clipping, she'd imagined Randall, scissors in hand, cutting it from the inky pages.

For a brief interlude she had seriously considered searching for Randall. It was 1972, the year she turned sixty, when all around her people were trying on new identities. That year, Elaine took her to a party where a barefoot man who had until recently been a banker played a dulcimer. Harriet's son, Stewart, Prudence's own age, extolled the EST seminars run by Werner Erhard, where Stewart claimed his entire personality had been ground to dust and he'd returned free of all hang-ups. Prudence had gone as far as calling a detective agency to make an appointment to discuss locating her brother, but she'd canceled before the meeting date.

Now she feels a moment of confusion. She wonders if perhaps she sent the newspaper clipping to Randall herself. After all, he had been born there too. Is that possible? That she is the one who cut it out? That she'd found his address? Sent Randall the very clipping Grace brought in the wooden box? The one on her library table now?

No, she did not. She's quite certain she did not.

# 14

# Grace & Garcia

After the faux-French-bistro lunch, Grace uses the excuse of errands to break off from the others, headed back to the hotel for the afternoon meetings. She enters Central Park from the south. Her grandfather had told her that on hot summer nights, he and his father would bring bedrolls and sleep in the park, the air cooler than in their fetid Hell's Kitchen rooms.

"Just you and your father?" Grace asked.

"My sister would beg to come, but my mother thought it unsafe for girls and women. Each time we returned, my father would say, 'Now, Bridget, Alice McDonnell was there with her husband and their five children, and you know that three of them is girls,' but my mother would have none of it."

His sister. Prudence. How strange, so many years later, to have a face to attach to her grandfather's story—a face, though, now of a very old woman, not a girl.

On occasion, her grandfather had told her, he would escort his sister across the park to the Tiffany mansion, their mother having strictly forbade her from crossing on her own. The house, as her grandfather described it, looked like a castle, with an iron portcullis and soaring turrets. An ominous castle, as though it housed a sorcerer who might dabble in dark magic.

Crossing now, west to east as her grandfather and Prudence would have done, it occurs to Grace that it's easier to imagine her grandfather's early years than her own. Her one visit to her mother, a day trip to Houston, shone little light on the eleven months she and Garcia had lived with their parents, that time seemingly buried for her mother in a thick sludge that had replaced her thoughts.

When Grace had once asked her grandfather how her parents had taken care of two babies with no electricity or running water, he'd shaken his head. "I wish I could tell you, Gracie. Your father would call every few weeks to let me know you were all still alive and to say hello to Angela. He never asked for money, but I assumed he and your mother needed it, and I would send a few twenties folded inside a piece of paper to a post office box your mother had opened in the town of Mendocino."

Grace doesn't recall the moldy smell of the blankets on her parents' bed or her mother crying all the time or the other women from the commune giving Garcia and her baths in the washing basin. At times, though, her skin spontaneously breaks into red welts, a bodily memory, she thinks, of the cabin floor always coated with dried dirt, of the dead flies on the windowsill. Even a decade later when she and Garcia were so well cared for by her grandfather and Angela, their rooms sunny and warm, their sheets washed with lavender water and ironed so they lay flat as stationery, she'd felt residues of that year hovering behind the eggs with tomatoes and peppers Angela would make Garcia and her each morning, the corn bread and fruit salads they would have after school, the dinners with glistening chicken pieces and yellow rice flecked with pimentos. Felt it in the gnawing in her stomach, from a place deeper than her gut, a feeling of danger, the world not right.

Not until Grace was three had she understood Angela was not her mother and Randall, whom she and Garcia called Pop, was not her father. With the realization had come the awareness that something was strange, something was alarming, about her grandfather's vigilance around water, always there, like a religious man's faith. She could sense it when she was offered a sip from a cup: her grandfather's fear that she or Garcia might swallow wrong and choke or aspirate the fluid. Bath time with her grandfather hovering in the doorway while Angela knelt by the tub, toys prohibited as dangerous distractions. The beach, even being wheeled by the boats in the Marina, strictly forbidden. Yet everywhere, surrounding them, water: the bay and ocean both visible from the roof deck, the sea mists that left a salty residue in the garden.

She gasped when years later Angela told her that her father had in high school taken up surfing. "He tried to hide it from me, changing back into his school clothes before he came home. But there was sand in his shoes, sand in the pockets of his sweatshirt. 'No, no,' he told me, he was not at the beach. They were playing in a sandbox in a park. 'Leo,' I said, 'I might not speak the best English, but I am not stupid. Big boys like you don't play in sandboxes.' Finally, he told me the truth, but only if I swore on his mother's grave that I wouldn't tell your grandfather."

Angela looked at her brown hands. "It is the only time I wasn't honest with your grandfather. I felt sick about it. I even went to confession to tell the priest. It was wrong to hide this from your grandfather, I told the priest, but I knew Leo was going to keep surfing no matter what I did. I was afraid your grandfather would have a heart attack if he found out."

"What did the priest say?"

"'God gave us lips so we can choose our words. Have you said anything untrue?'

"'No,' I said, 'but that's only because Mr. Randall would never ask me if Leo went surfing after school. He'd never think to ask that.'"

Angela shook her head. She still wore her hair in two braids as she had when she'd first come to work at the house forty-three years before. They swayed now across her broad back.

"'Well, daughter,' the priest said, 'then you are respecting his wishes.'"

By the time Grace began preschool, she understood that her father lived in Hawaii, but not that he began and ended every day with a joint and had taken up with a Persian girl whose mother was one of the countless cousins of the Shah or that after her father and the Persian girl split up, he still hung out with one of her brothers, a louche young man who would bring smokable heroin into Honolulu in a diplomatic pouch. Grace knew that her mother lived in Houston, but not that she was in and out of psychiatric hospitals for psychotic depressions, one of which had centered on her conviction that John Lennon had written "Woman Is the Nigger of the World" about her.

Up until then, occasional packages had arrived for Grace and Garcia from their mother: Christmas presents that would come in March or birthday presents a season late. Inside would be picture books her mother had drawn for them. Once, Grace still recalls, her mother sent a cassette tape of children's songs recorded by a woman whose twins Grace's mother used to babysit: "Itsy Bitsy Spider," "Twinkle, Twinkle, Little Star," "Hush, Little Baby," "John Jacob Jingleheimer Schmidt." In the parlor were photos of her father as a baby and child, many with his mother, her beautiful never-met grandmother Carolyn. But there was only one picture of her father with her own mother: her parents standing together in a field, her mother small and plump with wild curly hair and thick eyebrows and brown eyes like Grace's own. Someone, Grace had thought, who should sleep in a deep dark wood.

When she and Garcia were five, their father returned to San Francisco from Hawaii. For a few months, he lived with them on Locust Street. She remembers her father in the kitchen talking with Angela, racing down the Lyon Street steps with Garcia and her and then climbing back up with Garcia on his shoulders. She remembers him buying a drum set for Garcia and a child-size guitar for her, sitting between them on the couch while he read aloud some E. E. Cummings poems and "The Owl and the Pussycat": "In a beautiful pea-green boat . . . the land where the Bong-Tree grows . . . The moon, the moon, they danced by the light of the moon."

Then her father was gone again, though it would be many years before she knew that it was because her grandfather had kicked her father out after discovering him smoking heroin on the roof or that her father had remained in the city, crashing on his friend Shane's couch until Shane too threw him out, after which he'd stayed at a seedy hotel on Mission Street, enrolling intermittently in a detox program to clean up from what had by then become an intravenous heroin habit supported just barely by the nickel bags of pot he sold in Golden Gate Park.

At six, Grace began at the same private girls' school her grandmother Carolyn had attended and Garcia at the same private boys' school where their father and great-grandfather Gramps Winston had gone. The parallel, though, had stopped there. Whereas school had been effortless for Grace, Garcia was well into second grade before the letters on the page ceased looking like random squiggles. He couldn't keep straight 6 – 3 as opposed to 6 ÷ 3, and as hard as he tried, only half of what he brought to school—jackets, books, baseball gloves—made it back home. Although her grandfather responded with outrage, it had not been a surprise to either Grace or Garcia when at the end of third grade the headmaster of Garcia's school informed their grandfather that a school with a more flexible academic program would be a more suitable place for the boy.

As for Grace, her position at her own school was secured that same month when a girl with the residue of a harelip was teased by another girl. "Your lip's going to get hairy," the mean girl taunted, bringing the harelip girl to tears. Grace, who'd never hit anyone, slapped the taunter across the face so hard she left a welt. After that, one of the popular girls, both scared of and impressed by Grace, invited her to a sleepover birthday party, and Grace said she'd only come if the girl with the harelip was invited too—which she was.

During the year her grandfather hid their father's death from Garcia and her, they were nine, the same age their father had been when he'd lost his mother: old enough to sense something amiss, but young enough, for the most part, to stay tethered to the present, like drivers in dense fog who can see only six feet ahead.

When Garcia would ask about their father, their grandfather would respond tersely or pretend not to hear.

"Vietnam? Is my father in Vietnam?"

"No, he's not in Vietnam."

"Maybe he went there from Hawaii."

"Don't you remember? He came back from Hawaii. And Hawaii is nowhere near Vietnam."

She and Garcia were ten, in fifth grade, when their grandfather finally told them about their father's death. He drove them to Oakland to see their father's grave in the Mountain View Cemetery, designed by Frederick Law Olmsted with the plots overlooking the bay. Their father had been buried next to his mother, their grandmother Carolyn.

That night, her grandfather let Kate, already Grace's best friend, sleep over. Whispering together in Grace's enormous canopy bed, Grace had confided in Kate that her grandmother must have requested the cemetery. Her grandfather would never have chosen a place with views of the water.

And now here she is, in Central Park, designed too by Olmsted. She walks north through the Literary Walk, past statues of Robert Burns, Walter Scott, Shakespeare.

Looking back, it seems to Grace that after her grandfather told them about her father's death, he'd changed, particularly toward Garcia. He'd become more tolerant, supporting Garcia's move to a school with a gentler approach, letting him take up the drums, welcoming Garcia's new friends. It had come as a relief to no longer helplessly watch her brother trapped in a cycle of failing marks that led to her grandfather's disappointment, which only made Garcia more anxious and by consequence even less capable. To no longer feel that her every success was measured by its distance from Garcia's lack thereof.

To Grace's surprise, as a teenager she turned pretty. She had her mother's large brown eyes and olive skin tone and her father's slender frame and high cheekbones. She didn't care about clothes, but she knew that she was lucky, one of those girls who looked winsome in jeans that fell slightly off her hips and T-shirts that she filled out by fourteen. With a quick comb after a wash, her chestnut hair dried in smooth soft waves. Kate, then a brainy Math Team contestant with bushy hair and chunky legs, would moan, "I'd give up ten IQ points to have your body! Fifteen to have your hair . . ."

On Garcia, with the hint of a mustache and an extra seven inches of height, the features he shared with Grace had been so breathtaking her grandfather had worried homosexual men would approach him, but there'd never been any question about Garcia liking girls, and he'd had the good sense to prefer nice, quiet, smart girls like his sister, though he'd been too shy to pursue anyone with much success.

Grace had attracted a few of the more intellectual boys from the brother school to her own. With two of these boys, she'd attended proms in dresses Mrs. Cecelia Brown had taken her to I. Magnin to buy. After Grace's grandfather's death, Mrs. Brown had told Grace that her grandfather had once said that he was certain that had what happened with Garcia not happened, Grace would have married well: an intelligent man, not a player chasing sexy blondes or exotic brunettes, but a man who would have loved her for her fine mind and the kindness born from always watching after her twin.

Her first year of high school, Grace discovered in the long basement corridor that led to the locker room a photograph of the girls' division-championship 1937 volleyball team with her grandmother, looking slightly bored, in the front row. A few days later, Grace found a copy of the 1938 yearbook in the school library and read the entry for her father's mother:

> Carolyn Duprew: Co-Captain of Varsity Girls Volleyball,
> French Society, Art-Appreciation Club, Mills College.
> "The Soul selects her own Society."—Emily Dickinson

Sometimes at dinner Grace would read poems aloud to Garcia and her grandfather, who told her that her grandmother had done the same. Like her grandmother, Grace loved languages. Perhaps, a teacher suggested, she would study comparative literature in college.

One night, she read her grandfather and Garcia the translation of a poem by Lorca, "Gacela of the Dead Child," she'd learned in Honors Spanish.

> Each afternoon in Granada,
> a child dies each afternoon.

Each afternoon the water sits down
to chat with its companions.

When she looked up, Angela, who had been clearing their soup bowls, was wiping her eyes.

"Granada," her grandfather said. "Mrs. Brown took me there to see the Alhambra, which she says has the most beautiful gardens in the world. It reminded me of Laurelton Hall. Years later, I read that Tiffany had traveled there as a young man. So it was no coincidence. In his typical way, he plucked the extravagance and discarded the serenity."

"What's a *gacela*?" Garcia asked, and Grace was filled, as she often was, with sadness for the mismatch between his curious spirit and the machinery of his brain that made book learning hard for him.

"Our teacher explained that it's an ancient Arabic form of poetry. Lorca was from Andalucía, which she told us was for a long time the center of the Islamic world. She said that Lorca was paying respect to that part of his history."

After dinner, Grace went to the kitchen to ask Angela how she'd known the poem.

"Your grandmother, *niña*, loved Lorca. We translated his poems together when she was teaching me English. She was sixteen when he was murdered, and she told me she cried for days."

Angela turned off the sink and dried her hands on her apron. She took a deep breath and recited:

Todas las tardes en Granada,
todas las tardes se muere un niño.
Todas las tardes el agua se sienta
a conversar con sus amigos.

"I taught your father those lines."

Not wanting to go too far from her grandfather, by then seventy-nine, or from Garcia, who was planning to attend the College of

Marin's emergency medical technician program, Grace applied for early admission to Stanford, telling only Garcia, since she didn't want Cecelia Brown to exercise whatever influence she had.

A fat envelope from Stanford arrived a week before Christmas. She ripped it open, sitting on the edge of her bed with Garcia next to her. Reading it over her shoulder, he whooped.

Her eyes filled with tears at Garcia's generosity, at the way he never held it against her that she got all the commendations, awards, recognition.

"It doesn't make you feel bad?"

"Crazy, Sis. I'm so lucky to have you." Garcia hugged her. "You can do your junior year in Spain, in that city Pop was talking about, and I'll visit you and we can go see those gardens and drink sangria."

Her Spanish teacher had shown the class photographs of the Alhambra. Grace imagined sitting with Garcia in one of the tiled courtyards, by an oblong pool, listening to the soft gurgling of a fountain. Then she imagined further ahead, to Garcia working as an emergency medical technician: how he made people feel safe, how if she was ever hurt, she would want him helping her.

"What you're going to do is more important," she said.

"It's not what I do versus what you do. What matters is what we do. We're twins. We've been together what's for us literally forever. Do you think about that?"

"Sometimes."

"I think about it all the time. I know we're two separate people. But we're also one thing. One . . . what's the word?"

"*Entity*?"

"*Unity*. That's why it isn't what you do versus what I do. It's what we do."

Garcia held up his hands. He crossed the forefinger and middle finger on each, making twin Xs. And in that moment, she envisioned it: the man he could become. Still holding the acceptance letter, she wrapped her arms around Garcia's back, so much wider and meatier than hers. She could feel in his flesh the wisdom and tenderness, how good a husband he would be.

"I'm going to have to find a twin to marry," she whispered.

"A twin who has a sister who trained him," he said.

A month before they graduated from high school, Garcia told their grandfather his plan. "I want to take a road trip this summer, before I start college."

Garcia had followed their grandfather to his study, and Grace had come with him on Garcia's urging: "He won't go nuts with you in the room." Her grandfather's brow furrowed, and Grace knew he was thinking about their father—how he'd stepped off the expected track, spun into an orbit that spiraled more and more out of control. But Garcia was nothing like their father. He'd never snuck off to surf at Kelly's Cove. He'd worked Saturdays at their grandfather's shop. He'd never been drunk, never gone further with a girl than a French kiss.

"I've saved up money. I want to buy a car and drive cross-country with Jamie." Jamie was Garcia's best friend, a good-looking kid who lived with his widowed mother, worked afternoons at an auto-body shop, and was headed to San Francisco State to study business. "His college doesn't start until the last week of August. College of Marin starts after Labor Day, so we have plenty of time."

"Pop," she said. "You know Garcia's the best driver of all of us. And Jamie is a mature eighteen. You always talk about your trip cross-country, hitching trains. Garcia and I've been so sheltered. Neither of us has ever gone anywhere on our own. We've been so overprotected."

Her grandfather looked shell-shocked. She could see that he knew she was right, and that because he loved them so much, he wanted to do what was best for them even if it felt unbearable to do so.

The night before Garcia left, Grace made oatmeal-raisin cookies. Angela packed a cooler with the cookies, ham-and-cheese sandwiches, a corn bread, and a thermos of sweetened iced tea. At eight in the morning, Grace and Angela stood in front of the house while Grace's grandfather triple-checked that Garcia had the emergency kit, the list of phone numbers, the credit card, the book of traveler's checks. That the tires on Garcia's used (but not too used, because her grandfather had kicked in a thousand dollars) car were properly filled.

Garcia hugged her, lifting her a few inches off the ground. She inhaled the scent of him. "You be safe," she said.

"I will, Sis."

"Twin promise?"

"Twin promise."

A few days before Garcia left, her grandfather had shown them a book with the pictures of the loggia from Laurelton Hall installed at the Metropolitan Museum of Art. "I'll go see it when we get to New York!" Garcia had promised. Seated now on the steps of the museum Garcia never reached, watching a doo-wop group, painfully elegant in their striped suits and two-tone shoes, their beautiful voices offered up for pocket change, Grace realizes that after the hostility following her paper—the insistence that someone had to be right and someone had to be wrong, someone the fascist, someone the murderer—she no longer wants to go inside. Doesn't feel able today to view remains of the place where her grandfather and, it occurs to her now, Prudence too were born.

The Japanese girls a few feet away on the steps ignore the doo-wop group, instead making duck faces for the pictures they take of one another. Stretching south from the museum are vendors hawking silk-screened T-shirts Garcia would have bought: Che Guevara in his signature black beret, Alfred E. Neuman with his floppy ears.

It had taken several years to fill in the gaps between what Garcia told her about what had happened after he and Jamie left San Francisco and what she'd wanted to know but not wanted to cause him pain by asking. During the first few months she'd lived in Huntsville, she called Jamie repeatedly, hoping he would answer the questions she'd not pursued with Garcia, but each time Jamie's mother claimed he was out or in the shower or asleep.

She didn't talk with Jamie until she moved back to San Francisco. By then, he'd dropped out of college and was working full-time at the body shop where he'd had a job while he was in high school. When they met, at a bar near his mother's house, she was taken aback by his altered appearance: his hairline receded, his work shirt straining over his gut, the broken red capillaries across his cheeks. The slight tremor that made her wonder if he was on medication.

Jamie drank a beer and most of a second before he even looked at her.

She lightly touched his arm. "I'm sorry, Jamie. But I need to know. I need you to tell me what you know."

"Ask whatever you want."

"I remember Garcia telling my grandfather and me that you were going to stay that first night with your cousin, somewhere in Nevada."

"Yeah, we did. Want me to start there?"

"That would be good."

Jamie downed the remains of his beer. "Warren, he's my mother's cousin, has a house about twenty miles outside Las Vegas. Nice guy, but I warned Garcia, 'The guy talks nonstop, maybe because he lives alone.' It's like he's backed up with things to say. He took us for a steak dinner and then in the morning to a shooting range. I sucked, barely hit the target, but Garcia got a bull's-eye on his third shot."

Grace forced herself to smile. She wanted Jamie to understand that she was not going to attack him or accuse him or anything like that. He was clearly doing that plenty without her.

"Warren kept jabbering on about how Garcia with his marksmanship ability should try out for the police academy. Garcia was polite about it, but eventually he told Warren that he was going to become an EMT, kind of the opposite, he said, and that shut Warren up."

Jamie picked up his empty glass and signaled to the bartender for another. "Must be a million times I've gone over in my head that drive we made from Las Vegas to Phoenix."

He pulled out a cigarette pack. "You mind?"

She did mind, but she could tell he needed a smoke. She shook her head no.

He tapped a cigarette out from the pack and held it. "It was noon by the time we left Warren's. So fucking hot, we tied bandannas soaked in ice water around our necks and were talking just to keep from passing out. We got into all this serious shit. I remember Garcia saying how as soon as he had his EMT license, he was going to work in a war zone so he could help people when it was really a matter of life and death."

She wondered if she looked as destroyed to Jamie as he did to her.

"By the time we got to Phoenix, we were so fucked-up from the heat, we decided to stop. It was like six at night, and there was this thermometer on a bank that said one hundred and eight degrees. Since we hadn't spent anything the night before, we splurged and got a room at a place with a pool. It was still a dive, but at least we were able to cool off."

Jamie put the cigarette to his mouth and lit it. "There were these girls at the pool, on a road trip too, from Butte, Montana, prancing around in their bikinis. We started partying with them, nothing crazy, just drinking some beers and listening to music."

He paused and Grace could see him deliberating about what he could say.

"Go on."

"I kind of hooked up with one of them, this stupid chick named Nell. It was me, though, who acted stupid, and I ended up passed out in the bed in her and her friend's room. Her friend freaked out and called her mom, and the friend's mom started balling that she needed her to come home because her grandma was sick, some big mess."

Jamie took another drag from his cigarette, then smashed it out. "The car they were driving belonged to Nell. We came up with this plan that Garcia would take the friend to the bus station in town so she could go back to Butte and deal with her mom and grandma, and he'd drive on to Houston by himself. I'd leave by the afternoon with Nell, who was headed to her aunt's house in Galveston but was bitching about having to drive alone. She'd drop me in Houston on her way."

"We didn't know the two of you were going to Houston."

"Garcia never mentioned it until we got to Warren's house. I'm not sure if he'd even thought about it before then. He told me that he hadn't seen your mother since you were a baby. That the last letter you'd had from her was when you were like five or six. But he didn't talk much about it. It was, like, no point projecting since he had no idea what he'd find."

Grace nodded. This sounded like Garcia.

The bartender arrived with Jamie's third beer, and he drank half in one long gulp before continuing.

"For the first year after, I kept thinking it was the tattoo. The girl, Nell, she had this tattoo of a snake wound round a rose on her butt. I kept thinking it must have been some kind of voodoo magic thing that made me stay back with her, that if she hadn't had that devil tattoo, I would have left with Garcia."

Jamie looked down at the bar. His chin grazed the collar of his work shirt. She wished she could say, *It wasn't your fault,* but she couldn't make herself say that. He should never have let Garcia drive to Houston on his own. Garcia would never have done that to him.

"Garcia and I went back and forth about how to make a surefire plan for meeting up in Houston. It was Garcia who came up with the idea of the main courthouse. Any cop will know where that is, he said. We set a time. Five p.m. the next day. Saturday. Enough time, we thought, for us both to get there."

Grace felt her stomach clenching. For a moment, she thought maybe she should, after all, order a drink, but she hadn't had any alcohol since she'd left Huntsville, and she was afraid if she drank, she might miss something Jamie said.

"I got there early. The girl Nell and me drove pretty much straight through, so we got to the courthouse early. We sat on the steps, waiting until like eight. I kept saying, 'Maybe I got it wrong, maybe it was Sunday at five.' I came back by myself the next day, I was there by, like, four, and I sat there until it was way past dark."

Jamie seemed determined now to make it to the end of what he knew. "It was ten o'clock by the time I got back to this cheapo motel where Nell was waiting for me. She was pissed that I'd been gone so long. She kept trying to convince me that Garcia had probably just met someone and I should come with her to Galveston, but I refused, and then she got really pissed and called me a faggot and a dick 'cause I wasn't in the mood to screw."

He lit another cigarette. "The next morning, she left before I woke up without even saying goodbye. I spent the day wandering around downtown Houston searching for Garcia, asking guys selling sodas and derelicts hanging around in this park if they'd seen anyone who looked like him."

Jamie's voice caught, and Grace thought he might now break down. "I called your grandfather that night."

Grace had been in Paris with Kate, the two of them staying with Kate's aunt in her nineteenth-century apartment on the avenue de Wagram. It was Grace's second night of what was to have been a two-week trip when her grandfather phoned Kate's mother, who phoned Kate's aunt, who organized Grace's ticket to meet her grandfather in Sierra Blanca, Texas.

At a bar at Orly Airport, Kate's aunt had ordered Grace a brandy. It would help her sleep on the flight, Kate's aunt said. The plane was in turbulence over England when Grace threw it up in her airsick bag.

# 15

# Prudence

## London, L'Isle-sur-la-Sorgue, and New York, 1975 to Now

How different it had been to arrive by ship in Southampton with Carlton, to have him shepherd their luggage to the porters and onto the train to London and from there to their hotel, where they'd been served tea and cucumber sandwiches by a white-gloved butler before being escorted to their suite. Now, arriving alone at Heathrow for a solo holiday, Prudence joins the taxi queue, the bed-and-breakfast Elaine recommended heavy on charm and light on the ostentation she knows Prudence abhors.

The following day, Prudence takes the Underground to the Finchley Road station. She'd written to Dorothy, their first exchange since Dorothy's condolence note about Carlton's death, to ask if they might have a visit when Prudence would be in London in May. Dorothy promptly responded, inviting Prudence to come to 20 Maresfield Gardens. She walks from the station, through the leafy green streets, fragrant with cut grass and English roses.

Arriving, she is greeted by an elderly woman with a thick accent, the same maid, Prudence realizes with a start, who'd escorted Carlton and her inside for her interview with Miss Freud. Then Professor Freud was still alive and Dorothy lived down the lane. The woman gestures at the stairs, still with the window seat on the landing. Prudence follows her to the second floor and into a large bedroom overlooking the garden, where Dorothy, tiny as an elf, lies propped among the bed pillows.

The old heat rises up from Prudence's chest.

Dorothy waves a hand as if to wipe away Prudence's embarrassment at coming while she is in bed. "I have been looking forward to seeing you. Only my doctor and Anna are insisting I spend this week resting due to a mere cold. They still think of me as a tubercular invalid. But please, come sit. Miss Fichtl will bring us tea."

Prudence settles into an armchair pulled close enough that Dorothy could take a guest's hand.

"This was Anna's father's room. She moved me in here during the year I was bedridden, and I seem to have never left."

On the walls are photographs Prudence recognizes from CCB's apartment of the Four. There are other children too, who must be the children of the Four.

"Yes, I have thirteen grandchildren now." Dorothy points to a large box on top of a bureau. "I write each of them once a month. They don't all write back each time, but I keep all of their letters."

"Thirteen grandchildren! I still think of your children as young. I remember when you brought me some of Mabbie's art supplies."

Dorothy's face darkens, and Prudence immediately regrets her remark. Was it too intimate? Has Dorothy had a falling-out with her daughter?

"I'm sorry to have to tell you . . ." Dorothy takes a deep breath, then draws herself up in the bed. "But, of course, how would you have known? Mabbie committed suicide last July."

Prudence's hand flies to her mouth.

"It was a terrible shock to Anna and me too. She was here with us, having come back for the summer to be in analysis with Anna. She took an overdose of sleeping pills."

Dorothy pauses, and Prudence is filled with shame that Dorothy's thoughts seem to be on her and how she is absorbing this news.

"Mabbie's husband thinks it was a reaction to her brother Bob's death four years earlier. Bob died of a heart attack, but Mabbie believed he brought it on himself. Her husband thinks that in a horrid way, Mabbie was following her brother."

Prudence cannot speak—How can Dorothy have lost half of her children? How can the Four now be two?

Miss Fichtl arrives with the tea items. She sets the tray on the table next to Prudence.

"You can leave it," Dorothy says. "We'll serve ourselves."

"I am so very sorry," Prudence says when they are alone again. "I didn't know. I used to hear about your children through your father-in-law . . ."

"I'm glad CCB did not have to suffer Mabbie's or Bob's deaths. He loved my children so intensely. I always appreciated him for that."

"He did love them. He talked about them all the time." Prudence does not add, *Worried about them incessantly.*

"Please pour us the tea. If there is one thing I have learned living here in England, it is that there is very little that is not helped by a cup of tea. There were times during the Blitz when Anna and I would joke that our neighbors were more upset while we sheltered together in basements about missing their five o'clock tea than the blasts we could hear so close."

Dorothy smiles at Prudence. "Sometimes, I think it pathetic that we find comfort in leaves brewed in a pot of hot water. Other times, I think, this is civilization: we cleave to our rituals and aspire for graciousness even when bombs are dropping."

"What do you take in your tea?"

"Anna hates my having too much sugar, she thinks it's bad for my health, but two teaspoons would be lovely today."

Dorothy sips from the cup Prudence hands her. "Anna does not accept my interpretation of why Mabbie killed herself. She sees it as the consequence of Mabbie's guilt that her sexual desires for her husband were pulling her back home and away from her analysis. But I am the mother, and while it may sound arrogant, I believe that I know. Mabbie, like all of my children, felt profoundly wounded that I have made my life here instead of in the States with my grandchildren and them. Staying here last summer, with Anna and me, Mabbie must have felt the injury all the more intensely."

Dorothy leans back on her pillows. "And my children were right. I cannot sugarcoat the choices I've made. I have let Anna and our psychoanalytic work be primary. In a moment of supreme tactlessness, I once told them that they were grown and no longer needed me as they once had."

Dorothy points at the adjacent house, the top floors visible beyond the garden wall. "Anna and I ran a school for blind children there for many years. It did not take us long to realize that the children were suffering from a deprivation of all of their senses. There were no opportunities for them to discover what they were physically capable of doing. We believed that once an environment was created where they could run freely, their true personalities would emerge. And that's exactly what happened. The image I always had in mind was the gardens at Laurelton Hall: how when I was free to run in those woods and to climb trees and swim in the Sound, I discovered my own strength. For that, I have to thank my father, tyrannical as he could be."

Dorothy raises her eyebrows and taps her temple. "See how the mind works. Here I am, avoiding Mabbie with the blind children. It is ironic, I know, that what Anna and I concluded from our studies of the children we observed during the Blitz was that what mattered most was the relationship with the mother. Those children who were not separated from their mothers or for whom the separations were handled sensitively fared the best. And yet it is a lesson I ignored with my own children. Mabbie had a grown woman's body, but the character still of a girl."

Prudence has never before heard anyone indicting herself for own faults, as is Dorothy, without the accompanying excessive self-chastisement that always seems like a veiled plea for reassurance.

"I have been very lucky. One cannot have everything. I've had so much richness in my life here with Anna. Our work together. The work I've been able to help her with."

Dorothy drinks the remainder of her tea and places the empty cup on her bedside stand. "There are people who think I've been too submissive to Anna. But submission to another's needs is a component of healthy love. With my husband, given his illness . . ." Dorothy lowers her voice. "The times when he became violent . . . Submission to his wishes would have been so destructive to the children, and to me."

She studies Prudence, as though assessing the degree to which she understands. "With Anna, it is different. She has given me my life. There have been things I've had to forgo. Not having a home of my own where I could host guests when Anna insists on solitude, that has been a loss, but ultimately a trivial one. Living across an ocean from my children and grandchildren—that has not been trivial."

Prudence follows Dorothy's gaze to the garden. Once, CCB had told Prudence that Dorothy and Anna had become serious gardeners at their cottage on the North Sea.

"I cannot deny that I have had my regrets," Dorothy continues. "Very deep ones. But I have come to understand that there is grandiosity beneath regret: a fantasy about our own omnipotence. As though we could have made all the right choices."

Dorothy turns back to Prudence. "I think that is what your father was trying to tell me."

"My father?"

"Yes, that summer, when I clung to him because my own father was gone. I still remember how he said it. 'Miss Dorothy'—that's what he called me—'we must accept about our lives who we are.' Perhaps he even said 'what is our station.' I felt upset that he seemed to view himself in his very core as a servant. Later, when I saw him working inside, at my father's Madison Avenue house—which seemed so wrong, he should have been working outside—I was angry that he appeared to have accepted this: that my father had moved him and your family like pieces of his furniture from Oyster Bay to New York."

Prudence feels a pit in her stomach. *Like pieces of his furniture.* They'd been moved like chairs and armoires and settees from one of Louis C. Tiffany's houses to another.

"What saddens me most is that I replicated for my children what I experienced with my father. There was such enormity to his genius, he eclipsed everything around him. I knew since I was very young that I would always be in his shadow. It's a huge blow for a child."

Dorothy places the flat of her hand on her chest. "I achieved a fraction of what my father did, but for my children, my life too looked like it took place on a scale larger than theirs ever would. They saw themselves as satellites of Anna and me . . ."

Dorothy narrows her eyes. "In some ways, I'm envious of you.

Your father knew his children could have more than he did. That was what he was striving for."

Prudence feels flooded with remorse. Always, when she thinks of her parents, it is with regard to how she escaped their lives. Never has she placed much stock in what they gave her. The moments of joy she can still recall from when they lived at Laurelton Hall: the afternoons with Mr. T and his family away when her father would carry her into the sea, dunking her in and out of the gentle waves, her father seated on the wet sand, laughing while Prudence chased the advancing and receding seam of water. Her mother sucking the pit from an orchard plum and with a sticky stain on her thumb and forefinger giving Prudence the purple flesh with its burst of tart and sweet. After Prudence's father died, her mother (the only girl brave enough to ride a bike with Clara Driscoll around Grant's Tomb) so valiantly putting one foot in front of the other to keep the two of them afloat: frying oatcakes doused with cream and sugar, cheerfully setting off mornings to her job at Wanamaker's, sharing the spot of tea Sunday afternoons with Mr. Feeney. Never holding Prudence back: not when she wanted to enter the drawing contest, not when she enrolled at the New York School of Fine and Applied Art, not when she left to study in Paris even though, as her aunt later confided, it had plunged her mother into months of crying herself to sleep.

"Only now that I am so old," Dorothy says, "do I see that choice played such a small a role in my father's life. I don't mean to imply that he didn't have free will. But he was as enslaved by his perfectionism and talent as we were by its obsessive expression. After growing up with him, I was left feeling that it was a blessing not to have inherited his artistry."

Dorothy points at a watercolor on the wall behind Prudence. "Anna insisted on hanging that. It is something I did the year I was remanded to bed with the threat that if I didn't take my recuperation seriously, I would be a lifelong invalid. At one point, I was so tired of reading and knitting, I begged to be brought watercolors."

Prudence twists around to look at the picture. It is of the garden outside.

"You were drawing better than that when I met you as a child in my father's studio. My pathetic little piece is no more than inept copying. Like a cheap Polaroid."

Prudence turns back to Dorothy. "But my paintings were essentially the same. I spent so many years creating rooms for clients that were copies of what they'd seen in a magazine, I was never able to develop my own vision."

"Vision can be overrated. For my father, there was his vision and only his vision. When Theodore Roosevelt came to the White House, he's reported to have said about the glass screen my father had installed for President Arthur, '*Smash it to bits!*' My father railed that it was because Roosevelt hated his politics, but I always thought that it was because Roosevelt knew that what my father had created had not been for Chester Arthur, but for my father himself."

Prudence wonders if she should tell Dorothy that she'd heard this "Smash it to bits!" story from Harriet, who claimed the screen had been secreted away to a Washington warehouse, but it seems beside the point that Dorothy is marching toward.

"Thank goodness he switched to the glass business and left his interior design to his own homes. Who else would have wanted to live in rooms modeled after the Topkapi Palace? Or with collections of Native American artifacts?"

Dorothy sighs. "And then there were my father's parties. My daughter Tinky tells me people today would call them performance art. It boggles my mind to think about what he put into creating his Peacock Feast. He'd been disappointed by the outcome of the Egyptian Fete he'd thrown the year before. Some of the young socialites had abandoned his theme at the end of the evening and begun dancing, not as slaves entertaining Cleopatra and Mark Antony, but as themselves, and there were tradesmen there who drank too much and became raucous."

Dorothy pulls the coverlet up to her shoulders. "With his Peacock Feast, he was determined to have complete control. No female guests, only men of genius. The transport, the pergolas and flower beds, the organ music, the menu, the costumes, were all designed to create a unified effect. At precisely eleven, before anyone could break rank, the men were escorted back to the limousines. The evening ended with floodlights of different colors sweeping over the gardens and fountains as the limousines descended the drive.

"Once, when I showed Anna some photographs from that night, she said, 'What are peacocks if not symbols of phallic destructiveness?' I objected that they are also beautiful creatures. 'Yes,' she said. 'Your father produced a tableau of the cruelty veined in all beauty.'"

Dorothy laughs. "At the time, I chided Anna that even her father said a cigar is sometimes a cigar, but she's right. Behind every genius is a tyrant. And my father was that unapologetically. My sisters and I called him the Pasha of Perfection. Sometimes, I wonder how many generations it will take for us all to metabolize what he created and did. We are still living in his wake."

When Dorothy begins to cough, Prudence fears that Anna Freud will march in and demand that Dorothy now rest.

Still coughing, Dorothy points at her water carafe. Prudence fills the glass on the bedside stand and Dorothy drinks.

"I've overstayed my visit."

"No, please don't go. I know the coughing sounds awful, but I am fine. As fine as I ever am these days. There are so few people now who understand what I mean when I talk about my father. Not even Anna, really. Her father was a genius of an even greater magnitude than mine, but he intimidated Anna in a different way than my father did me."

Dorothy holds up her hand as she resumes coughing. After the coughing ceases, she drinks again, then continues: "Once, when Mabbie was very angry with me for having nixed a plan she and her siblings had devised of my buying a retreat in the States where we could all spend summers together, nixed it because I wouldn't be able to leave Anna long enough to make it worthwhile, she told me that it was the failure of my own analysis that kept me here. At the time, I dismissed it as something said in anger, but looking back, I would have to say that Mabbie was right. There is no one I have been closer to, felt more myself with, than Anna. But I have been as afraid to battle with her about certain things, including that retreat, as I was with my father."

Dorothy pauses and Prudence thinks, *Surely, now it is over.*

*Surely, now Dorothy will succumb to fatigue.* But after a moment, Dorothy goes on. "That summer, when my father was away, your father just listened while I blathered about how mean and unjust it was. He must have known I would never be able to say this directly to my own father. And, in the end, it was the same with Anna. I was unable to tell her that my wish to be near my children and grandchildren had the weight of hers to remain in the house where her father died."

Dorothy smiles. "You must think I am becoming a demented old lady. Talking about things that happened so long ago. Seeing you has shaken the dandelion so bits of my youth are floating around us. It's as if the repression has lifted. But now I've gone on too long. You must tell me about yourself, what brings you here."

Why is she here? Why?

All she can think of is how Dorothy had been unable to stand up to Anna, unable to assert that she wanted to be with her children.

"I did the same," Prudence says quietly. "Everyone assumed Carlton and I never had a baby because we were unable. But we were very much able. Carlton insisted he did not want children, and I never really stood up to him about it."

Prudence's eyes well. "It felt like a cruel joke that he died as my childbearing years were waning so even had I remarried, I would not have been able to undo that decision."

Dorothy looks intently at Prudence, but she does not say anything comforting. And this, Dorothy's knowing Prudence's wound and holding that knowledge without making light of its depth, is the most comforting response: the acceptance that there is no balm itself a balm.

Not until after she has left Hampstead does Prudence realize Dorothy mentioned Robert only once, when she said that submitting to his illness would have been harmful to her children. She wishes she had said to Dorothy, *You were so brave, you protected your children from their father. I was at CCB's house once when he had one of his episodes. I remember how frightening it was.*

Is it possible that Dorothy doesn't know that Prudence witnessed

Robert's jump from the window? That CCB had told Anna and she'd never told Dorothy? Does Dorothy know that Robert was wearing blue-and-white-striped pajamas? That his body hitting the pavement made a sound Prudence heard from across the street?

After Robert opened the window in CCB's library, he'd disappeared for a moment. Prudence wonders now what he did during that short interlude. Had he prayed? Looked into his own eyes in the bureau mirror? Kissed the photograph of Dorothy and their children he kept on his bedside stand?

In the morning, Prudence takes the train to Dover, and from there, the ferry to Calais and a second train on to Paris. She spends her first day in Paris in bed, battling a fatigue that feels like a flu but she knows is the aftermath of her visit with Dorothy: a battle inside herself to put the fathers Dorothy talked about—her own and Prudence's—side by side with the Mr. T her mother claimed had called her a dirty Irish pig, and the Eddie who'd swung at Randall and then vomited on himself.

Two days later, she takes a train to L'Isle-sur-la-Sorgue. She checks into the same hotel where she'd stayed with Claire and Claire's maid, where Jean-Christophe came in the middle of the night to give an emetic to Claire after she'd taken a bottle of Miltown. She thinks about Dorothy's daughter Mabbie having done the same with her sleeping pills. It had been shocking when Claire's maid banged on Prudence's door, but never had Prudence believed that Claire really wanted to die. Rather, the pills had seemed like Morse code sent to Claire's cheating husband: a telegram informing him that no number of Louis Quinze chairs and Provençal armoires would compensate for his nightclub singer. Had Mabbie been more serious than Claire or only less lucky?

Prudence brings a sheet of the hotel stationery and one of the envelopes to the café where she dines. It's a warm evening, and she sits at a table by windows that open like doors. She orders a soup and a paillard, then writes Jean-Christophe. She will be in L'Isle-sur-la-Sorgue for a few days. Might they meet for a coffee?

On her way back to the hotel, she takes a detour to the glove factory Jean-Christophe's father had converted to a clinic. The clinic is still there, now with Jean-Christophe's name and a second one below: Docteur Nicole de Grange. She slips the envelope under the door.

She cannot sleep. Jean-Christophe had asked that she not write to him. Perhaps he will be angered by her note. But that had been so long ago. Would not twenty-two years constitute having respected his wishes? Or perhaps he is away, at a conference or on holiday.

At nine, the phone in her room rings. Jean-Christophe's voice is deeper, muddier than she recalls. He is pleased she contacted him, he says. He still keeps a traditional schedule: seeing patients until one thirty, and then resuming at four thirty for evening hours. He suggests that they meet for lunch at two at a restaurant overlooking the river. He will reserve them a table.

After they hang up, she studies her face in the bathroom mirror. She is sixty-three. He is sixty. It seems foolish to be concerned about her appearance, but she is. She colors her hair so it is still red, though a bit lighter, more honeyed, than when he last saw her. She has her mother's fragile Irish skin, but she's taken better care of it than her mother had her own. And she is still slender, her body having never gone through childbirth, and menopause having slid over her without adding pounds. In New York, a taxi driver will still on occasion call her Miss.

When she arrives at two, Jean-Christophe is not at the restaurant. For a moment, she fears that he has sent her here as a vengeful trick. But the proprietress leads Prudence to a table she says Docteur Lemier has reserved for them on the terrace overlooking the canal.

A few minutes later, Prudence spots Jean-Christophe hurrying down the street. He is shorter than she remembers and considerably stouter, and when he leans down to kiss her cheeks, first left, then right, she sees that he has lost most of the hair on the top of his head.

"Forgive me. Right as we were closing, a mother rushed in with her young son, who had stepped on a nail in the garden. I had to clean the wound and give him a tetanus shot and three stitches too . . ."

He folds his hands on the table, and she sees the wedding band. How had this not occurred to her? That he would be married.

Or might this be the wedding band from his marriage to Anne? She can no longer remember if he had worn it so many years ago.

"But of course. An injured child has to come first."

"We doctors have always this same conflict. Our patients versus our own lives."

The waiter arrives, and Jean-Christophe asks her if they should have an aperitif first, before they order, and she says, if he has time. If he would like.

He orders pastis with a carafe of water and ice.

"My wife"—he pauses, acknowledging that this will be news to Prudence—"has never fully adjusted to having a husband with divided loyalties: family and patients. For my daughters, it is natural, all they have ever known, but not my wife. I don't mean to imply that she criticizes my work, only it still hurts her."

"You remarried."

He looks meaningfully at her. "The year after you were here. I believe you met her. Suzette, the music teacher from the school who was in my quartet."

Prudence vaguely recalls a woman with a round face who played the viola.

"She adopted Nicole and Simone, and we had a daughter together too. Renée."

"Three daughters?"

"Yes, but all grown now. Nicole is thirty-one with two sons of her own. She is a doctor too, in practice with me. She sees all of our female patients, gynecologist and general practitioner wrapped into one."

"I saw her name on your sign, but I didn't make the connection with your Nicole. And Simone?"

"She is an architect. She lives in Paris, but she has opened an office here as well, specializing in homes for holidayers. The area has become popular with the British who cherish their fantasies about our rural Provençal life. Renée, our youngest daughter, is a student in Avignon. She lives in the dormitories there, but we see her every Sunday. She's the godmother for Nicole's two sons and is very devoted to them."

Prudence does not ask about Suzette; she wonders, though, if she still teaches music, if she still plays in Jean-Christophe's quartet. If she has become the matriarch that Jean-Christophe's mother once was, caring for Nicole's two little boys, cooking midday meals with the help of a bonne. What reason Jean-Christophe gave her for not being at home today.

The pastis arrives. "May I?" Jean-Christophe asks. She nods and he pours the liqueur into their glasses, adds water, uses a long spoon to gently stir the cloudy liquid.

"*Salut*," he says, clinking his glass to hers.

"*Salut*."

He takes her hand between his two. From the way his thumbs and fingers trace her bones, she thinks he is content but not happy. He loves his wife but he is not in love with her.

Is anyone in love after twenty years? Perhaps not, but she feels certain that were she to ask Jean-Christophe, he would say that he never was.

Does it make a difference? Claire's husband had been in love with her once, and it had not prevented him from smashing their marriage or Claire herself to bits.

It makes a difference. Prudence, who'd felt the same about Carlton, knows it does.

Jean-Christophe is looking sadly at her. Yes, she is certain. He has grown to love his wife in the way some of her clients have grown attached to houses that never made their hearts sing.

"I could not have asked for a more devoted and generous wife than Suzette. Our daughters are grown and well and it is all because of Suzette."

Prudence fears that he will now ask about her. She cannot bear to tell him that there has been no other man since they parted. That no one has touched her intimately since he did in the very same hotel where she slept alone last night.

She sips her drink with her free hand. She drinks so sparingly, so rarely during the day, she feels even this tiny amount: her thoughts a bit indistinct, like a picture with the edges of things blurred.

"You are still beautiful," he whispers.

She can barely breathe. She imagines them going back to her room, Jean-Christophe naked atop her, heavier than he'd been before, his mouth on her breasts, the intense pleasure as he enters her.

Abruptly, he lets go of her hand. He is pushing back his chair.

His cheeks are flushed and she sees a bead of perspiration at his receded hairline. His pastis glass topples as he stands.

Jean-Christophe rights the glass, blots the wet spot with his napkin. He reaches into his pocket for a wad of francs he drops on the table.

When he leans over and kisses her forehead, she feels the moistness on his upper lip. "I must go, *ma chère. Immédiatement.*"

In the morning, she returned to Paris. For five days, she wandered the streets, unable to enter a restaurant, to take anything more than a café au lait she would drink standing at a *tabac* and a piece of bread or fruit she would pick at on a bench. She sat in the Parc Monceau and watched young mothers with their babies asleep in *poussettes*. She sat in the Jardin du Luxembourg and watched children with model sailboats. She sat in the Champ de Mars and watched boys kicking soccer balls.

Knowing Jean-Christophe as she had, she'd understood that if he'd gone to bed with her, it would have ripped something inside him: his belief that he honored his second wife's goodness, that he repaid what she'd given to him and their daughters with his fidelity. Sitting on those benches, Prudence remembered the sentences with which he'd once begged her to leap—to leave New York for L'Isle-sur-la-Sorgue, to be the mother to his girls. How cowardly she'd been compared with Dorothy, who could have settled in Connecticut with the Four: the Tiffanys and the Burlinghams remaining the warp and woof of her life; Robert, when he was sufficiently well, able to see his children on the weekends. Dorothy had leaped, and at much greater cost than there ever would have been for Prudence.

Seven years later, at seventy, she retired. For a few months, she tried again to paint. Her technical skills, she discovered, were better than they'd ever been, and they improved with the classes she resumed at the Art Students League. But fundamentally, nothing had changed. Her own vision remained inchoate.

She stopped attending the studios and classes at the Art Students League and instead took a volunteer job as a tutor at a school in East Harlem with children whose parents spoke little or no English. One second-grade boy, Bernardo, arrived each morning without a coat or a pencil. Meeting him in the library half an hour before the school day began, she could hear his stomach rumbling, but when she brought him an egg sandwich and a carton of orange juice, she was chastised: the children were not permitted to eat in the library; it was unfair to feed one but not all. The following week, her position was shifted to the afternoon, where she worked as a study-hall monitor, her interactions with the children limited to calling out the names of those who talked or threw objects or tapped their pencils on the desks.

She took an adult-education class at Hunter College on psychoanalysis, then another on Japanese art. She became a docent at the Cooper Hewitt Museum. She traveled with the Museum of Natural History to Japan and to India, with the Harvard Alumni Association, whose bulletins she received as Carlton's widow, to Machu Picchu and the Galápagos. Each trip felt like another pearl added to a strand, another wonder or marvel detached from anything inside herself, leaving her with photographs and travel mementos but no fingerprints on what Jean-Christophe would have called her soul.

It was then that she realized she'd begun to measure her life in decades rather than in years as she had when she'd worked for Harriet following Carlton's death, or in months as she had while Carlton was alive, or in weeks as she had as a girl after Randall left, or in days as she had when she and Randall shared a room in the Hell's Kitchen apartment. In hours as she had with her toes buried in the damp dirt, her father whistling as he weeded and pruned, in minutes as she had swinging her mother's hand at the edge of the sea, Laurelton Hall at their backs.

# 16

# An April Thursday, 2013

Grace and Prudence are seated side by side on Prudence's cream couch. With its high ceiling and curated furnishings, the room reminds Grace of Kate's aunt's apartment in Paris. Then, Grace had been too intimidated to touch the strange but wondrously beautiful pieces, each annotated by Kate's aunt: the Josef Hoffmann chairs she'd purchased in Vienna, a Le Corbusier lounge in black and white pony hair once used in the architect's parents' house on Lac Léman.

Prudence has taken the photograph of Randall as a small boy with two plump babies—one of them her, the other around her same age—from the wooden box, now open on the coffee table.

"There's an inscription on the back," Grace says.

Prudence turns the picture over. "'To Eddie and Bridget. With affection, Dorothy,'" she reads aloud. She looks over at Grace. "That would be Dorothy Tiffany, before her marriage. Before she left Laurelton Hall."

Prudence rests the picture on her lap. She imagines herself placed on a blanket next to Randall. Her mother hovering just outside the frame. Laughing, wetting her finger with the tip of her tongue to wipe a smudge—jam? chocolate?—off the skin next to Prudence's mouth. The mother of the other baby: Perhaps another upstairs maid? Or someone who helped in the kitchen?

"I was five or six," Grace says, "when I first saw that photo. In those days, I was always looking for twins, maybe to prove to myself that there was nothing abnormal about Garcia and me. I thought you and the other baby were twins."

"Dorothy was obsessed with twins. Her older sisters were twins. When I visited her once in Hampstead, she told me they used to tease her mercilessly because of her pleas to be included in their games. They had a special language, a way of communicating just between the two of them. Hearing it, she would burst into tears."

Prudence turns the photograph back over. The babies are dressed identically in what appear to be white nightgowns with white cotton caps tied under their chins. She'd assumed she was the baby closest to Randall, but looking more carefully now, she realizes she can't tell which of the two is her.

Grace insists on taking Prudence to a restaurant for dinner. Prudence wants to tell her it will be a waste, she eats so little, but it seems important to the girl. Young woman. Well, girl compared with her.

Grace holds her arm as they walk to the elevator. Prudence controls the impulse to shrug off Grace's hand, as she does on occasion with Maricel. The truth, though, is the world does unpredictably dip beneath her, not every day, not even every week, but when it does, there are black spots behind her eyes and a sense that her legs might give out.

The doorman hails them a cab. Once inside, Prudence leans back in the seat. There's a ringing, and for a moment she thinks it is coming from inside her head as happens on occasion, but then she sees Grace digging in her bag and pulling out her phone.

"David?" Grace sits up slightly taller and bites her lip.

With the street noises and the radio playing and Grace muffling her voice with her hand, Prudence doesn't hear anything more of the short conversation.

"Sorry," Grace says after she's put the phone back in her bag. "I wouldn't have picked up except that it was from the son of my patient who died earlier this month. Herman, the man I told you about whose sister made me think about trying to find you."

Prudence nods.

"All of us in the agency hear from family members for months, sometimes years, afterwards. We're there at such an intimate time in their lives. They feel like we've become part of their families."

Prudence wants to ask, *And why was he calling?*, but she fears overstepping, intruding into the privacy of Grace's work. Grace, though, continues, and Prudence thinks, *Of course she would. She's not the sort to open a door and leave her companion outside.*

"His aunt Rose asked him to invite me to a dinner she's making at her house on what would have been his father's ninetieth birthday."

There's a loud screeching and then a car horn.

"Will you go?" Prudence asks.

"I said I'd look at my calendar and get back to him, but I'll decline. We try to gently wean families from us."

Something, though, is niggling at Prudence. A thought that poked out its head and then slipped back into the recesses of her now too frequently too foggy mind. *Think*, she tells herself. *Concentrate.*

It's the way Grace said "David?" and then sat up slightly taller and bit her lip.

If a lifetime of caution had not left Prudence averse to prying, were she able to find a word other than the impossibly old-fashioned *suitor*, Prudence might ask Grace if she is certain the dinner is Aunt Rose's idea.

The vegan restaurant that Grace has apologetically chosen is surprisingly elegant, with white tablecloths and a sculptural floral arrangement at the hostess station. Prudence studies the menu. She doesn't know what any of it means: tempeh and buckwheat and quinoa. She thinks about how Carlton would have pursed his lips and tightly announced he would have just a tea.

"Could you pick something for me? Something light."

"I don't drink, but perhaps you'd like a cocktail or a glass of wine?"

"I'm afraid I'm beyond alcohol. It's hard enough without it for me to stay awake and keep my thoughts from wandering off."

"You are amazing. You have all your wits about you."

"My mind is so altered, but the cruel twist is, I still recall how it used to work."

"There was a period when I drank a lot," Grace says. "Every night. And then, one day, I just stopped. I thought, with my father having been an addict, it was something I should be careful about. I no longer feel at risk of my drinking getting out of control, but I don't like the way it makes me feel."

Grace sips her water. "I'm sure the discomfort comes from my grandfather. He revered beauty of all kinds, but he hated frivolity. I think the only person he was ever able to relax around and have fun with was my grandmother, mostly because he adored her so much and didn't want to be a killjoy for her. With us, though, after what he'd been through with my father, he was pretty much nose to the grindstone. He never made it a policy not to drink—he wouldn't have wanted to call attention to himself that way—but except for special occasions, when he might have a few sips of the champagne his friend Mrs. Brown would bring, he never did."

"He had good reason to abstain. Our father drank too much. In those days, half the men we knew did the same, but if he were alive today, he'd probably be considered an alcoholic."

Prudence surveys the room. Most of the other diners seem to be around Grace's age, though she does spot a couple who might be in their seventies. Still, though, a generation younger than herself. "I am glad you came this year. I doubt there will be too many more."

For Grace, it is of no help that death is her métier. She has to hold herself back from countering, *Don't say that, of course, there will be.*

The waiter arrives and Grace orders for the two of them: edamame to start, then a seitan stir-fry and leek lasagna she says they will share.

"Thank you," Prudence says after the waiter leaves.

Grace drinks half a glass of water. "I am debating whether to tell you about Garcia." She presses a finger against her bottom lip to prevent herself from chewing on it, a habit she developed while in Huntsville when she'd gnawed it so violently, it had become infected. "I want to, but then again, I don't."

Prudence looks at her so sadly, for a split second Grace thinks that she somehow already knows.

"Please tell me," Prudence says.

It took twenty-seven hours to get from Orly Airport in Paris, where Kate had tearfully hugged Grace goodbye, to El Paso, Texas, with the closest airport to the Hudspeth County jail in Sierra Blanca, where Garcia was being held. By then, her grandfather had hired Harlan McGinnety, the most expensive criminal attorney in the state of Texas. McGinnety's secretary arranged for the driver who met Grace at the airport and brought her directly to the jail to visit Garcia, who'd asked to see her alone.

She had expected Garcia to be broken: disheveled, wringing his hands, eyes darting. But behind the inch-thick glass, he was showered and shaved, with his dark, glossy hair neatly combed. It looked as though he'd dropped ten pounds in the week since she and Angela and her grandfather had watched him drive off with the credit card and traveler's checks and list of emergency numbers her grandfather had triple-checked. The pudginess was gone from his cheeks, his jawline sharp like their father's in the photos of him at the same age, and for an instant her heart soared and she thought, *Oh, this is just a kind of growth experience, like one of those Outward Bound trips some of the girls from school did.*

Garcia didn't say hello. He didn't smile at her. Instead, he pointed to the clock. "We have forty-five minutes. I've planned it out so I can tell you everything."

She wanted to press her mouth to the glass, to kiss her brother through it, but she only nodded. How many times had she helped Garcia organize an oral report or practice what he would say to a teacher? Now she was the audience.

"It started in Phoenix. Jamie and me met these girls, and we made this plan that he was going to drive with one of them to Houston and meet me there."

She held herself back from interjecting, *You never told me you were going to Houston. Going to see our mother. How could you not tell me that?* Garcia had just started his story, and clearly, more than anything else right now, he needed her to listen.

"It was my idea. I wanted to drive for a while on my own."

Grace nodded.

"I got on the road early, and I was feeling great, listening to cassettes of the music I figured our parents had liked: Jefferson Airplane, the Grateful Dead, early Beatles. I drove straight through to Tucson, easy, just two hours, and when I got there, I stopped to get some coffee. It wasn't long after, maybe ten miles past Tucson, I saw a kid sitting at the side of the road. He had this long blond hair pulled back into a ponytail, and he was playing a guitar. The case and a backpack were next to him on the ground."

Grace stared through the glass at her twin. She felt as though she could see the scene through his eyes: the shimmer of heat on the asphalt, the kid like a hippie Jesus with his high forehead and his skinny arms draped over the guitar.

"Pop had told me like a thousand times, 'Don't pick up hitchhikers,' so I just kept driving. But I couldn't stop thinking about him. I felt bad, leaving him there. It was starting to get hot, there weren't many cars on the road, and when I got to the next turnabout, I took it. He grinned like he knew I'd come back for him. He opened the rear door so he could put his guitar case and pack on the backseat. When he got in next to me, he didn't say anything, just kind of saluted me and settled in with his guitar on his knees.

"We drove for about an hour, and we were listening to music, not really talking. The cassette finished, and he started strumming his guitar, making different chords, so I didn't put another one in. After a while, he leaned over the seat and set the guitar in the case, and when he turned back around, he had a baggie with some pot in it. He rolled a joint, lit it, took a toke, and then offered it to me."

Garcia paused for a few seconds. "I'd tried pot my senior year. I didn't tell you because I knew you'd worry about it because of Dad. Two or three times in the basement of this kid's house."

It was the first time she knew of Garcia's keeping a secret from her.

"I was driving, so I said no. By then, though, we'd crossed into New Mexico, and the highway was so straight and empty, it didn't even feel like driving. There was nothing to do but keep my foot on the gas pedal. So, the second time he offered, I took a toke and then he introduced himself. 'Hey,' he said. 'I'm Hank.'

"I told him my name. That was about all we said at first. We passed the joint back and forth, and he fiddled with the radio, and then we started laughing about how it was a good thing the reception for the country music station was so crappy because that way we couldn't hear all the lousy lyrics. After a while, we stopped at a truck stop to get something to eat, and I realized I hadn't even asked him where he was going. 'Nowhere special,' he said. I told him I was headed to Houston. 'That's cool,' he said. 'Sounds like a good place to go.'

"We got back in the car and he took his guitar out again and he played and sang, some David Crosby and Jackson Browne songs, some Tom Waits, and I was thinking how he was pretty good, and then he put the guitar away and got this little pouch out from his backpack."

Garcia stopped. He seemed to be both checking out if she could hear the rest and shoring himself up to tell it.

"Go on."

He looked at her for a few seconds more before he continued. "Inside the pouch was a glass vial filled with white powder and a mirror and a razor blade and a tiny straw. Hank made some lines and did two, and then he held the mirror under my nose. I'd never done cocaine before, and I said I'd pass, but he said, 'It's cool. It'll help you drive, keep you alert. Like having six cups of coffee.' So I tried it, and it was incredible. My butt, sore from sitting since morning, stopped hurting and the radio started sounding fantastic, and after a while we got into this heavy conversation. I told him about our mother and how I was going to find her and meet my other set of grandparents, and he told me that he'd gotten into some trouble in Flagstaff, had to do sixty days in the county jail, and that his father had come back from Vietnam without a leg and was in a wheelchair and strung out on painkillers, and his sister was nineteen and having her second baby, and it was just too fucked-up so he was splitting town for a while.

"Around two in the afternoon, we crossed into Texas. Hank

asked me if I wanted him to drive for a while, and I said, 'Sure.' We pulled over to switch places and he gave me the pouch and showed me how to cut lines with the razor blade, and I was doing that and not paying attention to how fast he was driving until I heard a siren behind us."

Garcia licked his lips and then swallowed the way he did when his mouth was dry. She wished he could have a drink from the water fountain behind her.

"When I looked through the rearview mirror, I saw a trooper car approaching, and then I looked at the speedometer and I saw it was at ninety-five and Hank started yelling that I should throw everything out the window. He yanked his pack from the backseat and dropped it in my lap. 'Unzip it, motherfucker!' he screamed.

"I unzipped it. He was gunning the engine and steering with one hand and pawing through his backpack with the other. At first, I thought he was looking for the baggie of pot, but then he pulled out this pistol and handed it to me and started shouting, 'Shoot out their tires, man! *Shoot!*'

"Sweat was pouring down his face and I was afraid he was going to crash the car. 'Are you crazy?' I said. 'You can't shoot at a cop.'

"He began banging the dashboard with his fist. 'Shoot, asshole!' he yelled. 'We get pulled over with this shit, we're rotting in prison here.'"

Garcia pressed his fingertips to his eyes.

"My heart was pounding so hard from the cocaine, I thought I was going to have a heart attack. Hank was shucking the drug stuff out his window, and he was hollering, 'Shoot, asshole, shoot their tires.' He was still flooring it and I thought if he didn't crash, he was going to burn out the engine.

"The pistol was about the same size as the one Jamie's mother's cousin had taught me to use at this shooting range near where he lived. Hank grabbed it from me. 'I'm going to do it if you don't,' he said. I grabbed it back and turned around. The cops were gaining on us, and then I heard a shot. The cop in the passenger seat had shot his gun into the air as a warning.

"'*Fuck!*' Hank screamed. 'Shoot the fucking gun, you fucking asshole! Shoot or they're going to fucking kill us.'"

More than anything, Grace wanted to reach through the glass and wrap her arms around her twin.

"I put my head out the window and aimed at their tires. The car was shaking and I was shaking, but I hit something, maybe their fender. The cop who'd shot into the air, the one who wasn't driving, leaned out. He pointed his gun right at me."

Garcia looked straight in Grace's eyes. "McGinnety tried to get me to say I was still aiming for the tires, that the car was jerking every which way and I'd never touched a gun before that day with Jamie's mother's cousin, but I saw that cop's gun pointed at me and . . ."

Garcia closed his eyes for a few seconds. "It's a blur until I saw the officer slumped over, half hanging out of the trooper car. I was screaming, *'Stop, I think I shot him!'* Crying and begging Hank to stop, and then I crossed myself. I don't know why I did that, I'd never done that before.

"Hank looked at me like he'd turned into a werewolf. He jammed on the brakes and veered off the road, and then he jumped out of the car and started running across this field toward these trees on the other side."

Tears were streaming down Garcia's face.

"The cop who'd been driving had pulled over and laid the one I'd shot on the ground. He was pressing his hands on his chest. I wanted to help but I figured he'd kill me if I got out of my car, so I just sat there in the passenger seat, waiting for whoever he'd radioed to arrive."

When Grace finishes telling Prudence the story Garcia told her the first time she saw him in the Hudspeth County jail, tears are streaming down her own face. Prudence reaches across the table and dabs Grace's cheeks with her napkin. Seeing Prudence's eyes, dry but filled with sadness, Grace is overtaken with the awareness that this is her grandfather's sister. Prudence's sorrow is not only for her but for her grandfather too.

"That first week, my grandfather and I stayed at a motel in Sierra Blanca, just a short drive from the jail. Every morning, we met with McGinnety and the local Hudspeth County attorney, Ray Gardner, who McGinnety insisted we add to the team. McGinnety and Gardner had strongly recommended to Garcia that he enter a not-guilty plea. Not guilty because in the state of Texas killing a police officer was a capital-crime charge. But Garcia refused."

Grace breaks a roll in half from a basket she hadn't even noticed the waiter bring. She puts the two pieces on her plate.

"'Garcia's just stunned,' McGinnety told us. 'He'll come to his senses and agree to change his plea.' McGinnety went back to Dallas for a few days, leaving Gardner to handle the preliminary proceedings."

Grace picks up a piece of the roll, but then puts it down without taking a bite.

"When McGinnety came back, he met with Garcia at the jail and then with us in Gardner's office. There was a bottle of whiskey and two shot glasses on the desk, and I knew then the news was bad. McGinnety filled the two glasses. He handed my grandfather one and downed the other. 'Can't say this has ever happened to me before,' he said, 'but I've heard of it happening from colleagues who've had these kind of cases. Someone too remorseful to defend himself. That, sir,' he said, looking at my grandfather, 'is what we got ourselves here. A boy who believes he deserves to die.'"

Grace cannot bring herself to tell Prudence how, two months later, she'd held her grandfather's hand during Garcia's sentencing hearing. When the judge announced that Garcia was sentenced to death by lethal injection, her grandfather inhaled so deeply, not releasing his breath for so long, she'd feared he would pass out. Silver orbs had floated before her eyes, darkening to black pools. She'd gripped the seat to keep herself from keeling over and then stomped on her grandfather's foot to make him gasp and release his breath.

Across the courtroom, Garcia had been watching her, his sad, sweet eyes wet with what she knew was only concern for her grandfather and her. *Sis*, he mouthed. He crossed the forefinger and middle finger on both of his hands making their twin Xs.

The waiter sets a plate of edamame on the table between them. They look like green slugs, and Grace feels a swell of nausea that reminds her of how she'd felt for so many years following that day in the courtroom. Even if Prudence knows how to eat them, she won't want to any more than Grace does. Still, underneath the nausea, there's a sense of relief. She's told Prudence. The worst part of the telling is yet to come, but now Prudence knows where they are headed: down a long road leading nowhere anyone would ever want to go.

"In November, Garcia was moved across the state to the Ellis Unit, death row then for Texas male prisoners. I'd deferred starting at Stanford and I sent a letter withdrawing entirely. My grandfather tried to convince me to come home with him, we could each travel alternate weeks to visit Garcia, but there was no way I could be that far from Garcia."

Prudence nods.

"We were called the deathwatch relatives. There were about a dozen of us, mostly wives and girlfriends, living in Huntsville, the nearest town to the prison. Three of us in the same apartment complex. We rarely talked, but we all knew the status of each other's cases. They, of course, weren't our own cases, but we thought about them that way. Visiting hours were on Saturdays and Sundays, and we were each allowed one visit a week for forty-five minutes. A retired guard ran a van service out to the Ellis Unit, and he used to drive the three of us who lived in my apartment complex there each Saturday. We'd pay him sixty dollars, and he'd wait as long as it took.

"I got a job working the graveyard shift at a diner. My grandfather hated that I worked those hours, eleven at night until seven in the morning, but I couldn't sleep so it suited me. Sometimes, one of the other deathwatch relatives would come in, and whoever it was would make sure to sit at one of my tables. Usually, she wouldn't even say anything to me, but a couple of times someone handed me an article about a death row case or an editorial about capital punishment."

Grace wishes she could put her head on the table and rest for a while now, but even if that weren't too bizarre, even if it didn't alarm Prudence, it wouldn't change that she has to get to the finish.

"Each time my grandfather came, he would try to convince Garcia to withdraw his guilty plea and appeal for a new trial, but

Garcia was steadfast. 'I am guilty,' he'd repeat. 'I killed a policeman who was only doing his job. He had a wife. He had two children.'"

"But your brother was a child himself. That didn't hold any sway with the courts?"

"Not in Texas. They had executed seventeen-year-olds. Garcia was eighteen when he was arrested, twenty-one when they executed him. Legally an adult."

Prudence winces and Grace is certain that Prudence has never heard the word *executed* used in a sentence about anyone she knows. *Executed*. A euphemism for "murdered." The falsest word in the English language.

"I begged Garcia to make an appeal. 'You never wanted or planned to kill that man,' I would tell him. 'You were in an altered state of mind from the drugs. It was an accident.' But he never budged. All he'd say was 'I am guilty.' And then he'd repeat that the police officer had two kids. 'How does your dying right that?' I'd ask. 'Explain that to me.'"

Grace leans forward and cups her chin in her palm, the way she would listening to Garcia on the other side of the glass. "Only once did I sense a sliver of wavering in Garcia. 'Maybe if the police officer's wife told me she didn't want me to die,' he said, 'I might feel differently. But she hasn't. My death will bring her the relief that at least justice has been served.'"

The waiter approaches. "Everything okay, ladies?" He motions at the untouched edamame.

"Yes, but we're done." Grace glances at Prudence. "Unless you want some?"

Prudence shakes her head no. Grace waits for the perplexed waiter to clear their plates, relieved to have a moment to rest in her thoughts: the parts of the story she's never been able to tell anyone. How she would lie awake in the mornings after she returned from her job, practicing word for word the speeches she would give to Garcia on her Saturday visit. Couldn't he make an appeal for her sake? "Can't you do it for Pop and me?" How each time she said this, Garcia would stare at his hands splayed on the ledge, and she would feel wracked with guilt for asking him to give up the one thing he believed left him any dignity: that he was willing to be executed for what he had done.

Even then, once she'd understood this, she'd been unable to stop her pleas. "What if the policeman's wife said she wanted you tortured? What if she said she wanted Pop and me tortured? Would you go along with that?"

Garcia couldn't even look at her. And in that moment, she'd seen for the first time how she was torturing him.

She'd pressed the fronts of her hands against the glass, and Garcia had aligned his fingers with hers. "Gracey." His voice was gravelly through the microphone. "Please, stop fighting me. Let's just be together in the time we have left. Maybe you could read me poems like you used to when we were in high school. Or maybe the ones Dad read to us? Do you remember the one about the owl and the pussycat? How they danced by the light of the moon?"

*The light of the moon.*

"The *runcible spoon*. Do you remember that I asked you to look that up for me in the dictionary?"

"An eating utensil that is a fork and a spoon and a knife all in one."

"I was too embarrassed to tell anyone but you that all of those tiny words in the dictionary gave me a headache. But you understood. You could ask Pop to bring some of Dad's poetry books and you could read me the poems he liked."

That afternoon, Garcia had looked more sorrowful than she'd ever seen him. His days were literally numbered. He didn't want to spend them arguing with their grandfather and her.

She'd felt as though he were asking her to walk into a blazing fire. Or to put rocks in her boots and jump into an icy lake.

"And talk to Pop about what I said, okay? I can't have this conversation anymore."

Prudence again reaches across the table to wipe the tears that are again cascading down Grace's cheeks. How many times had her grandfather done the same? Wiped her face with a clump of napkins or his handkerchief? Only once, the terrible morning when she forced herself to talk to him as Garcia had asked, had it been her reaching across the table with the clump of napkins in her hand.

And now Prudence is asking about her grandfather. "My brother, how . . . how did he manage?"

Grace sees her grandfather, in the booth at the back of the diner, drinking his black coffee while he waited for her to punch out, cash in her tips, and join him. "I only witnessed him break down one time. After I told him that Garcia wanted us to stop talking with him about making an appeal."

"Oh my." Prudence closes her eyes as though she too is seeing what Grace now recalls: her grandfather's eighty-one-year-old face turned red. His clenched fists.

Grace's grandfather had buried his wife, the love of his life, when she was thirty-six. He'd raised their son, Grace's father, on his own, lost that son to addiction, then buried him. He'd raised Garcia and her.

"He said, 'No. *N-O.* I will not give in to Garcia's belief that he deserves to die. It is barbaric to kill a boy for a mistake he made at eighteen. I will not stand by and do nothing and just let them kill my grandson.'"

Her grandfather's shoulders shook. He hid his face in his hands, behind which came sounds like those of a wounded animal. It was the saddest thing she'd ever seen, this proud old man heaving with sobs. More than anything, she'd wanted to stop. To not say anything more. Not another word that would hurt the very person she loved more than anyone save Garcia.

Save Garcia. This was what she'd promised Garcia, her brother, her twin, that she would put an end to their talking about with him: attempting to save his life.

"I handed my grandfather a clump of napkins. 'Pop,' I said. 'Please try to understand this through Garcia's eyes. He wants to die for what he did. I don't believe he should any more than you do. He just wants to be with us during our visits. He doesn't want to talk about lawyers and strategies anymore.'"

"Did my brother agree?"

"He stopped talking with Garcia about an appeal. But he never accepted what Garcia was really asking: that we release him to die for what he'd done."

When their dinners come, Grace serves them each some of the seitan stir-fry and the leek lasagna. She nibbles at a piece of broccoli, eats a forkful of the lasagna. Then she continues.

"McGinnety had told us that five people from Garcia's visitation list would be allowed to witness the execution. I tried to convince my grandfather not to come, to spare himself, at his age, but he insisted, and so did Angela."

Angela, who'd been barred by Grace's grandfather from visiting Garcia but who'd refused at the end to take no for an answer, had flown in an airplane for the first time in her life to make sure Garcia's soul would not be waylaid.

"On the morning of his last day, Garcia was brought from the Ellis Unit to the old prison, in the center of town. That's where they did the executions, usually at sunset. He wasn't allowed any visitors that day aside from a clergyperson, and I didn't know if he would want a clergyperson, but it turned out he did."

The only other person Grace has ever told anything about Garcia's last day is Kate.

"I'd heard that the death row offenders were allowed to request a special last meal, and that it was a tradition to make extravagant orders: a steak and fried chicken and a pint of ice cream, that sort of thing. But I knew Garcia would not do that. All he'd requested, they told us, was a glass of orange juice and an apple."

Could she skip to the end? The afterward at the Mountain View Cemetery when Kate held her hand while Garcia was lowered into the plot her grandfather had intended for himself, between their father and their grandmother Carolyn. Each generation to its grave earlier than the prior.

But Prudence had said, "Tell me." When Grace lectures to nursing students on hospice work, she always begins by saying these are the two most important words one can say to a dying person: shorthand for "Tell me what you want another human being to know before you are gone." Only now, the *Tell me* is what Prudence wants to know while she's still here.

"A little before six, the four of us—my grandfather, Angela, McGinnety, and me—were brought into an observation room with a plate-glass window. There are days when I wish I could forget what happened next, and there are days when I am grateful that I never will because it is the last time I saw my brother."

*It's not the same,* Prudence thinks, not the same at all, those moments she spent with Randall perched on the side of her bed while he put his things into his rucksack: the sweater knitted by the grandmother neither of them had ever met, *The Call of the Wild*, the wooden box now on her coffee table. But she must have somehow known it would be the last time she'd see her brother because those moments have never left her, still vivid in the fog of her century-old brain.

"In the room on the other side of the glass, there was a gurney with wide leather straps and two phones mounted to the wall. One of them, McGinnety told us, was a direct line to the governor's office, and the other a direct line to the Texas attorney general, either of whom could issue a stay up until the very last minute. McGinnety stood on one side of my grandfather with his eyes locked on those phones, and Angela on the other, gripping his arm."

Grace had been too afraid that she might collapse and drag down her grandfather to stand at his side. Instead, she'd stood on the other side of Angela, squeezing her free hand. Angela with a determined look on her face and, hanging around her furrowed neck, the satchel of beans she'd soaked in rose water to catch any evil spirits that might trick Garcia from choosing the entrance to what she believed would be a better world.

"When Garcia was led in, he looked directly at us. I knew he was scared from the way he was pressing his thumb and forefinger together, but when he saw us, he smiled, and I could tell that it was genuine, not something he was forcing himself to do. He was truly happy to see us in what would be his last minutes.

"There were three correction officers there to strap Garcia onto the gurney as well as the warden and the clergyperson, but they wouldn't have needed anyone. Garcia climbed onto the gurney and he would have fastened the buckles himself had they asked. After he was strapped down, everyone except the clergyperson left and Garcia was allowed to make his final statement."

That night, Grace wrote down Garcia's final words so she would always have them. She has read them over and over so many times, she sees them now like the subtitles in a foreign film: *I am guilty of killing a police officer, a man who deserved only to be honored and respected. I know that I cannot lessen the suffering this has caused his family, but I want them to know that I am sorry in every fiber of my body and that I want to die for the crime I committed.*

"Lying on the gurney, Garcia couldn't see us, and that broke my heart, but then he turned his head so we could see the side of his face and he looked peaceful, and I thought maybe it was for the best that he couldn't see our faces. 'Pop,' he said, 'I love you. You gave me a wonderful childhood and you raised me to be a good person. What happened was not because of anything you did. It is my fault, one hundred percent.'"

Grace had been unable to look at her grandfather, had to trust that Angela and McGinnety would hold him up. "Garcia told Angela that she'd cared for us like we were her own children, and even though he'd always wished we could see our mother, because of her, he'd never felt like he was missing anything important."

Grace inhales deeply, the way Garcia had before his very last words.

"To me, he said, 'Grace, you have been the most generous sister anyone could ever have. I would need to be one of the poets you read to me to be able to express how much I love you. Remember how I always said we are a unity? Now you have to go on and live for the two of us. Please, Gracey, do that for me.'"

With Garcia's "Please, Gracey," she feels the crushing weight of grief. She wants to stop, but she knows that she must make it now to the end. To Garcia's end.

"McGinnety had warned us three drugs would be administered: first a sedative, then a drug that would paralyze Garcia, and then the drug that would kill him. I'd heard from the other deathwatch relatives that things sometimes went wrong. The needle had come out of one man's arm, the lethal injection had been too weak for another. But with Garcia, everything went as planned, and I have held on to the belief that he did not feel pain for very long. He twitched violently for what seemed like a minute and then he was still."

Grace studies Prudence's face. She knows Prudence is thinking of her own brother, eighty-two by then, lost in his black suit, watching his grandson's death.

"A few years later, Texas began allowing victims' relatives to also witness executions. I've always felt grateful that we didn't have to share Garcia's last moments with strangers. With people whose loss was as vast as our own."

"Did you go back to San Francisco?"

"Angela and my grandfather flew back the next morning, and I came two days later with Garcia's body."

Grace looks at the untouched seitan on Prudence's plate. It seems pointless to urge Prudence to try it.

"While I was living in Huntsville, I'd joined a group seeking clemency for an inmate Garcia had known, a cognitively impaired youth, who received the death penalty for a murder he'd committed at seventeen. My grandfather never understood how I could oppose capital punishment under any circumstances—view it as murder by the state—but respect Garcia's acceptance of his own sentence. But for me they are not contradictory: Garcia did not choose the death sentence. Rather, he believed that his acceptance of it was restitution for his crime."

Prudence nods, and Grace sees that more important than whether Prudence agrees with her—which Grace realizes she cannot say—Prudence understands what Grace thinks. How rare, how precious, Grace thinks, to know that someone else understands your point of view, whether or not it coincides with her own.

Grace spears a piece of leek with her fork, but cannot bring it to her mouth. Prudence has stopped even pretending that she might eat more.

Grace signals to the waiter. "We're done. Just a pot of Earl Grey tea, please."

"What happened to the retarded boy you were telling me about?" Prudence asks after the waiter has cleared their plates.

"The *cognitively impaired* boy. He was executed in 1992. When Bush became governor of Texas, all hope was lost. One hundred and fifty-two people were executed under his watch. Rumors were that he didn't even read the appeals."

How has she drifted so far afield? Correcting "retarded." Talking about George W. Bush. She corrals herself back. "My grandfather had a heart attack my second year of nursing school, and after that I stopped working with the clemency group. I still sent money and signed petitions, but I spent whatever free time I had with my grandfather. He'd come home from the hospital too weak to sit up, and once we accepted that he was not going to recover, we agreed on his entering a home hospice program."

With the mention of hospice, Grace is on easier ground. "I'd gone to nursing school with the plan of becoming a hospice nurse, but it wasn't until I experienced the program personally that I really understood what it meant. We had a sage nurse who encouraged us to have a rich goodbye. And we did, for the most part."

Grace pauses. She hears Prudence's *Tell me*, sees Prudence watching her with her still remarkably clear eyes. "I say 'for the most part' because some of the questions I would have liked to ask my grandfather didn't come to me until after he died. Maybe they were the ones that the pain to him of my asking would have outweighed the benefit to either of us of his answering."

"I understand." Prudence has had the same thought about Carlton: even if the circumstances of his death had been different and they'd had time together before he died, there would have been subjects he would not have wanted to discuss.

"My grandfather did talk with me about one very painful issue. He vehemently opposed Garcia's request that what would have been his inheritance be given to the family of the policeman he'd killed. I was so upset that he wouldn't honor Garcia's wish, but he viewed granting it as a kind of ratification of Garcia's death—and he had it stipulated in his will that the money could not be used this way."

Grace sighs. Her cheeks look hollow, and Prudence wishes she'd made more of an effort to eat because maybe Grace would have too. "After my grandfather died, I realized that I could get around this condition by using my portion of the inheritance as Garcia had wanted."

"How very difficult for you."

"It was hell. I hated myself for having found the loophole. It felt like I had to choose between my grandfather and Garcia."

"What did you do?"

"The Hudspeth County police force had set up a college fund for the officer's children, and I made an anonymous donation. I struggled over whether by making the donation anonymously, which I did out of respect for my grandfather, I was depriving the policeman's family of understanding Garcia's remorse, but I also thought that they might not have accepted the money had they known it came from our family."

The waiter arrives with the pot of tea and two mugs. Grace has said so much more than she's ever imagined telling anyone. What she's skirted over is herself: how she'd lived during the two years between the morning when Garcia was sentenced to death and the dusk when he was killed. That she's never talked about with anyone and can't imagine she ever will.

Grace glances at her watch. It's nearing nine.

"Am I keeping you out too late?"

"Not at all. We old people so often return to children's sleep cycles. It's good to resist that."

Grace points at the tea. "They won't have cream, but they'll have soy milk."

"I can't say I've ever had soy milk. But I'll try it."

Grace motions to the waiter. "Some soy milk, please, for my great-aunt's tea. And the check too."

It is the first time Prudence has heard Grace call her great-aunt. But then Prudence hasn't herself yet said *great-niece*.

Or *great-nephew*. She had a great-nephew too.

With her wind-beaten face and her body stripped of even an ounce of fat, Grace, her great-niece, looks like someone who's been living in a prison herself. Prudence wonders if Grace has ever let herself be angry at Garcia for what she lost because of him. Stanford, most certainly a marriage, children too. Were she to ask, Prudence feels certain how Grace would answer: Garcia wanted to die for his crime, but he wanted her to go on and live for them both. That was his last wish. How she's lived since he died is on her shoulders, not his.

Grace's shoulders. And, Prudence thinks, wasn't it the same for her? Carlton had refused to father a child. Is not the rest, everything else, on her own shoulders?

This sorrow, this lack of joy, this retreat from life: it's an even greater bond than their shared bloodline. A kind of arrogance, it seems now to Prudence. As though we are entitled to walk away from living fully if we don't like what comes our way. As though the retreat itself bestows superiority.

This sorrow, this lack of joy, Prudence thinks, it's a sin. Their shared sin.

When the bill arrives, Prudence reaches for her purse, but Grace makes a shooing motion.

Prudence does not object. For the first time, it occurs to her that with Grace, she now has an heir. In the morning, she will call Thomas. She will tell him to redraft her will. Grace will not use the money on herself. Whatever Prudence bequeaths to Grace, rather than going to the charitable organizations Prudence selected, will go to ones chosen by Grace.

It does not change that she, Prudence Theet, will exit this world like one of those dutiful campers who carefully bank their fires and port out their own waste and food detritus. Hardly a trace left behind.

# 17

# Grace

## Huntsville and San Francisco, 1988 to Now

A few days after Garcia's sentence, it dawned on Grace that she should go to Houston. Garcia had said that he thought of them as a unit. A unity. He could no longer visit their mother, so now it was up to her.

Not wanting to involve her grandfather by asking him for a phone number or address, she made a trip to the public library, where she found a Houston phone book with a listing for Helen and Norman Klein. That afternoon, she wrote them a letter: She was living in Huntsville. Might she come visit? A bus left Huntsville each morning at eight thirty and arrived in Houston at ten. If there was a day that would be good for them, she'd come then.

A week later, Grace received a card from Helen with a Chagall print on the front. This coming Monday would be ideal, Helen wrote. They would meet her at the bus depot.

It was easy to pick out Helen as she was the only white woman on the platform. Small and trim with charcoal hair clasped with a tortoiseshell barrette at her nape, she was standing under the corrugated awning.

"Grace?"

"Helen?"

Helen kissed Grace's cheek. When Helen stepped back, her eyes were damp. "Look at you . . . I can't say you look like your mother when she was your age, but you have her eyes. To me, it's cool today, but Norm thinks it's hot even when it's seventy degrees. He's in the car, keeping it refrigerated."

Grace followed Helen around the corner to a parking lot. The door of a powder-blue Cadillac opened and a large man with a bald top and coarse white hair that looped from his ears to his neck unfolded onto the blacktop. He reached out a hand—"Norm!" Helen chastised him—then withdrew it and gave Grace a stiff hug.

It was a twenty-minute drive to Helen and Norm's house, a kind of house Grace, raised in a neighborhood of Victorian homes, had only seen before on television: split-level with a picture window and flagstones that made an S-shaped path to the entrance. Helen led her into a room she called the den, with Scandinavian furniture and sliding glass doors that opened to a kidney-shaped pool.

Norm sank into a leather swivel chair and motioned for Grace to sit on the nubby low couch.

"We'll have lunch a bit later," Helen said. She arranged herself next to Grace and poured the iced tea from a pitcher she'd set on the glass coffee table. "I'm sure you want to hear about your mother."

Looking back, Grace can see how tightly swaddled Helen and Norm had kept her mother's story: a maneuver she's since grown familiar with from her hospice work, most commonly when the dying person has wronged the spouse or sibling or offspring holding the illness narrative. Then, at eighteen, with Garcia looming in her mind, she'd worried that she might ask the wrong question. Would Helen begin to weep? Would Norm stand and say, *I'm sorry, but you have to leave?*

She had not understood that all she had to do was listen to what they chose to tell her, which was, in fact, what she did while Helen described the day, seventeen years before, when Jacie, her stomach having been pumped of a bottle's worth of aspirin, had been admitted to the psych unit at the Fort Bragg hospital. That afternoon, Helen and Norm had flown to San Francisco, rented a car, and driven to Mendocino. Four days later, having arranged for Jacie's admission to a Houston psychiatric hospital, they brought her back on a private plane with an aide accompanying them.

"I wanted to take you and Garcia too," Helen said, "but your grandfather Randall refused. Jacie was crushed, but she believed that it would only be a matter of weeks before she would come get you herself."

Helen sipped her iced tea and dabbed her lips with a cocktail napkin that matched the throw pillows of the nubby low couch. She sighed. "Oh, it's a long downward spiral from there. The doctors were unable to stabilize Jacie's medications: she gained thirty pounds on the first antidepressant before surreptitiously taking herself off of it, after which she fell into a psychotic depression, during which she thought the electric toothbrush was sending her coded messages. The next medication made her manic, and she was arrested in a mall for harassing a mother with twins in a stroller, terrifying the woman by demanding her phone number so they could get together with their babies. By the end of her first five years back in Houston, she'd been in and out of the hospital fourteen times."

The doctors, Helen explained, no longer viewed Jacie's episodes of psychosis as caused by her depressions. Not only did the electric toothbrush talk to her, but she had developed the idea that she had a special connection with Stark Naked, a girl she'd met in San Francisco who'd earned her nickname after she'd climbed stark naked from Ken Kesey's psychedelic bus during its brief stop in Houston just weeks before Jacie left. Jacie was convinced that she and Stark Naked were one person living in two bodies with a single life passed back and forth between them.

When a bed on one of the long-term wards opened up three years ago, Helen and Norm followed the hospital's recommendation that they take it for Jacie. For a while, Helen had made the forty-minute trip to visit Jacie every other day, but now she went only once a week. On account of Norm's blood pressure, he visited once a month.

Norm drove Grace to the hospital. By then, her fear that he or Helen might ask why she was living in Huntsville or about Garcia had fallen away. Helen and Norm were not question askers, belonging to the large group of people who abide by the idea that if a person wants to tell you something, that person will tell you. It was a relief, but also a disappointment. On the plane to Paris, she and Kate had both read Milan Kundera's *Book of Laughter and Forgetting*, each independently underlining the sentence *Love is a constant interrogation*. The day before her grandfather called Kate's aunt and Grace's trip so abruptly halted, she and Kate had sat in the Tuileries Garden, vowing to each other that they'd only marry a man who embodied this idea: whose curiosity about them would be boundless.

"My mom is like that," Kate had said.

"With your dad?"

Kate looked horrified, but then, being compulsively honest as she was, answered, "Yes, with him. But with me too. I'm sorry. That must be hurtful, what with your not having a mom."

"I have a mom. I just don't know her." Kate had seemed so mortified that Grace had reached over and hugged her. "Don't feel bad. Between my grandfather and Garcia and Angela, I've never been short on love. The opposite: sometimes I feel like I am drowning in love. I'd sink if there was any more."

When they got to the hospital, Norm offered to come inside with Grace. Before Garcia's arrest, she would have been frightened to go alone into a psychiatric hospital, but she imagined it as not so different from her prison visits, which, surreal as they still seemed to her, were nonetheless now familiar. "I'm fine. I can go on my own."

Norm handed her a shopping bag Helen had packed. "There are some feminine hygiene products here for your mother. You can leave them at the nurses' station. And some cookies for the aides. Don't give them to your mother. She has elevated blood sugar. And there's a photo album too, from when you and your brother were babies. Jacie put it together while she was living with you on that commune. Helen thought it might be something the two of you could do together. Look through those pictures."

With the image of sitting so close to her mother that they could look together at photos, Grace's mouth turned dry. For a moment, she thought perhaps she should ask Norm to come inside with her.

Norm placed his hand on her knee. "Helen called the social worker a few days ago to tell her you'd be coming. The social worker said she would tell Jacie in advance, but it's sure to be a shock for her. I hope it goes well, but with Jacie, these days . . ." He looked out at the lawn surrounding the hospital. "You can never tell."

Entering the hospital did, in fact, feel like entering the prison for her Saturday visits to Garcia: the woman behind a glass barrier who requested government-issued identification, the clipboard with forms to fill out, the metal table on which her bag was emptied for inspection. Then, a long walk with many turns and two sets of stairs to her mother's ward.

A nurse unlocked the door and studied Grace's visitor pass. She peered at the paper, at Grace's face, back at the pass, and then pointed down a corridor lined with orange bucket chairs. "Jacie Klein. Last room on the right."

The doors to the rooms along the corridor were open. A woman was sitting on the floor, listening to a Walkman. A man was lying flat on a bed, lifting hand weights over his chest. Only the door to the last room on the right was shut.

Grace knocked.

"Yeah?"

It was hardly more than a grunt, but still her heart pounded. She'd not heard her mother's voice since she was eleven months old. "It's Grace."

"So come in."

Grace opened the door. A small woman, heavy, with unruly hair, was cross-legged on the bed with her back against the wall. Her eyes were hooded and a faint mustache darkened her upper lip. She glanced at Grace, then cocked her head at the desk chair in the corner. "You can sit there."

Grace pulled the chair out from under the desk. On top was a partially completed macramé planter, a box of pastel crayons, and a plastic carafe of water. She bit her lip to keep herself from crying.

The woman watched her. "I saw pictures of you—your grandfather would send them—but none since you were a kid. Didn't think you'd be skinny, but good for you that you're not a cow like me."

The woman—Grace's mother—made chewing motions with her mouth. "You look like your father when he was your age. He was seventeen when we met. A baby. I used to tease him that I'd robbed the cradle."

"I'll be nineteen next month."

"I know your birthday. February twenty-first."

Her mother's teeth were bad: stained yellow and with one missing on the bottom. She pointed at the shopping bag Grace had set on the floor. "Is that from Helen?"

"Yes."

"I'm not psychic. You just don't look like you shop at Neiman Marcus."

"I don't. I really don't like to shop at all."

"Neither did I. Unless it was flea markets or crafts fairs."

When her mother leaned over and took the bag, Grace felt unable to stop her. She watched helplessly while her mother opened the tin of cookies, then stuffed one whole into her mouth.

"Hand me some water, okay? All the crap they give me makes me thirsty. It's in a bottle in the bottom dresser drawer."

Grace opened the drawer and dug under the clothes, mostly men's undershirts and sweatpants, for the bottle. She gave it to her mother.

"This water is safe. I treat it myself. That"—her mother pointed to the plastic carafe on the desk—"is poisoned. They put sedatives in it to keep the animals quiet."

Her mother lifted the tin. "You want one?"

"No thank you. Actually, I was supposed to give them to the nurses. Your father said you have high blood sugar."

Her mother laughed. "He's Helen's toady. She hates me being so fat. But here, you can have them back. I don't want them blaming you."

She handed Grace the tin of cookies, then took the photo album out from the bag.

"This was my mother's idea?"

Grace nodded.

"I don't mean to sound nasty about her. She's got a heart as big as Texas, and I wouldn't be alive without her. I know I need the meds I take—well, most of them—but they make me logy and constipated and that makes me irritable."

Her mother drank her water, then sat silently, just watching Grace. "I don't want you thinking I was like this when I took care of you and Garcia. And I wasn't like this when I was your age. I know, looking at me now, it's hard to imagine, but I was this sweet, kinda innocent girl who just wanted to read by my parents' pool or draw with the twins I babysat next door. They were a boy and a girl too. It all changed when Stark Naked came to Houston and our animal spirits got mixed together."

Her mother opened the album. She examined the first page, then turned it so Grace could see.

The three photographs looked as if they were taken around the same time as the one of her parents standing in a field that Grace had grown up with at her grandfather's house. In these, though, instead of wearing jeans, her mother was wearing a sleeveless Indian dress; behind her was a cabin, and in the far distance a stand of tall trees.

"I was pregnant then. Not even two months and already a whale. Riva Krik. We thought it was going to be Eden on earth. Your father thought he'd be Bob Dylan and I thought I'd be Georgia O'Keeffe."

Jacie closed the album. "What a phony shithole."

She lay down, turned toward the wall, and pulled the blanket from the foot of the bed up to her chin. Then she let out a fart.

Grace pinched her nose. She couldn't tell if she was going to weep or vomit.

When her mother's breathing turned to jagged snores, Grace put the album and cookies back in the Neiman Marcus shopping bag. Should she kiss her sleeping mother's forehead before she left?

She decided not.

Helen and Norm asked her if she'd like to stay for dinner, but she begged off. Not wanting to say that she had to work at eleven, she said only that she had to get back to Huntsville. They made a polite invitation for her to come again, but she knew they knew that she wouldn't, and that although neither would say so aloud, not even to each other, they didn't really want her to.

Two days later, Grace went to a bar at happy hour. She'd never been to a happy hour. When the bartender asked what she'd like, she mumbled, "What do you recommend?" He brought her a pink lady with two maraschino cherries. A short man with short hair and broad shoulders, a regional sales director for roller towels, the kind you find in restrooms, he told her, bought her a second and a third and then took her back to his room. He did not say he was married and she did not say she was a virgin.

It hurt more than she expected and she had to bite her lip to keep from crying out. Even more surprising was that the man fell immediately to sleep. Stealthily, she dressed and gathered her things, making it back to her apartment in time to clean herself up before her 11:00 p.m. shift. In the morning, she bought a pocket notebook. On the first page, she wrote, *Number 1*, the man's name, and the date.

After that, she was careful to avoid the bars the correction officers from the prison frequented. Other than Number 9, whom she bumped into one day at the laundromat, she never saw any of the men again.

She met the last one, Number 16, two days before Garcia was executed. He bought her what had become her drink of choice, vodka and soda water, told her that he was an engineer, on his first job out of school. A sweet guy, not married, not with children waiting somewhere. She cried afterward, and from the way he held her, she could tell that he knew it had nothing to do with the mediocre sex they'd had or with anything he'd said or done. When he asked if he could see her again, as they almost all did if they didn't fall asleep before she left—Could he take her to dinner tomorrow?—she was tempted as she'd never before been. Perhaps it would help her not feel as if she were dead, but then she thought about how tomorrow would be Garcia's last full day alive, and she knew it would not.

Back at her apartment, she called in sick to work, unable to face the kids her own age who came at the beginning of her shift for burgers and onion rings following their movie or roller-skating dates, or the drunks who tumbled in after the bars closed, ambitiously ordering meat loaf or baked ziti they hardly touched, or the construction workers who arrived at five for their large, greasy breakfasts, the shift ending with the geriatric early risers with their bran flakes and stewed prunes. No, she could not serve any of them, not a one of them, on the day before her brother would be killed.

She wrote down the engineer's name next to the 16. She wrote down the date. Then she ripped the page out of the notebook and tore it to shreds. She poured the bottle of vodka she kept in her freezer down the sink, threw out everything in her refrigerator and cupboards, and packed her possessions in four book boxes. In the morning, before her grandfather and Angela arrived, she would go see the manager at the diner and quit. She would take the boxes to the post office and mail them to her grandfather's house. She would call McGinnety to inquire how Garcia's body could be brought back to San Francisco and book herself a ticket on the same plane.

Seven years passed before she slept with another man, and then whom did she choose? Sunny, who, Ben later told her, everyone but she and Sunny himself had known was gay. Since then, there've been a handful of other men—a law professor, a potter, an acupuncturist—but each had petered out more from entropy than drama, with the intervals between longer and longer, so that now three summers have gone by since she shared a bed.

Before Garcia's arrest, her grandfather had been a young seventy-nine, a slim man with thick salt-and-pepper hair who climbed the Lyon Street steps without getting winded and easily lifted the heavy flasks filled with flowers in and out of his shop's glass-front refrigerator. With Garcia's arrest, he'd turned gaunt, his hair wispy, his eyebrows snow-white. But not until Grace moved back into her grandfather's house and saw the neglected garden and learned that her grandfather had turned management of his shop over to his most senior florist did she apprehend the full extent to which he'd abandoned his life.

Angela fussed over him, as she'd once done with Grace's grandmother: squeezing fresh juices and pureeing his soups (all he wanted now at the dinner hour), insisting he go outside for fresh air every day, bringing cups of chamomile tea to his bedside to help him sleep.

Only on Sunday evenings, when Mrs. Cecelia Brown—by then well into her nineties but, aside from a hip replacement that had slowed her down for a few months, remarkably spry—always joined them for dinner, would Grace's grandfather attempt to eat a real meal.

Grace waited for one of these dinners to tell her grandfather her plan. "I'd like to go to nursing school," she announced.

Her grandfather put down his fork.

"Did you say nursing school, Gracey?" Cecelia asked.

"Yes. Nursing school."

"I thought you wanted to study literature," her grandfather said.

Grace poked around in the meatless portion of the Mexican stew Angela had made for her. She didn't want to say, *That was before. Back when reading gave me pleasure. Back when books made sense.* She didn't want to say that after three years in Huntsville, working the graveyard shift at the diner, visiting Garcia every Saturday, and then witnessing what she could only think of as her brother's murder, she felt too old for college. Too old to live in a dormitory, to attend parties and concerts, to take classes on Taoism in China or the German novel post–World War II. She didn't want to say that all she could imagine for herself was changing bandages and laying a cool cloth on a fevered forehead.

"Why not become a doctor, dear?" Cecelia asked. "You could do the premed program at Stanford. And they have such an excellent medical school."

"I don't want to be a doctor." Grace's words sounded too sharp. "I'm sorry. I didn't mean to say it that way. I meant to say that I want to become a nurse so I can work with hospice patients."

"Hospice patients?" her grandfather asked.

"Those are people who are dying, Randy. Explain it to your grandfather, Grace."

"Hospice is for patients who've accepted that they are dying and are no longer trying to be cured. The goal is to have as good an ending as possible."

From the way her grandfather's face tightened, Grace knew that he sensed that this new ambition of hers was a commentary about him. And if she was honest, it was. Her grandfather had abided by Garcia's wish that they cease talking with him about an appeal, but he'd never ceased his efforts to stop Garcia's execution. She had as critically judged his rejection of Garcia's wish to die for his crime as her grandfather had her acceptance of Garcia's wish to spend his last days at peace with them.

There were moments, including this one, when it felt unbearable to be in the same room with her grandfather, this man who loved her more than he loved anyone else still alive but saw her acquiescence to Garcia as resignation and her resignation as complicity. Complicity with the execution of his only grandson.

The week after her grandfather's death, Grace insisted that Angela move back into her own home: the apartment to which she'd never returned after Grace and Garcia had been left in their grandfather's front hall twenty-three years before. "It's not that I don't want you here," Grace explained. "And it's not that I don't still need you. I do. But it's time for you to have your own home." She'd thought, but not added, *To make your own life, not centered on us, which is now just me.* A month later, Grace put her grandfather's house on the market—the beauty of the Presidio neighborhood, the familiarity of the rooms where, aside from the time she'd spent in Huntsville, she'd lived since she was one, overshadowed now by the way the neighborhood felt like the set for a movie on which she'd failed to get a part, the house reminding her at every turn of Garcia.

It took a year to settle her grandfather's substantial estate: substantial because of his inheritance of her grandmother's money, which was now passed on to her save for the portion that would fund a pension for Angela. With the help of her grandfather's estate attorney, she set up a trust from which she would draw a modest income and create a sliding-scale hospice program once she completed nursing school.

She rented a small apartment by the beach in the Sunset. By the beach because after a childhood during which her grandfather had forbidden Garcia and her from going anywhere near the water, she discovered that the only thing that helped her to feel even the smallest bit alive was running at the ocean's edge: the sound of the surf, the cold damp sand on the bottoms of her feet, the taste of the salty air on her lips.

Every day at sunrise, she ran. Tuesday and Friday evenings, she went to the Integral Yoga Institute in the Mission, where she learned the Sanskrit chants and to do headstands. She took care of Kate's dog while Kate went on a trip to Australia with the man she would marry and then, after Kate returned and suggested Grace get a dog herself, had to explain to Kate that she could not have her own dog or cat or bird or fish or any living thing that she would have to keep caged in any way. She could barely tolerate a potted plant.

She read Epictetus on how happiness should only be based on that which is under one's control, on the illogic of mourning the death of a loved one, death being an expectable and uncontrollable outcome. She read accounts of people, some of them even scientists, who believed they could communicate with the deceased.

After she graduated from nursing school, she worked for two years for a well-established hospice agency. Spending time with families whose loved ones were in the terminal stages of an illness came easily to her, a relief to have death center stage rather than in the wings. At the classes run by the medical director of the agency, she learned to let go of many of the usual nursing dictums—to accept that for the dying, pushing fluids on them promotes further edema and only increases pain and suffering. Better to simply keep the mouth moist by swabbing inside with a wet sponge. From her Jamaican supervisor, she learned to recognize the Cheyne-Stokes breathing that often precedes the end.

On the sixth anniversary of Garcia's execution, she opened her own hospice agency. Now, sixteen years later, she can sense when death is close, knows as much about dying, she imagines, as anyone else still alive.

What her grandfather had never understood was that her acceptance of Garcia's wish to die in peace did not mean that she was at peace with his death. Had Garcia been killed that afternoon on the highway in Texas in a car crash or by the state troopers in the heat of the moment, it might have been possible. What she could not and would not ever, she is certain, be at peace with is that the country of which she is a citizen and to which she pays taxes and in which she votes, after presumed deliberation, murdered her twin for what was a terrible mistake, for which he had been deeply remorseful and would have dedicated the rest of his life—had they not taken it from him—attempting to make amends. That there was no compassion. That the killing of her beautiful brother with his beautiful soul had been construed as justice.

# 18

# Oyster Bay, an April Friday, 2013

"It will be so tiring for you, Mrs. P," Maricel objects when Prudence tells her about the trip Grace has organized to Oyster Bay to see what remains of Laurelton Hall.

"My great-niece is renting a car. She'll pick me up here. It will be very easy."

"It's too cold by the water. You'll catch a draft."

"I'll wear that puffy monstrosity. She wants to see where her grandfather was born."

"And you too . . . ," Grace had added.

At the edge of the narrow beach, Prudence lets Grace untie her shoes and roll up her slacks. Her feet, once so tiny and childlike they'd embarrassed her, are now disfigured by bunions and corns and yellow nails. Horrid, though not as bad as her mother's before she died when her toes turned black and gangrenous, at risk, the doctor warned, of snapping off like pea pods from a vine.

It is a warm day, in the sixties, but Prudence is indeed dressed in the puffy knee-length down coat she promised Maricel she would wear. While Grace sets up the canvas folding chairs Maricel's husband dropped off for them and Maricel insisted they bring, Prudence approaches the water. *I'm like one of those salmon Carlton talked about*, she thinks. *Traveling back to the very place where they were born to spawn and die. For me, though, there will be no spawn. Only die.*

When the cold water, so much colder than she expects, washes over the tops of her feet, Prudence sucks in her breath. The blue and gray of the sea and sky blacken as a wave of vertigo overtakes her and her knees buckle. Her bottom hits the ground, and then she hears Grace scream, feels the pounding in the sand as Grace runs to her.

"Aunt Prudence . . . Are you okay?"

Prudence looks up. Grace has one shoe on, one off. Her eyes are enormous.

"Yes." Prudence smiles. "I'm fine." She shakes sand off the sleeve of her coat. *I am fine, aren't I?* "The shock of the cold water made me lose my balance."

The ground is cold too, but she wants to stay here, with the water lapping her feet. She inhales the brackish air. Was it her mother who'd told her that the servants had used the beach when the Tiffany family was not in residence? In her memories, she sees both her mother and father here with her at the water's edge.

"I'm sorry for screaming. I panicked seeing you fall." Grace puts her hands under Prudence's armpits and hoists her to her feet. "I can't recall the last time I panicked. I'm known for staying calm." Grace brushes off the little stones that have stuck to Prudence's coat. "Did you get wet?"

"Not at all. This ridiculous coat. I was never particularly vain, but I did, in my time, pride myself on dressing tastefully. This looks like a life preserver."

"It served its purpose."

Holding Grace's arm, Prudence walks back to the folding chairs and the tote Maricel packed for them with a blanket and towels and a thermos of Earl Grey tea. To their left, Prudence can see what remains of the mansion: a few brick walls and the minaret that had housed the heating system.

"Why don't you take off your coat?" Grace says. "I can spread it out to dry. I think you'll be warm enough now that we're away from the water and in the sun."

Prudence nods. She'd remembered the minaret as taller and clad in tiles the same blue as the tableware at Jean-Christophe's mother's house. Now the tiles seem to be largely gone.

Grace helps Prudence out of her coat and into one of the chairs.

She unfolds the blanket and tucks it around Prudence, then kneels to dry off Prudence's feet with a towel.

"I can do that. You needn't do that."

"I'm a nurse. This is what we do. Bathe and dry people."

Prudence studies the gentle face of her great-niece. Why isn't she a mother, drying the wet heads and backs of children rather than worn-out bodies such as her own? Prudence's father had been one of seven children, her mother one of nine. How can it be that three generations later, the family line has come to an end, it seems, with Grace?

Grace lowers herself into the other chair. "My grandfather was always so terrified of the water. Not for himself. For us. As children, we weren't even allowed to go onto a beach. When my father was a teenager, he took up surfing, but he hid it from my grandfather. Angela figured it out, but she never told him. She was afraid he would have a heart attack."

Prudence feels a chill go through her. "We used to play on this beach." She crosses her arms in front of her and rubs the tops of each.

"Are you cold? We could go back to the car."

"No, I like being here. I can't believe I've never come back."

Grace leans over and swaddles Prudence's feet with the towel. She takes the thermos and mugs from the tote and pours them each a cup of the Earl Grey tea. Prudence nuzzles hers, letting the warmth bathe her face before she sips. Is it possible that she's not been on a picnic since the one Jean-Christophe had prepared the day he asked her to marry him?

"You cannot imagine how grand Laurelton Hall was," Prudence says. "Your grandfather was seven and I was four when we left, so mostly I know it from the photographs I've seen since. People now think of those kitschy lamps when they hear *Tiffany*, but this house was his masterpiece."

"My grandfather said Louis C. Tiffany was a very flawed man, but he can't be blamed for those lamps having been replicated for ice cream parlors and pizzerias from Florida to Washington State."

"The lamps were always commercial. Did I tell you that my mother worked in the factory before she was married?"

Grace shakes her head no.

"According to her, Tiffany didn't even design most of them. Most of them were designed by a woman who worked for him. Clara Driscoll."

"And he never gave her credit?"

"Not as much as she deserved."

Prudence sips her tea. How strange to be here now, after a century of splintered recollections: the Chinese lions, the fountain, a bride. The peacocks. The scent of an apple crate.

"That's terrible," Grace says. "Terrible but typical of the time."

"My mother didn't think he was a very nice man."

"Tiffany?"

"Mr. T we called him."

"Why was that?"

"She claimed he'd assaulted her."

Grace's brows knit. "Do you mean raped her?"

Prudence realizes she's never let herself even think that word. "By the time she told me, the cancer had spread to her brain. It was hard to know what to make of what she said about anything then."

Saying this, that she'd doubted her mother's story, assumed it delirium or less plausible because it would have taken place so many decades before, now seems monstrous. "Does that happen?" Prudence asks.

"Does what happen?"

Prudence feels confused herself as to what she is asking. The closest she can get is "How do you know if what people say before they die is true?"

Grace looks at her with what Prudence fears is pity. "Do you mean if we did an investigation into deathbed revelations and brought the findings before a court of law, would they be judged true?"

"I suppose that is what I am asking."

"My patient's son who is the evolutionary neuroscientist told me that one of the big questions in his field has to do with why we have false memories: whether there is any evolutionary advantage to this. So maybe yes, maybe no. But if you mean, are they true for the dying person . . ."

Grace's patient's son. Prudence can no longer recall his name. Only that he has an aunt who has invited Grace to dinner.

"For the dying person, they are true."

When they get back to Prudence's apartment, Maricel is there.

"What are you doing here at this hour?" Prudence asks after she has introduced Grace.

"I switched my morning and afternoon jobs. Do you think I'd sleep if I didn't know you were okay after your trip? And I knew you would want a hot shower after being out by the water. And some hot food."

Grace smiles at Maricel. Prudence is embarrassed that her great-niece has seen how Maricel treats her like a child. In truth, though, she is thankful to have Maricel here. Here now that her thoughts, since visiting the remains of the place where she and Randall were born, are straining on their tethers like boats at a dock with a hurricane approaching when God knows what will happen.

"My flight isn't until tomorrow evening. Perhaps I could come around noon to say goodbye?"

"I would like that," Prudence says. "Very much."

Maricel stands outside the bathroom while Prudence takes the long hot shower that Maricel is right that she wants. Afterward, there is the chicken-and-vegetable soup Maricel has made. At eight, Prudence shoos her out. "Thank you. But you have your husband to feed. I am fine. A hundred years past being a baby."

Lying in bed, Prudence thinks about Maricel sitting with her husband at the metal kitchen table where she once fed her three children too, and then about the food Grace told her the sister of her patient had brought to his bedside. The sister who wants Grace to come to her house so they can celebrate what would have been her brother's ninetieth birthday.

Had she not lost touch with Randall, perhaps she would have flown out to celebrate his birthday. Not his ninetieth, since he'd not lived that long, not his eightieth, since with Garcia in prison then, he had surely not wanted to celebrate that one, but perhaps his seventy-fifth. She would have sat at his table, the table his wife, Carolyn, had purchased so many years before, with Grace and Garcia, then fourteen she computes, and perhaps his friend Mrs. Cecelia Brown. Eaten the chicken with yellow rice Angela would have cooked, sung "Happy Birthday" with the candle flames wobbling in Angela's golden flan.

When Prudence wakes not at her usual 4:53 but two hours earlier with her heart pounding out of control, she thinks, *It is happening. I am dying.* She hears her mother's voice—"I wonder if he still has those red curls"—so clear she thinks, *Oh, I must have died already.*

Prudence sits up. Her nightgown is twisted and she feels the seam rubbing under her arm, so she must be alive. She lowers her feet onto the floor, counts to twenty as her doctor has advised to avoid fainting, and stands.

"Oliver," her mother had cried in her final days.

She moves to the window, parts the sheer curtains. With the nearly full moon, she can see the water towers on the roofs, the bushy tops of the trees in Riverside Park, the high-rises across the Hudson.

There'd been a full moon the night she and Carlton arrived in London, hovering between the towers of the Westminster Abbey. She'd lain awake, thinking about how her mother would have so loved to visit the cathedral, to see the Grave of the Unknown Warrior, where the woman who'd come to be known as the Queen Mother had on her wedding day laid her bouquet in memory of her war-lost brother. In the morning, Prudence and Carlton made the trip to Hampstead to bring papers to Dorothy, who disappointed Prudence by mistaking her mother for one of the other redheaded maids.

"Mark my words," Dorothy's sister Comfort had said. "She is having twins."

Prudence sees the minaret, the coarse white sand. The beached schooner she read about in the newspaper article. Feels the smooth wood under her feet as she and a little boy play on the deck.

The little boy is pretending he's a pirate. And Randall is there too. They're using peacock feathers as swords.

Randall's strong voice: "Ahoy, matey. Your turn, matey, to walk the wretched plank."

*Matey Oliver . . .*

Oliver.

## 19

# Oyster Bay, June 16, 1916

"Go," her mother says. She fixes her watery blue eyes on Randall. "Your father is in the back garden. Go play where he can keep a look on you. I have work to do and your sister is sick." She shoos the boys off. Prudence sees the peacock feathers her father gave them tucked in their trousers.

There is the sweet soapy smell of her mother's hair as Prudence is lifted from her bed and wrapped in a blanket, her rag doll inside. Carried from the gardener's cottage, where they live, down the flagstone path to the kitchen door. Her mother hands her to Molly, the cook, pads with a towel the inside of a crate that had held apples from the orchard, lays Prudence inside, then covers her with a shawl and smoothes her forehead. Folded into the shawl, the soapy scent of her mother. "Molly will watch you while I work upstairs. When Molly tells you to drink, you drink."

Molly is singing as she kneads dough for the teatime cinnamon rolls. Later, Molly carries her to the outhouse. There is a horribly loud sound—the world exploding?—and she grips Molly's arm, afraid Molly will let go of her and she will fall into the terrible black hole beneath her bottom.

"Awful, isn't it, dearie? Mr. T blowing up that beach so the regular people can't use it."

Then she is back dozing in the crate. The kitchen is warm. The door is open, a long triangle of sunlight on the stone floor. The air thick with buttery sugar. Underneath, the sour yeast of Molly's breath. She closes her eyes again. She is hot, then cold, then hot. She flings off her mother's shawl. There is a second explosion, even louder than before. The cups rattle on the shelves and the girl peeling the apples cries out, "Mary, Mother of God," and Molly lifts Prudence to sip cool water from a tin cup, wraps the shawl over her again.

She wakes to Randall's crying. He is clinging to Molly, hanging from her neck, and Molly is screaming at the apple girl, "Get Eddie. Get him now." Someone else has picked Prudence up, is covering her eyes, but it is too late. She has seen. Oliver's broken body, carried in by one of Mr. T's men. The white of his femur poking out through the skin, a swath of bloody skull exposed, the wet blue eye of the peacock feather plastered to his chest.

Then her father is there, in the kitchen, and behind him, her mother too. Her father is sobbing. "They were weeding the kohlrabi," he says over and over. "Both of 'em, there. Just twenty minutes ago, I made Oliver put his hat back on."

Her mother has sunk to the floor, next to Oliver. She is wailing, the most awful sound Prudence has ever heard, as though her mother's head, pressed against Oliver's heart, is being sawed off at the neck.

She knows. Even at four she understands. Her brothers had snuck off to play pirates in the schooner on the beach. They do it every day, the three of them, only today her throat hurts and her head is hot and she is here in the kitchen with Molly.

And now, standing at her window, Prudence sees it—her brothers hiding behind the rocks, watching as the men plant dynamite along the breakwater.

She feels it—the explosion. It shakes the apple crate, throws her brothers to the ground, sends the water rushing onto the beach.

Randall grabs Oliver's hand. He has it. He has Oliver's hand. He holds it tight, but there is another wave that hurls them both onto the rocks, and then he no longer has Oliver's hand . . .

They'd shared a bed, a carriage, a cradle.

They'd shared a womb.

Oliver, washed out to sea with the explosion and then flung back onto the rocks.

Oliver.
Her brother.
Her twin.

With the sheen on the water from what Prudence thinks must be a waning moon, she recalls a line from the poem she'd copied into her notebook so many years before:

the sea has nothing to give but a well excavated grave.

She looks at her bedside clock. It is nearly four. Soon the streetlights will switch off and the moon will disappear. She remembers first seeing the city lights, so very many of them, so astonishingly bright, through the window of the car that took them the night after the explosion to her aunt's house in Staten Island. The smell of the leather seats, of the whiskey someone had given her father to try to get her mother to drink. Randall holding a bucket for her when she got sick, and a strange man in the car, perhaps Mr. T's foreman or one of his lawyers. A man who must have told her father that reporting Oliver's death to the Oyster Bay police would not bring Oliver back, but the money—the envelopes that continued until Mr. T's death—and the job her father would be given at the Tiffany house on Madison Avenue would pay the Hell's Kitchen rent and buy Randall and her shoes and winter coats.

She remembers another two lines of the poem:

repression, however, is not the most obvious characteristic
of the sea;
the sea is a collector, quick to return a rapacious look.

# 20

# An April Saturday, 2013

When Grace's phone rings at dawn, as it often does with a patient's wife or daughter or caregiver, she knows that the person on the other end of the line has been watching the sky, waiting for a streak of light to signal that a call can be made. She knows not to ask questions, to simply pull on her yoga pants—as she does now following Prudence's "We said noon, but could you come now?"—and go.

Prudence greets her at the door. In her white nightgown with a pale shawl wrapped around her and her snowy hair combed back from her bony face, she looks like an apparition. She smiles feebly, lets Grace take her arm and lead her to the couch.

"Could you bring us some tea?" Prudence asks.

Grace arranges a tray: the thermos Maricel left the night before, a little pitcher with cream, two mugs. She pulls the slipper chair closer to the couch.

"I don't want to seem melodramatic, but . . . I woke in the middle of the night and thought I was dying." Prudence looks at Grace apologetically. "A line from a poem I'd once copied into my schoolgirl's notebook came back to me. 'Repression, however, is not the most obvious characteristic of the sea.'"

Grace recognizes the line as Marianne Moore's. While she'd lived in Huntsville, she'd asked her grandfather to send her father's poetry books, and she'd culled through them to find poems to read aloud to Garcia. She'd not read this poem to Garcia, but she'd read it herself several times.

"*Repression*," Prudence says. "The only other person I can recall ever using that word was Dorothy Tiffany. It was when I visited her in London, not long before she died. She told me that it was as though I'd shaken a dandelion and bits of her youth were suspended in the air between us."

Prudence gathers her shawl more tightly around her. "You've done the same. Last night, when I woke and thought I was dying, it seemed as though the repression had lifted and I could see what I've pushed out of mind now for nearly a century."

Grace pours the tea. How many millions of people, she wonders, across the millennia have managed moments such as this by busying their hands with serving tea? And is it not the difference between a garden and a desert that she now knows that her great-aunt takes cream and no sugar?

"In part, I fear telling you because it is also about your grandfather."

Grace hands a mug to Prudence. "Tell me."

"I feel certain now who the other baby was in that photo of your grandfather sitting on a blanket."

It is one thing, Prudence thinks, to feel certain, another to say it aloud.

"It was my twin, Oliver."

What looks at first like surprise and then the opposite crosses her great-niece's face.

"He must have died when Tiffany dynamited the breakwater in front of Laurelton Hall." Prudence closes her eyes for a few seconds. "I remembered my brother, your grandfather, weeping in the kitchen where I had been left with Molly, the cook, because I was sick that day."

She inhales deeply and makes herself go on. "A man carrying Oliver's body, bloody and battered from the sea."

Grace's eyes fill with tears. She bites her lower lip.

"My father was sobbing, my mother had her face buried in Oliver's crushed chest. I remembered all of us leaving that night. All of us except Oliver."

Grace sees in her mind's eye the photograph of her grandfather with the two babies at his sides. He'd been four or five, a carrottop, she's always assumed. On the day Louis C. Tiffany destroyed the beach, he would have been seven.

She sees her grandfather holding tight, as tightly as he possibly could, to his brother's hand in the wake of the explosion. Then, the water rushing over both of their heads and his brother's hand yanked away. Her grandfather diving and diving and diving for Oliver until he was dragged in and restrained by one of the men on the beach. She hears her grandfather screaming, *My brother. My brother.* Looking out and seeing nothing but the sea.

*The sea is a collector, quick to return a rapacious look.*

In school, she'd learned that twins run in families. She recalls at dinner having asked her grandfather, "Where are there twins in our family, before Garcia and me?" That her grandfather had not answered.

Grace forces herself to stop biting her lip, but now she is shivering, her teeth chattering uncontrollably as happened so many times in Texas when despite the hundred-degree heat, she'd have to wear a sweater over her waitress uniform. She moves onto the couch, rests her face on her great-aunt's bony shoulder.

Prudence untangles the side of her shawl and wraps it around Grace, cocooning them together. Could it be that she has never before held anyone who is crying?

Ella had cried as she talked about the boy she'd loved, but Prudence had only stroked her arm. Her mother had cried as she'd called out Oliver's name between death rattles, but Prudence had only adjusted her pillows and the compresses on her swollen abdomen. Jean-Christophe had cried when she'd said she couldn't stay, but then he'd comforted her, not she him.

She feels Grace's tears through her thin nightgown. She holds her great-niece and coos. Dove sounds from high in a dappled tree, from deep in a dank cave, from low in a quarry. Sounds without words attached.

Grace dabs at Prudence's shoulder with a tissue. "I've soaked your nightgown."

She kicks off her shoes and, turning to face Prudence, sits cross-legged on the couch. "Garcia and I could never understand why our grandfather wouldn't allow us around water. We tried to explain it as part of his being so overprotective because of our father and everything that happened with him. But that never really made sense since Angela had told us he'd been even worse when our father was young."

Randall, Prudence thinks. How brave he'd been: only fourteen when he put his belongings in a rucksack and stowed away on a train rather than punching their drunken father. How sad that she, who'd known him better as a boy than had anyone else, never knew him as a man.

"And you," Grace says. "I was ruined, losing my twin at twenty-one. But you were only four."

Prudence looks at Randall's box, closed on the coffee table. Maricel has put everything back inside and moved it here. Prudence lifts the lid and unpacks it, laying each item on the glass top.

She picks up the three white stones. They look like the stones she'd seen yesterday on the beach. Stones Randall would have collected while Oliver was still alive. Perhaps she'd been there, the three of them having snuck off to play pirates at the water's edge. A stone for them each.

She looks at the copy of the newspaper article captioned in Randall's hand: *The Peacock Feast, May 15, 1914.* The announcement, just two months later, of the marriage of Miss Dorothy Tiffany to Dr. Robert Burlingham. Dorothy, fleeing her father, whom she'd so generously viewed as equally enslaved by his artistic obsessions as he was the slave driver of others, for a husband whose mental instability had sent her across an ocean. Like the rabbit fleeing the mouth of the fox for the jaws of the wolf.

She finds the photo of Randall on a blanket with the two plump babies, reads afresh the inscription on the back: *To Eddie and Bridget. With affection, Dorothy.* Now she can see it: her mother, hovering just outside the frame, laughing, her spit-wet forefinger dabbing at the mouths of all three of her children.

Her mother's letters with the handwriting slanting willy-nilly from left to right and from right to left and the punctuation arbitrary, and then, after Prudence's father died and her mother pulled herself together, the letter with the sentences at the very end alone in black ink as though they'd been written at a later time:

> *it was a grate hardship for you that your father forbid you to speke of certen things. You thawt your father blamd you, but he knew deep down that you was a child.*

Which of them, Randall or her, she wonders now, had been better off? Randall had lived with the terrible knowledge of having let Oliver's hand slip away from his own, but she'd let the very knowledge of Oliver slip away from her.

Had she remembered Oliver, would her life have been different? Yes. She thinks yes. She cannot say why, not now after a night with so little sleep, and perhaps she won't ever be able to put it into words, but had she held on to her memories of Oliver, she feels certain that she would never have consented to abort the child she'd conceived with Carlton. This second amputation of a part of herself.

Had she remembered Oliver, would she have been able to risk being bound again to someone else the way they had once been to each other? Would she have taken a leap and made a life with Jean-Christophe and his daughters?

And Grace's father, Leo? Had he understood his father's fears, would he have forgone sneaking off to surf with his friends, not needed to take up with an unstable girl in order to captain his own ship?

Still be . . . alive?

How pointless, she knows, this infinity of ifs, so tantalizing, like pulling a thread to which there is no end until all of history is unraveled. If there had not been a turnaround on that stretch of Arizona highway and Garcia had not gone back for the blond boy with the guitar? If the dynamite Louis C. Tiffany had instructed his groundskeeper to use had been too damp to explode? If Oliver and Randall had not disobeyed their father, had stayed in the kohlrabi patch with Oliver's sun hat still on? If they'd remained at Laurelton Hall, her father the prized gardener, her mother promoted from upstairs to downstairs maid, Randall neither newsboy nor runaway?

There would not have been a Leo. There would not have been a Garcia. There would not have been a Grace.

Prudence's temples are throbbing. She wants to stop, but she cannot: her own breakwater dynamited, thoughts flooding her beach. Now, at 101, she understands that it is too simple, too schematic, to blame three generations of tragedy on a single explosion. No true story has a single plot. There were her genes, those intertwined DNA strands so magnificently discovered in her own lifetime. The physical environment in which her neurons, she has read, formed connections. The blueprint of humiliation: Even if her mother's story about Louis C. Tiffany was nothing more than the firings of a cancer-riddled brain, a recasting of the trauma she'd experienced losing Oliver and the blood she believed had been left on her employer's hands, even if no man had ever hoisted her mother's skirt over her hips and grunted, "Dirty thing," as a way of goading his climax, the words had still come from her mother's lips. They were the way she saw herself reflected in the eyes of a man who held her livelihood in his hands, who she was certain thought himself more human than her. The way she felt about herself when the money arrived the first of each month from Mr. T's offices to their Hell's Kitchen rooms.

Prudence puts the three stones back in her brother's box. She wonders if she and Randall had remained in each other's lives if they would have talked about any of this. Talked about how they, children of a woman convinced she'd been seen as an Irish pig, both married into families whose wealth had been made in part by slaves.

She chastises herself for seeking parallels between her life and Randall's: any similarities trivial next to the great divide between them. Her brother had been courageous. He'd loved his wife, his son, his grandson, then soldiered on after he'd lost them all—all save this extraordinary Grace, his legacy, now cross-legged on Prudence's living room couch, watching her. Watching without any sign of impatience as Prudence lays the peacock feather and the tile atop the stones.

*This must be*, Prudence thinks, *what Grace provides her dying patients: the comfort of her attention with the liberty to remain in their thoughts.*

She takes Grace's hands between her own. She remembers Jean-Christophe having done the same with her, but it's not a gesture she can recall having ever done herself. Not during the century she's spent in an isolation tank.

Not quite a century. Ninety-seven years. Before that, she and Oliver must have been always touching: hips, knees, toes. Bottoms, fingers, cheeks. Sharing a basket beside their parents' bed, a bath, a perch behind a potted lemon tree.

Oliver pressing against her when he saw the procession of girls with the roasted peacocks hoisted high on their shoulders.

Oliver poking his tongue into her palm when she clamped her hand over his mouth.

Her other leg.

Two pieces of a puzzle.

Two peas in a pod.

Oliver & Prudence.

Prudence & Oliver.

Prudence lifts Grace's hand to her own face. "I will most likely never see you again."

She kisses the tips of Grace's fingers. "I feel so grateful. Just a week ago, I didn't know that I had a great-niece . . . Or had a great-nephew."

"You would have liked Garcia. He was gentle and modest like you. Never smug or a braggart."

If Grace did not know death so intimately, if death had not been her lover now for so many years, she might say to Prudence, *I will come again. I will care for you at the end. I will be with you for your last exhale.* But she senses that for her great-aunt, there will be no stages of dying: no weeks during which she ceases eating and then drinking and then swims in and out of consciousness. No Cheyne-Stokes respiration. No time for Maricel to call Grace, for Grace to fly across the continent. Knowing death as she does, Grace feels certain that her great-aunt will simply, quietly, without fuss, lie down to sleep. There will be the terrifying moment when she feels her breath vanishing, feels as if she is, yes, suffocating, yes, drowning, and then the terror will vanish and her heart will stop.

"I love you," Grace says. "My grandfather loved you. I'm sure of that."

Prudence nods.

"Oliver loved you. He must have loved you the way Garcia loved me."

Prudence feels the sadness rising up from her throat, filling a hollow behind her eyes with ghost tears.

"Do you believe you will see him . . . see your parents, see Randall?"

"No. I wish I did, but I don't."

What Prudence most wishes is that she could die now, with Grace here—but then this moment, this sublime moment with her brother's granddaughter, her great-niece, would be over.

She wipes Grace's tears with the edge of her shawl. "There is something I want from you."

Grace feels her brow creasing, her throat tightening. She knows that she will have to say yes and that the yes will be to something she may not feel able to do but will now have to attempt with all of her might.

"I want you to live."

Grace closes her eyes. Garcia, strapped on a gurney, had said the same to her.

"I want you to let yourself be touched. I want you to risk everything to find love."

He wanted her to live. To live for the two of them.

"I let myself be crushed, and I didn't know why or even that I had. Half a lifetime without human touch, never understanding that we are neither souls nor animals but this mysterious marriage of the two. Carlton refused to accept this. He thought abstinence was a virtue and our animal natures could be overcome. And I let myself be convinced that he was right, that his aspirations were on a higher plane than changing a baby's diapers and making family meals and—I feel embarrassed to say this, we didn't speak of it in my day—having sexual relations. And you, dear Grace, you are living the same way. Crushed, like an invalid."

Prudence looks out at her perfectly decorated, perfectly balanced, perfectly cared-for apartment: not even in the same universe as the sweetness of Jean-Christophe's daughters radiating from every page of the little book they'd made for her about two sisters who bring their pet chicken to New York.

Grace nods, her hands now holding Prudence's arms. Prudence thinks about Grace sitting up taller and biting her lip when her patient's son called, about Grace saying that it's best for everyone to let go afterward.

"I want you to go to that dinner."

A look of confusion passes over Grace's face.

"At your patient's sister's house. Aunt . . ."

"Aunt Rose."

"Aunt Rose. With your patient's son."

"David." Grace flushes saying the name.

"I want you to go to a department store and let those nice girls who work in those places help you pick out an outfit and a lipstick too."

Prudence would add, *And get your hair cut and styled and some shoes, please, that are a bit less sensible*, but she does not want to go too far. Does not want to ruin the possibility that Grace might come to this herself.

"I want you to hold on, not let go."

"I understand," Grace says. "I do."

And Prudence sees that she does, that Grace does understand. The Marianne Moores and the Debussys and the Freuds and the Louis C. Tiffanys leave their work, but she, Prudence Theet, when her final breath comes, which it will soon, very soon, she knows, will not think of the rooms she decorated for sad Claire and her cheating husband, rooms undoubtedly long since trashed for some newer fashion, but of Grace. She, Prudence Theet, will know that she has left her mark on Grace, who leaves her mark every day on the dying, the good and the not-so-good, and their families, the loving and the not-so-loving.

"You and I, we've been too cautious, too elegant, too dignified."

"Yes," the younger woman says.

Grace is raising her arms over her head. A sweeping gesture, as though she might leap.

"Too much . . ."

A dancer, a fisherwoman, a reaper . . . A lover . . .

". . . prudence and grace."

# 21

# New York, 2013

*Grace had been right that there would be no time for Maricel to call her. Besides, it is a Sunday and Maricel is not there. But not even Grace, who has held so many hands at the end, knows what the passage will be like, and little else is as Grace imagined when her great-aunt arrives at the portal.*

*It is not the middle of the night, but dawn with the sky lightening and the birds newly chirping. There is no terrifying moment when Prudence feels her breath vanishing, fears she is drowning, suffocating. Instead, she opens her eyes and sees the plaster rosette surrounding the light over her bed, and the name of the leaves,* acanthus, *returns as she remembers a teacher with the improbable appellation of Mr. Vine showing them photographs of acanthus leaves applied to the capitals of Corinthian columns in ancient Greece. Ancient Greece, where she'd gone with Carlton, to Corinth, to see the Temple of Apollo . . . and then the thought swims into her mind:* We come from darkness.

*Inside the darkness, Oliver's bottom pressed against her belly, her mouth on the nub of his shoulder. She is certain now that he exited into the light first, that he ate the first half of the sweet plum her mother gave her, the pit sucked out and spit onto the dirt. She sees Dorothy's long hair entangled with peacock feathers, Oliver waving a discarded one as a sword. She hears Randall's "Ahoy, matey" . . . Oliver's "Ahoy, matey" in response. She smells the apple scent in the slats of the crate where she lies, the buttery cinnamon for the teatime rolls. Hears the explosion as Molly lifts her atop the outhouse seat.*

*The ground shakes.*

*Molly screams, "Get Eddie."*

*The wet blue eye plastered to Oliver's chest.*

*Then, even louder, "Get him now."*

*"Pru," Randall whispers. "You be good." Dorothy brings Mabbie's pastels, the chloroform mask over her mouth and nose, the tepid water from the kitchen pitcher before she creeps through the servants' entrance, the cool morning air on her burning cheeks as Robert appears and then disappears at the window. Carlton's bones picked clean in the belly button of a black ravine. Jean-Christophe's sisters debating the editorials in* Le Figaro *as the bonne clears the blue-and-white dishware and Jean-Christophe presses his thigh against hers. Maricel's burnished face clouded with regret when she says she might have gone to the Olympics for Guadeloupe, her pride when she mentions her children so well launched.*

*She sees Grace and Garcia, noses crusted with snot, the redwoods towering on the hillside behind them, Jacie with the chill she cannot shake and her stomach as distended as it was before she had her babies. She sees Leo, her brother's once-sweet son who wept with his face buried in his mother's cancerous belly and then banished her voice so he could dive into the Pacific's indifferent gray waves. She sees the plate of glass between Grace and Garcia as he begs her, "Let me die for what I've done," feels her skin wet with Grace's tears, the whoosh in the air as Grace's lovely arms sweep over her head.*

*Grace's voice in the calls she's made every few days these past two months. Her shy laugh when she says she did as she promised. Yes, she went to the dinner at Aunt Rose's house, and, yes, she wore a new outfit. A kelly-green pencil skirt that the salesperson said flatters Grace's slender legs with a coral lipstick the woman at the cosmetics counter proclaimed sets off Grace's chocolate eyes. And she ate everything: the chicken soup, the potato pancakes made with eggs, the asparagus tossed with butter. Everything except the pot roast. "I couldn't go that far." The girlish lilt a week later when she says David invited her on a hike up Mount Tamalpais and she said yes. Yes and then yes to a Jackson Browne concert and yes to a dinner they cooked together at his apartment, where she told him about Garcia and how she'd lived in Huntsville.*

*Prudence feels herself softly falling as the bed dissolves and above her are periwinkle clouds and beyond them a silver full moon and below her the shimmering surface of the river and then the pink floor of the sea, and she can no longer move, not even her eyelids.*

*She sees swallows slashing the sky in a V formation.*

*The words are growing dim, and someone else is saying them.*

Into darkness, *hears Prudence Theet, née Prudence O'Connor, and then there is silence and she is gone.*

# Acknowledgments

This is a work of fiction and, as such, all persons and events are fundamentally imagined. That said, my rule of thumb for characters who once lived and occasions that actually happened was to hew as closely as possible to the historical record. With respect to Louis Comfort Tiffany's life and work, the following books were invaluable: Alice Cooney Frelinghuysen's *Louis Comfort Tiffany and Laurelton Hall: An Artist's Country Estate* (the accompanying publication for a 2006–2007 exhibition of the same name at the Metropolitan Museum of Art, New York); Robert Koch's *Louis C. Tiffany, Rebel in Glass*; and Hugh F. McKean's *The "Lost" Treasures of Louis Comfort Tiffany*. Sheldon Finkelstein's article "Shattered Glass: Theodore Roosevelt, Louis Tiffany, and Unneighborly Litigation" provided important details concerning Tiffany's legal battle with the town of Oyster Bay over public access to the beach fronting Laurelton Hall. George Martin's *CCB: The Life and Century of Charles C. Burlingham, New York's First Citizen, 1858–1959* was an important source, as was the Oyster Bay Historical Society's *An "Upstairs, Downstairs" Look at Oyster Bay Estate Life*.

I am indebted to Michael John Burlingham for *The Last Tiffany: A Biography of Dorothy Tiffany Burlingham*, his sensitive and deeply researched account of his grandmother's remarkable life. Elisabeth Young-Bruehl's *Anna Freud: A Biography* offered another essential window into the relationship between Dorothy and Anna and their work together. Thanks are owed as well to Bryony Davies and the staff at the Freud Museum London, the former Freud family home, for granting me access to the letters and telegrams Dorothy wrote to Anna during their separation between August 1939 and April 1940.

My appreciation of Clara Driscoll, belatedly credited for her designs for Tiffany Studios, was enriched by The New-York Historical Society's 2007 exhibition and panel discussion, *A New Light on Tiffany: Clara Driscoll and the Tiffany Girls*. For my understanding of the history of interior design, I am grateful to the collection of the Cooper Hewitt, Smithsonian Design Library; Erica Brown's *Sixty Years of Interior Design: The World of McMillen*; and Adam Lewis's *The Great Lady Decorators: The Women Who Defined Interior Design, 1870–1955*. Thanks to fellow novelist and art aficionado Mary Kay Zuravleff for showing me Whistler's *Harmony in Blue and Gold: The Peacock Room* at the Freer Gallery of Art in Washington, D.C., which contextualized Tiffany's use of similar motifs and the extravagance of his interiors. Edith Wharton's first published book, the nonfiction *The Decoration of Houses* (coauthored with Ogden Codman Jr.), conveys the transition away from Victorian domestic mores and is ballast for the idea that the choices that guide the creation of homes express character in the largest sense.

Tom Wolfe's *The Electric Kool-Aid Acid Test* and Keith Melville's *Communes in the Counter Culture* fleshed out the 1960s history of San Francisco and the collective living experiments of the era, as did the website of Cathryn Casamo, aka "Stark Naked." Thanks to Sally Grigg of Howard Creek Ranch and Carmen Goodyear of Turtle Time Farm, who generously granted me interviews about life on the Mendocino communes, and to Goodyear's documentary in collaboration with Laurie York, *Women on the Land: Creating Conscious Community*.

For an understanding of the history of Texas death penalty cases involving juvenile offenders, I am beholden to Karen Olsson's 2001 editorial in *The Texas Observer* and Lianne Hart's 2002 article in the *Chicago Tribune*. I learned about hospice philosophy and practice from Maggie Callanan's *Final Journeys: A Practical Guide for Bringing Care and Comfort at the End of Life* and Michael Appleton's *Good End: End-of-Life Concerns and Conversations About Hospice and Palliative Care,* and then from sage hospice nurse Nina Schneider.

Heartfelt thanks to my wise and kind agent, Geri Thoma, for her faith in this novel over many years. She and the talented Andrea Morrison at Writers House patiently cleared away the brush and deftly added light to the darkness. My brilliant editor, Sarah Crichton, showed me what I couldn't see myself about this book, and in so doing transformed it. She and her expert team shepherded the novel to publication, with special appreciation due to my indefatigable publicist, Steve Weil; to Daniel del Valle for his creative marketing efforts; to Steve Boldt and Susan Goldfarb for their delicate copyediting; to Kate Sanford for guiding me through the minutiae; and to Marsha Sasmor for her early notes.

Thank you to my astute readers: Marian Gornick, Ken Hollenbeck, Jane Pollock, Jill Smolowe, Nancy Star, and Mary Kay Zuravleff. I am indebted as well to Lila Kalinich for her insights into the psychoanalytic meanings of peacocks and to George Makari for vetting the pages that concern Anna Freud.

Finally, thank you to Shira Nayman and Jill Smolowe for their support in all corners of my life, and to the Gornick women—Janet, Marian, and Vivian—for inspiring me by their deep engagement with work. And for making my world a bountiful feast, boundless gratitude to my husband, Ken, and my sons, Damon and Zack.